PRAISE FOR
Charleston Green

"I am always on the lookout for exciting new writers, and once I started reading *Charleston Green* by Stephanie Alexander, I was captivated. This novel leaves the reader entranced; the writing is skillful and clever and funny. I highly recommend this book."

—*New York Times Bestselling Author Elin Hilderbrand*

"With humor, heart and a heaping helping of Southern Charm, *Charleston Green* brings an entirely new meaning to the term 'unwanted house guests.' Tipsy is a lovable, flawed, complex heroine that readers will root for from the first page to the last—and pitch-perfect storytelling will leave fans begging for a sequel. This is Stephanie Alexander at her best!"

—*USA Today Bestselling Author of*
Feels Like Falling, *Kristy Woodson Harvey*

"An enchanting novel of a woman finding her way out of a midlife (and mid-death) crisis… Alexander blends the warm humor of her characters with balmy descriptions of her Southern gothic setting… In Tipsy and her ghosts, Alexander finds a story about the frustrations of love and aging, as well as the weight history places on the living, particularly, perhaps, in the South Carolina Lowcountry."

—*Kirkus Reviews*

Haint Blue

Haint Blue

A
TIPSY COLLINS
NOVEL

STEPHANIE ALEXANDER

Design and Distribution by Bublish, Inc.
Cover Art by Caroline Staley

ISBN: 978-1-64704-326-1 (Paperback)
ISBN: 978-1-64704-325-4 (eBook)

I know that you don't want to be
Out here forever on this road
Or live among the boxes
Where all my past lives have been stowed
Maybe you're thinking of someplace
With a garden by the sea
Where we could slow down
And you could put a little more work in on me

What with all my expectations long abandoned
And a future I no longer saw my hand in
How I found you is beyond my understanding
My stunning mystery companion

—Jackson Browne, My Stunning Mystery Companion

Do not be afraid of growing slowly, be afraid only of standing still.

—Chinese Proverb

The Southern love affair with pale blue paint originated with the enslaved Gullah-Geechee people of the South Carolina and Georgia Lowcountry. According to Gullah-Geechee tradition, ghosts—otherwise known as haints—cannot pass over water. Haints also rise into the clouds when they move on to the next world. By painting their houses to match the sea or sky, the Gullah-Geechee hoped to prevent haints from entering or trick them into moving on. Thus was born haint blue, a color now ubiquitous to piazza and verandah ceilings all over the South. The Gullah-Geechee further attempted to hold sway over the malicious or mischievous dead by trapping them in blue bottles. They hung the bottles in trees or crafted them into peculiar arboreal statues. Even in modern times one may still find bottle trees silently protecting homes throughout the Lowcountry.

Chapter 1

Almost two years after her ex-husband moved out, Tipsy Collins was still trying to figure out her life. She'd learned some handy lessons, for sure. When it comes to personal revelations, divorce is the gift that keeps on giving. For example, as her dating life collapsed around her like a house of unpleasantly prophetic tarot cards, she reached the liberating yet disheartening conclusion that she would never understand men, living or dead.

Like most women in their thirties, Tipsy had plenty of experience with the behavior of *living* men, but she only understood that *dead* men were just as flummoxing because she lived with one. After a lifetime of avoiding spirits, she'd inherited ghostly roommates when she had the good fortune to move into Miss Callie's house in the Old Village of Mount Pleasant, across the Ravenel Bridge from Charleston. Thanks to her former brother-in-law's generosity with his late mother's home, she didn't pay rent, but she had to share space with two cantankerous, kooky phantoms. Jane and Henry Mott hadn't escaped their miserable marriage with 'til death do us part, but with Tipsy's help and the mystery of their century-old murder solved, Jane had done the sensible thing. She moved on. A year later, Henry still lingered in Ms. Callie's house, as confounding as ever.

On this morning a few days after the Fourth of July, Tipsy brushed past him as she hustled her three children—Ayers, Mary Pratt, and Olivia Grace—out the door for camp. "Morning, Henry," she said under her breath.

Henry sat at the dining room table. He whispered to himself as he wrote in the air with one pale finger. His dark blue eyes followed his imaginary penmanship. Bright red, tousled hair hung in his face. He smiled, as if he'd just noticed Tipsy wrestling her three boisterous kids into submission in the foyer. "Good *morning*, Miss Tipsy," he said, "Where are y'all off to today?"

Dropping them at summer camp. Tipsy spoke in her mind. Henry would hear her as clearly as if she hollered through a bullhorn.

"Of course! How could I forget? I apologize, but this chapter of THE GREAT STORY is terribly demanding of my attention." Even when he was grinning like a fox in the early stages of rabies, Henry cut a dashing figure at Ms. Callie's antique mahogany table. In the age of kitchen islands, such edifices of formal meals were going the way of the flip phone. Meanwhile, neither Henry nor the furnishings had changed much since he died in 1923.

Which chapter now? Tipsy asked, although she pretty much knew the answer. Henry was compiling his mysterious magnum opus at a speed approximating that of a drunk slug crawling up a slippery wall.

"I'm *nearly* finished with chapter two!"

Another voice rose in Tipsy's mind. Her Granna, who had died years ago but shared her talent for seeing the dead and hence some of her headspace, spoke up with her usual country forthrightness. *It's taken him a year to finish two chapters,* said Granna. *He wants you to transcribe for him, but you'll have joined me in the afterlife before he's finished. Why doesn't he move on now that he can?*

I don't know, Granna, but if he wants to hang around haunting this place, that's his choice. She looked at the eccentric ghost like her own errant offspring. *Besides, I'm used to him at this point, bless his crazy ass heart.*

"Y'all have a nice day now," said Henry. "I'll take the basket of clean clothes to your room."

Tipsy gave him a subtle thumbs up. Henry's telekinetic powers definitely came in handy around the house.

He's more helpful than Big Ayers was, said Granna, in reference to Tipsy's famously self-centered ex-husband.

If I have to live with a man, I think I prefer a dead one. Living men drive me to drink.

Still getting the heebie-jeebies from Will?

That's as good a way as any to describe his vibes lately.

The kids' arguing recaptured her attention. Little Ayers had typical nine-year-old boy morning energy. He was singing a borderline inappropriate rap song he'd heard on YouTube at his father's house. He tugged one of Olivia Grace's curly brown pigtails while bouncing his soccer ball on his knee.

"Stop it," said O-liv.

"Ayers, stop it. Hold onto the ball. What's that song? I don't like the sound of it."

"It's the clean version, Mom."

He'd lately switched from *Mama* to *Mom*, reminding her that there was a lot more YouTube in her future.

Tipsy helped Mary Pratt sling her camp backpack over her shoulders. "Your bathing suit and towel are in—"

"Where's my lunchbox, Mama?" asked Mary Pratt. "Did you put fruit snacks in there?"

"Ayers, *staaaaap!*" Olivia Grace was about to lose it. While she was often the most compliant member of the Collins Kids Triad, she'd been known to clobber her siblings when they pushed her.

"Ayers Lee! You're almost ten years old, for heaven's sake. Leave your sister alone!"

"She started it! She called me a poophead!"

"Oh lord, are we revisiting poophead? O-liv, *no more poophead.*" Tipsy reached for M.P.'s lunchbox. She planned to head straight to Sullivan's Island to discuss a new painting commission after drop off, so she wore wedges and a long sundress. As a freelance artist, commissions were her most important source of income. She always dressed up to meet a potential client, but her outfit was not kid-friendly. As she handed over the pink rectangle, she stumbled on her hem and stepped on her own toe.

"Damnit!" she yelled. "Shit!"

The kids shut up mid-complaint.

"You okay, Mom?" Ayers flipped his shaggy blond hair out of his eyes.

"She cussed," Mary Pratt whispered to Olivia Grace. Olivia Grace grimaced in acknowledgement. The two girls, as identical at seven-years-old as they had been as newborns, didn't need to talk to communicate any more than Tipsy had to speak to talk to Henry or Granna.

Tipsy looked in the hallway mirror and straightened her dress. A tall, slim woman with wavy brown hair and gray eyes stared back at her. She appeared only mildly frazzled. No parenting induced eye tick yet, but hell, it wasn't even eight in the morning. Still plenty of time for her hair to stand on end and her mascara to run. She smiled at her reflection as if practicing for a television interview. Money was always tight in her post-divorce life, and she needed this commission.

Her phone dinged insistently as she gave Little A his water bottle. "Yes, buddies. I'm fine. I'm sorry I cursed, but y'all are driving me batty. Let's all try to chill out, okay?"

"Sorry," said Ayers. "Sorry, O-liv."

"S'okay," said Olivia Grace.

"I don't need fruit snacks," said Mary Pratt.

"All good, y'all. Please get in the car."

They meandered out the front door, chatting and laughing with the abrupt conviviality of children, while Tipsy grabbed her purse. She looked at her phone.

WILL GARRISON TEXT MESSAGE (2)

It's about time, she thought. He'd been distant the past week and hadn't texted a good morning. She swiped across the text.

WILL: DID YOU GO TO PAMELLA'S ABOUT THE COMMISSION YET?

TIPSY: NO, I TOLD YOU, I HAVE TO DROP OFF THE KIDS FIRST. DRIVING TO SULLIVAN'S AFTER.

The question irritated her. Will had connected her with Pamella Brewton, as he'd done carpentry work on her house. His sporadic communication of late harped on this meeting.

TIPSY: WHY DO YOU KEEP ASKING?

She stuck the phone in her purse and walked down Ms. Callie's front steps with the July sun baking her shoulders. She checked the kids' seatbelts and got into her old faithful Tahoe. Her phone dinged again as she buckled her belt. She tried and failed to ignore it. She couldn't stop herself. Her arm might as well have belonged to someone else.

She swiped across Will's next text.

JUST LET ME KNOW HOW IT GOES. AND CAN I COME OVER TONIGHT TO TALK?

Tipsy's heart sank. Will Garrison was no chatterbox. If he wanted to talk, it couldn't be good.

Tipsy dropped off the kids—the girls to swim camp and Little Ayers to soccer camp—without sending Will any messages demanding clarification. So frustrating of him to drop a "talk" on her with no context, but she refused to question him and then wait for another vague text that would likely increase her anxiety. She drove over the Ben Sawyer Bridge, but she didn't slow down to admire the stretch of picturesque marsh between Sullivan's Island and Mount Pleasant. Her mind raced over the past year as she crept through Sullivan's quaint business district, with its coffee-wielding pedestrians and stop-and-go golf cart traffic.

Will initially started acting weird around Thanksgiving. He'd cited his frustration at having a girlfriend to answer to during deer season, and she thought he was breaking up with her. She was crushed, until she realized he wasn't really going anywhere. She gave him space and he slowly came back around. By February, with deer season over and Will not much of a duck hunter, things almost returned to normal. Tipsy understandably felt more insecure about their relationship, however, and not only because of the break up scare. As their first bucolic summer together faded behind them, frustrating trends emerged that neither Tipsy nor Will seemed able to resolve.

When she was brutally honest with herself, she knew she'd always struggle to give Will the long leash he wanted. His idea of an appropriate leash was more like an invisible fence. She never understood where the boundaries were. Tipsy didn't think of herself as high-maintenance, but she did have expectations. She was happy for Will to spend time on the weekends hunting or fishing, as long as their relationship remained a priority. After all, she'd already been a deer stand widow in her marriage.

As for herself, she continued to wish Will would be more expressive. She thought with time and patient encouragement, he'd open up more, but she'd accepted that Will would never be one for effusive declarations of love or long, deep conversations about feelings. Tipsy had gone so long without any of that, she found herself craving it.

Maybe we'll never be able to make each other happy, she thought.

Her emotions did an about face, as they always did. She loved so many things about Will. He was as steady as a summer day was long. He was always there to help when she needed him, whether it be connecting her with new painting clients through his work as a residential contractor or fixing her garbage disposal. Most complicating of all, their lives were as entwined as the invasive vines that crept up the walls of Ms. Callie's house. The twins regularly had sleepovers with his two younger daughters. Her two best friends, Lindsey and Shelby, were married to his closest old friend (P.D.) and dating his closest new friend (Brian), respectively.

Lastly, and not unimportantly, they never lacked for physical chemistry. She still got the tingles when he ran his hand up her arm. Given the big messy picture, she'd decided the good outweighed the bad. She'd made the conscious decision to stick it out.

Am I settling or expecting too much? She'd never figured out the answer to that question. Granna, who married the first boy she ever kissed and lost him to bladder cancer twenty-some years later, didn't know either.

She missed Jane, Henry's wife. If she still haunted the house, Tipsy could talk to her about Will. Jane had always listened while offering snippets of practical advice. She was compassionate without being judgmental. Tipsy knew what Lindsey would say ("Just give him some time!") and what Shelby would say ("I love Will but if he's back on his bullshit, then screw him!").

I tend to agree with Shelby, said Granna.

Tipsy pondered as she drove past Sullivan's Island Baptist Church into the historic district known as Moultrieville. *Isn't there something in between? Between a mile long leash and screw you? Between settling for less and expecting perfection? And why am I still asking these questions?* Frustration roiled in her midsection. *I've been divorced for going on two years. Shouldn't my life be sorted out by now?*

Granna didn't provide an answer, which meant she didn't have a good one for those questions, either. Tipsy followed her phone's directions down Middle Street toward the south end of Sullivan's. While the northern Breach Inlet side of the island had a sparse, grassy beach town feel, the southern end had a small town *Steel Magnolias* vibe; that is, if Chinquapin Parish had included Revolutionary War fortifications. The oldest remaining homes were mostly tiny bungalows, but a few pseudo-plantation houses with traditional double-decker piazzas lingered on Officer's Row, a section of historic military housing on I'On Avenue. Ancient live oaks had observed the island's long, dark history, including a tragic stint as a quarantine station for enslaved Africans. Post-Civil War, an African American farming community had slowly transitioned to an exclusive seaside enclave. Brick ranchers from the 1960s with hodgepodge additions huddled beside towering contemporary board and baton mansions. As always, Sullivan's was proudly disorganized and eccentric. The architectural version of an academic convention; an eclectic mix of sleepy tenured professors and arrogant doctoral students.

She took a few sharp turns onto Thompson Avenue near Station 14, on the Intracoastal side of the island along the marsh. She looked up as her phone announced that she had arrived at her destination.

Will had told her that Pamella Brewton— Pam-ella, with two l's, don't forget— was a little eccentric.

From the looks of this place, said Granna, *he wasn't telling tales.*

7

The house was one of the island's clapboard senior citizens. Butterflies, moths, and fat bumble bees flittered over a front yard covered in white daisies and yellow brown-eyed susans. Purple wisteria blossoms and Confederate jasmine swarmed over the trellis above the front gate. The archway looked as if it were made of flowers instead of the same rotting wood that made up the fence. A cracked flagstone path led to a two-story house on raised pilings. Five crooked steps ended in a wide, slightly lopsided porch furnished with four red rocking chairs and a Charleston green joggling board. The strangest thing about the whole place, however, was the color.

Everything from the siding to the shutters to the fence itself was painted in shades of pale blue. Given the peeling state of it all, it was an old paint job, and a stubborn one. A bit of fading here and there, but otherwise that blue paint clung to the wood like a bad case of frostbite.

Haint blue? Tipsy asked Granna.

Looks like it, but my word, someone got a mite carried away.

Tipsy nodded her agreement. Normally haint blue—the shade of pale blue common to South Carolina porch ceilings—was one of her favorite colors. This house's color scheme reminded her of diluted toilet bowl cleaner, or mouthwash spit in a sink.

It took a moment to make sense of the darker blues and sea greens that interrupted all that used Listerine. At least ten bottle trees dotted the yard. They rose out of the flowers, iron crab legs capped with cobalt claws. A few were crafted from driftwood. Those upright arboreal skeletons reminded Tipsy of morbid Christmas trees decorated with spacy blue lights.

As she shut off the ignition, she read Will's text again. She swallowed the lump in her throat like an egret trying to gulp down a particularly large fish. She tossed the phone onto the passenger seat and got out of the truck.

Good decision. He threw the ingredients in the pot, said Granna. *Let him stew a while.*

She pulled the jasmine away from the weathered gray sign on the trellis. *True Blue Cottage.*

The bottle trees couldn't possibly be waving at her; they were made of metal or stiff dead wood. Still, something about the sunlight glinting off the blue glass made the whole yard seem topsy-turvy. *If I didn't know how such things worked, I'd think there were spirits moving around in there.*

So silly! said Granna. *Imagine trying to cram Henry Mott's lanky behind into one of those itty bitty bottles.*

Tipsy walked under the trellis and down the path. The brown-eyed susans bent toward one another as if they were gossiping about an unwelcome visitor. She climbed the creaky stairs, but when she got to the porch, she turned back to the yard. Sunshine on the pale blue fence created an unpleasant glare. She closed her eyes, but the shape of the bottles remained in splotchy blue streaks in the blackness. She rubbed her face.

The door swung open behind her. It banged against the exterior wall. "You *must* be Tipsy!"

Tipsy spun around. "Yes. Hey!" The woman before her was probably around fifty, even taller and thinner than Tipsy, with dark curly hair and bright green eyes. She wore a neon pink Bohemian tunic, green and yellow striped cropped jeans with fringe at the bottom, and a pair of sandals that wrapped halfway up her calf. Somehow, it all worked. "Pamella?"

"That's me, honey! Pam-*el-la*, with two l's!" Pamella grabbed her hand and squeezed, hard. Tipsy winced. Still, she couldn't help but smile back at this pretty woman who dripped enthusiasm like a leaky bucket of happiness.

"Come *on in.* I am so beyond happy to meet you! When we spoke on the phone, I knew you were the *perfect* artist for this project. Will Garrison had so many nice things to say about you. So did May Penny!"

"May Penny Collins?" asked Tipsy, surprised at the mention of her former mother-in-law.

"Yes! She and Tripp were friends of my late father." She peered over Tipsy's shoulder. Her voice dropped to a whisper, as if the spirits in the bottles might hear her. "It's pretty impressive to get a glowing reference from your *ex-husband's mother.*"

"Yeah, well, we've had our moments."

Pamella tugged her toward the threshold and then abruptly stopped. Tipsy bumped into her.

"Oh, wait. Listen, I inherited True Blue from my daddy a couple years ago. I *just* moved back to town from Atlanta. So good to be back in the *real South*." She wiggled her shoulders. While she didn't blink for emphasis the way Jane had, she added pizazz to words of import. Mostly in flailing hands, wagging eyebrows, and those shoulders that bounced like she danced to music only she could hear. Pamella talked as fast as a New Yorker, yet her husky voice retained its Southern twang. Like a taxicab horn crossed with a baying hound dog. "I know it looks like a *fricked up* version of the witch's house from Hansel and Gretel."

"It's truly blue, that's for sure."

"Hopefully I'll be able to change it soon, if this works out."

"Oh, jeez. I don't do exterior painting. Is that what—"

"Of course you don't! You're an *artiste extraordinaire!*" She dragged Tipsy into the house. True Blue had no foyer. Upon crossing the threshold, they were in the living room. A brown leather sofa and matching club chair sat around a hideous coffee table with a glass top and a base made from an old boat propeller. No carpets on the old hardwood floors. Faded beachy prints on the walls and a faint musty smell.

Pamella led her toward the kitchen in the back of the house. It was as fresh as the rest of the house was dated. White cabinets, white quartz countertops, and light wide plank wood floors courtesy of Will. An oyster shell chandelier hung over the island. All perfectly orderly, with the exception of two empty sauvignon blanc bottles and a wine glass in the sink. Pamella pointed at a bare expanse of wall behind the rustic kitchen table. "I'd like to hang it here."

"Perfect." Tipsy sized up the wall. "You want a painting of the front of the house with you and your father sitting on the stoop?"

"Yes. Or *maybe* the back. To get the marsh view? I'm not sure yet."

"I'll do a bunch of sketches to give you some ideas."

"Great. I want the figures to be me as a child and him as a younger man. I never knew my mother, so it was just me and Daddy."

"I'm sorry—"

"She ran out on us when I was a baby. No biggie."

Tipsy's own mother had left her, albeit as a teenager and not an infant. Even before her mother had really peaced out, Granna had basically raised Tipsy in her tiny, threadbare house in the rural upstate. Tipsy knew firsthand that maternal abandonment was kind of a biggie, but she didn't know Pamella from Adam so she kept her mouth shut.

"I can't believe I don't have a photo of me and Daddy outside!" said Pamella.

"It's okay. If you show me a couple pictures of the two of you from back then, it won't be a problem. I'll work y'all in however you want. Position, facial expression, whatever."

"That's pretty cool. Will said you could paint *anything*, but I didn't know he meant, like, *anything*." Cue shoulder wiggle.

Tipsy shrugged. She had no way to explain her supernaturally inspired ability to replicate life with paint.

Pamella gestured to the table. "Let's sit. Can I get you anything to drink?" The lady herself had a large Yeti tumbler. Tipsy shook her head as she joined her.

"I hope I'll be able to display the painting here." Pamella sipped from her Yeti. "But if I *have* to sell the house at least I can take something of it with me."

"You're thinking of selling? The market on the island is sure hot."

"I don't need to sell it for the money. I need to sell it… because… *you know*. The *you know what*."

"I do?"

"Will didn't tell you?"

"He told me I was coming out here to talk about a painting commission."

"You are… and we did talk about the painting. Of course I *want the painting*. But he didn't mention anything about my grandmother?"

"I'm sorry?"

Pamella leaned back in her chair. "My grandmother haunts this house. Will told me you have *some experience* with such things."

Tipsy about fainted. Her eyes bugged from her head like she was dead herself and someone needed to close them. No living person had ever frankly called out her talent for seeing the dead. She'd confided in exactly two people about it: Granna and Will. Yet Pamella was stating she had some experience with the paranormal in the same way she might ask to look at Tipsy's paintings on her Instagram feed.

She tried to eke moisture out of her suddenly parched mouth. Maybe she'd misinterpreted Pamella. "Will told you I have experience with what now?"

"Ghosts, lady. He told me you had a similar problem in your own house and you dealt with it." Pamella snapped her fingers.

"What else did he tell you?"

"Not much. Just that you'd found out *why* the ghosts in your house were stuck there, and then they moved on."

"Can I have some water?" Tipsy stood and walked past the kitchen island. She opened a few cabinets, and removed a tumbler. She ran lukewarm water from the tap. She needed to guzzle this water and the cold might make her head explode. How dare Will casually tell this woman about her lifelong secret?

Pamella started chattering behind her. "So. Right! My grandmother haunts the house—my father's mother. Ivy More Brewton. She died in 1944. Fell off the dock out back, bless her heart, when my father was only twelve. She—"

"Ma'am. Pamella. I need a minute. I came out here thinking this was a painting commission, not an invitation to conduct a séance."

"I *really, truly* do want the painting. But if you can help me with this other problem—"

"How do you even know the house is haunted? Can you see ghosts?"

"No, but I know she's here. Things happen in this house. Objects move. Doors open and shut. Sometimes, when she's angry—"

"She gets angry?"

"I think so. When I was a teenager Daddy and I got in an argument about my curfew one night. He was *so strict*. I was kind of, like, *a rebel*, but like in an eighties punk rock way that wasn't *that* rebellious. Like I wore leather jackets and once I dyed my hair jet black. I wanted to go to a party at— wait. Where was I? Oh, right. We were yellin' at each other and the coffee table flipped over. Magazines went everywhere. Daddy's bourbon all over the floor. Then the windows flat out *exploded*. I still have a scar, where glass hit me." She showed Tipsy a thin line on the side of her cheek. "It *was* a loud argument. I suppose we were disturbing her peace."

"How do you know it's your grandmother?"

"Daddy couldn't see ghosts, so he never actually laid eyes on her either. *His* grandmother, Ivy's mother Alma More, somehow knew it was Ivy. Maybe she saw ghosts."

Despite Tipsy's hesitation, the discovery of a kindred family caught her interest. "It does run in families, but not always in a straight line. My mother has no supernatural talent, but her mother, my Granna, she did."

"I didn't inherit anything from Ivy besides my face, from what photos tell me." She patted her cheek. "Anyway, after Ivy died, Alma warned Daddy about her haunting this place. Alma died long before I was born, so I never got to ask her any questions."

"So your grandmother—"

"*Meemaw.* I always wanted a grandmother to like, teach me to bake and sew and stuff. Ivy was as close as I could get. So I call her Meemaw."

"Meemaw. Okay. Pamella, listen. I'm sorry you're dealing with this. I'm sure it must be annoying—"

"It's gone beyond annoying. It's gotten worse over the years. When I was a child, Meemaw rarely got angry. By my thirties, it got *bad*. She'd go quiet for a few days and then she'd rage around like our family hurricane.

Daddy loved this place, but we couldn't stay here as often as he would have liked. That's why Daddy painted the *whole damn place* haint blue and set up all those frickin' bottle trees. You know the old stories. *Keep the spirits at bay. Trap them in bottles.* Yada-yada-yada."

Tipsy glowered, her sense of justice offended. "He wanted to trap his own mother in a bottle?"

"Is she still his *mother?* I don't know anything about this stuff. I've tried to do research, but there are a lot of charlatans out there. I mentioned to Will that the house is haunted. He's the first person that ever gave me any *real hope* something could be done about it."

"It seems pretty quiet here now."

"I've only been back for two months. I rented a townhouse downtown. I paid the kitchen contractors bonuses to get things done faster. But she's starting to get annoyed. I can *tell*. Two days ago, when I arrived, all the potted plants I'd set up on the porch were turned upside down. Dirt *everywhere*. Yesterday, I opened the back door, and even though it's a hundred degrees out, I felt a chill like I'd been plunked down in Antarctica."

Tipsy filled her water glass again and sat down. "If she's throwing things around and stuff like that, then she was a seer herself."

"What do you mean?"

"Only ghosts who were able to *see* ghosts as living beings have that kind of telekinetic power." Tipsy thought of Henry knocking over the bookshelf in her kitchen a few days after she moved to Miss Callie's. How afraid she'd been of his power. It sounded like this woman Ivy was just as volatile, if not more.

It's one thing dealing with your own restless spirits, said Granna. *But someone else's…*

That was enough for Tipsy. "I'm sorry. I hate that you're having these problems, but I don't think I can get involved."

"Please," said Pamella. "I *seriously* don't know what else to do. My father had three houses during my childhood. His family home downtown near the Battery, a new house in Atlanta where he did business, and this cottage. The house downtown was lovely, but I never missed it when he sold it. *Atlanta?* Not a second thought. Sold it myself when he passed. This place, though—it's *so special.* I want to make it happy and cozy again, like when I was little. I'd seriously like to live here, but I can't if Meemaw can't find peace. Poor woman, stuck here like a fly between a screen and glass. It's seriously *so* sad."

As much as instinct yelled at her to run out of this house, Tipsy felt the familiar burn of compassion for Pamella and her late grandmother. "I agree. The lingering dead are always sad, believe me. Maybe there's another way to get some peace around here." Even as she said it, Tipsy couldn't think of any other reasonable solution.

"I don't even know if I could sell the house. In my research I found a legal case from New York or somewhere, where someone got sued for not disclosing a haunted house! How can I sell a place and say, yeah, it needs a new roof, and my dead grandmother might hit you upside the head with a broom? *So tacky.* And potentially litigious."

"I get it. But I didn't give Will permission to tell anyone about my ghosts. It's a private matter—"

"I'll make it worth your while."

"It's not that—"

"Fifty thousand."

"Excuse me?"

"Fifty thousand dollars."

Tipsy about fell out. "Are you serious?"

"Let's say three thousand for the painting. Forty-seven for the exorcism!"

Tipsy sat back in her chair. Fifty thousand dollars would be life changing for her. She no longer suffered from painter's block and she'd been making decent money from her paintings, but she always watched her bank account like a hawk flying above a sneaky fish. Unlike other business endeavors, as an artist she was one person and she only produced so much. She refused to let the quality of her work suffer. That kind of money would finally give her a cushion. She could pay off her credit cards and start saving.

"If you're sure, and you really have fifty thousand dollars you can just hand over—"

Pamella grinned. "Don't you worry about that, lady. My daddy left me a *lot more* than a haunted cottage and a shed full of haint blue paint."

Chapter 2

ipsy and Pamella chatted as they walked into the backyard. Two live oaks and several crepe myrtles, all in need of pruning, cast their tired limbs over dried out grass. Four more bottle trees dotted the empty spaces between them. The living trees seemed to grow away from those unbending replicas, as if offended by their artificiality. The lot was long and skinny. A rickety dock stuck out into Cove Creek, the short, navigable rivulet leading to the Intracoastal Waterway.

"Once I know I'm keeping the place, I'll rebuild the dock. Put in a pool," Pamella said. She still sipped from her Yeti tumbler. Ice clanked softly against the metal as she tipped it back. At first Tipsy figured the tumbler contained water. A flash of color made her change her mind to lemonade. When she got a whiff of Pamella's breath when she opened the back door, she remembered the wine bottles on the counter. It was ten in the morning, but maybe Pamella was on Russian drinking time.

Pamella pointed at the houses on either side of her lot. Both had a boxy mid-century look. "We used to own all this," said Pamella, "but Daddy sold it before I was born. After his father died, it was *too much* for him to keep up a big piece of land out here and the house downtown. Grandpa Cam killed himself in 1952, when Daddy was twenty."

"Grandpa Cam and Meemaw," said Tipsy. "That's sweet. But sad for your father."

This is sounding more complicated by the minute, said Granna.

"Lots of sadness in Daddy's life. His parents died unexpectedly when he was young. Three divorces. I don't think he ever got over my mother running out on him. A lot of loss, indeed." She cleared her throat and smiled. "So, you need to know *how* Meemaw Ivy died in order to set her free? I always heard Grandpa Cam found her after she fell off the dock."

"Maybe, but if she's lingering that leads me to believe she has some unresolved issues."

"Meaning her death might be a little more *problematic* than a simple slip and fall?"

Tipsy nodded. "She won't remember what happened or the last week leading up to it."

"I see. I hope whatever happened to Meemaw wasn't too terrible."

Tipsy thought of Jane and Henry's tragic, multilayered murder. From her experience, hauntings weren't the result of peaceful deaths. She didn't see any reason to upset Pamella, so she nodded.

"What should we do now?" asked Pamella. "You tell me. You're the boss!"

"Maybe you should let me be for a while. I think ghosts sense me and they're curious. Or I can try to call her. But it would be weird, to like, talk to her while you're standing here. And it might make her upset."

"Whatever you say, but I feel guilty leaving you here alone with Meemaw."

"It's all part of the job, I guess."

Now it's a job, said Granna. *Ain't that an odd way to think of it.*

I'm going to kill Will.

Make sure you get paid before you go to jail.

Tipsy sat on a dilapidated picnic table under the shade of the largest oak tree. She checked her phone. It was almost noon. If she were sitting in the sun, she'd have already shriveled up. As it was, the breeze off the marsh and a glass of sweet tea made for a pleasant hour or so of watchful contemplation. She thought again of Pamella's morning wine and her exuberant persona. Something odd churned under all that bubbliness. She'd mentioned her two grown daughters, who both lived in Atlanta, and her third husband. She seemed to have a close relationship with her children, while she was estranged from her spouse.

"I was a good daughter," she said, as she downed a few mints before getting into her sporty blue BMW. "I think I've been a good mother. Both my girls have launched into the world, although they're propelled by their trust funds. Unfortunately, I'm *terrible* at choosing men."

Pamella might be odd, but we have something in common.

Not like you to be so defeatist, sugar, said Granna.

Tipsy thought of her impending conversation with Will. It would definitely be a rough one. There was no way she could let his betrayal of her trust go without calling him out, fifty thousand or not.

I'm annoyed with life, Granna. The past couple months I finally felt like I'd found a little stability. Selling paintings, getting along with Ayers, kids are good, Henry not too crazy, and Will seemed solid. Any one of those things goes sideways and I'm knocked back again.

That's life, honey, especially when you're trying to rebuild one.

But I've been trying so hard to do everything right, yet I never get ahead. Even this fifty-k. What a blessing, but why can't anything be easy? Now I have to wrangle some new, potentially crazier spirit—

Shhhh. You hear that?

Tipsy did. Soft singing. As the notes took shape, she picked out the tune. *Somewhere Over the Rainbow.*

The melodic alto voice came from everywhere and nowhere. A chill fell over Tipsy. She smelled cinnamon and nutmeg. Apple pies. Winter smells.

A woman stood framed against the green and brown marsh grass. She wore a short-sleeved blue and white floral dress with a cinched waist that ended just below her knees. Her black shoes had low heels. Her dark curly hair was pulled half up and tied with a ribbon. Tipsy could not see her face, as she was watching Cove Creek.

Despite her familiarity with the dead, the woman's stillness and her hidden face gave Tipsy the creeps. *Just a ghost,* she thought. *I've seen hundreds of them. I've lived with two of them.*

Tipsy eased off the table and walked toward the ghost. The woman's hair and skirt moved as if touched by a breeze Tipsy could not feel. Everything about her was gauzy, as if the humidity had further diluted her insubstantial form. Her arms hung limply at her sides.

Tipsy cleared her throat. "Excuse me. Ma'am? Are you Mrs. Brewton?"

The woman stopped singing.

"Ivy? Ivy More Brewton?"

Still nothing. Her skirt and hair swayed in the still air. Tipsy tried another route. "Meemaw?"

The ghost turned, as slowly as a flower looking for the sun.

Although the ghost had dark hair, Tipsy's mind had already formed some version of a grandmother. The woman who regarded her with steely eyes couldn't have been less grandmotherly.

Ivy More Brewton looked to be about forty. Like her granddaughter, she was taller than Tipsy. She had high cheekbones, full lips, and a heart-shaped face. Dark, thin, rounded eyebrows arched over reddish brown doe eyes. The rest of her was unusually hazy but sharp lines defined her face.

When confronted by this deathly pale impersonation of Pamella crossed with a 1940s screen siren, Tipsy was momentarily struck dumb. Finally, she croaked out again, "Meemaw?"

"That's what the young woman calls me. I believe she's the daughter of my son, Robert."

Tipsy had expected something like Jane's old Charleston drawl, but Ivy sounded more like Katharine Hepburn. Her teeth stayed clenched together so only her lips moved when she talked. "I saw you two talking earlier today, but I didn't realize you were here to call on me."

"Has anyone ever called on you before?"

"No. I thought my mother might pay me a visit, as she knew of the existence of ghosts as much as I did."

"Alma, right?"

"Yes. She wasn't a very powerful seer. She mostly saw shadows and light. But she taught me what her father taught her about spirits."

"What did she include in her lessons?"

"Don't tell anyone about it. Especially for the likes of us, it was dangerous."

"Why especially for the likes of y'all?"

"Poor people take the blame for everything, including the superstitious fear of others."

So Pamella might be rich, but she wasn't old money on Meemaw's side. "I see," said Tipsy. "Are you willing to talk to me?"

"Talking to you is about the strangest thing that's happened to me since death itself. I doubt I'll want to continue conversating, but…" She tapped one foot on the grass as if to tamp down her curiosity. It got the better of her. "What do you want?" she asked.

"Um…my name is Tipsy Collins. I'm about to try to help you move on from this haunting."

"What does *that* mean?" Her right eyebrow crept up her forehead. The wind picked up around her again.

She'd seemed relatively calm and rational, so Tipsy had started to let down her guard. A spurt of fear-induced adrenaline hit her veins. She had no idea what might provoke this ghost. She forced herself to speak firmly and simply.

"Your granddaughter Pamella asked me to help you move on. Since things sometimes get chaotic around here when you're disturbed. You break stuff. Toss stuff around. That sort of thing."

"I only do such things when living people are too loud." She crept toward Tipsy. "Always, you're yelling and banging and ruining my peace. When it gets intolerably noisy, I make my displeasure known. The living leave for a while. You probably think I'm terrible for doing so."

Surprising the ghost cared about Tipsy's opinion, given her aloof prickliness. "Not really. I don't know what it's like to be a ghost."

"Yet."

"I plan to die in my bed at age one hundred, thanks. No lingering for me."

"That's what we all plan, isn't it? I try to be patient with my granddaughter—Pamella? Her father, my son Bobby, he called her Pammy. Bobby passed away." Her voice cracked. "It's hard for me to remember when. But he was old. I know that much. He kept on going after I left him."

"I'm sorry. Even after death, I can't imagine losing a child."

Ivy's jaw clenched and she returned to business. "I try to be patient with Pammy, but I can only stand so much noise before it starts to cloud my thinking."

"Is that happening now, with Pamella back at the house and workers doing renovations?"

The eyebrow rose again. She'd passed on her overactive eyebrows to her granddaughter along with her supermodel height. "It's happening now, with you talking."

"Then let's get to it. I assume you don't remember your death?"

"Correct."

"If I touch you, I can see into your memories. See how you died and help you remember it. Once you understand what happened, you can move on." Tipsy thought of Henry's ability to leave Miss Callie's house for short periods of time. "Can you leave this place at all, like as a ghost?"

"No."

"Oh. Interesting. My friend was a seer like you and me when he was alive, and he can leave the house sometimes."

"That is curious. But can he do this?"

Ivy raised her hand. Her hair stood on end in a dark halo. The nearest tree limb bent toward her. It was the width of Tipsy's thigh. Ivy snapped her fingers and the limb cracked loose from the trunk. She flung the fifteen foot tree branch into the marsh behind them.

Holy shit, Tipsy thought. She'd seen Henry slam doors and knock things over, but she'd never seen anything like that.

I've told you, said Granna. *My talent ain't exactly yours, and Henry and Ivy might be different, too.*

You also told me some ghosts were dangerous.

Ummm…hmmm. I think we're looking at exactly what I meant.

"No, I don't think he can. Wow." Tipsy tried to maintain her small talk tone. "Overall you're pretty impressive. Most ghosts I've met are at least a little crazy."

Ivy More's eyebrows were punctuation on her forehead. The right one arched in a graceful question mark. "What makes you think I'm not crazy? Once things get too loud, you never know what I might do."

"All the more reason to move on and find peace. Let me see how you died and then you'll be on your way."

"I fell off the dock. I heard my son say it many times."

"Maybe you did, but I don't think that's the whole story. If you know it, you'll be free."

Ivy turned in a slow circle. "I admit, I'd like to leave here. I loved this place, but in the end, it was as sad as any of the other places in my life." She looked over her shoulder at Tipsy. "But I won't leave without my true love."

"Your late husband?"

"Camden? No."

"Uh…okay." Tipsy didn't consider Ayers her true love, so she didn't judge. "Who was it?"

"He's still somewhere on this island, according to my mother. She truly saw him, like a proper seer. She told me he's dead, yet he remains."

"So where do I find him? What's his name?"

"You'll know him when *you* see him. No woman could look at him and not fall in love. He was the only man I ever looked up to." She tilted her chin toward the sun. She hung her arms above her, as if she were slow dancing with a giant. "You can find him for me."

"But I'd need to know who he is. And where he is."

"I have nothing but time. You show me you can be of use and maybe I'll listen to you. But I'm telling you; I'm not going a damn place without him."

Ivy started spinning, arms akimbo, like a little girl trying to see how long she could twirl before dizziness knocked her down. Her hair and dress blew around her in a cloud. She disappeared in a swirl of bluish mist.

Without thinking, Tipsy attempted what could only be called an instinctive supernatural grab. She'd only done this once, when she'd pulled Henry into her presence when he didn't want to appear. This time, she tried to keep Ivy from going. She reached out with her own power, with no real idea of what she was doing, the same way she might reflexively grab a child by the shoulder to keep her from running into traffic. For a moment, she thought it would work. She felt Ivy hesitate, and her surprise at Tipsy's interference.

The moment didn't last. Ivy shoved Tipsy and the connection between them broke. Tipsy stumbled backward. Her ankle caught on a tree root. She landed on her back. Her butt struck another root. Pain shot up her tailbone and she gasped for air. Ivy's thrust had knocked the wind clean out of her.

As she lay there, gulping oxygen, Granna spoke up. *Yup, I did indeed say some spirits are dangerous.*

Tipsy rolled onto her stomach. Thank goodness she'd missed a fire ant hill a few feet to her right. She'd be adding inflamed red welts to her bruised butt-bone. *She's dangerous, all right,* Tipsy replied. She pushed herself to her feet. Foreboding washed over her as she hobbled toward the house. *But if I want the fifty-k, I'm stuck with her.*

Certainly an interesting day, sugar.

Tipsy checked her phone as she got into her car. She finally replied to Will's text.

Yes. Come over after the kids are asleep. The usual time.

Her interesting day wasn't over yet.

———◆✕◆———

Tipsy and Will sat on the joggling board on the front porch. She wanted to put a pillow under her sore tailbone, but that would require an explanation as to why her ass hurt. She wasn't in the mood for a darkly humorous story about today's spectral assault. Silence hung over them, as uncomfortable as the humidity that lingered even after the sun went down. Good memories were irritating gnats in the heavy air, taunting Tipsy with reminders of happier times. Tipsy usually did him the favor of starting the conversation, but tonight she was too frustrated and confused to know where to begin. He'd been acting so weird, and his betrayal of her trust added a new element to the unpleasantness.

She stood and grabbed the garden hose attached to a spigot under the joggling board. She sprayed water over the yard, as if she might drown out their problems and save their relationship as easily as she reinvigorated Miss Callie's dehydrated hydrangeas.

"You going to give me the silent treatment?" he asked.

She spun around and took the pressure off the nozzle but she splattered Will with water anyway. He leaned on his elbows, so she watched the top of his head. The same thick black hair Lindsey had described before they started dating. *He has good hair*, she'd said.

Great, Tipsy thought. *He also has a chiseled jawline and nice biceps and, oh, by the way, your standard male penchant for perplexing behavior.*

She lowered the hose like a sharpshooter re-holstering her gun. "I'm not giving you the silent treatment. I legit don't know what to say."

"I get it, but Pamella is paying you a ton of money—"

"Still, Will, it should have been my decision to tell her about my ghosts. You know how personal that is to me."

"If I asked you about it first you would have said no."

"Maybe I wouldn't with that kind of money in play. But you didn't give me the chance to decide."

"You're mad at me for hooking you up with fifty-k?" He snorted. "That makes no sense."

"It does make sense. This is about me trusting you with the biggest secret of my life, and you telling someone I don't know without asking me."

"I'm sorry I didn't ask, but I still don't see how you can be mad. I didn't ask because I knew you'd make a big deal about it."

"That's because it's a big deal. You do remember you didn't believe me last summer and accused me of lying, right? You made me feel crazy."

"You're bringing up that ancient argument?"

"No. I'm saying—"

"You're upset. Okay. But I feel like the end result is really good for you—"

"It is! But I can't just let it go that you didn't discuss it with me! What kind of trust precedent does that set, long term?"

"Long term?"

She backpedaled. "I, um… I mean if we're going to move forward."

He stared at the floor between his flip flops. Her stomach cramped as the silence stretched on.

"You wanted to talk," she finally said. "That must mean moving forward is not on the table."

"Tipsy. I love you. You know I do. But these kinds of things—I feel like nothing I do is ever right."

"Good lord. I'm not screaming at you." Even as she said it, her voice rose. "I'm telling you this is not some simple thing that can be resolved because I'm getting paid."

"That's the problem. As much as I care about you, everything is complicated with you."

"What's that supposed to mean?"

"Like, life in general. We don't see eye to eye on so many things. And then there's Ayers's drama, kid stress, work stress…freaking ghosts."

"You have your own baggage. *Hello!* Three kids and a recovering drug addict ex-wife? Most people our age have complications at this point. Comes with being an adult."

"I want simple."

"Whatever, Will. Things aren't just easy-peasy or an impossible deal breaker."

"I came over here to talk about how things have been and now it's a big philosophical discussion—"

"I'm glad you want to talk. Clearly, you've been festering about something. But you didn't even give me a heads up about Pamella. You think we're not going to discuss it now?"

"Damnit. I don't know. But right now I feel like crap."

"So do I! I want to help you feel better. You don't seem to want to help me."

They both went quiet again. This time Tipsy didn't let it last long.

"So we're breaking up?" she asked.

"Maybe we need to take a break. Like, cool things down for a bit."

Tipsy stood and put her hands on her hips. "Jeez. We've been a couple for over a year. I can't just walk back from that or sit around waiting for you to figure yourself out."

He got to his feet as well. "Fine, then. It's all or nothing with you?"

"No! It's all or nothing with *you*. Either I magically manage to have a relationship with you while having no expectations or—" She made air quotes with her fingers. "— *complications* or you break up with me."

He ran a hand over his hair. "So I'm supposed to keep going like this when I know I'm not giving you what you want?"

"It's not that hard. It's really not."

"Maybe for you it isn't. You always want me to tell you how I feel. Now I'm telling you and you're pissed."

"I'm clearly not giving you what you want, either. If you even know what that is."

"You're not asking too much, Tipsy. I know that, deep down. But I start feeling so hemmed in and I don't know how to stop feeling that way. I've been trying. I swear."

"I don't know what to say."

"Neither do I. I guess we do need to take a break. Can I call you tomorrow?"

She laughed. "No. If we're going to take a break then we're going to *take a break*."

"Like not talk at all?"

Oh lord, said Granna. *I sense there's some cake here, and he wants it in his belly and on the stand.*

The sadness in his voice pulled at her but she held her ground. "Not now. We both need to think about things."

Silence, *again.* She had to break it, which always seemed to be the woman's responsibility in tense conversations. "So what do we tell the kids? My girls are already asking when Rosie and Ella will be back with you so they can come over."

"We don't have to cut the kids off, do we? I'm happy to have the twins at my house."

She wanted to punch him, but at the same time, she didn't want to tell M.P. and O-liv that they suddenly couldn't spend time with Will's girls. It seemed heartless to take away a friendship she'd created. "We'll have to see."

They made small talk for a few minutes. Each sentence was more painful than the last—once again reminding her of how it could be, if only Will got his shit together.

Maybe he does just need time...

Uh, sugar. He's had plenty of time. If his doo-doo was going to do its thing, it would have done it.

Okay, Granna. Okay.

She walked to the edge of the porch. Will followed her. "Any updates on Henry's book?"

She shook her head.

"Is he—"

"I don't want to talk about Henry."

"I really am sorry I told Pamella. But when she said she'd pay any price, I knew—"

"What's done is done. Just go, okay?"

"Yeah." He reached out to hug her and she couldn't resist. She melted into his arms with her head on his chest. The tears she'd been holding back all day finally burst their banks. His pale blue polo shirt darkened under her face, from haint blue to bottle blue.

Too much blue, she thought. *It's like the sky is collapsing on me.*

"I'm sorry," he whispered.

She pulled back from him and sniffed. "Say goodnight."

She left him standing on the porch, slipped inside, and locked the door behind her. Chuffing sobs gathered in the back of her throat.

Nothing to be done now but let it out, sweet girl, said Granna.

So Tipsy did.

⸺◆✕◆⸺

She took care not to wake the kids, but she ran up the stairs to her bedroom and flopped on the bed. She sobbed like a nerdy teenager who had accepted that life wasn't a romantic comedy and the quarterback would always date the cheerleading captain. She cursed Will for his timing in coming into her life. When they started dating, she'd still been so relieved to be away from Ayers that she hadn't yet realized what it meant to be lonely. Damn Will for reminding her what it felt like to crave someone's company and then leaving her all alone.

She got up and checked on the kids when she finally cried herself dry. They'd slept serenely through her boo-hooing. She returned to her room, brushed her teeth and washed her face, and changed into a frumpy old nightdress she'd had since nursing Little Ayers. Decidedly unsexy, but who the hell did she have to be sexy for right now?

She picked up her phone.

WILL GARRISON TEXT MESSAGE (3)

AYERS COLLINS TEXT MESSAGE (2)

She figured she might as well see what Will wanted. She sighed as she read his messages.

I'M SORRY AGAIN.

I'M HERE IF YOU NEED ME.

GOODNIGHT

So now Will was offering her comfort from the heartache he'd foisted upon her. Sure, that made a lot of sense.

She dealt with Big Ayers next.

HEY

U AND ME NEED TO TALK

Tipsy covered her mouth with her hand to contain her giggles. She wondered what other dudes might send her such messages. Next thing she knew, she'd be getting a *we-need-to-talk* text from her estranged alcoholic father.

Henry materialized at the end of her bed. He sat elegantly, as he always did, with his legs crossed at the ankle. "I heard you crying, so I thought not to disturb you," he said. "Now you're laughing, so it seems appropriate."

Tipsy was too accustomed to Henry to care if he saw her in her Laura Ingalls Wilder nightgown with puffy eyes, a runny nose, and a few leftover mascara tears smudged across her cheeks. She tucked her bare feet under the covers because he gave off a chill. "All the other men in my life want to talk to me. Why not you, too?"

"I couldn't help but overhear your conversation with William." He said Will's name as if it were missing the letter L. Like maybe Pamella had borrowed one of them. *Wi-yum.* "It seems the two of you are breaking down?"

"The correct term is breaking up, but your version is more accurate. So yeah. He's kicked me to the curb."

Henry frowned. Before he asked for clarification, she said, "He didn't literally kick me. But it's over."

"He seems to be a very confused man."

"You're all confused. And confusing. Now I don't know what to do."

"What are your choices?"

"The first choice is to cut him off completely. No hanging out. No calls or texting. *Incommunicado*. The silent treatment. That's what Shelby would say. And that's what my Granna would say, if she were here."

"And the second choice?"

"Lindsey is more patient than they are. She's the one who told me to let Will be when he got all weird last time. He came around, like she said."

"While I cannot claim to understand all your newfangled ways of courting—your breaking down and up and sideways—I am of the mindset of Shelby and your grandmother. You let him be and he came around, yet here you are once more. It seems like you're kicking yourself in your own backside."

"You're right, but—"

"Tipsy, let me be frank. I had plenty of time over the past century. Rarely has a man been left with more time to understand his actions and emotions. You saw how much it helped me. I don't think you want to wait that long for Wi-yum to reach the right conclusion."

Tipsy wrapped her arms around her knees. "I know I have to try to cut him off. But it's so hard. Knowing he's there, but also not there."

"If Jane were here, she'd tell you I was a master at being there but not there."

"Henry, you clearly miss her. Have you thought any more about—"

"This is about you, not me." He stood and glided toward the head of the bed. She had to nestle down further into the covers to escape the minty, chilly breeze wafting off him.

"What you need to do is rest," he said.

"Okay, grandpa."

He scowled; his vanity clearly pricked. "I don't have a gray hair on my head."

The covers floated up around her chin and tucked themselves around her face, so she peered out at him like a teary angel sitting on a raincloud. "I have to reply to Ayers. He wants to talk to me, too."

"He can wait."

Henry's soothing voice, his minty scent, and the closely cuddled sheets lulled Tipsy, as if she were a tightly swaddled baby. Her eyelids felt heavy. "You're right. He'll just give me crap about something anyway." She opened one eye. "I saw a new ghost today. On Sullivan's. At the new commission. She's a piece of work. She's a seer, like us. She ripped a tree branch off and chucked it into the marsh like me tossing a sock in the laundry basket."

"Impressive. What do you know of her so far?"

"Supposedly she died when she fell off a dock. But her husband killed himself, and she claims another man was her true love…"

"Ah, I see. Death is often more complicated than we assume."

Tipsy closed her eyes again. "It's not just death. Life is the same way."

Chapter 3

When one is heartsore, the first moments after waking are the cruelest. As Tipsy's mind emerged from unsettling dreams of encroaching water, she had a few seconds of relief. Her house was not flooding. Before she opened her eyes, however, she remembered the sadness awaiting her in the real world.

Will broke up with me.

She lay in bed and blinked at the ceiling. She waited for the pain to slide down her throat through her chest with the burn of a shot of whiskey. It settled as a dull ache in her stomach. Her alarm sounded. She climbed out of bed to the sound of the kids rustling around in their rooms. She pushed through getting them and herself ready for the day. She donned running shorts and a ratty old tank top. Too grungy for the gym meant perfect for working on a painting. As she loaded two sketchpads and a canvas bag of pre-painting supplies into the back of her truck, she thanked the good lord for this job. She looked forward to starting on the painting, even if it included a supernatural Sherlock Holmes component. Despite her sadness about Will, her kids were healthy and happy and hopefully she had fifty-k on the way.

She walked the perimeter of the property when she got to True Blue, but she didn't see Ivy. She decided to focus on the painting instead. Maybe she was avoiding the inevitable, as approximately six percent of her fifty-k would come from the painting, but it was the least stressful six percent of the project. She walked through the back door into the kitchen. Pamella had texted that she'd left family pictures on the kitchen table.

She found a stack of old photos. First, a black and white picture of True Blue, long before the blue. An American flag with too few stars flew from a pole attached to one of the porch pillars of a neat white cottage with black shutters. Two men sat in rocking chairs on the front porch. They wore fedoras and their cigar smoke wafted around them, so Tipsy couldn't see their faces. There was writing along the white border: *C & J, Sept. 1928.* She found several other photos of the house from different angles and different decades. By the 1950s, someone had planted shrubs around the pilings and added a chain link fence. There was a photo from the back of the house after Hurricane Gracie, the 1959 storm that destroyed the dock but miraculously spared the cottage. In the 1970s, a long brown Plymouth parked in the middle of the front yard beside a white picket fence. Tipsy noticed two blue bottle trees, like the first of an invasive weed species. Pamella had stuck a sticky tab on a photo from 1989. *The year Daddy painted it blue. I started calling it True Blue and it stuck.*

In the 1989 shot, the bottle trees had multiplied. The house was blue, but the shutters were still black and the fence still white. A barrel-chested, white-haired man of about sixty stood in the front yard with his arms crossed over his chest. He wore loafers and a Citadel polo shirt. He stared unsmilingly at the camera. She couldn't see much resemblance to waifish Ivy or wiry Pamella in his serious, country club face, but she assumed he must be Pamella's father and Ivy's son, Robert "Bob" Brewton.

She found the resemblance to his mother and daughter in photos of the younger Robert. Even with a 1970s mustache and severely parted dark hair, he was a handsome man. He held little Pamella in his arms, resting her on one hip as easy as any mother would. Pammy, with her bouncy brown braids and long curly eyelashes, grinned so hard her nose wrinkled up like a growling puppy's. Bob stared into the lens, as if trying to guess the intentions of the person taking the photo. Another shot from the 1950s showed a clean shaven, strikingly attractive young man. He leaned against a convertible and glared at the world. Tipsy wondered if he knew how to smile.

Tipsy studied Pamella's childish face: the bright green color of her eyes, the way pieces of her curly hair escaped her braids. Her skinny frame clashed with her pudgy cheeks. Tipsy approached each picture with a mental camera. She pressed the shutter here and there to capture the shapes and shadows of Pamella's round face and the sharp angles of her late father's. She slowly created three dimensional models in her mind.

She'd have to ask Pamella what kind of expression she wanted for her father. Once Tipsy had a working mental picture, she'd understand how Bob Brewton's face would have twisted into a smile. How his chin would jut, his cheeks would plump out, and maybe his eyes would twinkle. On the other hand, if the man never smiled, Pamella might want something truer to life.

She pulled a small sketchpad from her bag and did a rough sketch of Bob's face, circa 1970, when he would have been about forty years old. He had a particularly strong jaw, and his thick black eyebrows added to the drama of his face. She wrote a note to herself. *Eye color?* While the figure in the painting probably wouldn't be close enough for eye color to matter much, for the sake of her mental picture, she'd ask Pamella.

Before she opened the second envelope, she read the note Pamella had stuck on it. *These aren't for the painting but thought they might be helpful anyway.* She slid several black and white photos onto the table.

They were all pictures of the gorgeous Ivy Brewton. While she looked nothing like Jane, who had sweetly rounded features, a cupid's bow mouth, and pale blue eyes, they shared a pre-1950s beauty. Something simpler or fresher. Neither woman would have had the benefit of Botox or highlighted hair or Instagram filters.

In the first photo, Ivy stood on the piazza of a house that had to be downtown somewhere. Outside of ancient Rome, only old Charleston had such pillars. She wore a dark pencil skirt and a tailored jacket. Her hair was pulled up in a mystifying 1940s hairstyle. It created tiered rolls above her forehead and at the nape of her neck, like loaves of pumpernickel bread. In an equally impressive fashion feat, a lacy white hat perched atop those dark rolls like a pat of butter.

A dark-haired boy of about ten stood in front of her in a pair of short pants and a button down white shirt. She had her gloved hands on his shoulders. To her left, a tall man wearing a dark suit. He must have been her husband, Camden Brewton. His hands were stuffed into his pockets. Despite his receding hairline, he was still comely. Camden smiled as if on his way to a church picnic, while stern Ivy and glum Robert looked to be headed to a funeral. It seemed as if Ivy and Robert were in one photo, and someone had glued the picture of Camden beside it. Husband and wife's hands were far apart, with hers clutching the child and his hidden from view in his trousers.

In the next photo, Ivy stood in a kitchen with her hands on a pot. She looked at the camera out of the corner of her eye. Tipsy detected a hint of humor there. As if the person taking the photo had told a crude joke and she didn't want to laugh.

So she's not all doom and gloom, Tipsy thought.

The last three photos were older. They were snapshots of a barefoot Ivy standing on the edge of the marsh in a simple light colored, calf length dress that emphasized her tiny waist. Her curly hair blew around her face. In the first photo she was laughing, her mouth wide open and her arms outstretched. In the second, she looked coyly over her shoulder while catching her hair behind one ear. In the third, she sat in the grass with her long legs stretched out before her. She leaned back on her hands and pursed her lips as if about to blow a kiss. Someone had written on the bottom of the first photo. *The most beautiful girl in the world. SI. Spring 1932.*

As Tipsy looked at those photos, curiosity overcame her that had nothing to do with her fifty-k. The happy young woman was nothing like the serious lady in the photo with Camden and Robert. Or the cold, irritable ghost she spoke with yesterday.

I know death changes people, Tipsy thought, *but with Ivy, clearly life changed her, too.*

Something tickled the back of Tipsy's mind. Like her supernatural abilities allowed her to remember every detail of a picture she wanted to paint, that same power caused her to vividly recall memories she sometimes wanted to forget. She'd long thought of them as her movie memories—scenes from her life that reminded her of the past at the strangest times. As she stood beside Pamella's kitchen table, she caught her own reflection in the ornate framed mirror over the sideboard. Just like that, her mind took her back to a different mirror. A much younger face, on the verge of so many changes.

———◆✕◆———

Tipsy stands in front of the bathroom mirror. She stares at her twelve-year-old self. She turns her head sideways to get a glimpse of her profile. Her eyes burn as she runs a finger down her nose. She hates the bump in the middle of it, no matter how much Granna tells her it's elegant. She thinks it's too damn big.

Other than her height, which she inherited from her daddy along with her nose, her beak is about the only thing on her that's too big. She looks down at her chest and her non-existent boobs. Her hips are too narrow. She looks like a boy in her jeans. Her long legs are as skinny as PopPop's old fishing poles.

She thinks about Tracy Scruggs and Jess Reedy, who are both blonde and short and have tiny noses and big boobs. No matter how much Granna tells her she'd blessed because someday those girls will be watching every calorie and it's not good to peak in the seventh grade, Tipsy wishes she looked like that with all her heart. Her own Mama had looked just so when she was a teenager, and she's still skinny.

That's because she don't eat anything, said Granna. Because she's got a problem.

Tipsy isn't exactly sure what Mama's problem is, but she thinks it has something to do with Daddy always telling her rail thin mother she's too fat. It makes no sense to Tipsy, but not much either of her parents does makes sense. Not like Granna, who always makes sense, even if Tipsy doesn't want to listen to her.

Granna knocks on the bathroom door. "Tipsy? What are you doing in there, sugar?"

"Nothing, Granna."

The door opens. Granna looks at her with those knowing gray eyes. "Nothing looks like it might be something. Something happen at school?"

"No. Yes. I guess." She bursts into tears.

Without saying a word, Granna wraps her arms around Tipsy and rubs her back. When Tipsy finally gets a hold of her waterworks, she closes the toilet seat and sits down. Granna sits on the edge of the bathtub. "You wanna talk about it? We don't have to if not."

Since Granna gives her an out, Tipsy wants to talk. "It's Missy. She's not talking to me."

"I thought y'all were best friends?"

Missy Roberts wasn't just Tipsy's best friend, she'd been her only friend for the past couple years. "Not anymore," says Tipsy. "Tracy and Jess asked her to sit at their lunch table. And they don't... want... me." The tears again.

"Oh, lord. Is there anything meaner in this world than a twelve-year-old girl?"

"Tracy and Jess said I'm white trash. And I'm a weirdo. Now all the sudden, Missy thinks so too."

"That sounds like the kiss of death at John C. Calhoun Middle School, now don't it." Granna puts a hand on Tipsy's knee. "Now listen. I've known Scruggs and Reedys and Roberts all my life. Ain't none of them so much better than us. A little more money, but if I remember correctly from my own school days, not a lot of brains in any of those families."

"It's not only being poor. I'm weird, too. I wish I'd been able to ignore the ghosts when I was younger."

"You had to learn how to avoid them. It's not easy. I know."

"But the other kids all saw me staring into space and hiding behind trees from no one. Like that darn dead girl at the park. Why'd she have to follow me around?"

"It's frustrating, but don't forget to have pity for the dead. They got it much worse than you."

"I'm ugly, weird, white trash. Maybe I'd rather be dead."

Granna grabs Tipsy's arm. She shocks Tipsy with the strength in her grip. "Don't you ever say that, girl. Don't you even think it, you hear me?"

Tipsy nods and bites her lip. Granna stands up. "Now I understand your feelings are hurt. Nothing hurts worse when you're young than being separate from other people your own age, no matter how I try to make you feel better. But I'm not going to tolerate any talk about you joining the dead." Granna's hands shake as she pulls a cigarette from the pack in her pocket. She holds the unlit white stick in her hand, as if it brings her comfort to know it's that much closer to her mouth. "And let me tell you about Tracy and Jess and Missy. I'll tell you where those girls will be ten years from now. Still here. Probably already married and divorced and living in a single wide trailer with a few babies on their hips. Now, you want to be like those cool girls, or you want to get out of this town?"

"I want to get out of this town," whispers Tipsy.

"Say what now?"

"I said I want to get out."

"That's better. Now you got six more years here. It might seem like an eternity to you, but I'm old, and besides, I've seen ghosts who are really facing eternity. Six years ain't nothing to me. Still, it will feel like a long time to you. You'll probably get hurt again along the way. But you keep at it with your painting and your good grades—the gifts God gave you in that head of yours—and you'll leave those mean girls in the dust." Granna's face softens. She rests her hand, the one still holding the cigarette, on Tipsy's head. Tipsy smells the faint, grassy scent of dry tobacco. "You can't give up because something knocks you down, honey. Living is like being in a hammock. Sometimes it's peaceful and pleasant. Sometimes it's swinging you back and forth enough to make you sick. Sometimes it even flips you right upside down just when you're getting comfortable. You get what I'm saying?"

Tipsy nods.

"I know it don't seem like it now, but the gorgeous woman you're going to become is on the verge of coming out. You might not believe me, but when I *look into your eyes, I can see her looking out at me." Granna winks. "You're going to leave those girls in the dust in more ways than one."*

Tipsy smiles. "Thanks, Granna."

"You feel any better? Any tougher?"

Tipsy nods, because she does feel tougher, and that makes her feel better.

"I'm going out back to smoke a ciggy, okay?"

"Yes, ma'am."

As Granna leaves the bathroom, Tipsy stands. She looks at herself in the mirror again. She still can't see this beautiful woman Granna is talking about, but she glares at the girl in the mirror. "You go to hell, Tracy Scruggs. You too, Jess." She chews her lip again. "And you too, Missy. If you're that kind of friend, I don't want you."

It sounds fierce and brave. Tipsy isn't sure if she'll ever be able to say it to their faces, but getting the words out of her own mouth is a start. Maybe she'll say them one day when she's driving away from Martinville. She'll yell them out the window, as she leaves Tracy, Jess, and Missy in the dust.

For now, though, she's got work to do. Tipsy sticks her tongue out at her reflection and giggles. Then she goes to her room and gets started on her math homework. Like Granna says, it's her brain that's going to get her places. She puts it to good use.

◆✕◆

By the end of the day, Tipsy completed head studies of Pamella and Bob and two drawings of the house. She left them on Pamella's kitchen table, gathered her things, and walked to her car. Ivy Brewton hadn't made an appearance, but Tipsy sensed the weight of her powerful presence even when she couldn't see her. She'd never felt that way about Jane or Henry. When she walked through the front door, the hot mugginess was a breath of fresh air after the tension in the house.

Pamella pulled into the driveway as Tipsy shut the Tahoe's rear hatch. She seemed to jump out of her car before she put it in park. She slung a leather bag over her shoulder and grabbed a pile of manila envelopes and folders. She tucked them under one arm and balanced her keys and her Yeti tumbler in the other hand. She gingerly approached Tipsy in jean overalls, a tight black tank top, and silver sneakers with a wedge heel. Her topknot hairdo was pulled so tight it gave her a homemade facelift.

The folders slid from under her elbow. Tipsy grabbed them before they spilled all over the dusty driveway. Pamella took a swig from her Yeti as Tipsy jiggled the folders back into a semi-neat stack.

"Hey, lady! I'm so glad you're still here," said Pamella. "I want to tell you something I remembered. Wait—how was it today? Did you see Meemaw again?"

Tipsy had texted Pamella the basics of her conversation with Ivy the day before. She was impressed Pamella took it all in stride, but then again, since she seemed to be three sheets to the wind most of the time, maybe she didn't upset easily.

"No. I feel like she was watching me—"

"That's *so creepy*. Like a horror movie. What do ghosts look like, anyway? Do they get it right in the scary movies?"

"I don't watch a lot of stuff about ghosts—"

"Of course. *Totally* makes sense. That would be like me watching reality shows about rich women who love wine."

"They look pretty normal to me. But she seems pretty powerful. I've never seen a ghost break a tree branch like she did—"

"*Damnit.* I have to call my lawn guy to get that thing pulled out of the marsh." Pamella stuffed the folders into her bag. "I got some great samples from interior designers if you want to see—"

"Thanks, but I really have to get the kids. You said you wanted to tell me something?"

"Ah, yes! You'll learn to remind me. I'm so ADD. I'm like a squirrel on cocaine."

Now that's an interesting analogy, said Granna.

"So about this *mystery man* of Meemaw's," said Pamella. "When I was about eight, Daddy caught me playing at the old barracks. I rode my bike down there—"

"The old barracks?"

"Yes. Just down the road, closer to the end of Cove Creek. Anyway, Daddy was so mad when he found me. *Pammy, you better stay away from there or I'll send you out to pick out your own switch!* Daddy only spanked me once in my whole life. When I was in kindergarten and I—"

"Why was he mad?" asked Tipsy. The squirrel had to be intercepted before it climbed up the wrong tree.

"Right. Yes. At first, I wasn't sure. I cried and hid in my room. But later that night, he sat me down. It was the first time he ever told me about how *Meemaw* caused all the weird things that happened in our house. He said I couldn't tell *anyone*. It was a *special secret*. That's when Daddy told me my great-grandmother Alma had *warned* him that Ivy might haunt the cottage. She brought it up at Ivy's funeral. Grandpa Cam got so mad, he pulled Alma aside and told her off. After that, Daddy never heard a word from Alma again."

"Wow. That's intense."

"My family is *nothing* if not intense. Anyway, Daddy also told me Alma wanted him to stay away from the barracks. Daddy was the spitting image of his mother, and Alma said something there might not appreciate seeing a little boy version of Ivy."

"Something, or someone."

"Right. I look a lot like Ivy myself, so when Daddy found out I was there alone—"

"He freaked out. Makes sense. No parent wants their child hanging around an angry ghost."

"It must be Meemaw's great love!"

"That's as good a clue as any we've got. Are the barracks part of Fort Moultrie? Or private homes now?"

"The barracks were built in the late 1800s, but the building has been abandoned since the thirties. The town refuses to allow it to be torn down or refurbished into condos. So there it sits, slowly falling into the marsh." She grinned, as if she'd found the first clue on a treasure map. "So you'll go check it out? See if you can find the ghost?"

Tipsy took out her phone. She checked her calendar. "I have to drop my kids off at my ex's right now. Tomorrow I'm supposed to work downtown at the Good Queen Bess. My friend Shelby's art gallery. We call it the GQB."

"So maybe tomorrow evening?"

"That should work." Tipsy added an event to her calendar at 6pm. *Go to old barracks/look for ghost. Tall. Male. Mid-century.* She chuckled.

"What is it?" asked Pamella.

"I never thought I'd be getting a reminder on my phone telling me to look for a ghost."

Pamella patted her arm. "Lady, you're a professional now."

As Tipsy backed down Pamella's driveway, her phone dinged. It was Big Ayers. As soon as she read his name, she remembered that she never replied to his text about talking.

AYERS: U STILL DROPPING THE KIDS OFF AFTER CAMP?

TIPSY: YES. GOING TO GET THEM NOW. SORRY I FORGOT TO REPLY LAST NIGHT. WHAT DID YOU WANT TO TALK ABOUT?

He still hadn't replied by the time she picked up the kids. She got the girls first, and then scooped up a sweaty Little A from soccer camp near the Ravenel Bridge. The kids chattered about their plans for the weekend as they drove across Mount Pleasant, toward Ayers's house off Long Point Road. Where Tipsy and Ayers had last lived together.

"Dad said we'll take the boat to Capers Island," said Little A.

"Uncle Jimmy's boat?" Tipsy's former brother-in-law and unofficial landlord, Jimmy, was married to Ayers's sister Mimi. Jimmy was a maritime attorney and his firm had assigned him to a big case out of Miami. With Mimi and Jimmy repairing their marriage after an extended rough patch, Mimi had decided to take her three kids and summer in Boca Raton. Tipsy was happy they were working it out, but she missed Mimi. She even missed May Penny, who was spending six weeks with

Mimi in Florida. Ayers's father, Tripp, stayed home. Tipsy got the sense he enjoyed a bit of a break from his notoriously high maintenance wife. She wondered how Mimi was handling so much May Penny time, but given her slowly improving relationship with her kids' grandmother, she hadn't asked. She'd decided to be Switzerland in the politics of the Collins family.

"Yeah. It's cool we can use it while they're gone," said Ayers. He looked up at her sheepishly. "Sorry, Mom. That sounded kind of jerky."

"I know you miss them, honey," said Tipsy.

"I can't wait to see them when we drive to Florida with BopBop!" Mary Pratt bounced in her seat. Tripp had volunteered to take the kids to Boca for a two week trip in August. The twins were counting down the days until they invaded Mimi and Jimmy's swanky canal-front, poolside rental house.

"Y'all will have a great time in Florida. And you'll have a great time this weekend! It's supposed to be great weather."

"Do you think Miss Kate will come on the boat?" asked Mary Pratt.

"Yeah," said Ayers. "Dad said she's coming so Tristan will be there."

"And Chloe!" said Olivia Grace.

"Tristan is a really good gamer," said Ayers.

Tipsy looked at them in the rear view mirror. "New friends of y'all's?"

"Yeah," said M.P. "Miss Kate is daddy's *giiiirlfrieeeeend.*"

Olivia Grace dissolved into giggles, as if the thought of her father with a girlfriend was the ultimate dad joke, but Ayers was old enough to sense it might be weird for Tipsy to hear.

"She's his girlfriend. But she's nice and so are her kids."

"That's great, y'all," said Tipsy. She couldn't care less if Ayers had a girlfriend, as long as the kids liked her. "Tell me about them."

They started chattering, and Tipsy quickly gathered that this Kate had two kids, a son a year older than Ayers, and a daughter a year older than the girls. Ayers had met Kate when they were picking up their sons from soccer camp.

"She's an a-counter," said Little Ayers. Tipsy guessed this meant she was an accountant. She'd moved to Charleston a couple years ago from "the place where they make all the country music," Little A's description of Nashville. Overall, it sounded like a positive situation, until pancakes came up.

"Miss Kate makes awesome pancakes with blueberries and whip cream," said O-liv. "She makes them every morning."

O-liv's comment struck Tipsy as odd. "Does she come over in the morning to make breakfast?"

"No," said M.P. "She spends the night."

Tipsy frowned. Her divorce settlement strictly forbade overnight visitors of the opposite sex, excepting a subsequent spouse. Unless Tipsy remarried, she'd be in contempt of court if she had a paramour spend the night. Same for Ayers. She and Will had never spent the night together with the kids, at either of their houses. Even without a court order, they agreed it wasn't a good idea for their kids' sakes. Some might think it old fashioned, but she'd voluntarily adopted the Charleston County Family Court's standard advice to refrain from having adult slumber parties with her kids around. Given her recent breakup, she was glad she'd stuck to her guns.

"She spends the night at Daddy's house?" asked Tipsy.

"Yeah," said Little Ayers. "It's fun. It's like a sleepover when we're at Dad's now."

"Do y'all ever sleep over at her house?"

"She lives in an apartment since she got divorced," said Ayers. "Dad says her old husband is an asshole." He clapped his hands over his mouth.

"Ayers Lee!"

"I'm sorry, Mom. It slipped out."

"Okay. But no more, mister." She turned up the radio as if to drown out her irritation. So now Big Ayers was basically living with this woman. He'd probably known her for about a month. The kids might find novel fun in it right now, but mom instinct and child psychology 101 told her it was a terrible idea.

Jesus pleasus, said Granna. *Now who's the asshole.*

Tipsy pulled into the driveway of her old house. She'd packed the kids' bags the night before, so as they piled out of the car, she pulled them out from around her painting supplies. She heard happy yelling and looked over her shoulder. A dark haired boy and girl waited for her kids on the front porch. Ayers came out as the children disappeared inside. As usual since his dark hair started thinning a couple years ago, he wore a baseball cap. He'd been working out lately, and had lost his pot belly. He had a dark tan from utilizing Jimmy's boat all summer. She had to acknowledge that he looked better than he had in years. A blonde woman followed him.

"Hey!" said Ayers, with an unusually jovial wave and a smile. "Let me help you with those bags."

Tipsy straightened as Ayers and his girlfriend walked toward her. She was what Tipsy thought of as a Charleston Dress Code Blonde: short, with wavy, light blonde hair, cute features, and a pretty obvious boob job. Tipsy easily imagined her in head-to-toe Lily Pulitzer, but her dress code also included an expensive looking white silk blouse, a red pencil skirt, and a pair of black Louboutin pumps. Tipsy was suddenly morbidly aware of her own professional attire: smelly tank top, booty shorts, and tennis shoes with a hole in the toe. She'd plopped a baseball cap on her sweaty hair, but she wasn't wearing a lick of makeup. This woman had the kind of cat-like eyeliner that defied Tipsy's artistic talents. If she tried it, she'd end up looking like a hungover raccoon.

"Uh, thanks," she said, as Ayers took the bags.

"Tipsy, this is Kate. Been meaning to introduce y'all."

Kate smiled at her. "So nice to meet you! Ayers told me you're an artist." She looked Tipsy up and down. It wasn't unfriendly—frankly, Tipsy didn't blame her—but it made Tipsy squirm nonetheless.

"Yup, I am. So nice to meet you, too!" Tipsy backed toward the driver's side of the truck and called over Kate's shoulder. "Ayers! Hey! I got to go. Don't forget to pack lunch for Little A tomorrow but the girls have pizza day."

Ayers said something from the house. Probably an acknowledgement, but it might have been a question. She didn't care. He could text her. He walked out the door again as Tipsy got into her truck. "So sorry to run," said Tipsy. "I have to make use of the free evening."

"I understand," said Kate. "My ex never helps with—"

Tipsy rolled up the window and cut her off. She pulled out of the cul de sac with her heart beating wildly in her chest. Annoyance, trepidation, and—she hated to admit it—not a little bit of jealousy.

Ayers knew he wasn't supposed to have paramours spend the night. He'd self-righteously hinted on numerous occasions that if he ever found out she'd shacked up with Will, he'd file a Rule to Show Cause with the family court and find her in contempt. He dared her to defy him, smug in his ability to hire an expensive attorney to take her down. Of course, now that he had someone he wanted to shack up with, he didn't care if it was good for the kids as long as it was good for him. Familiar feelings, as Ayers was typically annoying and trepidation inducing. Same old, same old.

The jealousy was new, and far more complicated. It sure didn't come from wanting anything to do with Ayers. Kate was welcome to him, and maybe he wouldn't give her so much grief if otherwise occupied. It was all the rest of it. Her pretty suburban house, where her hydrangeas still bloomed and she'd first rocked her kids to sleep on the front porch. Ayers and Kate would sit in the backyard on the flagstone patio Tipsy designed, sipping drinks and laughing while the kids ran around. Together in the quasi-family way that had brought her comfort when she spent time with Will.

In the meantime, she still lived in someone else's house, complete with someone else's furniture, and she was as single as an antisocial nun once again. Now Ayers had successful, professional, Charleston Blonde Kate. She'd probably change out of her classy business attire into a Lululemon outfit that cost more than Tipsy's entire drawerful of Target specials.

Tipsy.... Don't get bitter now. It's not like you, and it's surely not becoming.

Yes, ma'am, she said, because Granna was right. She was annoying herself with all her complaining in her own mind. She sought a distraction, but the other major new developments in her life— her newly single status and professional ghost hunting— required too much brain power and taxed her bruised heart. When she got to the stop sign, she sent a text to Shelby and Lindsey.

Hey y'all. Any interest in a heartbreak happy hour?

Chapter 4

She immediately noticed Shelby and Lindsey were a little dressed up for The Blind Tiger, one of the oldest pubs in Charleston. For years, The Blind Tiger hadn't even had a sign. You either knew it was there, hidden behind dingy windows on Broad Street, or you didn't. It wasn't particularly enticing from the sidewalk, but if you walked through the dark bar, the place opened up onto one of the most charming outdoor dining spaces in town. The patio and outside bar huddled behind mossy stone walls strung with white lights, giving it a pirate's cave meets fairy castle feeling. It seemed like the perfect place to meet the girls for a drink, until Tipsy noticed their strappy sundresses and heels.

Lindsey always wore heels, because she was barely over five feet tall. But these weren't her usual summer wedges. They were sparkly numbers with a stiletto heel. As for Shelby, she tended to stick to flip flops, so her selection of footwear was definitely outside of the norm. Shelby's white blonde hair hung in professionally crafted waves down her back and Lindsey's slightly darker, perfectly straight hair framed her face.

In an effort soothe her tender feelings and battered ego, Tipsy had gotten herself appropriately dolled up in trendy ripped jean shorts, dangly earrings, and a fun gold sleeveless top with an open back. She'd done her hair and makeup. She'd even worn wedges herself. She was about six feet tall in a three-inch heel, but she'd always worn heels until she started dating Will. One minor benefit of him smushing her heart like a rotten strawberry. At least she didn't have to worry about being taller than him.

Lindsey and Shelby waved and Tipsy joined them at their table. They both stood as she approached. "Sister... hugs," said Shelby.

Lindsey's lower lip stuck out in the universal sign of sympathy. "Will is such a moron."

"Thanks, y'all," Tipsy said as she sat. She pointed at their festive sundresses. "Hotties! What's the occasion?"

Shelby held up both hands. "The real question is, do you want to bitch about that clown? We got donkey ears if you do."

"Honestly, no. I'd rather pretend he doesn't exist."

"Good. It's five o'clock on Thursday evening," said Lindsey. She sipped a sweet tea since she was trying to get pregnant. "Prime Charleston drinking time for y'all and your off duty ovaries. Will Garrison can kiss our collective behinds. Let's not waste the opportunity to gossip on his sorry ass."

Tipsy ordered a Bud Light from a cute, shaggy haired server. She pulled a koozie out of her purse—from Group Therapy, a famous dive bar in the Five Points district of Columbia. She'd picked it up when the three couples attended a South Carolina football game last fall. She and Shelby got buzzed and nostalgic and insisted on revisiting their college stomping grounds.

Shelby tapped it. "Group Therapy! How appropriate!"

Lindsey laughed. "Such a fun weekend! When y'all started in with the KZ rush songs, and then Will—" She cut herself off. "Yeah, well. It was fun."

Tipsy took a sip of her beer. "I have gossip if y'all want it."

Lindsey's brown eyes widened. "Lay it on me, girl."

Tipsy filled them in on Ayers and his new lady friend. As she talked, they both whipped out their phones and started combing social media. Tipsy wasn't sure of her last name, but Lindsey was an Instagram sleuth. An expert in Facebook espionage.

"Is this her?" Lindsey handed her phone across the table. A blonde woman smiled up at Tipsy from a Facebook profile. The beachy profile photo included two dark-haired children. *Kate Lucas Brandt.*

"Bingo," said Tipsy.

"We have eighteen mutual friends," said Lindsey. She kept scrolling.

"For the love of god, don't accidentally like any of her pictures."

"Oh, please. I am a professional. If I ever need a side gig, I'm going to become a social media PI."

"So what are you going to do about Ayers?" asked Shelby. She adjusted her dress to give her famous cleavage a boost.

"I don't know. We've been getting along lately. I hate to rock the boat. At the same time, I don't want him living with this woman and my kids. I hope she's awesome; y'all know I'm all about strong women and she seems successful and put together. Plus she's a mom herself, so what more could I ask for? But still, they barely know each other. It's not good for the kids to see them, like, sleeping in the same bed and what not."

"Totally," said Lindsey. "After my parents' divorce, my mom's boyfriends sometimes slept over. So embarrassing. Once I threw up in the middle of the night and walked in on this guy's hairy—"

"Um, ew." Shelby gagged. "Blech. We get it. No need for a detailed visual."

"Prevention of childhood trauma aside," said Tipsy, "it's literally court-ordered that we don't."

"You could bring it up and see if he goes apeshit."

"That's like stepping on a snake you know is poisonous."

"Oh, look, y'all," said Lindsey. "She must be recently divorced. Here's a pic of her and her ex-husband from early last summer. Damn. He's cute. It looks like he's a doctor."

Tipsy glanced at the photo of Kate and her ex-husband at a medical university gala. He was indeed handsome.

"Whoo. Nice," said Shelby as she took a look. "She sure as hell downgraded to Ayers. She went from McDreamy to McDoofus."

"Come on now," said Lindsey. "Ayers looks pretty good on paper. He's lost some weight so he's back to being decent looking."

"*Ewwwww,*" said Shelby. "Sorry, Tips. I mean, Ayers was hot as Hades in a skillet back in the day. I'm just saying, poor Kate Lucas Brandt doesn't know what she's getting yet, bless her heart."

"That's true," said Tipsy. "Lord knows he can turn on the charm when he wants to. Anyway, I'll have to say something to him, but I can't handle it tonight when I've got so much else on my mind. So what's up with y'all?"

Shelby and Lindsey chattered on for a while about their daily lives. Lindsey about tracking her periods. Shelby about her recurring annoyance with Brian's mother.

"She's so overbearing, y'all. She's got an opinion about everything from my hair to my toenail polish. I don't know how he deals with her."

Tipsy and Lindsey glanced at each other across the table. Lindsey hid a smile behind a sip of tea. Shelby wasn't exactly known for keeping her opinions to herself.

Tipsy relaxed as she finished her beer. She figured she'd have one more. Plenty of time for any slight buzz to fizzle out. She waved to the server again, but Shelby cleared her throat. "Oh, sister. We have to go soon."

"Y'all do?" Tipsy realized they hadn't given her an explanation for being all trussed up. "Why?"

They looked across the table as if each wanted the other to spill some nasty beans. The kind that put you in the bathroom for hours. Lindsey bit the bullet when Shelby rustled around in her purse for her credit card.

"Well… uh, P.D. got a promotion at work. Regional Sales VP."

"That's great," said Tipsy. P.D. worked for a Black River Outdoor Company, a local company that specialized in all your saltwater sporting needs, from fishing poles to overpriced outdoorsy shirts with *BROCo* emblazoned on the sleeves.

"So…umm. We're going to dinner at Hall's."

"Oh." Tipsy looked between them. "Who all is going?"

"Me and Brian," said Shelby. She spritzed perfume on the tiny yin and yang tattoo on her wrist.

"And us, obviously," said Lindsey. "And Will is coming."

Tipsy forced out a reply. "Right. I see."

Lindsey raced on. "P.D. found out on Monday. We knew you and Will were having issues—"

"That's great. Since I didn't really know until yesterday."

"You know what she means, Tips," said Shelby. "Things have been weird with y'all lately."

"When P.D. made the reservation, Will said just make it for five."

So Will had already planned to break up with her earlier in the week. And now her two best friends and their significant others were going to dinner for a special occasion and including him, and she was out. "That's why y'all are all dressed up. What time is your reservation?"

"Quarter of eight," said Lindsey.

"It's only 6:30."

"We're meeting there for a drink beforehand."

Tipsy swallowed slowly, as if she had beer bubbles stuck in her throat. Hall's was one of the most popular restaurants in town. Famous for fabulous food and service and a lively pick up scene. During Thursday happy hour, the bar would be packed with single people on the prowl. Will would be one of them. Will who claimed he only wanted to *take a break*, but also didn't want her to come out for P.D.'s special dinner.

"Honey, I'm so sorry," said Lindsey. "We wanted to meet you anyway. I feel awful."

Tipsy smiled. She refused to cry. It wasn't really their fault. It was P.D.'s night and he wanted his buddies there. "Jeez. It's fine, y'all. No worries. I want to be at the GQB early tomorrow to get in some extra work on Pamella's drawings."

Shelby latched onto the change of topic as she gave the cutie her credit card. "How's it going?"

Let's see... I'm once again haunted by a crazed phantom with a mysterious backstory, but now I'm getting paid for it.

"It's going great. Still in the early stages, but Pamella seems super nice. Quirky, but nice."

The server came around to Tipsy's side of the table, but as she handed over her card, Shelby said, "No, no. I got it."

"No need. Pamella is paying me well."

"Seriously. I'll pick up the tab."

"I'll get you back later," said Lindsey.

Tipsy sat helplessly as the server whisked Shelby's card away with her pride. Shelby meant well, but now she was not only left out. She was a charity case.

They got up and walked through the dingy bar onto Broad Street. Shelby called an Uber. Lindsey hugged Tipsy. "You know what—are you sure you don't want to come for a drink? Screw Will."

"Thanks, Linds, but I'd rather eat lint."

"Let's do something this weekend, okay? You want to meet for spin class Saturday morning?"

"I have to be at Pamella's." Pride made her add, "I'll be there all day. She's paying top dollar so I have to put in the hours."

She thought Shelby would ask how much. Even though she'd have to answer some serious questions if she told them the true amount, she wanted to say it anyway. *Fifty-k! She's paying me fifty-k! I can afford a freakin' Bud Light at a happy hour price!*

The Uber app entranced Shelby. "He's on Meeting. Ronnie in a silver Town and Country. We're traveling in style." She looked up at Tipsy. "You sure you don't want to come for a drink?"

Tipsy hugged Shelby so she wouldn't see the tears in her eyes. "I'm good. Y'all have fun tonight!"

A beat up gray minivan pulled a U-turn and sidled up to the sidewalk. The fat man behind the wheel rolled down the window. "Your chariot awaits, ladies."

Shelby and Lindsey squeezed her hands and then scooted across the uneven sidewalk in their cute shoes. "Watch your ankles, y'all," Tipsy said, but Ronnie had already hit the button to close the minivan door. Shelby and Lindsey waved through the opaque windows.

Tipsy waved back. As they passed Church Street, Tipsy finally exhaled. She looked around the almost empty sidewalk. The old buildings on Broad Street housed many law firms, so once the lawyers finished their after-work drinks, it cleared out. A group of giggling young women approached The Blind Tiger. Perhaps they were going to see the cute server and hoped he'd ask for one of their numbers.

Maybe they'll write it on a napkin, thought Tipsy. *Do people still do that?*

She suddenly felt old and tired. No way in hell she'd go back into The Tiger and drink by herself, but she didn't want to go home yet. Even with Henry there, the house would feel too empty. She'd lie in bed and imagine Will sidled up to the bar or the grand piano. With his jawline and that damn thick black hair, he'd attract women like flies to a bug zapper.

She looked at her phone. She had a reminder notification about the mystery ghost at the old barracks. It wasn't even seven yet. This time of year, she'd have almost two hours of daylight left. Plenty of time to drive to Sullivan's and earn a little overtime.

Sunsets on Sullivan's Island are a sight for sore eyes, and Tipsy's were still swollen from her breakup cry. She figured even if she couldn't find a new ghost, she'd at least take in a wide scarlet and champagne sky and get her sob on again if she felt the urge. She turned on Thompson Avenue before she reached True Blue and found a spot on the road in front of the old barracks. The long, one-story clapboard building with crumbling porches and a single center turret looked like a shoebox crossed with a country schoolhouse. Tipsy imagined cigarette smoking soldiers sitting on the back porch, maybe playing cards when they had time off.

As she crept along the property line, she hoped this ghost's haunting hadn't trapped him inside the barracks. She didn't fancy going in there. It was probably inhabited by things more unpredictable, dangerous, and grosser than ghosts. Marsh rats, copperheads, and legions of palmetto bugs, Charleston's giant flying cockroaches. Those damn things would infest that rotting wood like miniscule soldiers in shiny brown armor.

She didn't see any no trespassing signs, so she walked toward the marsh. The remains of a dock jutted into the water, the pilings like broken piano keys. She spun in a slow circle with her hands shading her eyes. She didn't see anyone, alive or dead.

Damn, she thought. *What if I have to call him? I don't even know who I'm looking for.*

Before Granna answered, a pearly bluish glow on the dock caught her eye. She squinted, and the figure sharpened: a tall white man wearing a form-fitting dark blue polo shirt, a dark belt, and tan, wide-legged trousers. The setting sun behind him obscured his features, but from the glow on his head, he appeared to have blond hair.

"Target located. Here goes." She walked toward the dock with her heart beating like she'd attached a bicycle pump to it and started working it.

She patted her chest as if the old ticker needed a reminder that everything would be okay. *I've got to stop freaking out.*

You're a woman alone, approaching a strange man as it's starting to get dark, said Granna. *It would be freaky whether he's alive or dead.*

And I can't pepper spray this dude.

The man followed her progress as she approached, as if he realized she saw him. He took a few steps forward and narrowed the distance between them. As he moved out of the direct line of the sun, his features took shape. Tipsy slowed down. He looked oddly familiar.

He pushed his straight, thick hair away from his face. A few strands immediately fell across his forehead again. He had a square jaw with a dimple in his chin. Eyes so light blue she made out their color from twenty feet away.

She had seen him before. She's seen him in Henry's memories, and Jane's. She'd suspected him of killing them both. She'd even looked for him herself last summer, on the beach where he'd supposedly died.

"Holy shit," she whispered. "It's John Huger."

Tipsy's brain couldn't handle John Huger's abrupt entrance onto the stage. The role of anonymous dead man at the barracks should be played by a young soldier, or a poor farmer. Like something out of the old Irish ballads. Not the scion of one of Charleston's oldest families, Jane's dearest friend, and Henry's nemesis. She spun around on her heels and power walked back to the truck with Granna's flummoxed admonishments ringing in her ears. She got in the truck, started the engine, and peeled wheels away from the old barracks. She didn't look in the rear view mirror to see if John Huger stood on the front porch looking after her—a crazy woman who had shown up out of nowhere, looked him in the eye, and then disappeared like a startled fish swimming into deeper water.

You found him, silly! You ain't even going to talk to him?

This is, like, a totally complicated development, Granna! I need time to think.

Her mind raced. Ivy was gorgeous, but from what she knew, John Huger had been a top of the food chain kind of guy.

Ivy landed another rich guy in Camden Brewton, said Granna.

True, but still….

Proctor James, Jane and Henry's deceased minister who haunted the graveyard at St. Philip's Church, once told her John wasn't the marrying type. From what she'd seen, he was the playboy type. She'd watched him in action herself in Henry's memories, sidled up to a gorgeous blonde woman at his birthday party in his parents' mansion. She found it hard to believe he'd been deeply in love with a girl from the kind of humble background Ivy had hinted at, even an achingly beautiful one.

She went home and snuck past Henry as he talked to himself about THE GREAT STORY in the living room. Maybe he'd ultimately be able to help her out with some information, but for now she had enough to process on her own. In addition to the seeming unlikelihood of John being Ivy's long lost true love, he shouldn't even be there.

Proctor had told her John died on Sullivan's, but he drowned while swimming in the ocean. He should haunt the spot where he died, so she'd looked for him last year on the beach. It wasn't her finest moment, but she'd been at a low point in her search for answers to Henry and Jane's mystery. She'd been seized by the familiar urge to do something—anything—to fix her problem. She'd almost gotten herself struck by lightning trying to find John on that beach. In the meantime, he was haunting the old barracks on the Intracoastal Waterway side of the island.

So he died at the barracks? But how? And why would he be at the barracks at all? Pamella said the place was abandoned by the 1930s. It seemed sort of odd for John to be hanging around abandoned military housing, just for a whim. She opened her eyes and stared at the ceiling. Besides, if he died swimming, why would he be wearing clothes and shoes? Wouldn't he be barefoot and sporting one of those cringy old-fashioned men's one piece bathing suits that look like a cross between a romper and a wetsuit?

She struggled to stay awake, but try as she might, her brain got fuzzy. Thoughts of John walking toward her on the dock mixed together with images of Big Ayers jogging toward the car to get the kids' bags. At one point she jerked as she half-dreamed she tripped trying to get away from both of them. Eventually, the emotional fog of the breakup, the revelation of the new twist in the never-ending saga of co-parenting with Ayers, John Huger's unexpected debut as a new player in her first paying supernatural gig, and her single Bud Light all caught up with her. She gave up and fell asleep.

She woke early, but as was often the case when she felt sad or stressed, she had no appetite. Over the years she'd learned to lay off exercise until she got her head right or she'd quickly get too skinny. She took a shower, donned a black sundress that wouldn't show charcoal smudges, and drove downtown to Shelby's art gallery in the French Quarter, the Good Queen Bess. She hadn't been working as many hours since she'd been regularly producing paintings, but she usually went in a couple times a week to help out Shelby. Shelby had yet to find a new salesperson with any knowledge of art who didn't either show up late or always want to leave early. Or, in the unfortunate instance of an art history major from the College of Charleston, smoke weed in the bathroom.

She unlocked the gallery and prepped for opening: sweeping and dusting, adjusting lighting, and making sure the bathrooms were clean. She took pride in her own wall in the main showroom. She reread the small placard beside one of her pieces.

A native of the South Carolina upstate (Martinville, SC), Tiffany "Tipsy" Denning-Collins attended the University of South Carolina on a full scholarship and holds a BA in Fine Art, Summa Cum Laude. She has lived in Charleston for over a decade and has found her artistic home in the beauty of the Lowcountry. She is the recipient of numerous art awards, including Young Artist of the Year (Southeast), and her work has been featured in Southern Living, Garden and Gun, Charleston Magazine, and at the Southeastern Wildlife Exposition (SEWE). "Tipsy's work is noted for an intense realism infused with an almost supernatural air of feeling and mystery, from her beautiful yet flawed figures to landscapes that have the observer breathing marsh air, often with a wry sense of subtle social commentary." – Elizabeth Patterson, guest art critic for the Charleston Post & Courier.

Tipsy read the placard every time she came into the GQB. It reminded her of her accomplishments whenever she felt overwhelmed, even if Shelby's mother Elizabeth Patterson had discovered Tipsy, so naturally she was sort of biased.

She also liked to read her full name, *Tiffany Denning-Collins*. She hadn't dropped Collins officially, because she'd sold her first few paintings in the past year under that name, and because the twins had expressed sadness when she told them she was changing her name.

"You don't want to be a Collins like us?" asked M.P.

"It's not that, baby," Tipsy said.

"Then what is it?" asked Olivia Grace.

In the end, it had been too complicated to explain to her daughters why she wanted to return to her maiden name. Instead, she decided to hyphenate it, with the result being that most people still thought of her as Tipsy Collins. Still, she knew the truth, and she'd already hinted to her girls that they didn't have to change their names when they got married. "I'll only change my name if my husband is famous so I can get free stuff," Mary Pratt had replied, much to Tipsy's amusement.

She set up her sketchpads on the drawing desk beside the front door. It was a quiet morning, with only a few casual shoppers popping in to admire the paintings and watch her sketch studies of little Pamella. She didn't have the emotional space to think about much else when she was drawing, but by the time her hand cramped up around noon, she couldn't ignore the appearance of John Huger in her mystery any longer. She accepted it as a stroke of luck, because Henry might very well be able to give her insight.

As if he sensed her thinking about him, Henry materialized beside a mixed media piece made of recycled beer and soda cans. "Anything can be art these days, can't it?" he asked.

"We have plenty of trash. Got to do something with it." Tipsy spoke aloud in the empty gallery. "How do you do that, by the way? Show up when I need you."

"I have a touch of writer's block, so I decided to get out of the house. Do you need me?"

"Yeah. I think you can help me." She waved her pencil at him. "But you better be ready for a shocker. This one might be enough to make you blow these paintings right off the walls."

Henry sat on the window ledge as Tipsy filled him in on her potential big money payout and Ivy's long lost love. "You'll *never* guess who her mystery man is. It's... wait a sec." She took a blank canvas from under the desk and held it before her like a shield. "It's... John Huger."

Henry's face darkened, but there was no blast of cold minty air. The paintings stayed firmly on the walls. "Really," he said. "That is interesting."

"Damn. I thought you'd be more worked up."

"You told me John died eight or nine years after me and Jane, correct? He drowned on Sullivan's?"

"That's what Proctor told me. But his death—his haunting. Something isn't right." She told Henry her suspicions about John's inappropriate location and clothing. "And on top of that, this woman— the ghost, she just *does not* seem like John's type. She's beautiful, but she grew up dirt poor in Mount Pleasant. Can you imagine John with a woman like that? I picture him with someone glamorous, like Jean Harlow, or—"

"What's this ghost's name?"

"Her maiden name was Ivy More."

At the mention of Ivy's name, Tipsy got a better reaction. Henry's mouth hung open in confusion. A couple of bottle tops loosened themselves from the mixed media piece and pinged off the hardwood floors. "I'll be damned. What a pair they would be."

Tipsy dropped her pencil. "You knew Ivy?"

"Not terribly well, but yes. She lived with her family at the foot of the Pitt Street Bridge. Her father was an oysterman. Her brother did odd jobs for Jane and I sometimes. If I remember correctly, her mother was rather eccentric. The village oddball. Ivy worked at Patjen's Grocery Store."

"Oh. My. God." Tipsy was wildly excited. She stood and scooped up the bottle caps. "What else do you know about her?"

"She must have been about nineteen or twenty when Jane and I died. You know how dedicated I am to my wife—"

"Yes, yes. Everyone knows you're a one woman man."

"But still. Ivy was the kind of beauty no man could ignore. She was shy the first few times we came into the store. Not surprising, given our different stations in life, but Jane was so friendly with everyone, rich or poor. She was sweet and talkative after we got to know her." He smiled. "Actually rather sassy. She called me Mr. Carrot Top. You know how prickly I was... am... but when Ivy teased me about my hair, it was endearing, not insulting." He shook his head. "Still, it's confounding to me that she and John were lovers."

"She describes him as the great love of her life. Not like, a hook up—a casual thing. She won't even leave her haunting without him."

"As a ghost, I should accept that nearly anything is possible. Even John Huger madly in love."

"Was he that bad? Like, objectively, Henry. I know y'all had your issues."

"Objectively, John was…" He took a thoughtful pause. "In the eyes of everyone we knew, John was everything. He was good looking and rich, but it was more than that. He was charming, and gregarious, and loved to laugh. He was a great tennis player. He tore around the woods at his family's farm on horseback like he was part Comanche. He shot clay pigeons out of the sky on a windy day. He even sang well." Henry glowered. "I suppose all the men wanted to be him and all the women wanted to marry him."

"But you didn't like him."

"I found him to lack substance. Maybe because his life was too perfect. He never had to think about anything. Everything was all cigars and roses for John."

"I saw him in one of Jane's memories. He seemed pretty thoughtful."

"If he had that in him somewhere, he was too manly to show it very often."

"He and Jane seemed as tight as two sides of a zipper."

Henry nodded. "She called him her big brother. I was jealous of their closeness. Hard to believe she wanted me, not him. Another reason I couldn't stand him. Not as intellectually noble, but it's true. If every woman in town lusted after him, why would Jane be any different?"

"Clearly, she was, since she married you." Tipsy thought for a moment. "But John never married."

"Never showed the slightest interest in the institution, despite the eternal maneuvering of all the young women in town and their families. John's parents, R.J. and Colleen, were desperate for him to marry for years. They had no other children. He was the only heir to the family fortune."

"His father was a bootlegger, right? That's sort of unsavory."

"During the Prohibition days, bootleggers were almost heroic. A happily accepted crime among people with money and an unslakable thirst." Henry shrugged. "The John I knew didn't pay any mind to his parents bothering him to marry. He cheerfully ignored all propositions, but he had endless trysts. More than a few scandals and broken hearts. Ruined reputations. The women, not John. He was always forgiven and never lost his appeal."

"All hail the double standard." Tipsy rolled her eyes. "Maybe a different kind of woman finally caught his heart. Then he died before they could be married. It's tragic."

"What happened to Ivy after John died? What led her to fall off a dock on Sullivan's Island and get herself killed?"

"From what I know, she married this guy Camden Brewton—"

"Stop." Henry held up one hand. "Camden Brewton? The plot thickens. I feel my writer's block lifting at the thought."

"What's the big deal?"

"Camden and John were first cousins on their mother's side. They were very close. Camden was a few years younger than us. He worshipped John. Followed him everywhere his whole life. Even grew up to look like him, although no one was quite as handsome as Johnny."

"Hold up. Hold up." Tipsy pressed her fingers into her temples. "John and Ivy are madly in love. She's the wrong kind of girl—"

"Absolutely. I cannot imagine John's family approving. Her dotty mother spent time in an asylum. Her father Bubba More claimed to be a preacher, but he was a mean, nasty bastard. The definition of uncouth, as classified by my own dear old mother."

"So John and Ivy fall for each other, then John dies suddenly. And Ivy marries his cousin, who was like his brother. And also rich, right?"

"Yes. Not as rich as John, or Jane's family, but richer than my family."

"I wonder why his family agreed to let them get married? That's almost as weird as why they got married in the first place."

"Maybe Camden loved her, too. Like I said, she was the kind of woman some men would fall in love with just looking at her."

"Still, I wonder—"

The front door bonged out a warning. Tipsy looked out the window as Henry disappeared. An older couple were chatting in the threshold. The man opened the door and wiped his brow.

Tipsy smiled and got up from the desk to show them around. As she chatted about the artists and their work, she barely heard the customers' questions. Fortunately, her brain could answer them on autopilot.

You got yourself another ghostly love triangle, said Granna.

Sure do. Henry is right. This plot is as thick as cold grits.

Granna chuckled. *And just as difficult to swallow.*

Chapter 5

Tipsy swiped across texts from Shelby and Lindsey as she packed up at the end of the day. She smiled when she read their messages. The ladies wanted to meet for happy hour. Maybe they felt remorse about last night and the Hall's incident, but Tipsy didn't care if it was guilt induced. She dreaded the thought of a weekend without her kids. With Shelby and Linds, she'd be less likely to cave and text Will out of loneliness.

It was a beautiful night, so she suggested one of their favorite spots on Shem Creek. LET'S DO IT! I NEED A VODKA TONIC. TAVERN AND TABLE? TIME?

SHELBY: EARLIER THE BETTER. TIRED!

LINDSEY: SAME. 5:30?

Their tiredness caused a twinge of annoyance, because it directly correlated with their late night partying at Hall's. Still, Tipsy wasn't going to douse their happy hour in flat tonic water before it even started. She agreed to half past five and zipped home feeling pretty good, all things considered. She showered and donned a red maxi dress that passed Henry's inspection as not too scandalous. It had cooled down so she walked down Bennett Street toward Shem Creek.

She found a few spots at Tavern and Table's crowded outside bar overlooking the creek. She ordered a VT, a Mich Ultra for Shelby, and a sweet tea for Lindsey. She set her purse on one seat to her left and the silk shawl she'd brought for the walk home on the one to her right. She watched the boats go by until Shelby made her typically flamboyant entrance. She bounced down the stairs leading from the restaurant to the bar in her white booty shorts with her flip flops flapping against her feet and her cleavage jiggling.

"Hey, sister." She took a swig of beer before her butt had fully settled on the stool beside Tipsy. "I have to tell you about Glen and his ex."

"Hey to you, too. She's really his ex this time?" Tipsy asked.

Shelby nodded. She never got tired of disturbing stories about Glen, the jerk who broke her heart last summer when he went back to his supposed ex-wife. Upon further analysis, she was less an ex and more a plain old wife. "So Glen told Will and Will told P.D and P.D told Lindsey…"

Tipsy took a moment to let the mention of Will go in and out of her heart like a rusty arrow. She sipped her drink and looked around the bar.

"…Glen went back to the house to get stuff after he moved out. Clothes. Tools. His laptop computer. She didn't want to give him the laptop. So he grabs it…"

Lindsey was at the end of the bar talking to a tall guy with shaggy blond hair.

"…and the wife calls the cops and chases him out of the house. She's got the computer cord and she jumps on his back. And get this—she tries to strangle him with the cord."

This caught Tipsy's attention. "Holy crap. For real?"

"Lit-er-ally." Shelby put her hands on her own throat. She stuck out her tongue and gagged.

"You okay, miss?" asked the bartender.

"She's fine," said Tipsy. "Just impersonating strangulation by HDMI."

"So they're wrestlin' on the ground. It's the WWF come to Mount Pleasant." When Shelby got excited her accent got thicker, even though she grew up downtown and shouldn't have much of a twang. Any sort of drama took her back to her years in Columbia, where she'd been surrounded by people from towns like Barnwell and Walterboro and Cheraw, and Tipsy herself from upstate. "They're rollin' and floppin' in the grass when the police show up. Computer cord around his throat like an Easter necktie. The police officer had to drag her off him, kickin' and screamin'." Shelby started laughing. "Here's the best part."

"It gets better?"

"Somehow the computer got knocked over and turned on. The cop picks it up and *boo-ya*. There are pics of Glen on the desktop.... in a rather *delicate* position."

Tipsy giggled. "Oh lord, with who?"

"Who knows? Whoever he was cheating on his wife with, bless her heart. But can you imagine..." Shelby laughed harder. "That poor cop. He had to break up a potential MacBook Murder and see pictures of Glen's skinny white butt to boot."

Tears ran down Tipsy's face as she pictured a bald, beefy cop being involuntarily subjected to Glen's amateur hour.

Lindsey left the guy at the end of the bar and pushed through the crowd. She was so short she disappeared a few times. She slid into her stool.

"I missed the giggles," she said.

"You already know the story," said Shelby. "Glen being asphyxiated and outed as a porn star in one incident."

"Oh, that! He deserved it, the loser." She leaned in closer. "Did y'all see who I was talking to?"

"Who is he? I can't decide if he's cute or not." Shelby's forehead about touched Lindsey's as they conferred. Tipsy leaned back to get out of their way.

"That's P.D.'s boss."

"Interesting. He doesn't look like a zillionaire."

"He's not a zillionaire, but he's rollin' in it. So much money in fishing, y'all. He founded BROCo right out of college. Now it's a national company."

"Where's he from?" asked Shelby. "He has a Charleston-ish look."

"Georgetown. Still Lowcountry."

Tipsy watched the guy at the end of the bar. He looked to be in his early forties. He wore a wrinkled, untucked button down shirt, rumpled khakis, and flip flops. Georgetown was an old mill town about an hour north of Charleston, between Mount Pleasant and the sleepy beach towns of Pawley's Island and Litchfield. It had a pretty waterfront district, but on the whole, it was a little neglected and run down. Dude slapped a visor over his messy hair. He might be rich, but he definitely repped his hometown's vibe.

"What's his name again?" asked Shelby.

"Clar-is Andrews."

"*Clar-is?*" Tipsy tried to picture the name.

"Right, but get this. It's spelled like *Clarice,* but it's pronounced *Clar-is.*"

"Good grief," said Shelby. "That's more Southern than Tiffany Lynn here being described as a state of intoxication her entire life."

Tipsy swatted Shelby, but she said, "It is pretty weird. Like, can you imagine being a man named Clarice? I don't care how you pronounce it. You better get tough or die trying."

"Like the Johnny Cash song," said Shelby.

Tipsy nodded. "A Boy Named Sue. Not many people can pull that off."

"He pulls it off, all right," said Lindsey. "He's got women falling out of his pockets like spare change."

"Just because he's rich?" Tipsy asked.

"Uh, honey, that's not a bad reason," said Shelby.

"His money has something to do with it, but there's more to it. I know he doesn't look like much from here, but—"

"Yikes, here he comes," said Shelby.

Clarice elbowed his way through the crowd toward them. He met Tipsy's eye as he approached. She looked away and studied the ice and the squished lime in her glass.

"Hey, y'all," he said, as he sidled closer. "Sorry to disturb your chat, but I forgot to mention, Lindsey, can you and P.D. join me on the boat next Friday for cocktails with a new buyer?"

"Sure," said Lindsey. "We'd love to. Clarice, these are my girls. Shelby—"

Shelby reached across Tipsy and shook his hand. "Hey there."

"—and Tipsy."

"Nice to meet y'all." The guy's eyes were an interesting blueish hazel. He regarded Tipsy as if she were some kind of trophy fish he couldn't quite place. He wasn't classically good looking, but for whatever reason, she found herself blushing. He had a deeper voice than she expected from a guy who was, upon closer examination, sort of skinny.

"You too, Clarice." She pronounced it the correct way, so it didn't sound like a woman's name. Granna laughed in her head. *A man named Clarice! Whoo-hoo, I ain't never heard the like.*

"Y'all having a nice night?" He asked them all, but Tipsy was pretty sure he looked at her. She leaned across the bar and flagged down the bartender.

"Yup," said Shelby. "Just catching up and drinkin' up."

"Let me buy y'all a round," said Clarice.

Tipsy looked over her shoulder. "You don't have to do that."

"Sure I do. Y'all are too pretty to buy your own drinks." He waved at the bartender.

"You got off cheap with my ice tea," said Lindsey. "But BROCo has great health insurance, so you've put in your contribution to my wellbeing. Thanks."

"No problem. Have a good night, ladies." He tipped his visor at them and made his way back to the end of the bar.

Shelby poked Tipsy. "A Boy Named Clarice was checking you out."

"Listen, Tips." Lindsey put a hand on Tipsy's shoulder. "You know normally I'm all for exploring your options, especially post-breakup, but Clarice is a big fat no-no."

"Why?" asked Shelby.

"He had a *nasty* divorce. He's a nice guy, but it screwed him up bigtime. He's told P.D. he has no interest in having a girlfriend. He hops from one woman to the next. From what P.D. says, all these women still hang around and take whatever attention he'll dole out."

"I can see why. In a weird way, he's sexy as hell." Shelby grinned. "Pre-Brian, sounds like the kind of dysfunctional scenario I would dive into with my eyes closed and holding my nose."

Tipsy sipped her drink. "I'm not into seeing anyone right now."

"Of course. It's too soon," said Lindsey. "Although, Will didn't flirt with anyone last night. Even though the Botox sharks were circling. Not at all."

Shelby rolled her eyes. "So what?"

"Isn't it weird? He breaks up with Tipsy and then sits there mooning around like a monk with good hair."

"Great," said Shelby. "Maybe he should go on some dates and see what kind of wackos are out there."

"He didn't talk to anyone?" asked Tipsy. "That's sort of a relief."

Tipsy! Don't you even think about letting that man off the hook because he didn't immediately run out and harpoon a Botox shark!

Granna was right and so was Shelby. "You know what—who cares? He can do what he wants and so can I. I just don't feel like doing *anything*, yet."

They chatted for another hour and shared a couple more soothing laughs. Whenever she cast a glance in Clarice's direction, he looked in hers. That certainly didn't make her feel worse.

"I'm wiped, y'all," Lindsey finally said. "Plus it's prime ovulation time. I can't let my ovaries get tired."

"You got a husband seduction outfit planned?" asked Shelby.

"I doubt she needs to seduce P.D.," said Tipsy.

"I might. He was hurting this morning and he's on the sofa right now." Lindsey scowled. "His swimmers better not be hungover."

Tipsy burst out laughing. She called for her check before Shelby grabbed it. As she waited for the bartender to return her card, she noticed that A Boy Named Clarice had called it an early night, too. Or at least moved on to the next drinking spot.

She took out her phone and noted texts from May Penny and Jimmy, her former brother-in-law and landlord. Nothing from Big Ayers. That was a relief. She'd had a nice evening. She didn't want to ruin it with his bad attitude or any ruminations on his newly sinful living situation.

Shelby offered her a ride, but Tipsy decided to walk home in the slowly softening light. She had to watch her step through the bumpy parking lot, but once she got to the sidewalk, she read her texts. She smiled at the message from May Penny. Mimi's kids had introduced her to Bitmojis. She'd sent this one to Tipsy and Mimi. It showed a cartoon version of her former mother-in-law (complete with tennis skirt, bobbed blonde hair, and giant sunglasses) raising a glass of wine. *TGIF!* was written in bubble letters over the cartoon May Penny's head. Tipsy replied with her own high-fiving cartoon self. How things had changed. A year ago, she thought May Penny had always disliked her and always would. Somehow, they'd come to a place of mutual respect, and dare she say it, enjoyment of each other.

She looked up at Miss Callie's house toward the end of the street. She admired the bright white paint job contrasting with the Charleston green shutters. Jimmy had painted the whole place before he left for Florida. To her relief, his repairs had gone agonizingly slowly because he and his siblings fought over everything. She estimated that at this rate, she'd have at least another year in the house. Their family strife gave her more time to save money, but she'd also come to love the place. In her fantasies she won the lottery and bought it herself.

She swiped on Jimmy's message and slowed to a stop. He usually texted in the short, clippie way typical of men. She doubted he'd ever sent a text with a period.

JIMMY: HEY TIPSY. SORRY TO HAVE TO TELL YOU THIS, BUT MY FAMILY IS FIGHTING BAD ABOUT MAMA'S HOUSE. I'M TRYING TO MANAGE THEM, BUT AT THIS POINT I HAVE TO THROW THEM A BONE. THEY'RE ALWAYS ON ME ABOUT WHO PAYS FOR WHAT REPAIRS. MY SISTER ELLEN DECIDED THE BEST WAY TO HANDLE EVERYTHING IS TO GET A RENTER IN WHO CAN PAY. ESPECIALLY WITH THE KITCHEN RENO COMING UP.

Tipsy bit her lip. Maybe things would move faster than she thought.

JIMMY: I WANT TO GIVE YOU FIRST DIBS ON STAYING IN THE HOUSE. BUT I'M GOING TO HAVE TO START CHARGING YOU RENT. ARE YOU OK WITH THAT?

She typed a quick reply as she entered the yard. OF COURSE IT'S UP TO YOU AND YOUR FAMILY AND I TOTALLY UNDERSTAND. WHAT ARE YOU THINKING?

JIMMY: I THINK I TALKED THEM DOWN TO A GOOD PRICE. DOES $2600 SOUND OKAY?

Tipsy walked onto the porch. She sat on the joggling board. Twenty-six hundred was more than generous. Jimmy could probably get almost twice that for the place based on the location.

She wiped her eyes. Unfortunately, generous or not, she still wasn't sure how she'd pay so much long term. Thank goodness for Pamella's fifty-k. Without it, there was no way she could afford it. Still, she replied to Jimmy in the affirmative. I'LL MAKE IT WORK, THANK YOU!!! ☺

She couldn't hide her trepidation from the person who knew her best and resided in her head. *Granna, we got to figure out Ms. Ivy's story or we'll be moving.*

The night is young, sugar. Plenty of time to get going on figuring out.

We're not figuring out anything without John Huger. Tipsy pulled her keys out of her purse. She was in for another evening on Sullivan's Island, and unfortunately it wasn't an extension of her Friday Happy Hour.

This time, when Tipsy walked across the overgrown grass surrounding the old soldiers' barracks, she knew who she wanted to find. Not a young sergeant in uniform, but a full grown man in what looked to be the 1930s version of business casual.

Tipsy thought back to her first attempt to find Jane's niece Luisa Bishop last summer. It was her first attempt to find any ghost, ever. She closed her eyes and tapped her fingers on her thighs. One-two-three-four-five-four-three-two-one. She paused on each number. Her pulse slowed and her mind emptied. She called out in the same way she called to Luisa.

John Huger? Are you here? I'm a friend of Jane Mott. Can you hear me?

Nothing.

She moved closer to the building, until she could have reached out and touched the peeling, grayish paint. The fading sun darkened an already murky window. Her eyes followed several cracks like a jagged mountain-scape on the glass. This time she shouted.

Hey, John! John Huger!

She jumped when a white face appeared behind the window. The cracked glass momentarily gave the impression of wrinkles, as if she were looking at an old man. He sidestepped and the John she recognized from Jane and Henry's memories came into focus.

"Who's this?" His bright blue eyes narrowed. "I *don't know* you. Who… are… you?" John sounded rather like the persnickety hookah-smoking caterpillar from *Alice in Wonderland*.

You better get to explaining, sugar, said Granna, *he doesn't look too excited to see you.*

"Right," said Tipsy, and then, "Hey, John. My name is Tipsy Collins. I'm friends with Jane—"

"Jane has been dead for many years. She died before me. Yet *you* claim to know her?"

"I do. I know her as a ghost. I also know Ivy—"

"Ivy must be very old. Wouldn't she be?" He looked over his shoulder, as if conferring with someone Tipsy couldn't see.

"Ummm… your understanding of time is off by a few years. If Ivy were alive, she'd be about the oldest person in the world. Except for maybe one of those Japanese people who live on seaweed."

John stepped through the barracks wall. He had to be six foot four. Probably taller. Tipsy almost covered her eyes, lest he be decapitated by the broken glass, before she remembered that John could walk through a minefield with no ill effects.

His hands clenched in fists. "Is that supposed to be funny? There's nothing funny about Ivy, or time, or Orientals. Nothing is funny at all! Now *who are you?*"

Once again, Tipsy thought of the disgruntled, puffed up caterpillar, who was *exac-a-tally* three inches high.

Tipsy fought nervous giggles as John glared down at her from his full height.

You always start twittering when ain't nothin' funny, said Granna. *He's not turning into a butterfly. He's getting irater by the second and he's fixin' to disappear.*

He definitely got up on the wrong side of the coffin. I thought John was supposed to be charming and gracious.

I'd be grumpy too if I were trapped in this dilapidated, moldy old shack for ninety years. Now focus!

Tipsy tried again. "I'm sorry. You're right. Not funny. I know Jane because she used to haunt my house. I know Ivy, because she's also a ghost—"

John's expression abruptly flipped from anger to anguish, from one comic strip panel to the next. "Have mercy. My poor sweet love. Where is she?" He turned back toward the barracks. "Did y'all hear her? Ivy is trapped. We're all trapped." He slapped his thighs. If he had substance, he would have given himself a hematoma.

Whoa. So much for Ivy being his side chick. No one freaks out like that over a booty call. And who the hell is he talking to?

Maybe try to talk to him like you did with the girls, said Granna, *when they were little and pitching a fit.*

Tipsy tried to imagine John as a giant toddler, mid-conniption. She needed to be stern, yet entice him. "John, come on now. Don't get hysterical. If you can't calm down, I can't tell you anything about Ivy."

That got through to him. Again, his expression flipped from sad to glumly suspicious with disorienting speed. He muttered to himself.

"John, is there another ghost here? Who are you talking to?"

"No other ghosts. Talking to my friends."

"Your friends—"

He responded in a singsong voice. "Fur. Feathers. Scales."

Oh, hell. Caterpillars be damned. This is lions and tigers and bears, oh my. He really is nuts, Granna.

Sounds more like possums, rats, and snakes, replied Granna. *Don't poke him. Just wait.*

John talked to himself, or maybe he was talking to the mosquitos. "Remember, Ivy said I should listen to everything around me. Everything! So talk, whoever you are. Since Ivy said I should keep my ears open."

"That's uh… good advice—"

"Ivy didn't say I had to listen for long."

Tipsy took the hint. She gave him a brief version of how she came to know Ivy Brewton, and of Ivy's current predicament. He didn't blink, flinch, or react in any way. After his hysterical response to hearing Ivy's name and his chattering with his animal friends like the ghost of Dr. Doolittle, it unnerved her. She found herself intimidated by this ghost, although not as much as Ivy flat out scared her. John had no supernatural power, so he couldn't physically hurt her. Still, she didn't have any illusions of befriending either of them in the way she'd become buddies with Jane and Henry.

It bummed her out some, at least in John's case. She'd liked the guy she'd seen in Jane's memory. He seemed like the kind of person who looked out for his friends, and who would be fun to have a beer with. Still, of all the ghosts she'd known so far, John was the most secluded. For someone as gregarious as he'd been in life, the solitude must have been torture. No wonder he talked to the palmetto bugs.

"…. So Ivy knows you're a ghost, too. But she didn't know where to find you."

"I remember the day Ivy's mother visited," said John. "She came here to pick blackberries from the bushes behind the barracks. I walked up behind her, although I didn't think she'd see me. No one had seen me before, nor since, until today. But Alma rubbed her arms as if touched by cold breeze. Then she turned around and looked me right in the eye. She screamed and dropped her berry basket. Ran off baying like a coonhound in the moonlight."

"That sounds a little dramatic."

"Alma was an odd bird." His face softened as he talked, like a tight bud relaxing into a blossom. "Still, I hoped she'd come back. Odd or not, it would have been nice to have someone to talk to. But she never returned."

Tipsy felt judgmental in a way only people who share a talent can be. "Supposedly Alma wasn't a powerful seer, but there's no need to lose your shit about seeing a ghost."

"Pardon?"

"Never mind. I want to help Ivy move on. If I want *her* to move on, I have to help *you* move on, too, apparently."

"Where would I go?"

"I'm not sure where it is, or what it is, but I know Jane happily moved on. She understood her death and she found peace. That was that."

"She understood that devil she married murdered her?"

"He didn't."

"I'm sure he did! Everyone knew he did it."

"Look, I'll explain what happened to Jane and Henry another time. I want to know what happened to *you*. Do you have any ideas? Most of the ghosts I know have, like, problem deaths. Agony, violence, things left unresolved. Can you think of anything like that?"

"My parents wouldn't accept my love for Ivy, but…" Curiosity had replaced hostility in his eyes, but the suspicion came back like a fever after the Tylenol wears off. "Why *do* you want to help us? What's in it for you? Maybe you want to keep us apart!"

"I'm doing some work for the current owner of Ivy's house, but I feel sorry for y'all. You're so close to one another, yet so far away."

"I don't need your pity."

"Do you want my help or not? If you do, maybe be nicer."

John took two steps toward her. He towered over her, tall and thin and grayish purple in the fading light, like a crumbling skyscraper. Even if she wore heels, she'd still have to look up at him. He was taller than Big Ayers. Taller than she remembered her daddy being when she was a child and she thought him the biggest man in the world.

She held her ground and reminded herself that John was no seer in life. He might be huge and grumpy as hell, but he could do nothing more than give her the chills.

He glowered down at her long enough for his lavender glow to darken a few shades as the sun kept setting. "All right," he finally said. "Tipsy, your name is? Show me what to do."

"Sit down," Tipsy said. She sat in the grass and he followed her. She hadn't done this since she witnessed Jane and Henry's gruesome murder. She tried to remember how she'd braced herself last summer so she didn't fall over when she lost consciousness. She thought of the rent coming due and took a deep breath. "This might be kind of weird, but it's the only way I can see what happened. Hold your hand up to mine," she said.

The sunset raged behind John's head like he was being burned at the stake. He raised one purplish white hand. She'd never seen hands so big on a man. Once again, she thought of her father. In those long ago and rare times when he'd held her hand, she thought his looked like a bear's paw. John's fingers engulfed hers. Night fell over Tipsy's mind as if their supernatural connection had hastened the setting sun.

———✶✦✶———

It's exactly like when she peered into Jane and Henry's memories. Yellow flashing lights cut through the black, and she opens her eyes. She stands in a manicured garden enclosed by brick walls topped with iron spikes. To her right, a sprawling brick mansion with four story white piazzas. Shaggy Confederate jasmine clings to the garden walls. The white blossoms spray their fragrance over the yard like tiny vintage perfume bottles.

John stands in the springy grass, grousing at an older, shorter man with a shock of salt and pepper hair. They don't look much alike, but there's something familiar in the way both men stand with their shoulders thrown back and their chins lifted, looking down on the world. Tipsy guesses it's John's father—R.J. Huger, Henry had called him. Both men wear white trousers, white shoes, and white polo shirts.

"Son," R.J. says, clearly exasperated. "I don't want to talk about this again. If we're going to get to the Smith's on time, we need to leave."

"I don't care about another damn picnic." John peeks over his shoulder. "Maybe I should have talked to Mama first instead of you. She'd understand."

"Don't you dare upset her like that. Her asthma is bad this time of year. She can't tolerate an attack." R.J. crosses his arms over his chest. "What has gotten into you?"

John laughs. "I'm sure about something for the first time in my life that wasn't your idea. Mama has been wanting me to get married for years! Begging me! She'll be happy!"

"You don't understand your own mother. She asked you to marry Annie Rose Middleton, or one of the Gaillards. She wanted you to marry one of the Robinette girls—"

"That again? Jane and Connie were like my sisters! I'd never marry either of them."

"Maybe if you'd married Jane, she'd still be alive."

John's face flames. Tipsy can feel his shock and rage and grief as if they were her own emotions. She gasps at the intensity of his feelings. She'd forgotten this part; this emotional voyeurism. It's as overwhelming now as it was in Jane and Henry's memories. She bites her lip to keep from screaming at R.J. herself.

"A low blow, Daddy. Below the belt."

"Maybe so, but it's true. But now we're talking about the future, not the past. Mother wants you to marry the right kind of girl."

"Ivy is the right kind of girl! She's the most wonderful person I've ever—"

"She's a marsh Baptist. She probably speaks in tongues."

"There's nothing you can say that will make me change my mind."

R.J. tries to reroute the conversation. "What about Daisy Lamboll?"

"What about her?

"You know exactly what about her, after last summer. Her father's been hinting around asking when you're going to make an honest woman of her. She's twenty-two. She needs a husband and she's not going to wait forever."

"That was just a summer fling."

"Daisy didn't think so. She was pretty torn up when you stopped calling on her last fall."

John's face reddens, as if he's ashamed of his behavior in retrospect. "I'm sorry, but I never had any intention of—"

"Of marrying her? Or any of the other girls you dallied with over the years? Listen, son. I have a few too many friends who have looked the other way after you dangled their daughters on a line. Daisy Lamboll is a lovely girl. You've known her for years. She's sweet. Knows how to run a house. Y'all would have some pretty babies."

"No, Daddy. I'm not marrying Daisy Lamboll."

"Because of this Ivy person? You're going to break Daisy's heart, and insult another of my oldest friends to boot, because you're infatuated with a white trash gal you just met."

John takes two steps toward his father, with his fists balled at his side.

"You going to hit me now, son?"

John's arms flop at his sides. He looks at the blue springtime sky above him. "No, sir. Of course not."

"There's a showing of good sense, finally. Now, I'm glad you want to settle down—"

"Meet her. Please? I know you'll love her."

R.J.'s mouth sets in a stern line. "We've gone 'round and round about this for a week. You're a blackfly biting a horse's ass, and then you wonder why it's kickin'. I told you, no."

"I'll talk to Mama—"

R.J. points a finger in his face. "You say one word to your mother and your monthly allowance might just run dry. You'll be asking that girl's piece of trash father to give you a job shucking oysters!"

John's chest rises and falls with his harsh breathing. Tipsy wonders if he might split his nice white shirt.

"Damnit." R.J. storms toward the stairs. "We're walking to the Smiths in ten minutes. You fix a smile on your face. I'll not have your sour puss ruining our afternoon."

As R.J. stomps up the steps, another man clips down them. "Afternoon, Uncle R.J.," says this new man, who resembles John, but a few inches shorter with blonder hair and not as strong a jaw.

"Afternoon, Camden," says R.J. as he passes. He slams the door behind him.

The new guy joins John in the garden. "It didn't go so well this time, either?"

"I don't know what to do, Cam. He won't listen to me. And damn him for using money to control my life. I'm tired of it."

"Come on, Johnny. Did you expect him to approve? You might as well try to make mud pies in a drought."

John is desperate for a way to make it all work in his own mind. "I don't think Mama would feel the same way Daddy does. She's too kindhearted, and she... she..."

"She's never said no to you in your life?" Camden says, and chuckles. "I know you're not used to anything blocking your road, but somethings aren't meant to be, cousin. Maybe you need to find another path. Lord knows there are plenty of other girls."

"Not like this one."

"I admit, she's pretty, but when we talked to her at the grocery, she barely said a word."

"What do you expect? She's not used to people like us, and her family doesn't exactly gather at lawn parties making small talk. She's a bit shy at first, but she's more than just a pretty face. She's tougher than most men I know, growing up how she has. She asks questions about everything. She makes me think. She's got the best laugh—it's like—like—"

"A coot with a broken wing?"

"Damnit, Cam. It's not funny. She knows more about the wild things that roam the marshes than you and I could ever learn in a lifetime of sitting in a duck blind. And she..." John's own statement is a revelation to him. "She makes me feel like life can mean something."

"It's taken a girl who kills chickens with her bare hands to make you think life means something?" Camden points at the house and the surrounding gardens. "Look how blessed we are."

"That's just it. What the hell am I doing every day, living in this big old house? Going to parties. Sitting through sermons no one in church takes to heart. Chasing women like poor silly Daisy Lamboll, who never thought of a damn thing beyond dresses, hats, and landing a husband."

"Aww, don't knock Daisy. She's turned out like her parents planned."

"If Daisy thumbed her nose at all of them, maybe she'd have some fire in her belly. Then again, who am I to talk? I'm always at my father's command. I remember before Janie died, she asked me an odd question. Johnny, she said, why do I always do what everyone wants me to do?"

"Jane married Henry Mott despite her family's misgivings. Look how that turned out. I wouldn't mention Jane when you're trying to bring people to your way of thinking."

"I understand what Jane meant. I've probably been stewing over my own version of that question for years, even if I didn't know it. Running out to Sullivan's to escape all this. With Ivy by my side, I finally found a way to live with it all and still have some peace."

"That's a lot of responsibility for one person." Camden punches John's arm in an attempt to lighten the mood. "What's she getting out of this arrangement? Aside from your muscles and your money."

"She doesn't care about the money. I don't think she knows a Huger from a Robinette from a Rutledge. As for why she loves me... well, I certainly like the person I am when I'm with her better than the person I've been."

"I'm teasing you, Johnny. Everyone loves you, especially women. Ivy More surely won't be any different or any—"

"I want to protect her."

"You just said she's tougher than both of us. Who does she need protecting from?"

"Her father. Not everyone has a family like ours. Ivy's daddy is a damn brute."

"Gallant of you, but also sounds like that might come with some white trash problems. You want to inherit her mess?"

John is bent on ignoring Camden's logic. "I never knew someone could love me like she does. Much less that I could love someone like I love her."

It's almost as if he's as flummoxed by his newfound love and the emotions that go along with it as his father and Camden are. "I never planned any of this, but the best gifts are the surprise ones."

"Good lord. I hear you. You're madly in love. You're the South Battery Romeo. But I'm telling you, R.J. will never accept it. Your mother won't either, kindhearted or not. If you want to marry that girl, you better plan to live in her shack with her and her ornery daddy. You can't always get your way."

"You can think what you will, but I promised her. We're going to be married." He strides toward the staircase. "Now come on. It's the end of the month and I'm running low on pocket money. I need to fix my face up right for the Smiths damn garden party."

Camden follows him. "John. Be realistic—"

John stops in the middle of the staircase. "I don't think I will be realistic, Camden. You insinuated that I always get my way, and you're right." He takes the last steps two at a time. "I plan on keeping it that way."

They disappear into the house. Like the slam of the screen door shutting out the hungry spring mosquitos, Tipsy is abruptly cut off from the past.

———✄———

When Tipsy opened her eyes, she was staring into John Huger's solemn face.

"Well," he said. "What happened?"

Tipsy must have grabbed the grass to hold herself up while she was out. She disengaged her fingers and wiped her hands on her thigh. The aftereffect paled in comparison to her first supernatural interactions with Jane and Henry, but she still felt like she'd stepped off a roller coaster.

The sun had set while she visited that bright spring morning in the 1930's. John glowed blueish in the moonlight. She thought of the strips of colored LED lights Little Ayers had begged her to hang up in his bedroom. They made the room feel like the command deck on an alien spaceship. John looked like he'd attached LED lights to the insides of his head and they were shining out through his eyeballs.

When the world stopped spinning, she told him what she'd seen in his memory. As she talked, she thought of Henry's opinion of John, the supposed shallow, pampered dandy. The guy she'd seen in the memory might have had a seemingly perfect life from the outside, but he'd clearly gone through some internal turmoil.

"That argument happened over a month before I died," he said as she finished, with obvious disappointment. "On the day of Nora and Lou Smith's annual garden party. How is it helpful?"

She shrugged. "Did anything happen at the party?"

"No. Camden and I went with my parents and his mother. A pleasantly boring affair. You didn't see Ivy in the memory?"

"No. Your father. You. And Camden."

"Good old Cam. The brother I never had." John finally sounded like the amiable man who had counseled Jane. "Sometimes I wonder what happened to him. I can only hope he lived a long, happy life."

"You don't know? Oh. I suppose you wouldn't." Tipsy didn't necessarily want to be the one to tell John Huger how his cousin Camden's life turned out. She stood. "I should get going."

John suddenly stood next to her, although she hadn't seen him get up. First frame; sitting in the grass. Second frame; looming beside her like an elegant gargoyle. "Do you know anything about Cousin Camden's life?"

"Uh… I don't know much."

"Tell me. Please."

"It's getting late. This kind of thing tires me out." She walked to the street. John followed her, but once he hit the spot where the grass met asphalt, he had to stop.

"Tipsy—that's your name, correct? Please tell me. I know nothing of my friends or family."

She sighed. "You're not going to like it."

"Did he die young?"

"Not as young as you. He lived twenty years or so."

"How did he die?"

"He had his own tragedies." She swallowed. "He passed after his wife died."

"Oh, no. Who did he marry? I'm glad he found someone. He was like me before I met Ivy. Inclined to be a bit of a cad, I'm ashamed to say."

Yikes, said Granna. *You better take a step back.*

"He married…" Tipsy indeed took a step back, and then another for good measure. "He married Ivy, John."

The smile left John's face. She almost heard a newly enraged expression snap into place, like when an optometrist switches the little glass plates during an eye exam. Smile—click—scowl. "Ivy More."

"Yes."

The blue light leaked from John's eyes down his arms to his huge hands as if someone had filled his veins with antifreeze. He vibrated like a revved engine. Tipsy instinctually raised her arms to cover her face, lest the ghost of John Huger explode and pepper her with spectral ooze, like in the Ghostbusters movies.

Ectoplasm, she thought. Ironically, the real Bill Murray indeed lived somewhere on Sullivan's Island. *Help me, Dr. Venkman!*

"Camden Brewton married Ivy More?" John's giant fists clench up. He looked around as if he were talking to the fireflies. "Did you hear that, y'all? Camden *Brewton* married Ivy *More!*"

"I'm sorry to be the one to tell you. I know it must be painful—"

"I'll kill him! I'll kill them both!"

"They're already dead—"

John raged along the edge of the road like a silverback gorilla behind glass. Tipsy was the zookeeper who had provoked him.

"John!" she said. "John—calm down, please."

"My own *cousin* took up with the only woman I ever loved after my death?" He pointed at Tipsy. "And you! Have you come here to torture me with this knowledge?"

"No! I didn't want to tell you, but I suppose I had to. If I'm going to free Ivy—"

"Let her rot! Unfaithful tramp!"

"Did you expect her to join a convent?"

"No!" John started crying, in the kind of strangled way of men who are both unused to tears and ashamed of them. "But Camden? My cousin?" He grabbed his hair and pulled. "My own flesh and blood?"

He spun around and stormed toward the barracks. He gesticulated wildly to his imaginary friends and trailed blue mist in his wake like a spilled Kamikaze shot.

"John!" she yelled. "Hey! Come back!"

"You need some help, miss?"

Tipsy spun around. An older man stood on his front porch. The porchlight backlit his face, so she couldn't see him clearly.

Maybe it's Bill Murray, she thought.

Or maybe he's going to call the cops if you don't get it together, said Granna.

"Oh, no sir. Sorry! I'm looking for... my cat. John. John the cat."

"That's more original than Fluffy," said the man. "What's the cat look like? I'll keep an eye out."

"He's big, and…. grayish… and kind of mean. I wouldn't get too close to him." She walked toward her car. "He always comes home eventually."

"Cats are like that. Can't get rid of 'em once you feed 'em!" He turned toward his house. "You have a nice night now."

"You too!" Tipsy hit the unlock button. Her car chirped like a big metal mockingbird, or maybe a coot with a broken wing. The lights flashed and she winced. She had a bit of a headache, but like her nausea, it was nothing like those early supernatural time hops. She felt perverse pride for having mastered the art of looking into a ghost's head.

When you're a clairvoyant for hire, said Granna, *you better be ready to learn something new every day.*

Chapter 6

T ipsy slept later than she planned, even for a Saturday without kids. She was a little queasy and barely choked down a protein bar, so she decided to forego exercise and go straight to Pamella's to work out something with Ivy Brewton.

As she drove onto the island, she thought about the best way to approach the skittish ghost. It was no joke trying to negotiate with such a powerful spirit. As much as Tipsy wanted information, common sense and her still achy tailbone told her that only slow and steady would win this race. She didn't want to end up in the marsh with the unfortunate oak limb.

She brought her sketchpads, so she planned to shoot two coots with one arrow by working on her sketches in a conspicuous ghost watching location. She walked around the back of the house and sat on the picnic table under the live oak with a sketchpad on her lap. She resisted calling out to Ivy. If she sat long enough, hopefully the ghost would emerge on her own. That strategy worked for Ayers and Will when they sat in a deer stand and waited for the bucks to come for the corn. Like the nosy gentleman last night had said, it worked with stray cats after a feeding.

After about thirty minutes of sketching, the chirping birds, boat engines, and the laughter of a few children in the adjoining backyard blended together like natural elevator music. She finally looked up when a new melody interrupted the neighborhood's everyday harmony.

Ivy More sang to herself as she wandered across the yard. Ivy's rendition of *Somewhere Over the Rainbow* wasn't as perfect as Judy Garland's, but it was close, and it had the same sense of plaintive longing.

Her misty dress fluttered around her legs like the wings of the bluebirds that should be flying out of the trees to perch on her shoulder.

Tipsy watched her out of the corner of her eye. Ivy cut her own gaze in Tipsy's direction before looking back at the marsh. She almost seemed to dare Tipsy to call out to her. Over the next hour Ivy added other songs to her repertoire. Tipsy recognized a couple of them, like *Pennies from Heaven*. She broke into *Amazing Grace*, a song that never failed to make Tipsy tear up.

They made awkward eye contact a few times, like two strangers sharing a cramped elevator. Each time their eyes met they both looked away as if afraid of hypnosis. Finally, Ivy floated toward Tipsy. She cleared her throat.

Tipsy looked up from her sketching and smiled, as if she hadn't been playing hide and seek in plain daylight with this ghost. "Hey, Ivy. Pretty morning, isn't it? Your singing voice is nice."

Ivy gave her a pursed lipped smile that did not touch her cold eyes. "Thank you, Miss... what was it?"

"Tipsy. Tipsy Denning-Collins. I know it's an unusual name—"

"My grandfather was called Abundance Chapman."

"Ah. So your threshold for unusual is pretty high." She returned to her sketch of Robert Brewton's face and forced Ivy to do the talking.

"So. Ahem. Miss Denning-Collins. It seems my granddaughter is paying you a large amount of money to remove me from this house."

"Jeez. That's kind of harsh. She's trying to set you free. She doesn't exactly like the idea of her grandmother being trapped in purgatory in her backyard." Tipsy set her sketchpad on the table beside her. "I found the love of your life."

"Did you now?"

"John Huger."

Ivy's hair blew around her head despite the lack of breeze. Her skirt floated around her legs like laundry dancing on a line. "You *really* found him?"

"Y'all are two peas in a pod with your suspicions. Yes. For one, how would I even know who he was if I hadn't?" Tipsy sounded more confident than she felt. Her foot tapped anxiously against the picnic table bench.

Ivy spoke through clenched teeth. Her voice tightened into painful propriety. "I suppose that is true. How is he? *Where* is he?"

Tipsy gave Ivy a summary of her conversation with John, ending with the memory of him arguing with his father. As she talked, Ivy's hair and skirt relaxed until everything was hanging off her as if the laws of physics still mattered. Tipsy took it as a hopeful sign that the ghost was settling down.

"Did you ever have any suspicions about John's death?" asked Tipsy.

Ivy shook her head. "Never had any reason to suspect anything. Johnny loved his swims. It made me nervous, him swimming by himself. Sometimes at night. The currents on this end of the island are fierce. Even in the creeks, I worried about the gators. But there was no telling my Johnny anything." Her mouth turned up at the corners. That hint of humor reminded Tipsy of the photo of Ivy with the giant pot.

Tipsy thought of Camden's observations. "He always got his way?"

Ivy forced her mouth back into a prim line, as if she'd spent her whole life and death working against emotion. "He did. But he wasn't a bully. He was *good*. He wanted everyone to be happy, and mostly, everyone was, when he was around. He was just… like gravity. You couldn't fight him, but without him, life would be all wrong. Everything out of place. That's how it was for me. Once I met John, nothing was right without him."

Tipsy's heart ached for her; this bitter version of the pretty, laughing woman in the older black and white photos. "Why don't you show me what happened to you first? You can go on and wait for him."

"I won't go on when he has to stay here. I told you that." Her dress blew around her legs again. She held it down, like a dark haired Marilyn Monroe standing over a subway grate.

Oh, dear. Thar she blows, said Granna.

"Then I guess we're all stuck for now," said Tipsy. "You're stuck. John's stuck. I'm stuck figuring out what happened without much cooperation from you."

Ivy approached the picnic table. Each time Ivy's personal wind blew, her billowing skirt came closer to Tipsy. It gave off a misty aura. If Tipsy was right, she merely needed to get close enough for her own skin to meet that gauzy layer. Despite her fear of Ivy's volatility, she subtly shifted in the ghost's direction as if her butt had fallen asleep.

"You know...even if I touch you," she said casually. "It's not like you would just disappear into the next life. It's still a choice you make."

"I'm not taking any chances. Now did John have any words for me?"

"Uh... well." Tipsy scooted toward Ivy's fluttering skirts. "He clearly loves you. I told you what he said about you in his memory. Those were about the sweetest words I've ever heard anyone say."

"But did he have a message for me now?" Ivy's skirts tossed about irritably, born on the gathering clouds of her annoyance.

Tipsy, be careful!

I have to try, Granna!

"He was sad to hear you're trapped. But he was surprised. And... kind of mad. About Camden—"

"You told him I married Camden?"

"I had to when he asked if I knew how y'all's lives had turned out—"

"How dare you tell him!"

Pamella had set up a dining table with a green and white striped umbrella on the cracked cement patio. The umbrella abruptly snapped shut and shot into the air like a canvas rocket. It soared up about twenty feet before losing momentum, hovering for a second, and dropping back to earth pole first.

It hit the ground with a crack and the pole exploded. Shards of wood flew across the lawn. Distance protected Tipsy from the carnage, but she automatically turned away with her arms over her head. Even Ivy seemed surprised. She lurched backward. If she were solid, she would have run into the table, but instead, she stepped through it. Tipsy's upraised elbow passed through the fluttery spectral edges of Ivy's blue and white dress. The familiar darkness closed over her.

———◆✕◆———

Tipsy stands beside a one story whitewashed cottage with a brick chimney overlooking the marsh. She turns to get her bearings. There's a skinny, low bridge a hundred or so yards to her right. It connects two marshy patches of land separated by a narrow body of water. It's the Old Pitt Street Bridge, the only connection between Mount Pleasant and Sullivan's Island in this day. Two cars putter across it. A man in a broad hat has stopped in the middle of the bridge to watch a fishing boat squeeze underneath it. Beyond the bridge is the open harbor.

She's in the Old Village, just across the Intracoastal Waterway from Sullivan's Island near the end of Pitt Street. She walks around the side of the building. There's the skeleton of an old wooden boat, propped up on cinderblocks, in the backyard. There's a wooden cross at the edge of the marsh with a bible verse painted on it. Genesis 9:2. Tipsy has no idea what that means. Granna made her go to youth group but Tipsy never paid much attention to anything but the cute boys and free pizza. Still, she commits it to memory.

This must be Ivy's family home. It's a long, skinny place. Halfway down the side, there's a narrow porch. Tipsy catches her breath. John and Ivy sit on the steps, not five feet away from her. She's wearing a light green dress. His tan trousers are rolled up. The sleeves of his white shirt reveal muscular forearms. They're both barefoot. Their feet covered in sand.

As she creeps closer, Tipsy wonders if people were more attractive in the past, or if there's something about seeing a real live person after seeing the pale, sunken-eyed version of him or her. Ivy's nose is dusted with freckles. Her light brown eyes are chestnut in the sun. She has the kind of full, pretty lips Tipsy envies—the ones that stay red even without lipstick. A few tears have tracked down her face. Her hair floats around her head, lifted on a real breeze, not the weird spectral wind that blew her skirt up against Tipsy and brought her here.

John reaches over and tucks her rebellious curls behind her ears. He takes her hands in his; those same huge hands Tipsy thought might crush her own. Instead of being pale polar bear paws, they're tanned from hours under the South Carolina sun. She once thought he reminded her of Peter O'Toole, circa Lawrence of Arabia. That resemblance is still there in his chiseled jaw and bright blue eyes lined with dark curling lashes, but there's a bit of Paul Newman in there, too.

"Please don't cry, sweetheart," he says. "This isn't my brave Ivy. I can't stand to see you so sad. Everything will be well. I promise."

"I want to believe you, Johnny. But I just can't see how we'll manage. Your parents ain't—aren't—going to accept me. My father knows about us." This young Ivy hasn't yet learned to squelch her accent. It isn't exactly like John's; it's somehow thicker. More country. *"You don't know what this fear is like. There's always more at stake for a woman. Especially one like me."*

"What do you mean, a woman like you?" He smiles. "A wonderful, amazing woman?"

Ivy can't help but smile back at his positivity. Ivy's emotions wash over Tipsy, and she understands how much Ivy loves this about John. His firm belief that everything will always be well and good. It makes Ivy, who has lived her whole life feeling quite the opposite, feel hopeful.

"You're a wonderful, amazing man. Even if you are sometimes a bit foolish."

"I'm a fool in love! Now come on, sweetheart. We only need a bit more time."

Ivy rests a hand on his cheek. "You want that to be true, so you believe it."

John stands and tugs her to her feet. "I swear on my soul we'll be married. Please say you believe me."

He kisses her, and apparently, there's enough in the kiss to convince her. She pulls away, breathing hard. "I believe you."

"I'll protect you; I swear it." There's a wild desperation on his face. "Don't doubt me. Don't doubt us."

"I don't doubt us. I doubt everyone around us. I doubt the world that's working against us."

"Goddamn the world."

"It's so easy for you to say so, when the world has always cooperated with you."

"I'll make it happen. I will. All our dreams will come true. In a year, you'll be sitting on a piazza downtown. The lady of the house."

"Do you think your neighbors will appreciate that? I'm not sure how I fit into your life. Besides, I'll miss the marsh."

"Ivy, it will be our life, together. As for the neighbors, we might raise some eyebrows at first, but they'll love you once they get to know you. Just like my family will, and all my friends."

"I hope they do. I want to make you proud."

"I couldn't be prouder of anyone. I know it will be an adjustment for you, but we'll manage it together. And we'll go out to the island whenever you need to get away. Stay at our cottage." He taps her nose. *"I'll put a sign on the front gate that says—"* He waves his hands with the flourish of someone painting a warning in all capital letters. *"BUBBA BEGONE."*

She laughs, and Tipsy sees the girl from the old photos. She grins in a way that's hard to rectify with the terse spirit Tipsy knows. She bops John's nose herself. It's a sweet gesture between two people who are as natural together as the ocean meeting the shore. *"No sign ever kept my daddy out."*

John scowled. *"Has he roughed you up again?"*

"Not lately—"

"Damn, it's hard for me to hear that. That man is the devil." John runs a hand over his wind tossed hair. *"I wish you'd let me set you up somewhere else. If he touches you again—"*

As if on cue, new voices enter the conversation. A man yells, *"Ivy? Where you at, gal?"*

A woman is chattering in the background. Ivy's eyes widen. She grabs John's shoulder. *"Go, Johnny."*

John turns toward the voice. *"Maybe I can talk to him this time. I'll be friendly as a spaniel puppy. I promise."* He shrugs off her hand and fixes a smile on his face. That expression has never failed him before. He's sure he can charm anyone.

A man and woman come around the corner. It's difficult to tell how old they are, but it's clear life has been hard on them. The woman is shorter than Ivy, but she has the same curly dark hair. Hers is shot through with streaks of gray. She's thin, wearing a gray dress, an apron, and beat up shoes with laces. She waves to Ivy, but when she sees John, her smile freezes on her face.

The man's skin is cracked and weathered from endless days under the sun, working on boats and harvesting oysters. He's tall and rangy with lank, straight black hair and a receding chin. The only thing about him that smacks of a relation to Ivy are his big brown eyes, but while on her they're lovely and doe-like, on him they're the goggle eyes of a malnourished frog.

John clears his throat. "Hello Miss Alma... Bubba—or it's George, right? Now I know you're surprised to see me—"

Bubba More pauses for a split second, before striding across the yard. He passes John's outstretched hand, offered in peace like a well-muscled olive branch, and grabs his daughter's elbow. "What in the name of the Holy Ghost is this rich turd doing in my yard again?"

John's chin juts, but Ivy says, "It's all right, Johnny. Go along now."

"I told you! I don't want him around this house, or you!"

Alma freezes in place. She wrings her hands. "Now, now," she says. Tipsy hopes for more from her, but she keeps repeating that ineffective placeholder.

"Sir," says John. "I'm going to ask you once to take your hands off Ivy—"

"You think I'm afraid of you? I killed alligators with my bare hands while you were sitting on your daddy's knee, reading bedtime stories."

"My daddy's stories taught me it's not right for a man to put his hands on a woman."

"I'll do what I want with my own daughter. Now you get your ass on out of here."

This comment kills John's attempt at civility. "Who do you think you're talking to, cracker?"

Bubba lets go of Ivy and rushes at John. He's nowhere near as big, and he has to be at least ten years older, but he's much nastier. He shoves John, and John stumbles backward. For a second, he stands there in shock, as if one of his own gundogs attacked him. The second doesn't last, though, and *he lunges at Bubba. The two men fall to the ground in a flailing mass of flying fists and jabbing knees.*

Alma More flinches and turns away, muttering to herself, but Ivy runs across the yard. John is on top of Bubba, punching him in the face. She tugs at his shoulder. "John. Johnny, please. Please stop."

He pulls away, heaving and gasping. His lip is bleeding, and there are scratches on his neck. He grabs Ivy's shoulders. "Come with me. Come home with me now. I don't care what my parents say. We'll tell them our plans and they'll let you stay at our house, and—"

A sharp click makes them both freeze. Bubba is pointing a shotgun at John's face. His left eye is already swollen shut, and there's blood on his teeth when he smiles.

"If this son of a bitch ain't off my land by the time I count to ten, Ivy, I'm blowing his pretty blond head off."

Alma starts praying. Her Our Father grates on Tipsy's nerves like a child's whining.

"Go," Ivy says to John. "I'll manage him. I've been doing it for years."

"If he hits you, I swear to God—"

"...four... five... six..."

"Go now, Johnny! This will only make things worse."

His eyes are desperate. "All right. But I'll be back for you tomorrow. Or the next day. I swear it. I'm getting you away from him." He kisses her.

"I love you," she says.

John backs up with his hands up. "Big man with the gun, aren't you?"

"If I see you around here again, Huger, I'll kill you. And I won't need no gun." Bubba grins. "I got ways of killing you, like them gators, where no one will ever know. So you best stay... the hell... away."

John grabs his boots from the bottom of the porch and backs up. His eyes bore into Ivy's until he disappears around the corner.

Bubba lowers his gun. "What did I tell you, Ivy? He's a coward. He don't want you. Or if he does, it's for one thing."

"We're going to be married," she whispers, as Alma hustles over and starts rubbing her arm.

"Haha! You think that man wants to marry your scrawny ass? You're an idiot. Always have been. And you missed bible study. You need to come inside and cook something and repent."

She glares at him from beneath her wild curls, and Tipsy knows she's no damsel in distress. Ivy looks like she might kill Bubba herself. Grab him around the throat, like one of those gators, and strangle the life out of him.

"You got something you want to say, Sister Ivy?"

Alma whispers a soft warning and Ivy shakes her head. "I'll make biscuits and gravy. Will that suit you?"

"Ain't got no chicken?"

"Haven't killed one this week." She drops her voice to a whisper. "You know how to ring a bird's neck yourself, don't you?"

Alma laughs, in that uncomfortable way of people trying to make everyone see the humor in a very unfunny situation. She finally speaks up loud enough for Tipsy to hear her. "Hush now, Ivy girl. Don't sass your daddy."

"Whatever you're mumbling, you're surely lucky I got water in my ears," says Bubba, as he walks up the stairs. "How'd the lord see fit to send me a stupid daughter who whores around with rich men? No better than Mary Magdalene before our Lord forgave her. Surely there's a lesson for me."

"You study on it, Daddy." Ivy whispers through clenched teeth, as if practicing for her Katharine Hepburn impersonation. "Nose deep in your good book. I won't be here to hear your sermon."

Tipsy feels Ivy's pain, and most of all, her faith that John's love will deliver her from this man. She's ready to put aside the warped teachings of her father, once and for all.

Bubba stops on the top step. "I meant it, Ivy. I'll kill that bastard if I see him again. He deserves it, and I ain't afraid to do it."

When he disappears inside the house, Ivy sits on the steps. Alma sits beside her. "Why you prodding your father?" she asks in a soft voice.

"I'm tired of him. His mean words and his heavy hands. Why should I have to put up with it?"

Alma puts a finger under Ivy's chin. "I think Mr. Huger is putting words in your mouth."

"I got my own mind, Mama. John loves that about me."

"Ivy. You need to be careful with your heart. We don't know John's intentions."

"John wants to marry me. He's told me."

"Wanting and doing are two different things. As it is, this carrying on between y'all ain't fitting for a young lady."

Ivy laughs and stands. She sashays before her mother and twirls her curls with one finger. "I got enough eggs on my platter without worrying about being ladylike."

"Mr. Huger will want his wife to be a lady. All those rich people in their big houses with their colored servants." Alma laughs. "How you going to give orders to servants when you've lived like one yourself?"

"John loves me as I am," Ivy says, but Tipsy feels a hint of trepidation about her fairy tale ending. She expressed those same concerns to John herself, and now Alma is making her question John's reassurance.

"If you love that man, you'll stay away from him so Daddy don't put a bullet in him."

"Daddy wouldn't really do that." She pauses, as if waiting for Alma to agree that Bubba was all bark and no bite, but all she gets from her mother is a noncommittal sniff. She changes the subject to something less distressing. "How'd Saul end up so different from him?"

"He's the baby of the family. A last born boy is always a sweet child."

"I'm glad he's moving to Georgetown soon for that mill job. No need for him to stay around here and turn into Daddy." She wipes her eyes. "But I'll miss him."

"You're crying about missing your brother even as you're talking about leaving me."

Ivy sits beside her again. "I'm not leaving you, Mama."

"That's sure what it sounds like to me. None of your big plans involve your old Ma."

"No, silly. Marrying John doesn't mean deserting you." She smiles. "Maybe you can come with me."

Alma vehemently shakes her head. "Oh, no, no. Missus Alma More would get lost in one of those houses."

"But who will I talk to about all our secrets?"

"It's true that you'll be on your own there. I doubt any of those rich Charleston ladies see ghosts."

"Why not? Is it a gift God only gives to the poor?"

Alma shrugs. "The trapped dead have suffered. Why would God give such a gift to those who can't understand their pain? Now you think about that wisdom, child. Mama ain't all crazy."

"You're not crazy," Ivy says, but she doesn't sound convincing to Tipsy.

"Crazy is in god's eye, ain't it?" Her face darkens and she makes a cross in the air. "Today is a good day. But there's always tomorrow."

"If you feel the darkness coming again," Ivy says, trying to contain her alarm, "you got to fight it."

"Can't fight sadness like John Huger punching your daddy in the face. Can't make my thoughts do right when they don't make sense. Lord, lord." She closes her eyes and rocks in place.

"Mama." Ivy snaps her fingers. "Let's go inside now."

Alma's eyes open. "No one is sure of a bright tomorrow when the darkness is lurking. But I'm glad I been here to pass on what my papa told me about all the strange things that exist in the world beyond most people's understanding. He'd be proud of you, powerful as your sight is."

"Is it something to be proud of?"

"Lordy, girl. Sure. Look at me. I only seen one true spirit in my life. My friend Lorraine, haunting her parent's house. You're like Papa. Vision so bright you're practically seeing into heaven. You're rare, like the white dolphin folks see playing in the creek sometimes. You told Mr. Huger about your gift?"

"Not yet. I've never talked to anyone about it but you and Saul."

"Be careful. A man can do terrible things to a woman he thinks is crazy. Don't I know."

"You mean when daddy sent you away to that hospital when you first saw Lorraine's ghost?"

Alma nods. *"My fault, letting my nerves get the best of me, but more so, my fault for letting him know why."*

"I'm used to it. I'll never have a conniption at the sight of a ghost. Don't you worry now."

"Worrying is what mothers do. You best guard your secrets. And your heart."

Ivy wants to tell John about the ghosts, but Alma's advice makes her nervous. Tipsy knows the feeling. She told Will, and look how that turned out.

"Yes, Mama," says Ivy. Part of her is annoyed with her mother for raining on her parade. Alma's doubts and suspicions about John and her unwelcome doses of reality about what it will mean to be his wife. At the same time, she feels guilty and worried about leaving her mother. She resolves to talk to John about it as soon as he returns. She craves his support and his reassurance and his undying positivity.

It was all too much to think about. Tipsy knows that feeling as well. She doesn't blame Ivy for shifting her mind to something simple. Something with definitively measured ingredients and a familiar, predictable outcome.

"I have a hankering for cornbread. Will you measure out the sugar for me?" She tugs her petite mother to her feet. Alma only comes up to Ivy's shoulder, but she rests her head on her daughter's arm and squeezes her waist. Tipsy thinks about everything Ivy is juggling. Her awful father, her fragile mother, and the unexpected whirlwind arrival of John Huger in her life.

Young Ivy cannot fathom the tragedies before her. She does not understand that her trajectory has irrevocably changed. As they disappear into the house, Tipsy's heart breaks for her, and as always, the memory fades.

When Tipsy woke up, she was leaning over with her hands on her knees like a drunk teenager about to hurl up a few spiked seltzers. She slowly straightened and peered around the yard; a myopic owl confused by the daylight. The pastel edges of True Blue blurred like flowing water. A breeze whispered conspiratorially as it drifted over the grass. Even though most of the bottle trees were made of inflexible iron, she swore she heard the tinkle of glass against glass.

After a few blinks, the world settled into place. Ivy was gone, so Tipsy finished her drawings and left them on the kitchen table for Pamella's review. She got into her truck and wiggled her stiff fingers before turning the ignition key. She thought about strangling alligators. Ivy's father Bubba was something else. He flat out threatened to kill John, a solid clue as to what really happened to him. Maybe solving John's mystery would be relatively simple, but it didn't help her with Ivy's conundrum. It wouldn't explain how she ended up trapped in her haunting. While it might not be as important, good old inquisitiveness also demanded an answer as to why Ivy married Camden.

Mayhap they're connected. She's trapped by the shame of betraying John by marrying Camden?

It's possible, Granna, but did she really betray him? A marriage to a man like John or Camden might have been the only way she could escape Bubba. Her options were pretty limited, given her background, the times, and her obligation to protect her mother.

Tipsy turned onto Ben Sawyer Boulevard. She drove up the drawbridge's incline. *Poor Ivy. She's not the friendliest lady, but she clearly had a rough go of it. Not like Jane's turn of the century princess life. That's enough to wear the charm out of anyone.* She stepped on the gas, but the Tahoe didn't accelerate. *What the heck is up with this damn truck?*

She pushed the pedal to the metal. The engine revved, but the truck didn't speed up.

Even on the downhill, it was stuck in low gear.

Sugar, I think you need to pull over. Something ain't right—

The Tahoe lurched and started vibrating.

"Shit!" Tipsy hit the hazard lights. The guy in the Mercedes behind her honked. She was slowing the already poky Saturday progress of traffic off the island.

She wasn't even going fifteen miles per hour. Mercedes man blasted his horn again. She yelled over her shoulder. "Chill out, asshole!"

STEPHANIE ALEXANDER

She crept along, mortified by the curious people watching her from the other lane. The traffic jammed up behind her as if she were leading a late Fourth of July parade. She made it to the parking lot of Mainland Container Company, a popular restaurant built on the grounds of an old putt-putt golf course. She turned off the engine and rested her head against the window.

Car problems? Really?

Call a tow, said Granna. *Nothing else for it.*

She found a tow company on Google, and the guy who answered said he'd be there in forty-five minutes. Foreboding swelled in her chest. She'd been blissfully free of car problems and a car payment for several years. Rent, and now this?

How about you get a drink, since you're here.

Good idea, Granna.

Tipsy walked to the outdoor bar. Tables dotted the patio around a young guy playing Dave Matthews covers on an acoustic guitar. Kids goofed off in the grass behind the bar while their parents sipped beers and ate truffle fries. Tipsy and Will had brought their crew here several times.

She pulled out her phone to distract herself from such thoughts and ordered a Bud Light from the busty blonde woman behind the bar. The bartender handed over Tipsy's beer then poured herself a shot. "Cheers."

As she clinked her can against the woman's tiny glass, Tipsy read the small tattoo on her forearm. *Proverbs 31:7.*

"What's that bible verse mean?" she asked.

"Let him drink, and forget his poverty, and remember his misery no more."

"Amen to that." Tipsy thought about the quote on the cross in Bubba More's yard. "I was a slacker in bible school. Can I run a verse by you?"

"My mama didn't tolerate bible slackers. But if I know it, you have to take a shot."

"Genesis, nine, two."

The bartender smiled. She had crooked front teeth. *"The fear of you and the dread of you shall be on every beast of the earth, on every bird of*

100

the air, on all that move on the earth, and on all the fish of the sea. Into your hand they are delivered."

Tipsy gave the woman a high-five. "Impressive."

Not surprising Mr. Nice Guy Bubba More would choose such an uplifting verse, said Granna.

Maybe he wanted to intimidate his neighbors. And the oysters.

"Make it a gentle one," Tipsy said to the bartender.

The bartender poured her a small shot of reddish brown liquor. "A Fireball shot never hurt anybody."

Tipsy took the shot and sipped at it. The spicy flavor burned her throat. The bartender turned away and Tipsy dumped it in the grass below her. When she turned around again Tipsy presented her with an empty glass. She checked the time. Still half an hour before the tow truck arrived. She opened Instagram and started scrolling.

She immediately recognized it as a bad idea, but like the rubberneckers who had gawked at her car limping down Ben Sawyer Boulevard, she couldn't turn away. She glanced over happy families lounging on beaches and beside pools. She watched a few videos of kids bouncing along behind boats on inner tubes.

How is this my life? she asked Granna. *I'm sitting at a bar in the middle of the afternoon on a Saturday, drinking alone.*

It's the car, Tipsy.

Still, I did not sign up for this. This is not how my life is supposed to be.

She scrolled past a meme about day drinking. She paused on a post from a woman she didn't know very well. Lindsey's aesthetician, Julia Something-or-Other. Lindsey had given Tipsy a facial for her thirty-fifth birthday, and the woman had been super chatty. She asked Tipsy about her kids and her art and everything else under the sun. So much so, Tipsy found the whole experience rather unrelaxing. Still, she knew a lot of people. Tipsy always needed to get the word out about her art, so they'd connected on social media.

Tipsy shaded her phone from the sun's glare and the post came into focus. Her heart about stopped.

A bunch of people on a boat. Julia held up her phone to take a selfie. Behind her Lindsey, P.D., Shelby, and Brian smiled for the camera.

Will leaned into the photo from the edge of the group. He wore dark glasses and a hat, but there was no mistaking that jawline.

Her heart started beating again. Way too fast, as if to make up for precious lost seconds. She tapped the photo and some tagging came up. It looked like P.D.'s boat. Aside from her friends, there were three other women and a guy she didn't know. She read the caption.

Thanks so much to @designchicklindsey and @shelbypattersonart for taking us out on the boat for my birthday! Such a beautiful day on the water with great friends old and new! I love my clients! #boatlife #charleston #lovewhereyoulive #birthdaygirl #thebig27

Tipsy swallowed the rest of her beer. Her heartbeat became an alternating staccato of hurt and anger. Her best friends took a bunch of random people on the boat and invited Will for good measure? She thought to text Shelby and Lindsey, but paused and rested the phone on her paint splattered shorts. She *had* told them she'd be working all day. Her phone dinged. She opened a text from Pamella.

How did it go today? ☺

Tipsy blinked back tears. Great. I left a few sketches.

Awesome! FYI, painters are coming out to give me a quote on scraping off the blue and repainting. Gonna get rid of some of the bottle trees too. So watch out for restless spirits other than Meemaw, hahaha!

I'll keep an eye out. She wasn't sure why she kept going. Probably pure old loneliness. My car broke down and I'm waiting for a tow at Mainland. And I just saw a pic of my ex-boyfriend on a boat with a bunch of women who look to have an average age of twenty-five.

Pamella: Oh no! Honey do you need a ride?

Tipsy: No, thank you. Tow truck is going to drop me at a garage near my house.

Pamella: Ok... but let's meet for a drink tonight! High Thyme at 6. Come on, you need to commiserate!

The tow truck pulled into the gravel driveway. Tipsy closed the apps on her phone. As she flicked Instagram into cyber silence, she got a glance at Will's smiling face.

She returned to Pamella's text. SOUNDS GOOD. ☺ I'LL SEE YOU THEN.

Chapter 7

Tipsy called an Uber at five o'clock, but apparently so did everyone else in Mount Pleasant. She sat on the front porch and watched the tiny car on the Uber app crawl along East Bay Street toward the Ravenel Bridge. She sipped a beer. She'd be sitting here for a while if the closest Uber driver had to make it across the bridge and past the traffic jammed up around Shem Creek.

Henry appeared on the joggling board beside her. "You look pretty this evening," he said. "New gentleman coming to call?"

"Thanks. And no. Just a girls' night with my new boss, since Shelby and Lindsey are busy entertaining my ex-boyfriend. I hope P.D.'s boat sinks." She smiled. "Wait—you might be able to help me."

"Tipsy, you know I'm at your disposal, but I wasn't a murderer in life, as we've proved, and I don't want to start in death."

"What? No! Good lord, Henry. I'm not asking you to sink anyone's ship, literally or figuratively. I mean with my ghost conundrum."

She explained the visions she'd seen in John's memory, and Ivy's.

"That all certainly does sound complicated. It's still odd to me that John is a trapped spirit. I never would have thought him complex enough to linger. One has to have the capacity to dwell on life, don't you think?"

"Jeez, Henry. That's kind of an asshole thing to say."

"John wasn't one to perseverate on life."

"Maybe there was more to him than you think. From what I've seen, he was having his own existential crisis, even if he wasn't using stories or paintings to figure it all out."

"Meh. Hmph."

"Even if you can't stand him, you know him better than I do. Any ideas about how to make him cooperate?"

"This ghost sounds nothing like the living man I knew. John was pushy and arrogant, but always pleasantly so. I can't imagine him as belligerent or suspicious. He just happily mowed down anyone or anything in his way."

"What about his cousin, Camden? Did you know him?"

"I knew him well enough when we were children. He used to tease me even though I was much bigger than him."

"That was ballsy. Was he following John's lead?"

"John didn't have to tease anyone. Zeus didn't pay much mind to the mortals."

"So what was Camden's problem?"

"Camden was a more average child. Averagely handsome, averagely charming, fair at sports. And he was trying to keep up with John and his friends. The perfect recipe for a nasty child, but he wasn't the only one who treated me unkindly. Looking back, I can hardly blame them. I didn't do much to endear myself to anyone. Still, of the many who pestered little Henry, only Camden owned up to it."

"What do you mean?"

Henry raised his hand. "Would you like to see?"

Tipsy looked at her phone. She still had over twenty minutes before the Uber showed up. She'd been managing her supernatural time travels pretty well, and her sleuthing had to take precedence over socializing.

She nodded. Her hand met Henry's as if they were playing a children's clapping game. Tipsy closed her eyes and whispered to herself. "Miss Susie had a steamboat… the steamboat had a bell… Miss Susie went to heaven… the steamboat went to hell…."

Tipsy stands on Church Street, outside St. Philip's Church. She's stood here once before, when she saw into Jane's memory of a cold winter day. Judging from the attire of the people streaming out of the church, it's a different season and an earlier time. There are no coats and woolen caps, only springtime dresses. It must be before the flapper era, because the women's dresses have cinched waists and longer hems. Tipsy can just see their ankles. Their hair is longer too, mostly wrapped in chignons at the base of their skulls. Their warm weather bonnets have flat brims in a variety of widths. The men all wear dark suits and bowler hats with a few straw boater hats mixed in.

Henry clips down the stairs with a brown bowler in his hands. He looks to be about twenty. He's dashingly exotic—tall and slender with bright red, perfectly combed hair that's in stark contrast to the messy curls Tipsy knows. He's looking over the crowd for someone. No one speaks to him, but most people look up as he passes.

A younger man pushes through the throng. He stands behind Henry, shifting on his feet, as if afraid to speak to him. He taps Henry's shoulder. Henry turns around, but he's clearly expecting someone else. He looks at the young man with no recognition and poorly disguised annoyance.

"Henry?" the young man asks. He's maybe seventeen, still gangly but with the potential for handsomeness in his straight nose and blue eyes.

"Yes?" Henry is already looking past the boy.

"I heard you returned from France, and I—"

"I'm sorry, but who are you?"

"I'm Camden Brewton. You might not remember me, but—"

Henry's nostrils flare. "Yes. I remember you. It's hard to forget those who harass you."

"That's what I wanted to talk to you about—"

Henry towers over him by about half a foot. "I don't think you want to revisit those times, son. Boarding school is a jungle populated with vicious heathens. The pubs of London are not for the faint of heart, either. I wouldn't feel bad punching you in the mouth. You're old enough now."

"No. Of course not. I have no intention of—"

"Of calling me a ginger freak? Shooting spitballs at me? Sneaking under my desk and tying my shoelaces together?"

"Henry——"

"I don't know why I didn't pummel you then. Probably because I didn't want to incur your cousin's wrath. It must be nice to have someone to hide behind your whole life." He starts to turn away.

"I'm sorry." Camden stuffs his hands in his pockets. "I'm sorry I was so cruel to you. I don't know what was the matter with me."

"You're... apologizing?"

Camden nods. "I keep thinking about how awfully I treated you. We all did. Except Janie of course."

"John left me alone."

"But he didn't stop the rest of us. If I had a son, and he treated another child that way, I'd take my hand to his backside."

Henry is shocked into silence.

"That's all I wanted to say. I'm sorry I bothered you. Welcome home, anyway." Camden's cheeks are the color of Henry's hair.

"No. Wait. I'm merely... ah, surprised."

They stand there for a few uneasy seconds, before Camden sticks out his hand. Henry slowly offers his own. "Thank you. For your welcome. I appreciate it."

"You're welcome. I'll see you around." Camden backs away. He bumps into a pretty, petite, dark-haired woman. Tipsy feels the urge to cry as she recognizes Jane. Her flashing blue eyes and her wide smile, complete with deep dimples in both cheeks.

"Excuse me, Janie," says Camden.

"Of course, Cam. Tell your mother hello for me."

Camden nods and disappears into the crowd. Jane smiles up at Henry. "Henry, darling. Will y'all come to our house for lunch? Mama said I could invite... what's wrong? Oh, dearest. You're not smiling."

He grabs both her hands and kisses them. A few of the surrounding ladies twitter their disapproval, and two little girls start giggling. Henry *drags Jane across the street. They stand beside the cemetery gate. Henry kisses Jane's hand again.*

"Are you crying?" She wipes at his eyes.

He shakes his head and sniffs. "It's the sunlight."

"Henry. Remember what we promised one another."

"Always tell the truth. But this truth makes me feel ridiculous."

"What is it?"

"Camden Brewton apologized for being cruel to me when we were children."

"Goodness. That's rather surprising. But very nice, isn't it?"

Henry bites his lip and nods. Jane presses against him.

"Be careful," he whispers. "Your parents won't want us making a spectacle."

"I don't care. I want the whole world to know how much I love you."

He cups her cheek in his hand. "I swear to god, Jane Robinette. You are an angel out of heaven and I don't deserve you."

You got that right, *thinks Tipsy.*

"Now tell me why you're upset." She wants to know. Even though it's Henry's memory, so his emotions dominate it, Tipsy can tell. It's written all over her eager face. She's not merely asking to sooth him. She wants to know everything about this enigmatic man in front of her.

"I suppose—I just... damnit. Why is it so much easier to write than to speak?" He takes a deep breath. Tipsy feels his sorrow. Years of wanting to fit in and failing and retreating into his imagination. Feeling sure he was crazy, and forcing himself to ignore the dead people no one else saw. Telling stories in his mind to make it all make sense, because at least he could control the plotlines and the dialogue, whereas real life was terrifyingly unpredictable. The ghosts of his childhood are swirling around him. "All those years of the children being cruel to me. I told myself I didn't care back then, and thirty minutes ago, I would have said I didn't care now. But Camden reminded me of the truth."

Jane squeezes his hand. "You cared very much."

"Maybe part of me feels like I'm still that odd little boy no one liked and everyone teased. Except you. You never teased me, Jane. You were the only one who ever stood up for me."

"I don't hold with meanness. It's not Christian."

Henry pulls her into his arms. "You've always been brave. Much braver than me."

"You're the one who traveled around Europe on his own with a war on."

"That's a simple thing, compared to standing up for the person everyone else disdains. Thank you, my love. For everything. For being here right now."

"I'll always be with you, Henry. Always."

———◆✖◆———

Tipsy opened her eyes. She was looking up at Ms. Callie's haint blue porch ceiling. The whirling of the ancient ceiling fan made her eyes cross. When she lowered her chin, she got the spins. She smacked her dry tongue around in her mouth.

"You're crying," said Henry. "A symptom of your visions?"

"Not usually." She thought of Jane's pretty smile as she ran her hands over her wet cheeks. "I guess I miss Jane."

"Ah. Those sentiments I understand. Did you see Camden apologizing as well?"

Tipsy nodded. "I saw exactly what you wanted me to see. I wish it was always that easy."

"I knew what I wanted to show you. That differs from trying to piece together memories to reveal something unrecalled."

"Camden seemed like a decent guy. It took gumption to come up to you in public and say that. You were sort of intimidating."

"Was I?"

"You know exactly how you were. Everyone was watching you. You loved it."

Henry chuckled and laced his hands behind his head. "You know me too well. Although, at the time I didn't realize I wanted to look intimidating."

"You and Jane," she said. She didn't need to elaborate.

"Yes. We were something, weren't we? You didn't need to see the last bit, but I wanted to show you how we were before I ruined everything."

"She told me how much y'all loved each other. Nice to see it from your perspective." She returned to the conundrum at hand. "Did you and Camden become friends?"

"I didn't have friends. But we were cordial. I didn't detest him, as I did John."

"I know you hated John, but you still need to help me free him. If I can't get this job done for Pamella, I'm definitely going to have to move."

Henry frowned. "I certainly don't want that. Besides, the young, foolish, living me detested John. I have no reason to hate him now. He's simply another sad man, like myself, trapped by his past pain."

"I think he felt genuine pain over Ivy. He seemed so passionate and dedicated in his memories. And he was crushed when he found out she married Camden."

"If there's one thing I cannot doubt, it's how much Camden and John loved each other. Even after Jane and I were married, Camden was attached to John like wool on a sheep. I can't imagine two brothers more loyal to each other. My brother Edward and I would sooner watch each other drown than throw out a line."

"I had a thought. It's not the nicest thing to think of Ivy, but maybe she used Camden to escape her father. She thought she had a way out by marrying John, then he died. Maybe if Ivy couldn't have John, she, like, seduced Camden."

"It's possible. Wouldn't be the first time in history a woman used the gifts god gave her to elevate herself through marriage."

"Just ask Anne Boleyn."

"Oh, I have. I spoke to her ghost in London."

Tipsy's eyes widened. "What the hell—"

"A tale for another time. As to Ivy's predicament, I remember Bubba More. Mean as a lightning strike, but not nearly as pretty. It must have been terrible being under his thumb night and day."

"He could have killed John by the barracks and then dumped his body in the ocean. That would explain the body in one place and the ghost in the other." Her phone dinged as her Uber pulled up in front of the house. "Have a good night. I might be late. I'll stop by and see Ivy after my drinks. And maybe John."

She descended the stairs and then turned around. She walked backward so the Uber driver couldn't see her talking to thin air. "Wait—Henry. Come with me to see John. Maybe he'll listen to you."

"Why would he do that?"

"I don't know. At least you'd be a known entity."

Henry shifted uncomfortably, like she'd asked him to kiss a fat auntie with bad breath. "If you think it would help."

"You haven't seen anyone from your life other than Jane in almost a hundred years! It might be fun." Fun was a stretch, given the men had disliked one another their entire lives, but desperate times called for desperate alliances.

The Uber driver yelled out the window. "Ma'am! You coming?"

Tipsy blew air kisses at Henry before he argued with her. "Kay thanks. Gotta-go-love-ya-bye!"

A bright red blush colored Henry's pallor like messy lipstick.

"Oh lord, Henry. It's not a marriage proclamation!"

"I *am* already married, Tipsy."

"These days, men and women can tell each other they love each other. As friends."

He smiled. "Oh, good. That's actually very nice. I love you as a friend, too. You're the only one I've ever had."

She laughed as she walked down the garden path. She really did love Henry, undead wacko or not.

Chapter 8

Tipsy sat across from Pamella at the crowded L-shaped bar at High Thyme Cuisine, a cozy restaurant that was part fine dining, part local hangout. The bartender cruised past them and topped off Pamella's sav blanc without even asking. Friends and acquaintances waved and reached around one another to shake hands and give air kisses in a friendly game of salutation Twister.

Pamella wore a long, white, shapeless dress, as if decked out in a disposable Target bag. Her gold strappy shoes had a four inch stiletto heel and rainbow pompoms dangled over her electric blue toenails. Her earrings were tufts of pink lace. Tipsy would have laughed her ass off if a salesperson suggested this ensemble to her, but Tipsy was not Pamella Brewton.

One of Pamella's long legs poked from a high slit in the sack dress when she stood to greet someone. She towered over the rest of the diners at approximately six foot three. She didn't look like a high-end bag lady. She looked like a retired supermodel. The people around them turned and ogled. A few whispered as if they were trying to place someone famous.

Tipsy looked down at her white shorts and navy blue tank top and her nude wedges. She wore the simple gold hoops Ayers gave her for Valentine's Day about ten years ago. When she put her outfit together, she'd been inspired by a classic nautical feel. She bit her lip to keep from laughing as the pompoms on Pamella's shoes bounced in time to her toe-tapping.

I'm so basic!

Granna sniffed. *Kind of tacky to call attention to yourself through gaudy clothes.*

Okay, Mother Teresa, Tipsy fondly replied. *If I could pull off a getup like that, I would.*

Either Pamella didn't notice or she was too used to it to care. She sat down again and crossed her legs. The bag dress fell in elegant layers on either side of her, like she'd sliced a slit into Cinderella's petticoats. "Now tell me aaaaall about your *bad day,* lady."

Tipsy ordered a Bud Light when the bartender cruised past them. She gave Pamella a truncated version of her no good, very bad few days. Pamella listened politely and offered some unrealistic advice.

On rent: "What about those condos at the foot of the Ravenel? They have great water views!"

On cars: "Your car is *eight* years old? Oh, lady. It's on its last legs and one of them is a wooden peg. You need a new car."

On men: "I don't see how a girl like you could even *consider* dating someone under six feet tall."

Tipsy eventually turned the conversation to the update Pamella wanted.

"So," she said. "Let's talk Meemaw."

Pamella clapped. Tipsy's car, rent, and man problems were forgotten. Tipsy gave Pamella the basics about John and Ivy.

"Goodness gracious! How romantic." Pamella put her hand to her forehead in a mock swoon. "My sweet Meemaw who grew up in a shack and a dashing, rich man from downtown Charleston. Torn apart forever, yet right down the road from one another. And then she married Grandpa Cam, his cousin? Lord-a-mercy. The tragedy of it all is almost too much!" She paused. "You said Huger, right? Grandpa Cam inherited money from his uncle, remember? He was a Huger."

"Yeah. I thought of that. Sounds like Camden got John's inheritance."

"But he also inherited True Blue. It came to Grandpa Cam through his mother's side of the family—"

"Right! Their mothers were sisters. John's family had a cottage. So *True Blue* was John's family house! Wow!" Tipsy thought of the photo Pamella had shown her of the cottage, from 1928. *C and J.* She'd probably unknowingly seen a photo of John and Camden on the porch smoking cigars a few years before John died. No wonder she hadn't been able to come up with the property last summer by searching the records for *Huger*. If it came through John's mother's family line to Camden Brewton, there would be no record of any Hugers owning it.

"So this guy John Huger would be like, my cousin a bunch of times removed or something—oh, speaking of family trees, I started a family tree on Ancestry.com. It might connect me with relatives. Maybe someone knows something about Meemaw that we don't."

"Oh, wow. You want to go there?"

"You got me thinking about Meemaw's family. It might be a bust, but if it is, no harm done. I'm still alone in the world, except for my daughters."

"It can't hurt. I wish Ivy would cooperate. I've always avoided ghosts because most of them won't leave me alone once they recognize my talent. They want to tell me their sad stories. Not so your Meemaw."

"It doesn't surprise me. Daddy described her as a sad, reclusive lady."

"She had a sad backstory, but once she got married, she surely didn't have any money problems."

"You can still be miserable with lots of money. Some of the *gloomiest* people I know are rich."

"If I'm going to be miserable, better to be rich and miserable than broke and miserable."

"Careful what you wish for, lady." Pamella sipped her wine. "She was especially melancholy at the house downtown. The historical name is the Joseph George Huger House. It's on Meeting Street near South Battery. Camden inherited the Huger House from his uncle, too, you know."

Another of the photos explained. Ivy, Bobby, and Camden were standing on the porch of the house where John grew up. Tipsy wasn't sure if that was creepy or poignant. Probably both.

"According to Daddy, Meemaw didn't like being downtown. She never fit in with the other women, who were *ladies* in the way old

Charleston defined them. Even on her better days, Daddy said she drank too much. The last few years of her life, she was on the sauce more often than she was off it. Drunk as a coot when she fell off the dock."

"How sad for your father."

"I get the impression Grandpa Cam tried to be there for Daddy, but he was lonely after his mother died. He always had a rather solitary nature. Few friends. No family on the Brewton side. Ivy's family had all moved away from Charleston."

"In Ivy's memory, she talked about her younger brother Saul moving to Georgetown. But Bubba and Alma moved up there too?"

"Maybe. Daddy only met Ivy's family a few times before she died. Bubba disowned her when she married Camden Brewton. Remember, Grandpa Cam and Alma got in a big tiff at Ivy's funeral. That was the last he saw of any of the Mores."

"He never tried to reach out to them when he was grown himself?"

"Not that I know of. Ivy's family kind of embarrassed Daddy. It's not like he was going to invite them to Easter brunch at the Yacht Club."

"Pammy?" A tanned hand with pale pink fingernails closed on Pamella's shoulder. A Charleston Dress Code Blonde who appeared to be somewhere between Pamella and Tipsy in age stood behind her in a pair of skin tight white jeans. Her bright yellow tube top looked ready to explode from the pressure of her breasts behind it.

"Kim!" Pamella stood to hug her. Kim was short, so she ended up placing her head on Pamella's chest like a child hugging her mother.

"Tipsy, this is my friend Kim Nowak. This is Tipsy Collins. The artist working on the painting of my house!"

Kim smiled. "Oooooh. I can't wait to see the finished product!"

"Kimmy's a real estate agent. Best in town."

"Oh, pooh, you're so sweet."

"Did you come for drinks?"

"We're waiting on a table. It's Lucy Murphy's birthday—"

"How is she?"

"She's good." Kim dropped her voice to a whisper. "Don't say anything, but she's about to send her teenage son to boarding school. He drove the golf cart into the East Lake in I'On when he was drunk."

"Yikes," said Tipsy. I'On was a upscale neighborhood off Mathis Ferry Road. It was a retro downtown Charleston, complete with mansions, narrow roads, and terrible parking. Probably the second swankiest neighborhood in Mount Pleasant after the Old Village, and one of the gossipiest.

"The kid had to climb on top of the cart and sleep there to avoid a circling gator. All the neighbors saw him out there the next morning."

"Poor thing," said Pamella, but Tipsy wasn't sure if she meant the kid or his mom.

"Anyway, some of us are meeting for dinner—" She waved. "Clarice! Over here!"

Tipsy's head swung toward the door. Clarice Andrews stood beside the hostess table, looking as sexily disheveled as ever. He waved and walked toward them.

Kim elbowed Pamella. "You remember I told you about my friend Clarice."

"Yes. Still can't believe your friend named *Clarice* is a man."

Clarice joined them beside the bar. Kim introduced Pamella, but before she did the same for Tipsy, he said, "Tipsy, right? Small world."

Tipsy smiled. "In Charleston, it's always a small world."

"Y'all know each other?" asked Kim. Her own smile stiffened. Tipsy immediately sensed Kim sizing up the competition, whether Tipsy thought of herself as competition or not.

"We met last night," he said. "Mutual friends."

Kim's phone dinged. "Our table is ready on the patio. Lucy and them are parking. So good to see you, Pammy. Let's get together this week and catch up." She tapped Tipsy's shoulder. "And nice to meet you!"

"Y'all want to join us for dinner?" asked Clarice. "We can squeeze in two more."

Pamella looked at Tipsy. "Ummm…"

Tipsy thought of her plan to talk to Ivy and John and shook her head. A food coma would surely follow if she ordered High Thyme's deliciously decadent lasagna. "I wish I could, but I have to get up early tomorrow to deal with my car. But you go ahead, Pamella."

"You sure?" asked Pamella.

"Yes! Go have fun."

Pamella handed her card to the bartender. "I'll get the check."

"You don't have to—"

"Come on," said Clarice. "I'll buy you another drink."

His statement annoyed Tipsy. Everyone in Charleston thought she couldn't pay for her drinks. Did she look that desperate?

"I can't, but thanks so much for asking."

Kim tugged at Clarice's arm. "We'll meet you at the table, Pammy. So nice to meet you again, Tipsy!" She dragged him through the crowd.

The bartender returned Pamella's card and she tucked it into her tiny sequined bag. "A man named Clarice. Still, there's something about him, don't you think?"

"I think he's arrogant," said Tipsy, for no particular reason. "He's used to getting what he wants."

"He's surely getting it from Kim. Love her though, bless her heart."

How southern, said Granna. *She's fabulous, but she's sort of a tramp.*

Tipsy felt wary compassion for Kim as she remembered Lindsey's comments about Clarice and his fan club. It wasn't a stretch to surmise that Kim had fallen prey to Charleston's greatest urban legend, the mythical Lack of Men. The resulting female panic often made women turn on their fellow ladies to stake tenuous, vindictive claims to the available bachelors.

I wish we could see each other as allies, not rivals, Granna.

"I'll go by True Blue when I leave," said Tipsy. "See if Meemaw is in a chatty mood for once."

"Sure, lady. Too bad we can't give her a glass of wine to lighten her up."

"Probably not a great idea, since apparently that contributed to her death."

117

Pamella laughed and sipped her own wine as if she saw no comparison between her own drinking and her grandmother's death.

The crowd parted before Pamella as she made her way to the door. Tipsy followed her like a lady-in-waiting behind the queen. They stepped onto the patio. Pamella eased past the other tables with her wine glass held high. The birthday gathering congregated at a round table in the corner. Four women and three men were already seated. A mylar balloon in the shape of a champagne bottle floated over their heads.

The celebrants were chatting amongst themselves and saying hello to Pamella, but Clarice Andrews wasn't talking. He was watching Tipsy. He raised his hand and then ran it through his hair. She guessed he was trying to cover up his wave.

She gave him a closed mouth, quasi-smile and walked down the stairs. She slipped off her wedges and donned the pair of flip-flops she'd put in her purse. As all professional clairvoyants know, wedges are not appropriate ghost hunting footwear.

It was still light when Tipsy arrived at True Blue. She sat on the picnic table bench, but Ivy didn't appear. She checked the shed, thinking Ivy might be hiding inside. Nope. Nothing in there but a mishmash of home improvement implements. She returned to the yard and stood with her hands on her hips. Ivy probably saw her.

She thought about trying to force Ivy to come out, but the last time she'd intervened, Ivy shot her across the yard like a Styrofoam bullet from one of Little A's Nerf guns.

She cleared her throat. "Ivy? I know you can hear me. Can you come out?"

Nothing.

"Look, I told you I can't *make* you move on. Seeing into your memory isn't like pushing you off a cliff into the afterlife." She wandered over to the picnic table again and sat on the tabletop. "I can prove it, because I *already* saw one of your memories. And you're still here. I know you are."

Ivy materialized in front of her. "You looked into my past?"

"Your skirt brushed against me when you sent the umbrella flying. John said some more sweet things about you. You want to hear about it?"

Ivy tugged at her skirt, as if she might disrobe herself of her own curiosity, but she couldn't resist a bedtime story about her own life. "Tell me about me and Johnny."

Whew, thought Tipsy. So far, needling Ivy into cooperating took longer than dragging her into the open, but it was certainly safer. *No need for another supernatural standoff.*

Granna, ever the harbinger of realistic observations, spoke up. *Not yet, anyway.*

So Tipsy described the memory she'd seen. Ivy had a distracting way of silently mouthing Tipsy's words as she spoke. Tipsy turned toward the marsh. A dolphin family was taking an evening swim through the slick waters of Cove Creek. It was hard to observe so much beauty and tell such a sad tale. Enough to make the most stoic supernatural voyeur tear up.

"The memory ended when you and your mother walked inside." Tipsy turned back toward the house. To her surprise Ivy sat right beside her on the table and sniffled along with her.

"Wish I could give you a tissue," said Tipsy.

Ivy looked at her blankly.

"Like… a handkerchief."

"A Kleenex?"

"Ah, yes. You're a little more up to date than Jane and Henry."

"Jane and Henry?" Ivy's eyes widened. "Not Jane and Henry *Mott*?"

"Yeah. Since you won't talk to me, I haven't had a chance to tell you we have friends in common. Everyone in Charleston knows someone who knows someone. Even across a century."

Ivy's lips twitched. "Jane was such a lovely lady, and Henry… once I got him laughing, he wasn't too bad." Her burgeoning smile melted before it solidified. The frown returned. "Didn't Henry kill Jane and then kill himself? That's what John believed."

"No. Henry never could have killed her. He loved her too much in his weird way. Everyone loved her. I... I really miss her." Tipsy sucked in a building sob. "I'm sorry. It's not like me to be so blubbery."

"It's kind of you to help the dead."

"I had to help Henry and Jane because living with them made me sick. But the more I got to know them... helping them was probably one of the best things I've done in my life."

Ivy watched a heron creep along the waterline in a guerilla warfare battle against the minnows. Her jaw relaxed. "I never saw John again after that day. He disappeared two days later."

"Oh, lord. I'm sorry."

"After they found his body, I couldn't get out of bed for a week. I stayed under the covers even when my father threatened to kill me if I didn't get up. It's the one time my mother talked back to him. She said she'd poison him if he didn't let me be. Mama might not have been very good at seeing ghosts but she had plenty of other country skills. She mixed up all manner of old medicines and concoctions. It was enough to make Daddy leave me alone for a while."

"But how did you end up married to Camden? I don't get it."

"John's death was terrible for him, too. We shared each other's pain, and my father was so angry with me for how I'd carried on with John. Camden knew John had wanted to keep me safe, so he offered marriage. I accepted."

"His family allowed it? John's father was so opposed."

"Camden's father was dead. His mother was a sickly, mousy woman. After John died, no one cared who Camden married, as long as he stayed close by. R.J. and Colleen Huger clung to Camden. They'd lost John. All they had left was a nephew who resembled him. A family with a giant hole no one could fill. All three of them—John's parents, Camden's mother—died before Bobby turned five."

"So Camden inherited everything. Did you ever love him?"

She shook her head. "I suppose I tried, but…not truly. The first few years were tolerable. We both loved our son Bobby. He came along within a year of us getting married and everyone doted on him. Uncle R.J., Aunt Colleen, Cam's mother Millie. But we didn't have any more children, even though we both wanted them. I think Camden blamed me."

"That's not fair."

"It's always the womb's fault, isn't it?"

"Another one for Anne Boleyn. So y'all drifted apart?"

"Drifted isn't the right word. More like a flood tide. Whatever kinship we shared over John's loss faded with the doldrums of everyday life. Sometimes he tried to be tender to me, but I missed John too much to return it. I felt as if I lived with an actor playing a poor impression of him. Camden finally realized he was truly stuck with me."

"Right. Divorce was illegal in South Carolina back then."

"We barely spoke. I'm sure he saw other women but I didn't care."

"Sounds awful."

"It wasn't awful for Bobby. His father adored him. He went to private school. He went to The Citadel after I died." Ivy's eyes sparkled with pride. "He looked so handsome when he turned up at the cottage in his uniform. He inherited all this land out here and the cottage, and the house downtown, and of course the money. I was a good mother, too, at least until the end." That happy twinkle dimmed. "I drank too much. Bobby knew it. Of course, I left him too soon."

The heron took off. Ivy's jaw clenched again as it disappeared into the tall grass on the other side of the creek. "I've never really spoken to anyone about all this."

"From what Pammy told me, it didn't sound like you had a lot of confidants among the South of Broad set."

"I did not. I tried for years, for Bobby. I tried to speak properly and be gracious to everyone. I tried to make them forget where I came from. But they have long memories in Charleston. I simply wasn't what Camden and his people expected me to be."

"John wanted that for you too, right? A Charleston society housewife, entertaining on the piazza. Hope you don't mind me saying so, but I got the impression you shared some of your mother's misgivings about all that."

"It's true. I was intimidated, and Mama's doubts didn't help. But John made me feel like anything was possible. I never knew anyone who looked life in the eye like Johnny Huger. He dared the world to try and throw him off his tracks. Never met anyone like him since. With John, maybe I could have made a home. His family might have loved me. I might have made friends."

"Because everyone loved him so much?"

She nodded. "But mostly because of how we loved *each other*. He would have been patient with me. Explained things to me and stood beside me. Camden expected me to know what to do and say. He was always dragging me into those old houses for one party or another. I hated it. So many lingering, tormented spirits."

"I bet. I grew up in the country. Not as many people means fewer ghosts."

"I tried, but it wore me out, pretending I didn't see them. Especially the colored people." She drew in a sharp breath, although she didn't need air. "Once at a Christmas dinner on Legare Street I saw a lovely colored woman, with a kerchief and a homespun dress. She followed me and begged me to help her find her son. *Mississippi! Mississippi! Sold south to Mississippi!* And me trying to ignore her and talk about cake recipes with women who hated me. I learned to stare straight ahead like a horse with blinders. It's been easier since I died. No spirits haunt me, except myself."

"I take it you never told Camden about your talent."

"No. I'm sure I would have told John, eventually, but I never told Camden. It was just me and the ghosts. I missed being able to talk to Mama about it all."

"This probably sounds weird, but I can hear my Granna in my mind. It's a comfort to me."

"Not much sounds weird to me. But I've never heard my mother speaking in my head. Like I said, she was a poor seer."

"But you said she saw John, right?"

"Yes, when she and Saul were visiting from Georgetown. John, dead as a stump but walking around as if taking a Sunday stroll. The only other ghost she ever saw so plain was her friend Lorraine."

"What happened when she saw Lorraine? In your memory, you said your father sent her away."

"Saul was only about a year old. I was ten. We heard a rumor Lorraine was pregnant with a bastard child. She hung herself in her parent's barn. Mama walked past the house, and there's Lorraine's ghost. Just sitting on the porch. She couldn't tolerate seeing her dear friend like that. She had a fit of hysterics. Daddy sent her to the state asylum, but it was too much for him working and taking care of us. So he brought Mama back about two months later. She wasn't ever the same though. She spent most of her time collecting plants and berries around the marsh. She didn't see other people except to go to church. I became the woman of the house. She was my helper with the cooking and washing and mending. She didn't teach me anything other than lessons about otherworldly things. Thank goodness she did though, because the lord knows I would have been right confused without her."

"I kind of wondered why she got so worked up over seeing Lorraine," said Tipsy, "but I've never seen someone I knew in life after they turned into a ghost. That would be pretty freaky. Maybe she saw John and Lorraine so clearly because she knew them both."

"She always *wanted* to see spirits clearly, but I suppose Lorraine being her first when she was already a grown woman, with a grown woman's view of the world, was too much for her."

"Did she have another fit of hysterics when she saw John?"

"At first she was excited she'd seen him—like we were two girls sharing a secret. As if she was proud of herself for rummaging up the power to finally see another ghost. But then she clammed up. Wouldn't tell me where he was. She feared I'd refuse to leave him or even kill myself."

"Could you have killed yourself?"

Ivy took a thoughtful moment. "It seems like jumping off a dock at low tide wouldn't be a very certain way to kill myself. Break a leg, yes. But I would have had to hit my head just so—"

"You're right. A long shot."

"This is so strange. I haven't spoken so plainly since John died."

"I hope it feels good, but I can *truly* help you if I see into your memory."

"I hear you. I do." Ivy's voice sounded less like the transatlantic accent of an old movie star and more like the drawl Tipsy had seen in her memory. "But I need you to help Johnny first."

"You don't trust me to help him once I find out what happened to you?"

Too late. Ivy disappeared.

Tipsy sighed. At least they'd had a decent conversation. She rubbed her eyes. *Maybe I should visit John.*

Her phone dinged. It was Big Ayers. She couldn't ignore him. It might be about the kids.

She immediately surmised that Ayers had not written the message by himself. His new lady had at least proofread it for him.

AYERS: KATE AND I ARE MOVING FORWARD WITH OUR LIVES TOGETHER. SHE'S A WONDERFUL PERSON AND A GREAT MOM. SHE LOVES OUR KIDS AND WILL BE GOOD TO THEM. WE'LL BE GETTING MARRIED, BUT WE AREN'T IN A RUSH. WE WANT TO DO WHAT'S BEST FOR OUR FAMILY. IN THE FUTURE, I'LL BE CONSIDERING HER AND CONSULTING HER WHEN I MAKE DECISIONS. I HEARD YOU AND THAT WILL GUY BROKE UP. SORRY FOR YOU ABOUT THAT, BUT I ALWAYS THOUGHT HE WAS SKETCHY. I HOPE YOU CAN BE HAPPY FOR ME, LIKE I'D BE HAPPY FOR YOU IF YOU FIND THE RIGHT PERSON. THANKS. I'LL DROP THE KIDS OFF USUAL TIME TOMORROW.

Tipsy reread the message three or four times, but she still couldn't process it. *Moving on with our lives... I'll be consulting her...* and last but certainly not least... *I always thought he was sketchy.*

Suddenly, she could not handle the thought of visiting John Huger and getting screamed at some more. A decent conversation with Ivy would have to be her accomplishment of the day. She put her phone in her purse and called an Uber.

Tipsy was not prone to anger. It wasn't an emotion that came naturally to her, like for example, compassion, curiosity, or her old friend, excessive rumination. She snapped at her kids when they were driving her nuts like any human being with the good fortune to parent small children, but when it came to legitimate reasons to be infuriated—like her parents abandoning her, or her ex-husband thumbing his nose at the family court system—she inevitably talked herself out of being angry. She focused on the other person's feelings and needs, or told herself whatever pissed her off wasn't that bad in the grand scheme of umbrages, affronts, or transgressions. She'd gotten more comfortable with rage since she separated from Ayers. Proximity from his constant irritability had allowed her to breathe into her own petty annoyances.

By the time she got home after her chat with Ivy, a rare, full blown fury consumed her. She stalked into Miss Callie's house. When she reached her bedroom, she immediately tossed her boring nautical-themed outfit in the hamper. She donned her frumpy old nightgown, washed her face, and laid on her bed. She was too worked up to sleep, so she jumped up, stomped down the stairs, and turned on the TV in the family room. None of the endless stream of entertainment options appealed to her.

She was too mad at life. Here she was, sitting in Miss Callie's place. The house she'd fantasized about making her own. What a ridiculous waste of a fantasy. The car problems, the rent, Will breaking up with her, Ayers back with the same bullshit on a different day. She'd been doing okay. She'd been feeling okay. Now, just when she was getting ahead, she was back to square one on basically everything.

When she chose to end her marriage, she knew it wouldn't be easy to start over. But Ayers had moved out almost two years ago. Why was she still in this limbo? She'd been working her ass off, putting her kids first, being a reasonable co-parent even when she wanted to kill Ayers. She'd produced paintings, sold them, and made decent money. She could finally afford health insurance a few months ago. Now she was looking at buying a new car and paying Mount Pleasant rent. Even if she moved out of Miss Callie's and into an apartment, and even with Pamella's fifty-k, she'd be back to scraping by. Somehow, she had to quickly finish Pamella's painting, find new commissions, and paint more pieces for the GQB.

All while freeing a couple of star-crossed lovers from their hauntings. Let's not forget that little conundrum. If she didn't solve The Twin Mysteries of the Man Who Drowned (But Maybe Not) and the Woman Who Pitched Off the Dock (Or Did She Though?), she was more than screwed.

Money thoughts overwhelmed her, so she turned to her equally overwhelming personal life. She'd been a good girlfriend to Will. She'd gone out of her way to make sure she wasn't one of those needy, clingy women everyone insisted she must not be. But must she have no needs at all? The more patient and understanding she was, the less he gave. An inch and a mile, all that. Everything revolved around Will's feelings. God forbid he feel pressured or trapped.

A frustrating revelation came over her. She had let Will's feelings dominate her life, just like she'd let Ayers's emotions do the same. They were very different men, so they were very different emotions. Tipsy herself was the common denominator.

I'm terrible at relationships. That's the bottom line.

Let's not get ahead of ourselves now—

I can't stand it anymore, Granna! My life should be fixed by now. She leaned against a scratchy wool pillow and tears ran down her cheeks. *There has to be something I can do to make things better. Or at least feel better right now.*

Tipsy sat up. She grabbed her phone. She found Will's last texts—his messages offering to be there for her after he dumped her on her ass. She began typing furiously.

TIPSY: HOPE YOU HAD AN AMAZING DAY ON THE BOAT WITH MY BEST FRIENDS AND A BUNCH OF RANDOM BOAT FLIES. SINCE YOU CLAIM TO CARE ABOUT ME, I'D APPRECIATE IT IF YOU AVOID SHOWING UP ON MY SOCIAL MEDIA FEEDS. IT'S PRETTY PAINFUL SEEING STUFF LIKE THAT.

It didn't make sense, since no one can control other people's postings, but Tipsy didn't care. Will had stuck his damn head into Julia Whoever's photo like he was laid out on a guillotine.

She hit send, then realized she had more to say.

I TAKE THAT BACK. YOU CLEARLY DON'T CARE, SINCE YOU HAVEN'T REACHED OUT TO CHECK ON ME IN TWO WEEKS. SO GO AHEAD AND DO WHATEVER WITH WHOEVER. JUMP ON TINDER WHILE YOU'RE AT IT. Send.

She cried harder. I CAN'T BELIEVE YOU. I CAN'T BELIEVE YOU THREW EVERYTHING OUT THE WINDOW. YOU DON'T CARE AT ALL. Send. Send.

To her surprise, his typing bubble lit up. She held her breath.

TIPSY I'M SORRY YOU'RE UPSET. YOU DIDN'T REPLY TO ME AND YOU HAVEN'T REACHED OUT EITHER. YOU'RE THE ONE WHO SAID WE SHOULDN'T TALK. I'M TRYING TO RESPECT WHAT YOU ASKED ME TO DO.

She bit her lip as tears coursed down her face.

TIPSY: I DON'T KNOW WHAT TO DO. THIS IS SO HARD.

WILL: IT'S HARD FOR ME TOO.

TIPSY: I DON'T UNDERSTAND! YOU'RE THE ONE MAKING IT HARD?! IT DOESN'T HAVE TO BE!

WILL: BECAUSE I KNOW IT'S NOT RIGHT BETWEEN US. JUST BECAUSE WE CARE ABOUT EACH OTHER DOESN'T MEAN IT'S RIGHT. I KNOW I'M NOT MAKING YOU HAPPY.

TIPSY: YOU JUST HAVE TO BE YOURSELF AND BE WITH ME!

WILL: THIS IS MYSELF. I'VE BEEN TELLING YOU SINCE WE FIRST HAD THAT CONVERSATION IN YOUR KITCHEN AFTER YOU TOLD ME ABOUT THE GHOSTS. I WANTED IT TO WORK AND I'VE BEEN TRYING, BUT IT DOESN'T SEEM TO BE WORKING FOR EITHER OF US. WE'VE BEEN OVER THIS A THOUSAND TIMES.

TIPSY: YOU DIDN'T TRY HARD ENOUGH.

WILL: I DON'T THINK WE SHOULD HAVE TO TRY SO HARD. DO YOU?

Tipsy was sad and afraid and lonely, so that annoyingly correct logic didn't totally break through her fog. I MISS YOU, she typed. Tears plopped onto her phone screen. She wiped it with her nightgown.

WILL: I MISS YOU TOO. I TOLD YOU, I'M HERE FOR YOU IF WE CAN TRY TO BE FRIENDS. I HATE TOTALLY LOSING YOU.

TIPSY: IS THAT REALISTIC? HOW CAN WE GO FROM WHAT WE'VE BEEN TO FRIENDS?

WILL: I DON'T KNOW IF IT'S REALISTIC. BUT I'LL GIVE IT A TRY IF YOU WILL.

TIPSY: ARE YOU SEEING ANYONE ELSE? WHAT ABOUT THAT JULIA WOMAN?

WILL: NO. I'M NOT SEEING ANYONE ELSE. I JUST MET JULIA TODAY. SHE'S NICE, BUT I'M NOT INTERESTED IN HER.

TIPSY: OKAY. I'LL TRY TO BE FRIENDS.

WILL: WANT TO START BY GETTING THE GIRLS TOGETHER SOON?

TIPSY: I GUESS SO. I'M SORRY I FREAKED OUT.

WILL: IT'S OKAY. I UNDERSTAND. I HOPE WE CAN FIGURE OUT A WAY TO STAY FRIENDS. GET SOME SLEEP, OKAY? WE CAN TALK TOMORROW.

TIPSY: OKAY. GOODNIGHT.

WILL: GOODNIGHT ☺

Tipsy set down her phone and curled into a ball. She felt better. Even if she'd started out intent on standing up for herself, and hence fixing one of her problems, when the ultimate effect of her tirade would be to drag out her agony.

She sensed Granna fixing to speak up, so she talked first.

I'm sorry, Granna. I meant to give him a piece of my mind. Now somehow, I'm planning a playdate. Maybe I'm so stressed out that I can't be alone.

I'm not judging you, sugar, said Granna. *But you're still alone. He's not coming back. He's sitting on the fence. You're letting him sit there when you should push him off.*

Remember, it took me sixteen years to finally put Ayers in his place, and I don't know if it helped much. I'm back to trying to figure out how to handle him.

That's different. You and Ayers have three kids. You have to deal with him for the rest of your life. Not so Mr. Will Garrison.

Let me get through this. Then I'll cut him off. I promise.

Careful what you promise. And I don't mean the promises you make to me. The broken promises you make to yourself can be much heavier.

Yes, ma'am. I'll be careful. As she closed her eyes, Tipsy felt sorry for those who truly had to say goodbye to their loved ones, because on days like this, she didn't know what she'd do without Granna.

Tipsy is eighteen and she's packing up her grandmother's house. Her mother Denise Denning inherited the place, and she plans to sell it as soon as she can. The house is on ten acres on a state road outside of Martinville, Podunk Capital of South Carolina, so it's not like there are buyers lined up. Still, Mama made it pretty clear that the sale of the land PopPop scrounged his whole life to buy must pay for her own life in Charlotte, North Carolina. Mama is still married to Tipsy's daddy, Randy Denning. As far as Tipsy knows, he works at the county landfill up there. Regardless, Denise insists she's in the poorhouse so the house and the land have to go.

Tipsy stands in the little living room. It's meticulously clean, as always. Filled with the kinds of funny knick-knacks older ladies accumulate that no one really wants. Prime example—Granna's collection of china elephants. When Tipsy took her United States government class in the ninth grade, it dawned on her that maybe Granna had those elephants because she was a Republican. She never talked much about politics. So Tipsy asked her, and Granna had tsk-ed. "I ain't a Republican, nor a Democrat, neither. What's any of that have to do with me? State Capitol in Columbia is a long way from State Road 62, much less Washington, D.C."

Tipsy, full of civic duty and patriotic pride, had replied, "It's got a lot to do with us, Granna. Who pays for the state road? Or makes the laws? Or declares war?"

"Your grandfather mowed the grass on the side of the state road himself. Now those people down the way do it, bless them." Those people *were the black family that had moved in when Tipsy was twelve. At first, Granna fretted about having black neighbors, even as she reminded Tipsy that she was not a racist and she admired Dr. King above all others. Once they started mowing and she got a taste of Mrs. Jenkins's fried chicken, however, she accepted them for the most part.*

"As for declaring war," said Granna, "the men in Washington sent my only brother to Vietnam and he never came back. That's what people like them *do to people like* us. *"*

Four years later, Tipsy is on her way to becoming people like them. *She has no interest in remaining in the impoverished, hillbilly club Granna considered people like* us. *She has a scholarship to the University of South Carolina. She's moving into the dorm in a month. She'd argued her mother into a few weeks to clean out the place and keep a roof over her head. Mama had said she'd come help, but Tipsy hadn't seen hide nor feathered hair of her. Thank the lord for Granna's life insurance money. It let her buy supplies for her dorm and some new clothes on sale at Belk. Granna died of lung cancer four weeks ago, not long after making her last public appearance as the lone family member at Tipsy's graduation. Tipsy's eyes burned whenever she thought of Granna with her oxygen tank. She'd held her hands over her head and clapped as Tipsy walked across the stage with her National Merit Society sash over her graduation robe. The principal had announced her award for High School Artist of the Year from the South Carolina Arts Council, along with her scholarship and her diploma.*

She knew Granna wanted to jump up and scream, but the cancer wouldn't let her. Granna's co-workers at the Piggly Wiggly had wheeled her into the Martinville High School gym. After she died, they started a meal drive for Tipsy. Her freezer is overflowing with casseroles. Tasty, but none of them were her grandmother's homemade baked mac and cheese.

She covers her face with her hands. Oh, Granna, *she thinks.* What will I do without you?

The mac and cheese recipe is in my blue box, sugar.

Tipsy screams. If the Jenkins were any closer, they would have come running to see what had happened to looney ol' Miss Stella's equally looney granddaughter.

She spins around with her heart racing. It sounded like Granna was right beside her. The smell of Prell shampoo engulfs her. She can almost taste puffed wheat, the cardboard-like cereal Granna kept in a plastic bin on the counter.

No need to get jumpy. It's only me.

Oh, lord. I'm losing it. *She'd read about schizophrenia in her AP Psychology class. It often hit people in early adulthood.*

Tipsy, you are not losing it. It's no more lost than it's always been.

"Granna?" Tipsy says, out loud. "Is that you?"

Sure is, sugar.

I don't understand. *She looks around her. A terrible thought strikes her. How had she—who had been seeing ghosts her whole life—not thought about it?* Are you stuck here as a ghost? Where are you?

I'm not a ghost of the kind you and I have always seen. I'm not trapped in between one place and another.

But where are you?

I've moved on.

To where?

You wouldn't understand, *Granna says.* It's the kind of thing you have to experience to know.

But you're here, too?

Suppose I am. I just realized it. Seems to be another benefit of our talent.

Why didn't you tell me before you died?

Didn't know. I'm as surprised as you are. None of my dead relations ever spoke up in my head. You and me, though, we've always been two peas in a pod. *She chuckles.* The pod being your noggin these days, apparently.

So I'm not alone?

I'll never leave you alone. You are my most special girl.

Thank you, Granna. Thank you!

Now then. *Granna is all business, like she's telling Tipsy she better get in there and clean up her room.* Looks like you got a lot of work to do. Don't count on your mama to help you.

I don't know what to save and what to throw out.

Throw out most of it, sugar. Don't hang onto these old things because of me.

Now that you're here, I don't have to.

Suddenly, Tipsy knows what she has to do. The urge to get this sad process over with seizes her. She finds a trash hauling company in the phone book. She'll get a portable dumpster and ask the Jenkins boys down the street to help her get rid of the furniture, unless Mrs. Jenkins wants any of it. She'll keep the photo albums and framed photos, and her favorite blue and white porcelain elephant. Granna didn't have any jewelry except her gold wedding band, and she'd been buried with it. The rest of it is going.

Where will you stay for the holidays and the summer? *asks Granna.*

Tipsy walks into the kitchen and starts opening cabinets. I don't know yet. But it will sort itself out. I can't be the only college student who is homeless between semesters. *She feels brave. After all, how many people can say their dead grandmother is looking out for them?*

She picks up a framed picture of herself and Granna from an art competition a few years ago. Tipsy is smiling at the camera and Granna is smiling up at Tipsy. Her award winning piece—an oil painting of Granna and two of her old lady friends sitting in the front pew at their church—is behind them.

Granna's love and confidence has flushed the fear and paralysis from her system. I'm starting over and I'm going to keep making you proud.

I know you will, sugar, *Granna says.* I know you will.

Tipsy dozed off on the couch. As had often happened since she moved into this house, she woke up to a chill and a pale face glowing in the darkness. She pushed herself up on one elbow.

"Henry," she said. "What time is it?"

"I'm not sure. I haven't yet figured out how to use our powers to operate your watch-telephone-writing gadget."

She reached for her phone on the end table. She pressed the home button and the light about blinded her. She closed her eyes and held it up to Henry. "What does it say?"

"Two thirty-seven."

"Oh, hell," she said as she sat up. "I got to go to bed. I have to deal with the car tomorrow and go to the grocery store before the kids get home. And work on Pamella's painting. Oh, and last but not least, figure out how two people died in separate odd circumstances decades ago."

"I thought about your request for me to speak to John," said Henry. "If it will help you, of course I'll talk to him. Besides, even if I disliked him, Jane loved him. She'd hate to know I didn't help him."

"Thanks. I'm planning to go Sullivan's tomorrow if you can meet me there." She stood and stretched.

Henry followed her to the foot of the stairs. "I have no other plans."

"Great. I'd give you a high five but it might send me into the past. I'm too tired for that."

"High five is when you—" He held up one glowing hand, palm outward, like a spectral school crossing guard.

"Yes. It's like, *whoo-hoo, let's do this.*"

"Was this gesture around when John died? I could high-five when I see him. To crack the iceberg."

"It's *break the ice.*"

"I know. We used that phrase in my day. But with me and John, this reunion will be of Titanic proportions."

Chapter 9

ipsy got up early despite her exhaustion. She packed up an easel, a large sketch pad, and some watercolor paintbrushes. An Uber dropped her off at the old barracks. She lugged her art supplies around the back of the building, out of sight of the road, and set up like she was painting the marsh. She stuck earbuds in her ears. Anyone who happened to wander back there or pass by boat would see a woman singing along to her favorite jams whilst creating a masterpiece. Not a crazy lady wandering an abandoned property and talking to herself.

Henry appeared beside her while she clipped the sketchpad to the easel. "Good morning," she said.

"Morning," said Henry, with uncharacteristic gruffness. He sounded more like a teenager who had been forced out of bed than a Southern gothic gentleman. These trips outside the house were taxing for him on a normal day. An unlikely ghostly reunion gave him additional reason to be uncomfortable.

"How long can you stay?" she asked.

"About half an hour. Although if I become distressed it may be harder to ignore the call of the house."

"Let's do this then. Last time I had to scream for him to hear me." She closed her eyes and screamed in her mind like a supernatural yodeler.

John Huger! Come out! It's Tipsy Collins! I need to talk to you!

Henry covered his ears and doubled over but Tipsy kept yelling.

John! John! John Huger!

John appeared in front of her with his uncanny, flip-of-a-switch speed. He scowled. "You're back. I thought I made it clear—"

"Hello, John." Henry straightened out of his protective hunch. His eyes widened, as if he'd forgotten what John looked like. The moment passed, and he fixed his usual arrogant half smile on his face.

As for John, his mouth hung open. "What the hell? What *in* the *hell.*" The Contrary Caterpillar had returned. "What. The. Hell—"

"Now, sir," said Henry. "I understand. Tipsy—what do people say nowadays when they're shocked or dismayed? Something about actuality?"

"I think you mean *what the actual f-bomb.*"

"Yes. I've heard your former husband say such."

John snarled like a cornered bush hog. "You murdering bastard. You dare speak to me, after you killed Janie—"

"John, he didn't kill Jane," said Tipsy.

"Lies! Everyone knew you killed her!" John rushed at Henry, but Henry disappeared and reappeared three feet away. John's grasping arms closed around empty air.

"I know you believe I did," said Henry, "but I didn't kill her. Nor myself."

"Who did then?"

"We don't have time for that," said Tipsy. "Henry can't stay long and we have to—"

"How is he here at all?"

"Because I was like Tipsy during my life. I saw spirits."

Recognition dawned on John's face. "When we were children, and you used to talk to people who weren't there..."

Henry nodded.

"That's why you were such an odd little bastard."

"If you must put it that way, then yes. That ability from life allows me limited mobility in death."

"How do I know I can believe you? Either of you?"

"John. I did not kill Jane." The haughtiness left Henry's voice and posture. "The reason I know the truth is because Tipsy here helped us understand what happened. She can help you, too. You must listen to us even if you had no fondness for me when we were alive—"

"I never had any *un*-fondness for you. You were the one who hated me and all the rest of the fellows."

"The rest of the fellows harassed me constantly. I don't remember you telling them to stop, even though they would have listened to you—"

"Y'all," said Tipsy. "I know you have a century of catching up to do, including some murder updates and a childhood therapy session, but can we concentrate on the issue at hand?"

"I know Ivy More was your sweetheart," said Henry. "Tipsy can set y'all free, but it's not only about you. Tipsy needs money, and Ivy's granddaughter is willing to pay her to free Ivy and bring peace to your old cottage—"

"Ivy is at our cottage?"

"Camden inherited everything from your father," said Tipsy, "including your family's cottage on Sullivan's. That's where Ivy died."

"Good ol' Cam inherited a lot after I died. Houses, money. My woman." John's eyes narrowed as new reasons for wariness dawned on him. "How does the granddaughter know Ivy's there? No one but Tipsy and Alma More has ever seen me. Are you telling me the granddaughter is a seer, too?"

"No," said Tipsy. "Pamella isn't a seer. But Ivy was."

"Good grief. How many secrets did Ivy have? And she betrayed me. Why should I help her move on?"

"That's the most selfish thing I've ever heard! That woman is over there—" Tipsy pointed in the direction of True Blue. "—hiding from me. She'd rather be stuck haunting that house for all eternity than go on to peace without you. And you're doubting her love for you?"

"But she married Camden! My cousin!"

"Oh, good lord. Henry. Please. Talk some sense into him."

Henry slowly approached John. "Johnny. I know how you feel. Jane broke my heart once and I thought the anger itself would kill me. I suppose in a way, it did. But once I understood her side of the story, I forgave her. Or more accurately, I realized I had nothing to forgive. She made choices based on what life handed her. If you loved this woman so much, can you not give her the benefit of the doubt?"

John's eyes watered with glittery tears. "I don't know. I'm so angry all the time. The mice and the snakes; their voices confuse me but they never let up. The days and nights run together and I can't do anything but watch the light change and listen to them. Then when I learned this..."

"Shhh." Henry spoke as if placating the little boy he never had. "I understand, man. But this anger and suspicion isn't the good 'ol John I knew."

"You're a good man," said Tipsy. "Ivy told me so."

"Am I? Sometimes, I can't remember. There's so much I can't remember. Other things never leave me. Like the loneliness. And missing her."

"You can see her again," said Tipsy. "Y'all can be together."

John pointed at the marsh. "I've watched the sunset out here so many times, I know how the shape of the creek has changed. I've always wondered, why here? I have no real association with this place that I remember. Except that Ivy and I met here a few times. I kissed her on the porch. Is that why I'm here?"

"Will you let us try to find out?" Tipsy asked gently.

John whispered under his breath. Tipsy wondered which of his make-believe friends he was palavering with—opossum? Mosquito? Maybe a seagull? Thankfully, it was a sensible imaginary animal. John nodded. "Yes. It can't hurt to try. I apologize for my hesitation. And my rudeness."

"Death does strange things to people," said Henry.

"So you need to touch me again, Miss Tipsy?"

"Yes. Hopefully I'll see something that can explain your death."

The two men walked toward her like the remnants of pagan gods. John was Thor without his hammer, while Henry was a diminished Apollo. Tipsy gripped the side of the easel. John looked to Henry for guidance, and Henry nodded. John's thick fingers enclosed hers. Henry put one hand on his old rival's shoulder. With his other hand, he touched Tipsy's wrist. His dark blue eyes widened as darkness fell over them both.

———◆✕◆———

Tipsy and Henry are in a room with tall ceilings and crowded bookshelves, beside a dark wooden desk. John and Camden sit in leather club chairs across from one another. They're both sweating, despite the whirring electric floor fan. The windows are open to catch a breeze. The two green marble fireplaces are quiet, as if they know their presence reminds people of the oppressive heat. John is smoking a cigarette. Tipsy wrinkles her nose at the smell. It always made her gag when Granna smoked during the summer. How could anyone inhale smoke when the world is already on fire?

"I can't talk you out of this," Camden says. He holds a glass of iced bourbon.

John blows smoke toward the ceiling. "You cannot. I have the marriage license under my mattress. Ivy will sign when we go to the courthouse. The deal will be done."

"Uncle R.J. is going to blow his stack."

"He won't. You'll see. My parents will be happy once we're married."

"You're delusional."

"I'm in love, Camden. If that makes me delusional, so be it." He taps his cigarette on a thick clamshell ashtray. "But there's still one problem. Bubba More."

"He's her father. If you're marrying her, you'll have to tolerate him."

"No, no. He'll never accept me." John smiles, and Tipsy doesn't like that cold grin. His emotions make her feel sort of sick. She'd expect nasty ol' Bubba More himself to give off these vibes, not John. She's uncomfortable in the same way she used to squirm when she watched a movie sex scene on the couch beside Granna.

"That's why I need your help." John smushes out his cigarette and lights another. "I need you to ask Bubba More to meet me and talk about Ivy. Maybe hint that there will indeed be money involved if he's willing to let her go."

"Where are you going to get enough cash to bribe that bugger? Uncle R.J. isn't going to fork over the greenbacks once he realizes you've gone against him."

"Cash can't solve every problem, Camden."

"Now you're not making sense. Will cash solve this one, or won't it?"

"I'll use his greed to get him to talk to me."

"Then what?"

"That bastard threatened to kill me. He's beat my Ivy since she was a little girl!"

"We've established he's a bad seed."

"Sometimes it's better to pick the bad seeds out of the crop and get rid of them altogether."

Comprehension dawns on Camden's face. "You don't mean—"

"We get him alone, and then we get rid of him. Don't worry. It will never come back to us."

"That's murder, John. Murder."

"No one will care! His own family detests him."

"A judge will care. I'm not getting sent to prison as an accomplice—"

John reaches out and grabs Camden by his shirt. "You think I want to do any of this? Of course I don't. But it's the only way to make things right for me and Ivy." Tipsy can feel Ivy in John's very veins. She's creeping, like her namesake, through every inch of his being. Strong enough to slowly crack the bricks of his morals and upbringing and maybe even his sanity.

"Bubba More won't just let you kill him. You said yourself, he's as vicious as a hurricane gale. Look at those scratches on your face. Your lip is swollen up like a dead fish. He won't go down easy. Besides, you think this girl wants you to kill her own daddy?"

"I won't tell her. Not now anyway. Maybe someday. Believe me, she'll be happy he's gone."

"This is too much, John." Camden is getting desperate. "Once y'all are married, you won't have to worry about Bubba More. Go on and marry her and forget about him."

"No. When I left there yesterday, I realized I'll have to take unusual measures."

"I hate to see you put so much at risk—"

"I thought you were my brother, different mamas aside."

"I am, Johnny. That's why I'm telling you this is insanity."

"When you love someone like I love her, you'll understand. What kind of man am I if I let her daddy hit her? Or let my fear of my own father ruin our lives?"

The clock on the wall ticks loudly behind them. Finally, Camden says, "If this is what you insist. You're my blood. I'll help you get him there. But I'm not doing the dirty work."

"I knew I could count on you. We'll take the ferry to Mount Pleasant tomorrow and stay at the cottage. By Monday morning, Bubba More will be crab bait." John blows smoke through his nose in a bullish blast. It changes color as it wafts around the room, from soft gray to deep blue. Tipsy wants to trap John's intentions and his plan in a bottle, like one of the old people trying to catch errant spirits. She might stop the train cars from piling up behind his doomed steam engine. As it is, the smoke darkens until the view disappears altogether. Tipsy is sent back to her life, while Henry must return to his death.

Henry sat on the grass with his head between his knees while Tipsy explained the vision to John. The growing confusion on John's face might have been comical under other circumstances. He went from the discerning judge to the impassioned prosecutor to the flabbergasted, wrongly convicted defendant.

"I understand my own distress," said John, "but I cannot believe I wanted to kill someone. That seems unlike me. The living me, anyway."

"Obviously, your plan never came to fruition," said Tipsy, "since you died and Bubba lived on. Something went awry. After seeing Ivy's memory, I had a hunch Bubba might be involved. Maybe he killed you first."

"Perhaps," said John. "These are odd conversations."

Henry stood. "Tipsy and I are accustomed to them. I must leave you both. My own afterlife prison cell is calling me."

"Henry—wait. It was good to see you. I'm glad you didn't kill Janie."

"It was good to see you, too. Believe me, no one is happier than me to know I didn't kill my wife."

"We can talk tonight, Henry," said Tipsy. She wanted Henry to admit he'd been wrong about John's lack of emotional depth. "About all that *deep thinking* John did in that memory. We can, like, *perseverate* on what we saw."

Henry scowled. He wasn't ready to own his own unfair prejudice yet. "That sounds *lovely*. I'll see you at home."

John chewed on his lip as Henry disappeared. He turned to Tipsy with a questioning look on his face.

"I'll need some recovery time before we look again," she said. "This kind of thing still exhausts me and I have a lot to get done today."

"Then you should come back soon."

"Tomorrow, hopefully."

"Well… until then." He started to fade, but then zapped back into focus. "Tipsy, I must say, I feel more like myself right now than I have in years."

She folded up her easel, tucked her sketchpad under her arm, and balanced her phone on her box of watercolor pencils. "I'm glad. I wish I could say the same."

Over the next few days, Tipsy kept waiting for the other shoe to fall. Instead of stomping on her, however, it commenced grinding her down like a bug to be squished. The mechanic called and informed her that her transmission was shot. There were also other issues with the engine. Grand total for repairs: fifty-four-hundred dollars. She rented a bare bones Jeep Cherokee that reminded her of a gas guzzling golf cart. It would take two weeks to repair the Tahoe, so the rental put her out another grand or so. Still, better than having to figure out how to buy a new car.

Her luck was short-lived, because when she and Henry went back to the barracks to see into John's memory again, she found the door between herself and the past securely shut. When she tried to enter, she pictured a medieval castle with a huge beam across its iron gate, behind a raised drawbridge, surrounded by a deep moat infested with piranhas. Neither Tipsy nor Henry could catapult their collective consciousness over the battlements.

"What do we do now?" John asked her, as the three of them sat in a circle in the grass beside the marsh like a preschool class on an ecology fieldtrip.

"Henry, remember how we needed both you and Jane to see the memory of how you died?"

Henry nodded.

She thought hard for a moment. "When I freed Luisa Bishop, I didn't need to find anyone else. Proctor James heard about his own death, and he can go on whenever he wants to. He chooses to stay. You and Jane had a more complex demise. I couldn't only rely on your suppressed memories, or hers."

"We both had something to add to get the complete picture."

"Exactly." She turned to John. "I think there's someone else involved. Which makes it even less likely you died on a solitary evening swim."

"If we need someone else, we're most likely out of luck," said John. "Whoever it is would be long dead."

"And probably not a ghost." Tipsy leaned back on her elbows, thoroughly deflated. "What the actual f-bomb."

"We have some idea of who might be involved. If Bubba More killed John, or did other terrible things, perhaps he's a ghost," said Henry.

"He moved away before Ivy even died. We'd never find him."

"Camden?" Henry asked. "He killed himself, correct? A decent recipe for a haunting. It sounds like he may have been one of the last people to see John alive."

"My guess is Camden backed out," said John. "He wasn't a coward, but he cared deeply about appearances. A murder conviction wouldn't have endeared him to the other members of the St. Cecilia Society. Besides, he was a gentle person at heart."

"It can't hurt to look for him," said Tipsy. "I'll go back to the College of Charleston library and look at the old newspapers. Seems like there would have been something about your death in the paper."

"This meeting is adjourned then," said Henry. "Until further discovery of potential murder suspects."

A couple days later, Tipsy drove from the GQB to Mount Pleasant with a terrible mix of anticipation and dread churning in her stomach. A strange way to feel on her way to get the girls from a playdate, but Will had picked up the twins from camp after he got his own kids. They were at Will's place, and she hadn't seen Will in three weeks.

Her phone dinged as she sat at a light on Johnnie Dodds Boulevard. She swiped across a text from Pamella.

OMG! GUESS WHAT? I HAVE COUSINS! IN GEORGETOWN AND PAWLEYS IS. AND MURRELL'S INLET! LIKE, I HAVE ACTUAL FAMILY!

She included a gif of a woman joyfully jumping up and down.

TIPSY: THAT'S SUPER COOL!

PAMELLA: GUESS WHAT'S EVEN COOLER? I MESSAGED ONE OF THEM THROUGH THE GENEALOGY SITE AND GOT REPLIES!

Now that was pretty cool, and potentially helpful. Tipsy typed a quick text. DO THEY KNOW ANYTHING ABOUT BUBBA MORE OR THE REST OF IVY'S FAMILY??

The light turned green, so she drove for a few hundred yards, but this time of day, Johnnie Dodds came with a lot of stops.

PAMELLA: I THINK THEY DO! MY COUSIN, THIS GUY NAMED SANDY MORE, IS THE SON OF HER BROTHER SAUL! CAN YOU BELIEVE IT? HE SAID HE'D BE HAPPY TO GET TOGETHER AND TALK FAMILY STUFF!

TIPSY: FINALLY! AN ACTUAL BREAKTHROUGH. SHOULD WE DRIVE UP THERE FOR THE DAY?

PAMELLA: I MAY HAVE A BETTER PLAN. STAY TUNED!

The idea of making progress on Ivy's mystery briefly distracted her, but as she pulled into Will's driveway, her stomach turned into a hollow bagel hole in her tense midsection. Will walked out of his garage as she put the rental Jeep in park. He wore a baseball cap, an old BROCo tee-shirt and a pair of gym shorts. He was barefoot and had bits of grass stuck to his legs. Tipsy herself had strategically chosen a cute outfit, but not too cute. She didn't want to look like she was trying too hard. She'd damn sure run a brush through her hair and put on lip gloss.

Must be nice to be a dude. No need to worry about getting fancied up to see your ex for the first time in weeks. Or maybe he doesn't care.

He's even shorter without shoes on, said Granna with a sniff.

Thanks for reminding me.

She rolled down the window. Will walked toward the rental with his usual crooked half smile. He rubbed his chin and pursed his lips like MC Middle-Aged White Guy. "They see me rollin', they hatin'…"

"Yup," said Tipsy. "You caught me ridin' dirty."

"Does it go over forty?"

"Not if I forget to charge the battery."

"Be careful. That thing won't stand a chance in a fender bender with an F-250."

"I will. How'd they do?"

"Reunion successful. They're in the backyard on the trampoline. Now we have to drag them off it."

"I already thought about it," she said. "I'm using dinner bribery."

"Chick-fil-A?"

"Works every time."

Silence fell over them. Will crossed his arms over his chest. "You doing okay?"

She nodded. "You?"

"Yeah. Keeping busy."

She wanted to ask who was keeping him busy, but she let it lie.

"You want to walk back there with me?" he asked. "We can give them the twenty-minute warning and have a beer. Catch up on the past few weeks."

"I still have to pick up Little Ayers from his friend's house. Why don't you get the girls? I'll wait here." To her horror, a tear snuck out of one eye.

Will rested his hands on the top of the car door. "Tips…"

"It's okay." She swiped furiously. "I'm fine. It's just weird."

"Yeah. It is." He backed away. "Hold tight. I'll round them up. Can I tell them they'll get milkshakes?"

"Yup. It's that kind of evening."

A few minutes later, Mary Pratt and Olivia Grace burst from Will's house with their camp backpacks. They piled into the rental car and rolled down the windows. Will's two little ones stood on the front step. They waved furiously.

"Bye, Rosie! Bye, Ella!" shouted Olivia Grace.

"We miss you already!" added Mary Pratt.

"We'll come to y'all's house next time!" said Ella.

Rosie ran into the yard. She blew kisses, as if the Jeep Cherokee was a covered wagon bearing her loved ones away across the plains, never to be seen again. Mary Pratt broke the Manifest Destiny illusion. "My mom will text your dad!"

The girls chattered happily about their reunion playdate. Since they weren't arguing, Tipsy had a chance to think as they sat in the Chick-fil-A drive through line before picking up Little Ayers. She wasn't sure what she'd expected from Will. Maybe she thought he'd realized how much he missed her and he'd declare his undying love. That wasn't the case, as he hadn't even showered before she got there.

I don't know that Will Garrison has ever made a declaration about anything, said Granna. *That's part of the problem.*

Tipsy leaned her head against the window. *Even if he is sad, he's not going to show it.*

You want to be with someone who can't show it, sugar?

A tap on the window saved her from having to answer. She gave her order to the cheerful teenage girl with the iPad.

"Anything else, ma'am?" the girl asked.

The lingering emptiness in her stomach refused to be filled with food. "Just a large Coke."

"Can I have a name for the order?"

"Tipsy."

"Ma'am?"

"Sorry. Tiffany." She must be out of it if she'd given this poor girl her lifelong nickname instead of her given name.

"Okay, Miss Tiffany. For a second I thought you said Tipsy. Like..." She rolled her eyes and stuck out her tongue.

"Wouldn't that be crazy. Thank you."

"My pleasure!"

Tipsy rolled up the window against the summer heat.

"My pleasure! My pleasure!" said Mary Pratt.

"M.P., don't make fun," said Tipsy.

"I'm not! I'm practicing so I can work at Chick-fil-A someday!"

"Yeah, Mama," added O-liv. "I bet they pay you in nuggets!"

Tipsy blessed her girls for providing her with a reason to laugh. They stopped again while the employees ran food between the cars, so she swiped across her phone. She had two texts from Will, one from Pamella, and another from a number she didn't recognize.

She read Will's first.

Sorry I didn't say goodbye. You were already gone when I came out.

Thanks for letting them come over. They had fun ☺

Irritation bubbled in her stomach, as if she were already sipping her Coke. *Well, that's blasé,* she thought. *Can Will really be that dense? Or unemotional?*

Uh, yeah. He can, said Granna. *He always is. Why expect anything different?*

She read Pamella's text next. Let's plan a quick girls' trip! Clarice Andrews said we can stay at his house in DeBordieu. We can relax some

AND MEET MY COUSIN IN MURRELL'S INLET. WHAT DO YOU THINK? BTW, CLARICE ASKED ME FOR YOUR NUMBER. HOPE YOU DON'T MIND!

Tipsy opened the text from the unknown number. HEY TIPSY. THIS IS CLARICE. HAPPY TO LET YOU AND PAMELLA USE MY HOUSE FOR SOME RNR ANYTIME. ALSO I'M PLANNING TO TAKE THE BOAT TO CAPERS THIS SATURDAY IF YOU WANT TO COME. I'D LIKE TO GET TO KNOW YOU. I HOPE THAT'S NOT TOO FORWARD, BUT I DON'T LIKE TO BEAT AROUND THE BUSH. HAVE A GREAT EVENING.

Whoa. That is pretty forward. Tipsy thought about Lindsey's warning about Clarice Andrews being a big no-no. She also recalled Kim from High Thyme clinging to his arm like a barnacle, although she had described him as just a friend.

On the flip side, Tipsy hadn't been out on the boat much this season. The idea of an afternoon at Capers sounded like heaven. Ayers wanted to take the kids overnight on Saturday for his birthday. So she would be free. Maybe Clarice Andrews would be a fun distraction.

If I recall, Will started out as a fun distraction, said Granna.

This is different. There were red flags with Will early on, but they were subtle. Lindsey's impression of Clarice is a matador's banner. I'd go into it with my eyes wide open, unlike Miss Kim. If I know he isn't potential relationship material, that actually makes him safer than someone like Will.

I suppose your logic holds some water, but don't let the boat spring a leak.

I won't, Granna. I got this.

As for Mr. Wi-yum Garrison, he said he'd been keeping busy. No reason for Tipsy to sit home by herself on a pretty Saturday afternoon without kids.

A Chick-fil-A attendant handed her a warm bag of food, three small milkshakes, and her giant Coke. She fished around in the bag and checked her order.

What about staying in Clarice's house? asked Granna. *Seems a little more personal.*

Yeah, but if he's offering, why not? Finding Pamella's cousin is a big break. I'll ask Ayers to take the kids a couple days early and we can go Thursday. I've taken lots of extra time for him when he's hunting and fishing.

Tipsy stepped on the gas and the Cherokee buzzed like a housefly. She'd been to DeBordieu Colony, between Georgetown and Pawleys Island, years ago. It was a lovely, quiet gated beach community. Why should she feel bad about a nice boat ride with a friend and an overnight stay at the beach? No complications. No sweat off her back. As Tripp Collins would have said, everything was as easy as okra and tomatoes.

That's what she told herself, anyway.

Chapter 10

A yers agreed to keep the kids from Thursday morning through Sunday. Tipsy confirmed with Clarice that she and Pamella would take him up on his gracious offer to stay at his house and she'd take him up on his equally kind offer of a Saturday boat day. By the standards of Tipsy's usual parenting-driven routine, it was setting up to be an exciting week. She focused on the kids since she'd have less time with them, but as for her three little peeps, they were happy to have extra time with Kate's children. From what Tipsy garnered, Kate and her kids had all but moved into Ayers's house. She needed to discuss that touchy topic with him soon. For now, in order to make progress toward her fifty-k and ultimately maintain her own stable living situation, she needed Ayers to cooperate with her.

It's always a dance with Ayers, Granna, she thought as she drove downtown to the GQB after dropping the kids at camp on Wednesday morning. *I make a lot of decisions where both of my choices are kind of shitty.*

That's the nature of that gum-smacking, deer-shooting, contrarian beast. Always has been.

Tipsy dipped into the College of Charleston library during her lunchbreak. She searched microfiche editions of the July 1932 News & Courier. Déjà vu rolled over her as she inhaled the smell of decaying film, like rotten vinaigrette salad dressing. The last time she'd come here, she'd found only Jane and Henry's obituaries. This time she found a full page article. She read it a few times, printed it off, and took it home to share with Henry.

That evening, while the kids were watching their wind down Disney shows, Tipsy and Henry sat on Miss Callie's front porch. Tipsy took a corner chair facing the windows so she could chat freely with Henry without looking like a nutjob to any passersby. Henry sat across from her with one leg draped languidly over the other. Tipsy imagined F. Scott Fitzgerald must have had the same aura of elegant melancholy.

"Read it to me again," he said.

"Can't you read it yourself?"

"The print is tiny and I can't put on spectacles."

"Okay, okay." Tipsy balanced the article on her thighs. In the accompanying portrait John wore a formal suit and a solemn countenance.

Henry peered into her lap. "It's unnatural for a man to be so handsome."

Surprisingly, his statement seemed an observation, not a criticism. She shrugged and started reading.

"Prominent Charlestonian Drowns in the Atlantic
R. John Huger, member of the Huguenot Society,
the Saint Camellia Society, and St. Philip's
Church, perishes after a routine evening swim

The body of Robert John Huger, Jr., known as John, was found on the beach on the south side of Sullivan's Island on Wednesday, July 13, 1932. He was last seen on Sunday, July 10, leaving church, having told his parents, Mr. Robert John Huger, Sr., and Mrs. Colleen Stoney Huger, that he was going to the family's Sullivan's Island cottage to fish and planned to stay the night. His cousin, Mr. Camden Brewton, planned to meet him for a supper of fresh flounder, but upon arrival, Mr. Huger, Jr., was nowhere to be found and the family's jon boat was tied to the dock. Mr. Brewton assumed Mr. Huger had gone for his daily swim, as he was wont to do during his stays at the rustic retreat. Mr. Brewton didn't start worrying until late that evening. Tragically, no one ever saw R. John Huger, Jr., alive again.

A search party of concerned friends assembled on the island and combed the shores and marsh for any sign of him. On Wednesday morning, the sad truth made itself known: Mr. Huger drowned while taking a routine swim. A famously strong swimmer but sometimes weak in the stomach, the family speculates he may have seized up with a cramp and been washed out on a rip current.

"It was the worst moment of my life," said Mr. Brewton, who found his cousin's body floating in the surf a dozen yards offshore. "If not for his red striped swimming costume, I might not have seen him at all."

Tipsy looked up. "The rest is about how everyone loved John, who was apparently the greatest guy to ever live, and the funeral arrangements. So, Camden found John on the beach in a bathing suit. He clearly died somewhere else, and he wasn't wearing a bathing suit when he died."

"That's a blessing. Can you imagine being stuck in a bathing costume for eternity? How humiliating. It's bad enough for me with this hair."

"That means someone killed him, put him into a bathing suit, and dumped him in the ocean. How morbid!"

"Bubba More strikes me as a rather morbid fellow."

"Ugh. I wish we could find him. Any luck with Camden?"

"Not yet, but the old Huger House is one of the biggest downtown. It's four stories and has several outbuildings. I'm combing the house room by room. Funny to think that in a hundred years, I've never seen another spirit besides Jane. Now I'm searching for ghosts."

"I feel like my whole life is about trying to understand ghosts lately. The ones like you and Jane, and Ivy and John. Literally haunting me."

"As Miss Dickinson said, one need not be a chamber to be haunted."

"Right. But it's more than that."

"Ah, I sense a metaphor there."

She smiled. "A little inspiration for THE GREAT STORY, right? The Geechee people were trying to understand ghosts too, with all their stories."

"Haint blue to stop the spirits crossing the threshold. Bottle trees to trap them. But Miss Callie's porch ceiling has been painted haint blue for approximately one hundred and twenty years. Didn't stop me and Jane from getting stuck here."

"And like Granna said, you're a tall drink of water to fit inside a bottle. I guess no one has a good solution. I keep trying to stuff different parts of my life into blue bottles anyway. Hoping to understand all my ghosts, literal and figurative." Tipsy pulled her bare feet up under her. "Of course you remain the most puzzling ghost in my life. I figured out how to set you free, and you refuse to go."

"Puzzling?" Henry closed one eye. "Eh. I prefer bewildering. Perhaps mystifying? At the very least, perplexing."

The screen door opened and Mary Pratt stuck her head outside. "Mama. Can I have ice cream? Please, please, please, please—"

"Yes, yes, yes, yes, silly." Tipsy set the article on the table and got up. "Duty calls," she said in Henry's general direction.

"It always does, yet it takes many forms."

"What's that supposed to mean?" Tipsy asked, after Mary Pratt disappeared inside the house.

"Another metaphor, perhaps."

"Perplexing as ever, Mr. Mott."

"Go on now, Mama. The child needs her treat, and I need to write."

Tipsy blew him a kiss. To her amusement, he caught it and slapped it on his cheek. Tipsy left him to his allegories. As Henry returned to his never-ending story, she went inside to scoop ice cream.

DeBordieu is one of those South Carolina words that people from out-of-state can't pronounce. It's French, so everyone wants to put a bougie spin on it, as if it's a variety of fine red wine. Those in the know are aware of the local pronunciation, which is usually *Debi-doo*, or if your tongue is feeling really lazy, *Deba-doo*. It's the epitome of a hidden gem, just past a double-humped bridge that hops across the confluence of the Waccamaw and Great Pee Dee Rivers as they spill into the Winyah Bay.

"There it is," said Pamella, as they passed a nondescript green and white marker. She took the next right. A larger sign, *DeBordieu Colony*, sat back from the road, partially hidden amidst an overflowing bed of marsh grass as if to conceal the community from those who didn't belong. Pamella smilingly told the guard at the gate that Clarice Andrews had called them in. He gave them an overnight pass and they drove toward the oceanfront.

As Tipsy looked through the windows of Pammy's BMW, she figured DeBordieu was a cross between Sullivan's Island and Kiawah. Exclusive and walled off, yet shabby chic. The whole place oozed family wholesomeness, albeit the kind of upright living that included a lot of drinking. Most of the preppy looking people who zipped by in their golf carts gripped wine glasses and koozie clad beer cans. Herons, egrets, deer, and gators observed them with healthy suspicion, as if they'd finally accepted these noisy human interlopers in their world.

They pulled into Clarice's driveway. His beachfront house had a farmhouse look about it, with natural gray siding and simple porches. Tipsy and Pamella got out of the car with their overnight bags. Pamella found the key under the mat and opened the door.

The house was furnished in a cutesy but dated coastal style, with yellow walls, light wood floors, and brightly colored sofas and chairs. An airy kitchen eased into a wall of windows and a wide back porch overlooking the dunes and the peaceful ocean.

"He got this place in his divorce," said Pamella.

Tipsy set her bag on the counter. While she wasn't a big one for architectural interior design—an artform she'd never mastered—she noticed the countertops. "Wow. Are these real oyster shells? And sea glass?"

Pamella ran her fingers over the counter. "Looks like it."

Tipsy squinted at the blue and green glass, like bits of Bob Brewton's ghost-catching bottles trapped in stone. "Gorgeous."

They found two guest rooms on the second floor. Tipsy got a text from Clarice as she plugged in her phone.

CLARICE: DID Y'ALL GET THROUGH THE GATE OKAY?

TIPSY: YES! WE'RE HERE! IT'S A LOVELY HOUSE! THANKS SOOOO MUCH FOR LETTING US STAY HERE TONIGHT!

CLARICE: SURE, ANYTIME ☺ Y'ALL ARE WELCOME TO GET DRINKS/FOOD AT THE BEACH CLUB. USE MY ACCOUNT, THEY DON'T TAKE CASH OR CARDS.

"Hey Pammy, Clarice said we can use his account at the Beach Club." It sounded like a great idea, but Tipsy didn't want to push his generosity or be beholden to him. "Do you think we should?"

Pamella stuck her head into Tipsy's bedroom. "Uh, hell yeah."

"I mean, if they accepted cash or cards I wouldn't, but—"

"Get dressed, lady. I already found the golf cart down in the garage. That bad boy is chaaaaarged up!" She wiggled her skinny butt.

Tipsy laughed. "You win."

She texted Clarice a thank you, brushed her hair and teeth and put on lip gloss, and changed into a casual striped sundress and cute flip flops. In her full length yellow jumpsuit and wedges with tiny leather sunflowers all over them, Pamella looked ready for a night out in Miami. She refreshed her Yeti from one of the three bottles of wine she'd brought in a cooler. She backed the golf cart out of the garage. Tipsy winced as she almost hit the mailbox.

After a harrowing golf cart joy ride, they pulled up to the Blue Heron Grill, the casual beachfront restaurant and tiki bar beside the swankier clubhouse. Kids were tossing footballs and doing cartwheels in the grass, running back and forth from the beach in wet bathing suits, and waving drippy ice cream cones. Families sat at long tables eating pizzas and burgers. A crowd clustered around the tiki bar; a mix of retired couples, multigenerational families, and teenagers trying to look old enough to score a drink. There was a pleasant breeze and the sunset was fixing to be a nice one. Tipsy did a quick scan and didn't see any ghosts anywhere. A bonus, as she had no patience for extra spectral activity.

Pamella chattered away about a friend of hers as they ordered drinks and found a space at the bar. This nameless lady had recently had some misadventures in plastic surgery. "It's the lips," said Pamella. "If she'd left those alone, the rest of it might have turned out all right. Now she looks like a premenopausal salamander, bless her heart. I always say, Botox, a little filler, *all good* now. Have a facelift if your wattle is *waddling* too much, but leave the lips alone. Have you had anything done yet?"

"Me? Uh, no." Tipsy pointed at the line between her eyebrows. "I'd love to fill in the Grand Canyon, but it's not in the budget right now."

"If it bothers you, do it. You *deserve* it." Once again, Pamella spoke with the casual comfort of one who had never worried about money. A haunted house, yes. But Botox money, no. "You have three kids! Parenthood is the river that carves the deepest canyons on a woman's face. Although marriage is right up there. Speaking of, Doug keeps calling me. Asking to visit."

"Your ex?"

"He's not technically my ex yet. He's my *almost*-ex."

"You going to see him?"

"I don't know." She sighed. "I left him for a reason. He's insensitive and he's messy and he plays too much golf. He drives me *batshit*, but I'm fifty-one. Dating is a nightmare. I've been on Bumble, but I haven't met anyone interesting enough to distract me from him. What's your favorite dating app?"

"Oh, jeez. I haven't been on one yet."

"Now that you're single again, you should do it. A little *rumble* on the *Bumble*. You know what they say about smooching frogs, so put on some Chapstick. Although… *I don't know*." Her perfectly micro-bladed brows wagged. "*Clarice* seems interested. I'm pretty sure he only offered the house because I said you were coming with me."

"Meh. Will and I just broke up. Plus I have too many things on my mind to worry about dating."

"Have you talked to your ex-husband yet about his *co-habi-ta-tion?*" She said it as if were a Southern version of a multisyllabic French word, sort of like *Debi-doo*.

"No, but it's coming. I have my kids about eighty percent of the time, but I need extra help from him right now. I'm so busy with painting, working with Shelby, and trying to figure out the John and Ivy debacle, he has to pick up some parenting slack. Another reason the sooner I can figure out this mystery, the better."

"Are you going to file something with the court?"

"That's the most direct option but also the most expensive one."

"I'd be careful if I were you. And not only because of the money. You've told me about this guy. He seems like a loose cannon."

"He is. I always say that Ayers is predictably unpredictable. I would have thought he'd have a stream of chicks in and out of his life, but he's been pretty conservative about dating. I mean the grapevine is never silent, so I know he's seen a few women, but this is the first one he's brought around the kids. And he flat out told me he's planning to marry her, but he's not in a rush."

Pamella sipped her wine. "So that tells me he's pretty serious about her, but it's good he doesn't want to rush it. He does not need to be marrying her so quickly, for your kids' sake or for the sake of his own dumbass."

"If he got remarried under the right circumstances, I'd be all for it. He needs a steadying hand. She seems like a great potential candidate so far, but who knows? She might be nuts under her snazzy professional outfits. And she surely doesn't have the whole picture of him yet. If they get married and it falls apart, my kids are the ones who will suffer."

"All excellent points, and it sounds like *you* know him, even if she doesn't. Now think about it, lady, with that big old brain of yours. What do you think he'll do if you back him into the corner?"

"He'll be so pissed." Cold realization chilled Tipsy. "He'll probably head to the courthouse and marry her that day."

"It's a lot easier for them to break up if they get to know each other and it's not right, rather than go through another divorce."

"Damnit. You're right. Once again, I'm choosing between two crappy scenarios. Leave it alone and he keeps living with her, to hell with the court order and what's good for the kids. Make a fuss and I'll have a shotgun wedding on my hands."

"In this case, the less crappy choice will be to let them figure out if they should get married or not. At least she has her own kids and she won't want more. And she'll understand his life. Not like women his age who have never had children and expect the world to revolve around them." Pamella tapped Tipsy's arm. "Same for you. You're much better off with the baggage of a divorced father than the baggage of a lifelong bachelor."

"Too bad Will doesn't realize my baggage is preferable to a younger woman's ticking biological clock."

"No better way for him to figure it out than to live it. Look at me, with my two and a half ex-husbands and all the wisdom that comes with 'em."

"You are wise, my friend," said Tipsy. She felt a jolt of affection for Pamella. She did indeed seem full of wisdom, even if she couldn't apply it to her own life.

Pamella drained her wine glass and caught the attention of the bartender with a snap of her fingers that would have been annoying if not for her warm smile. She added another glass of wine to Clarice's tab and then giggled in delight as she recognized the women across the bar. "Oh my god! Old friends from UGA!"

"Go say hi," said Tipsy. "I'm going to order nachos. You want anything?"

"Nope. I'm good!" Pamella hopped around to the other side of the bar. Tipsy pulled out her phone and swiped on a text from Clarice.

Sunset?

She took a picture of the pinkish sky and sent it to him. He replied right away.

Wish I was there to see it in person.

Tipsy paused. There was an expectation she'd write back with something indicating she wished he was there, too. She wasn't playing into that game. It's beautiful! ☺ Thanks again for letting us use the house and for the drinks/snacks.

She returned her attention to the dunes and the ocean and the chatter of the happy people around her. As her mental camera scanned the crowd, she stopped on the man playing acoustic guitar on the patio beside the restaurant. She spun the imaginary lens. The man's grayish beard and his big fingers, toughened by the strings, came into focus. He sang *Carolina in My Mind* by James Taylor. A little girl of about three in a pink gingham dress and bare feet had stopped before him, mesmerized.

Tipsy wondered if anyone beyond the child's parents noticed the beautiful moment. Her imaginary shutter clicked and she stored the image in her mind. It would make a lovely painting once she finished Pamella's project.

At least I don't have painter's block anymore.

Thank the lord for that, said Granna. *And thank Jane and Henry.*

Tipsy raised her beer in a salute to her ghostly friends and her new friend, Pamella. She toasted the lovely sunset that Clarice would not see.

The next morning, Tipsy and Pamella took a long, chatty walk on the beach that soothed Tipsy in the way only a girlfriend talk can. As she got dressed after her shower, she realized how long it had been since she'd taken a girls' trip. This one overnight felt like a weeklong spa getaway.

Pamella knocked on her door. "I put this on and I don't really like it. You want to wear it?"

She held out a sea green sleeveless brocade and lace top. As Tipsy took it, the detail told her it was expensive. "Seems sort of fancy for Murrell's Inlet."

"You have jean shorts? It would look awesome with those and…" She disappeared and returned with a pair of camel-colored wedges with an ankle strap and a buckle in the shape of a heart. "These!"

"I mean—I love it. But do you have something else to wear?"

"My overnight satchel is like Mary Poppins's bag. I got *all kinds* of shit in there. And I keep a few extra things in the trunk."

Tipsy pulled out her shorts and went into the bathroom. She tried on the whole outfit. Exactly what her style would be, if she had a lot of money. She smiled at her reflection and walked into the bedroom. "What do you think?"

Pamella looked up from her phone. "Gorgeous! Such a good color on you. Keep it!"

"What? No. I'll wear it today, but—"

"Seriously, Tipsy. I have so many tops. I never wear half of them. This one is made for you." She patted Tipsy's shoulder. "*Keep it.*"

Tipsy picked up on the friendly bossiness in Pamella's voice. She looked in the mirror again.

If she really wants me to have it...

You know I'm not one for handouts, said Granna, *but when the handout is that pretty, I'll make an exception.*

"If you truly don't want it," she said. "Thanks so much."

"No problem! It's the perfect outfit for the *Loooooove* Shak!" Pamella said, as she sashayed out the bedroom door. She called over her shoulder. "Bubba's Love Shak. Kind of ironic, isn't it?"

Tipsy laughed at the comparison between the popular restaurant in Murrell's Inlet and Ivy's miserable upbringing. "Meemaw didn't have a lot of love, but she had the Bubba and the shack."

Twenty minutes later, they were in the car, heading to the waterfront town of Murrell's Inlet, fifteen miles north of DeBordieu past Pawleys and Litchfield Beach. Murrell's Inlet had a couple unofficial town mottos: *Seafood Capital of the World!* and *Murrell's Inlet, a drinking village with a fishing problem.* The town sat tucked back from the open ocean on a pleasantly protected saltwater cove. It was famous for its seafood production and the waterfront boardwalk known as the Marshwalk. The Marshwalk connected thriving restaurants that pumped out delicious food and live music from morning until long past dark seven days a week. The police didn't care if the visitors walked between restaurants with open drinks, so they did so with relish. The crowd was bizarrely eclectic, from bachelorette parties to charter fishing groups to bikers who came down from Myrtle Beach to sample the Inlet's biker bars.

Pamella pulled into the parking lot behind Bubba's Love Shak. Tipsy noticed her hands were shaking as she put the car in park. "You okay?"

Pamella nodded. "But I'm nervous. Meeting Daddy's first cousin is sort of weird. What if he doesn't like me?" She looked down at her white linen pants and beaded sandals. She fingered the delicate diamond necklace she always wore. It had tiny stones strung on a platinum chain. "Maybe I should have worn something else."

Tipsy patted her arm. "Pammy, everyone loves you. You're one of the most charming people I know. Your cousin will love you, too. He might not have any other relatives like you—"

"Oh, hell. He'll hate me! He'll think I'm a snob."

"No. He won't." Tipsy opened the door, and then gently said. "A little advice. Don't *insist* on paying for the drinks. Offer if you want, but don't demand it. People have pride, you know?"

"I will be *seriously* down to earth."

"Just be yourself. Now come on. Let's meet Meemaw's nephew."

They walked around to the Marshwalk side of the restaurant, past the hanging sign for Bubba's Love Shak. It was a brightly painted but roughly hewn one-story building. A line of colorful rocking chairs and picnic tables on the patio overlooked the waterfront. Servers rushed around taking orders while food runners dropped off baskets of fried seafood and liquor drinks in plastic cups.

Tipsy shaded her eyes and squinted out over the Inlet at the line of houses across the water in Garden City. As boats cruised toward the Marshwalk they passed a tiny island inhabited by a family of goats. The town removed those hardy critters each winter and redeposited them in the spring. Laughing groups of people clustered along the boardwalk. Kids raced between strolling couples like little human barrel racers.

Pamella grabbed Tipsy's arm as they walked up the stairs. "I think that's him, from the Facebook pictures." She pointed out an older man

at a picnic table. He had a can of Coors Light in front of him. He wore
a tee-shirt, jean shorts, and flip flops. He had a gray ponytail.

"Eeek. I'm too dressed up," said Pamella.

"Can't change now. Come on."

Pamella smiled as they approached the table. "Sandy?"

Sandy appeared to be in his seventies but was thin as a rail. He
grinned and stood. "Pamella? Hello, cousin!" He had pale raccoon
circles around his hazel eyes from his sunglasses. He pumped Pamella's
hand up and down. With each friendly jerk, her nervous smile widened.

"Sit down." He waved to the server. "Misty! Get these ladies a drink."

Misty, a tough looking woman with a pot belly, clearly knew Sandy
and felt no need to jump when he called. "Hold your horses, Mr. More."

Pamella sat on the bench beside him. "Mr. More. With one *O*,
I assume?"

Sandy nodded. "Been spelling it all my life."

"I love to hear that! This is my friend Tipsy, the… uh… genealogist
I told you about."

"Hopefully I can help you dig up some new roots under the ol'
family tree, but let's get to know each other first."

Misty took their drink order and Tipsy listened as Pamella and Sandy
traded truncated life stories. Sandy, or Saul Junior, was the son of Ivy's
brother, Saul More, Senior, long deceased. Sandy and his son owned
More & More Marine, a boat maintenance and repair shop.

"Nice living to be made between the fishermen and the pleasure
boaters," said Sandy as Misty dropped off their beverages. "So… this
poking around in the family closets. Why now, if I might ask?"

"Oh, well. You know!" Pamella sipped cheap chardonnay from
a plastic cup. "Genealogy is all the rage these days! Can you tell me
anything about the Mores? Like, did you know your grandfather? My
great-grandfather George. They called him Bubba."

Sandy sucked air through his teeth in a universal sign of disdain.
"Oh, boy. Grandpa Bubba." He pointed at the sign over the restaurant's
entrance. It read *Ain't No Love Like Bubba Love*. "Bubba Love he was not."

"So you knew him pretty well?" asked Tipsy.

Sandy nodded. "He died when I was... oh, about fifteen. Grandma Alma died a few years before. They both died of lung cancer.

"My Granna died of the same cancer."

"Brutal. That's why even in my hippy days, I never smoked a cigarette. Might have smoked other things, but never touched a Camel or a Marlborough."

"Did Bubba and Alma live with your father?" asked Tipsy.

"Yup. Big Saul moved to Georgetown to get away from Bubba, but Bubba and Alma followed him up here when Ivy got married."

"My father told me he met Big Saul a couple times before Ivy died," said Pamella.

"Yeah. Ivy passed away before I was born. But my Daddy told me about her. He adored his big sister. She was more like a mother than goofy old Grandma Alma. After Ivy got married, Saul used to take Alma down to Charleston to see her about once a year. What was her husband's name?"

"Camden Brewton," said Pamella.

"Right. If I remember correctly, she had a romantic thing with another man before Camden. A relation of his?"

Tipsy nodded. "Yes! John Huger."

"Bubba hated that John Huger. Then he died, and within a week or two, Ivy runs off and marries his cousin. Bubba went off like a dry firecracker and completely disowned her. Refused to speak to her or see her."

"That makes sense," said Pamella. "I remember my father talking about Grandma Alma and Uncle Saul, but he never mentioned meeting Bubba."

Tipsy frowned. "Kind of extreme to disown your child because you don't like her spouse."

"Bubba was an extreme person," said Sandy. "She flat out disobeyed him, and in his mind, his daughter was sleeping around with rich men. That didn't reflect too well on a man who claimed to love his bible.

Besides, he couldn't tolerate wealthy people, because he *wasn't* rich and never figured out how to *get* rich."

"Seems dumb if she was so rich and he was so poor," said Tipsy. "I could have done with some well off relations in my early years."

"Bubba wasn't stupid. Far from it. But he had the kind of weird pride that comes from everyone always looking down on you." Sandy drained the rest of his beer and waved to Misty. "Funny enough, I did hear stories about the bruhaha when Ivy died. A few days before, Ivy's husband asked Saul to come to Charleston because Ivy was drinking so much and wandering around like a possum in the daylight. Mr. Brewton had to call in reinforcements. He considered having her committed."

"Wow," said Pamella. "So Saul came to Charleston to help out?"

"Yup. Supposedly he and Alma were in town when she passed away. Apparently, Grandma Alma went off the reservation when Ivy died. Not the first time. Alma was always kind of..." He pursed his lips. "... whoo-hooo! It wasn't her fault, really. It's hard to be a real world psychic."

Tipsy choked on her beer. "A real world what?"

"Like, a psychic or something. Big Saul always said his mother was touched by the other world." He wagged finger at Pamella. "You might not know it, but Aunt Ivy was, too."

"Ha!" Tipsy said, loud enough to make Misty the waitress jump in place at the next table. "Right. A psychic. You never heard that, have you Pamella?"

"Come on, Tipsy." Pamella leaned across the table. "If he knows, he knows."

"Oh, lord. Fine," said Tipsy. "Yeah. We've heard it."

"And?" Pamella poked Tipsy's shoulder.

"And I... um... I have the same... issue."

"You're a psychic?" asked Sandy. "Like one of those people on TV?"

"No. Not like that at all. But I can... do... I see things. Stuff."

"She sees ghosts," said Pamella. "And the real reason we're here is... Ivy haunts my house. I'm trying to get rid of her!"

Sandy sat in stunned silence for a moment. Then he grinned. "Well, damn! That's awesome! Big Saul was always on me for not showing any kind of psychic ability—"

"I prefer the term clairvoyance," said Tipsy.

"Like I was a family disappointment. The power came through Alma's father's side. The Chapmans from Beaufort. Grandma Alma originally came from down that way."

"I didn't know that," said Pamella.

"She moved to Charleston as a teenager to find work. Met Bubba. Got married. But she had deep Beaufort roots."

"Such a pretty town," said Tipsy, as she pictured the charming waterfront village seventy miles south of Charleston, just north of Hilton Head. "Like a mini-Charleston."

"It's pretty, but there's also a lot of hoodoo shit down in Beaufort County. You know, I always wondered if Alma had some Gullah-Geechee in her somewhere way back in the gene pool. It wasn't only the psychic stuff. All her country cures and curses. That woman was a walking superstition. White people didn't have that kind of root doctor knowledge. It was passed on in families."

Tipsy thought about Ivy's dark curls and her full lips. She was as fair as Tipsy even in life, from what Tipsy had seen in her memory. Still, given South Carolina's long, complex, and often dismal history, that didn't necessarily rule out Gullah-Geechee heritage.

"Supposedly Alma only had a touch of the sight," said Tipsy. "But Ivy herself is powerful. We're trying to figure out how she really died, so we can set her free."

"Is that how it works? That's interesting. Y'all got any theories?"

"Not really." Tipsy explained how they had a hunch Bubba More had been involved in the death of Ivy's lover, John.

"You might be on to something. If anyone was capable of murder, it was good ol' Grandpa Bubba."

"That's good to hear, in a warped way," said Tipsy. "But as far as Ivy, all we got is a dock dive. Can you tell us anything else that might help?"

"Not that I can recollect. But I can look around in the old family albums. Stuff like that."

"I'd like to see them someday," said Pamella.

"You should come to my house for supper. Meet my wife and my kids and grandkids."

"That would be nice." Pamella smiled, but Tipsy sensed hesitation on her part.

They had another beer and chatted about simpler things than old murders and secret family psychic histories. Before long, the people around them started getting rowdy. Tipsy looked at her phone when Sandy stepped aside to talk to someone. "We should get going. I want to get back to town pretty early. Boat ride with Clarice tomorrow."

"Oh, right!" said Pamella, ever the hopeful matchmaker. "You need your beauty rest!"

Fifteen minutes later, they'd said goodbye to Sandy and they were in the car. Tipsy insisted on driving, as she'd had two and a half watery beers over three hours and Pamella had consumed an unknown quantity of wine.

"That was interesting," Tipsy said as they drove through Murrell's Inlet. "No big revelations, but we got some dirt on Meemaw's family from the horse's mouth. You going to take Sandy up on his offer of supper?"

Pamella rested her head against the window and yawned. "Interesting, yup. Dinner... maybe? We'll see. I'm tired. I'll doze off if you don't mind."

"Sure. Go for it." An hour-plus car ride would give Tipsy time to think. There didn't seem to be enough hours in the day for all her thoughts lately.

Don't think yourself into a corner, said Granna. *Why not turn on some music and just enjoy the scenery?*

Tipsy humored Granna and flipped on the radio. *Let It Be* by the Beatles wafted through the car. She smiled. *You're my Mother Mary, with your words of wisdom.*

Paul McCartney knew what he was talking about.

Tipsy cruised along listening to Paul's soothing tenor for a while. When she hit a stoplight in Pawley's Island, she checked her phone. Her pulse picked up. She tapped a new text from Will.

WILL: HEY! HOPE YOUR WEEK IS GOING GREAT! WANT TO GET THE GIRLS TOGETHER THIS EVENING? I'LL GRILL BURGERS AND WE CAN HAVE A BEER. I'M TAKING MY THREE TO ISABEL'S SOCCER TOURNAMENT IN COLUMBIA TOMORROW SO IT WOULD HAVE TO BE TONIGHT.

Confusing emotions trapped Tipsy. Of course she *wanted* to hang out with him and the kids, but his message annoyed her on multiple levels. The last minute request to get together. His casual tone, as if he were texting one of the soccer dads. Did he want her at his beck and call for occasional family-friendly evenings?

The driver behind her honked. The light had turned green while she ruminated. She drove a couple miles to the next light. Part of her wanted to call him out, but she decided to keep it simple for now. She decided to let it be, as Paul suggested.

HEY, MY WEEK IS GOING GREAT. HOPE YOURS IS TOO. AYERS HAS THE KIDS THIS WEEKEND FOR HIS BIRTHDAY. THANKS FOR THE INVITE!

Will replied by the time she stopped again. OKAY BUMMER! ANOTHER TIME!

Fortuitous that the kids were with Ayers so she wouldn't be tempted to bake the cake Will wanted to simultaneously consume and display on the stand. She didn't reply to his last text. She kept on driving and tried to follow Paul's advice.

Chapter 11

A t noon on Saturday Tipsy took an Uber to Clarice's house in Toler's Cove, a gated community across the Intracoastal Waterway from Sullivan's near the Ben Sawyer Bridge. A dozen skinny houses and several condo buildings snuggled against one another and the marsh. Yachts and deep sea fishing boats lined the community docks.

Tipsy guessed which house belonged to Clarice before she pulled up to it. Smack on the Intracoastal with some of the best views on this side of town. Yellow paint that needed a touch up and a good power washing. A ten-year-old Chevy Silverado pickup and a shiny new Mercedes sedan sat in the cracked driveway.

She walked up the stairs to the front porch and rang the doorbell. A dog barked and she heard Clarice yelling. The door opened and a grinning furry face appeared in the crack. A chocolate lab bounced by Clarice's side.

"Mooch! Get back. Down, damnit!"

Tipsy took hold of the door as Clarice dragged the dog away.

"It's okay," said Tipsy. "Let him say hello."

Clarice released Mooch and he ran all up on Tipsy's legs. He slurped her hands and spun in a circle, as if in apology for his rude greeting. Another *woof* sounded from the living room to her right. An ancient Boykin spaniel, the chocolate colored, curly haired state dog of South Carolina, lifted his head and regarded her with milky eyes.

"That's Rooster," said Clarice. "He's my kids' old dog. Mooch is my kids' young dog."

"Ah. Do your kids live with you?"

"They're in college. They're back and forth between my house and their mom's in the summer." He smiled. "The dogs are products of my divorce. I got Rooster because my ex didn't want to deal with him. I got Mooch last year as my single dad guilt Christmas present."

"I thought about getting a dog to keep me company when mine are at their dad's, but I can't handle it right now."

"Wise choice. I can't handle it either, but here I am covered in brown fur and drool."

Tipsy laughed. "Thanks again for letting us use the DeBordieu house."

"No problem. Hope y'all had time to chill. Everything is more relaxing at the Dew. You want a beer?"

She held up her cooler and her beach bag. "I brought some."

"Great… well, we can get going. The guys have the cooler filled and the boat gassed up. Let me grab my wallet."

Tipsy looked around as she followed him into the kitchen. Like the outside of the house, the interior was high-end yet neglected. The living room contained a giant leather sectional sofa and a huge television, but no other furniture. The kitchen had quartz countertops and high-end appliances, but no kitchen table in the breakfast nook. Photos of his two sons covered the table in the foyer.

Clarice reappeared from the mudroom off the kitchen. He led her out the back door and across a boardwalk. Two dockhands stood beside a pale blue center console fishing boat with *Ol' Black Water II*, *Mount Pleasant, SC* emblazoned across the back. The boat had to be close to forty feet long. It seemed brand new, with its blinding white seats and stereo system like something out of an LA nightclub. Tipsy tried not to stare as she climbed aboard.

"It's really pretty." She used the same casual tone when she complimented Pamella's couture outfits.

"I like it. Got it this season. I moved my other boat up to a marina in Georgetown for when I'm in DeBordieu."

"You like the Doobie Brothers?"

"Hell, yeah. All things classic rock for this guy. Plus it just fits. Black River Outdoor Company, and I grew up on that river."

As Tipsy self-consciously stripped down to her bikini she reminded herself that it was over ninety degrees, and in Charleston, boats and bikinis were intrinsically linked. As Clarice steered the boat away from the dock, she wondered where he expected her to sit. There were three captain's seats. Should she sit there, or on the loungers on the bow? If she sat in the captain's seat, should she sit beside him or with a seat between them?

Oh, lord. So weird! Help, Granna!

Tipsy, I can't help you. I couldn't even swim. I surely never rode around on a boat worth half a million dollars.

"Come on up here." Clarice patted the seat beside him, but she didn't want to squeeze in close to him. She sat with one butt cheek on the middle seat and one on the far seat.

They pulled into the Intracoastal, but Clarice kept the engine low so they could chat. Tipsy cracked a beer and handed him one from the stocked cooler. He turned on the stereo and Crosby, Stills & Nash waxed poetic about the Southern Cross. They made casual conversation as the boat slid through the water.

"How do you like the Old Village?" he asked.

"I love it. I adore my house. Although it's not really mine." She filled him in on the basics of her living situation. "I hope I can live there for another year, before Jimmy's family figures out what they want to do with it. Then we'll see. Maybe I'll move back over around Long Point. That's where my ex lives."

"Ayers Collins, right?"

"That's him." She should be used to everyone knowing Ayers, but it still made her uneasy.

"I remember him from college. He pledged my fraternity my senior year."

"Ah. Sigma Alpha Order forever."

"Eh, it's kind of bullshit, but it was fun then. If I remember, he had a big mouth."

"Yeah, he still does."

"Y'all get along?"

"It's been okay lately. He's dating someone new and pushing her on my kids. Things could get complicated again."

"My ex is remarried."

Tipsy pretended like Lindsey hadn't given her any input. "Y'all get along?"

"Nope. We're still in lawsuits two years later. Now we're waiting on a hearing in the Court of Appeals. She wants some of BROCo, even though I started it before we were married. She left me for her personal trainer. What a cliché, right?"

"That's terrible. But do you really want to keep fighting her? Can you, like, buy her out?"

"I'd rather pay lawyers forever than give her another cent."

Ouch, Tipsy thought. *Lindsey was right.* "Where does she live?"

"I got the Dew house and then bought mine on Toler's. She got our old house on the Isle of Palms." With his thick Georgetown drawl, it came out like the *Ah-la Palms.* "We'll pass the house. It's just past the connector, across from Goat. I considered buying a weekend place on Goat, right across from it. Thought we'd be close for the kids."

Goat Island was a tiny slip of land across the Intracoastal from the Isle of Palms accessible only by boat. "I guess for someone like you, getting back and forth by boat wouldn't be a big deal."

"Right. The kids could take the jon boat across—but then I found out about her affair. Since then, we haven't been able to talk at all. Now she lives in my old house with her new man."

"If Ayers marries his girlfriend, I'll be in the same boat."

Clarice held up his beer. "Cheers to our exes moving on. May they be as miserable as they made us."

Tipsy clinked her drink against his but his bitterness was a turnoff. She didn't care about Ayers moving on. Not in the same way he did.

"I won't bite, you know," he said.

She swallowed. "Sorry. I mean. No. Not sorry—"

He laughed, but it wasn't unkind. "Sorry, not sorry? Relax, okay? We're just going for a cruise." One eyebrow peeked over his Ray Bans. "What did Lindsey and Pamella tell you about me, anyway?"

"Pamella didn't tell me anything."

"But Lindsey did."

"I don't want to throw Lindsey under the bus."

"I won't be mad. You're her friend."

"She told me to be careful with you. She said you're... uh... kind of popular. With women."

"I have a lot of friends."

"Friends with benefits?"

"Maybe. I'm always up front with women I go out with."

"Right...." The brutal honesty of the conversation helped Tipsy relax. Or maybe it was the beer she was slurping down. "You don't like to beat around the bush."

"Exactly."

"Lindsey said you're not interested in dating anyone seriously."

He shrugged. "Like I said. I'm always up front with people."

"But you said you wanted to get to know me."

"I do. You're a gorgeous artist with a mysterious smile."

Tipsy punched his arm. "You have no idea how mysterious I am. Take it from me. Once one mystery is solved, another will raise its enigmatic head."

"Damn. Your vocabulary turns me on."

She pushed him again. "I'm getting another beer, silly."

As she popped the top, the soothing sound of Stevie Nicks's voice floated through the speakers. She warbled about thunder, rain, and players playing their games. She crooned hypnotically about her crystal visions as Tipsy returned to her seat.

"You have any dreams you'd like to sell?" Clarice asked.

Tipsy gave him a half smile. "I keep my visions to myself."

"Still mysterious."

"Like I said, you don't even know."

They kept chatting as the boat cut through the Intracoastal Waterway like a fiberglass barracuda. Tipsy loved the stretch of the Intracoastal from Sullivan's to Capers. She never tired of the landmarks. They passed Breach Inlet, which divided Sullivan's from the Ah-la Palms. Goat Island, with its rustic cottages and ramshackle docks, sat proudly across from the mansions lining the water on IOP. It was like a standoff between the country club uncle and his rowdy, redneck brother at a family barbeque. Everyone wanted to have a good time but they approached it differently. Kids jumped off the docks into the gray green water and flopped around on floats. A homemade vessel that looked like a floating tiki bar cruised past blaring Jimmy Buffet.

"I love taking the kids to the Marina for ice cream," Tipsy said as they passed the bustling IOP Marina.

"We had some fun times there, too. We used to take the kids in the golf cart when they were little."

Clearly, *we* meant his ex-wife.

He is so not over his divorce.

I wouldn't say you're over it either, sugar.

Yeah, but I'm not stuck on the pronoun "we" to describe the state of me and Ayers.

Past the golf community of Wild Dunes, IOP ended and they were back in the wilds of the Intracoastal. They entered the inlet between Capers Island and Dewees Island, two blots of marshy land encircled by beaches and cut off from the mainland. Dewees housed a small population of hearty islanders, but Capers was wholly uninhabited.

Dozens of boats full of buff dudes and thong-wearing women crowded Dewees's white beach. Throbbing base beats carried across the inlet.

"I remember when there was never anyone on Dewees," Tipsy said. "Now it's party central for the under thirty set."

"I take it you want to head this way?" He pointed to the shore of Capers, where there were nearly as many boats, but kids ran around and families had set up umbrellas and picnic lunches. There were a lot more beer bellies and covered behinds.

"I'd rather. Seems like more our scene. The downside is we'll probably see people we know."

"Why is that a downside?"

"Sometimes this town is just too damn small."

It started out as a typical fun afternoon on Capers Island. People lounged on their boats or congregated in the warm, shallow water. Kids swam in hidden creeks behind the beach. They chucked mud at each other and floated on ancient palmetto tree trunks like little pirates. As Clarice backed the boat toward the beach, she was reminded that Capers wasn't only for families. There were several boats full of happily hammered single people and couples, but they were harmless by the standards of Charleston partygoers. No fistfights. Not too many thongs. Music relatively tame. Only a few gaudy political flags.

The air smelled clean and fishy, with a hint of boat fuel. Tipsy's skin felt tight and dry from the salty water. She wiped her sunglasses on a towel when they fogged up and reapplied sunscreen a couple times. By beer number three, she took a break and downed a bottle of water.

They hung out in the water behind Clarice's boat and chatted with people who strolled past. As predicted, they both ran into friends and acquaintances, but nothing terribly awkward. Thankfully, Lindsey and P.D. were at a wedding, Shelby had taken Brian to her family's lake house, and Will would be sweating his ass off at the soccer tournament in Columbia. The thought of running into them all having fun on the boat together was about as appealing as a bad sunburn.

Tipsy got a few curious looks, but no one asked questions about her appearance with a notoriously eligible bachelor. As for Clarice himself, he kept a respectful distance, until he reached down to pull her up from the ladder.

"Let me help you."

She took his outstretched hand. He tugged harder than needed. She shot into the boat and lost her balance. He caught her with his hands on her waist. Their wet torsos came together and he slid his arm around her back. He pulled her closer. She looked up at him. He'd removed his sunglasses. Curly eyelashes framed his blueish hazel eyes.

"You okay?" he asked, in his ridiculously deep voice. His face was dangerously close to hers, and damn, if she didn't have the urge to kiss him.

She pulled away and swatted him. "Of course I am." She laughed and tried to dispel the tension. "This ain't my first waterborne rodeo."

She walked to the front of the boat and grabbed another water bottle from the cooler. Clarice followed her. She removed her sunglasses and set them on the seat beside her. She wasn't sure why she had jitters. Because it was weird to think of kissing someone other than Will? Because she was afraid people would see her? Or because for a minute, she forgot Clarice Andrews was supposed to be off limits?

"Hey," said Clarice. "I didn't mean to freak you out."

She opened the water and took a swig, hoping to cool off in more ways than one. Another vessel backed into an empty spot a few boats over as she rested the bottle against the side of her neck.

Tipsy gasped.

It was Jimmy's boat. Ayers was driving and Charleston Blonde Kate sat in the seat beside him. The five kids were crowded around the bow.

"Holy hell," she whispered. She almost poked herself in the eye shoving her sunglasses onto her face. She scooted behind the console and tugged her baseball cap down over her forehead, so it touched her glasses.

"Tipsy." Clarice put his hand on her shoulder. "Hey—all good?"

She stepped away from him. "We have to leave."

"Uh, okay. Did I do something?"

"No. Yes. No, but that Cobia that just pulled in? It's Ayers."

Clarice looked over his shoulder. "Damn. So it is. He's going bald? That sucks."

"I don't care about Ayers's freaking hairline. I don't want my kids to see me."

"Oh. Okay. But we're just two friends hanging out, right?"

"Sure. Two friends, *hanging out*. But they've only ever seen me *hanging out* with one other man. My ex-boyfriend Will. I haven't even discussed that breakup with them." She heard the twins laughing and yelling as they ran onto the beach. "Can we go, please?"

"That's fine. I'll pull up the anchors."

Tipsy grabbed the sweatshirt she'd brought in case the ride home got chilly. She clumsily pulled it on over her hat and tucked her hair into the collar. She crept to the bow and lay down on the loungers where no one could see her. She pulled a towel up around her face.

"You're not playing," said Clarice as the anchor whizzed up its automatic pully. "You sure you're not a secret agent? Or a ninja?"

"I'm not a secret agent but I am from Martinville. If you don't drive, I will cut you."

"Let me get a beer for the ride at least."

Little Ayers's incensed voice floated up from the beach. "Dad! Mary Pratt put pluff mud down my bathing suit!"

"I swear, Clarice Andrews, go now or I will cut your ass."

"Yes, ma'am." He shut the cooler and started the engine. "I know better than to risk an ass cutting from a country girl."

They slowly pulled away from the beach. Tipsy stared up at the late afternoon sky through her foggy sunglasses. She wanted to cry. Once again, she asked herself, *how is this my life? Hiding from my kids on a giant boat so they don't see me with a strange man? While Ayers plays happy family with Charleston Blonde Kate?*

If I may interject—

You will anyway, Granna.

Not trying to take up for Ayers, but you played happy family with Will.

Before Tipsy replied, Clarice yelled, "We're clear if you want to come out!"

She sat up and looked around. Capers faded behind them, along with the booming bass from Dewees. She was out of beers, so she opened the cooler and grabbed a White Claw. Normally she hated this sticky sweet stuff, but beggars who need a drink can't be choosers.

"You want to sit back here with me?"

"I'll stay up here," she said. She didn't feel like chatting.

As the boat picked up speed, Blue Oyster Cult's cowbell-driven homage to the Grim Reaper carried over the wind. The lyrics reminded her that Romeo and Juliet were together in eternity. Maybe it was supposed to be a positive message, but Tipsy knew better.

Her eyes welled up. *John and Ivy aren't together in eternity,* she thought. *Neither are Henry and Jane.* They were all kept apart by unexpected circumstances and weird supernatural laws that Tipsy couldn't quite figure out. As for Tipsy's own existence, she wasn't trapped in a haunting, but she sure didn't feel like she'd mastered the rules of life.

Granna cleared her throat. *As I was saying about playing family....*

You're right. Tipsy's sharp voice hurt her own head. *I did play family with Will. It blew up in my face so now I have to tell my kids he's not in my life anymore. Looks like Ayers one upped me. He didn't introduce anyone to the kids until he was talking marriage.*

Good grief. It's not a contest, Tipsy.

It feels like one right now.

You can't always be a perfect parent. Ayers isn't always a bad one. Being a parent is all about making more good choices than bad ones.

Tipsy lay down and pulled the towel over her head again.

For heaven's sake, I did the best I could with your mother. Look how she turned out. Pregnant and unmarried at eighteen, shotgun wedding to Randy Dwayne Denning, who sure as hell wasn't father of the year. But I got you. It all turned out just right. You never know when your flubs are going to turn into wonderful.

I get it, but I feel like no matter what I do—no matter how hard I try to make things better—I end up screwing everything up!

Beating yourself up will definitely not make anything better.

Tipsy nodded under the towel, but while she understood Granna, she still couldn't fathom how she'd gotten to this place. She had to explain another failed relationship to her kids, she was jealous of Ayers, and she was hiding under a towel with a fading buzz on a luxury boat driven by the biggest player in town.

The cowbell kept on dinging, and the song's inherent melancholy lulled her until she dozed off. She sensed the boat slowing down and sat up. They were pulling into Toler's Cove. Sunset was still a couple hours off, but the light had changed to a beautiful cast that covered everything in a layer of pinkish gauze. Like the lord had picked up a celestial makeup brush and dabbed cotton candy blush all over the water, the marsh, and the air itself.

"Hey, sleeping beauty."

"I wasn't really asleep," Tipsy muttered, but the yucky taste in her dry mouth said otherwise. She stood and walked toward Clarice. All that remained of her buzz had faded. She was just tired and heartsore and sort of humiliated.

"Want another drink?" he asked.

"No way. Just water."

He handed her a bottle and set about tossing lines to the dockhands. They secured the boat and moved on to the next yacht. Clarice cracked another beer while she drained her water. She felt better once she washed away the medicinal aftertaste of those few sips of White Claw.

"It's nice now that it's cooled off," said Clarice. "I love this time of evening."

"Me too. I'm sorry. It probably seemed like I was overreacting."

"I get it. I overreact about stuff related to my ex all the time."

They listened to the clink-clunk of the hull against tiny waves stirred up by passing boats. She looked up at him. "You're actually nice for a notorious womanizer."

"Thanks." He brushed her hair away from her face and set his beer in the cupholder. Her pulse picked up as he pulled her toward him. "You look like you need a hug."

She did need a hug, so she let him put his arms around her. Before she realized what was happening, he was kissing her.

"I need to get going." She pulled away from him.

"Hey, it's okay—"

Her temper flared. "No, Clarice. Stop saying that. It's actually not okay."

"I'm sorry. I thought—"

"You think I'm attracted to you? Yeah. I am. Like every other woman you bring out here on this boat."

"Listen. I told you where I stand—"

"You want to add me to your Rolodex of chicks you call up when you want to get laid?"

"That's harsh."

"But it's true."

"We don't have to do anything. But you are right—I'm really attracted to you. I was the second I saw you. And you're very cool. But I don't want anything serious."

She laughed. "Who said I want anything from you?"

"I don't know. Most women do. That's why I try to be straight up."

"You're so *screwed* up."

"Because I know what I want and I don't want? Look, it would be easy to come on strong, romance you, and get what I want and move on."

"You think so?" Tipsy was fuming, even as part of her acknowledged he might be right. She was in an emotionally vulnerable place. Would she have been able to resist Clarice if he had tried to sweep her off her feet? It was infuriating.

"That's how it usually is. Or was, when I first started dating."

"It's not going to be that way with me."

"I don't do that kind of thing anymore. I got into bad situations. Rushed in. Too much drama and I hurt people. So I stopped."

"But women still hang out with you? Like this?"

He shrugged.

"I'm not going there, Clarice. I am not."

"I know you aren't. You've made that pretty obvious." He smiled. "Maybe someday I'll be in a different emotional place."

"Hopefully I will not be available."

"I kind of hope you are."

She gathered her bag and little cooler. "Keep hoping, brother. It will be a long ass time before I'm available to anybody, for anything."

Clarice wanted to drive her home, but Tipsy insisted on taking an Uber. She didn't want to create any opportunities for him to kiss her again. Not with her bed in close proximity.

As she watched Ben Sawyer Boulevard turn into Coleman Boulevard through the window of a beat up Kia, she wondered about Henry's reaction should she invite a strange man into the house. They had a longstanding, unspoken agreement about privacy and she never worried about him spying on her. He was touchingly devoted to Jane in his weird way. The sibling affection between them felt as solid as her living bones, but that only added to her trepidation about hosting any one night stands at the house. Henry might take it as if someone were deflowering his sister. One of Tipsy's paintings might fall off the wall onto the guy's head.

One night stands, she thought. *Has it come that?*

Tipsy thought about her dating life since she left Ayers. She'd had a brief, intense romance with another well-known single guy, one not as rich as Clarice but better looking. When she thought back on the guy Shelby had dubbed St. Dave for his hypocritical professed dedication to a suspect set of Christian values, she wondered why she'd found him appealing. Dave was hot, but in retrospect, he wasn't the brightest bulb and he was terribly conceited. Maybe just the newness of dating again after so many years with Ayers. She bit her lip to keep from giggling when she thought of Dave's ineptitude in the romance department. She contrasted him with Clarice, who was nowhere near as buff or handsome, but was—she hated to admit it—sex on wheels. Everything about him was understated but powerful, from his careless clothes to his too deep voice to his gorgeous yet simple house. Even his honesty about what he wanted. She grudgingly respected him for it. Not many men would have the balls to lay it out there. If that's truly what he wanted, it was ultimately better to tell it like it was than to lead someone on.

She hadn't exactly been a nun dating between Dave and meeting Will, but she'd known better than to pee in her own pool, so to speak. She avoided the legions of single guys in their thirties and forties who lived in Mount Pleasant or on the surrounding islands. She'd purposely stayed below the gossip radar screens. Going to Capers with Clarice Andrews was definitely not flying below the radar. People were going to talk.

Tipsy didn't want to be someone people talked about. She knew enough from Shelby's escapades and the gossip she heard from friends. Everyone in Charleston intersected with everyone else in an incestuous circle of dating, marriage, affairs, and more dating. Lindsey had the right idea. Before she married P.D., she stuck to much younger men for her single lady conquests. No one other than her closest friends ever knew anything about it.

Great. Does this mean I'm back to fraternity parties?

Granna spoke up for the first time in a while. *How about you take a break? A real break? You surely got a lot on your plate right now.*

Tipsy rested her head against the window. *That's looking better and better, Granna.*

The Uber driver pulled up to her house. She trudged up the walkway and climbed the stairs. The doorknob jiggled as she fished for her key. The door opened to a seemingly empty hallway.

"Thanks, Henry," she said.

He was perched on the edge of the sofa in the sitting room where he died. "I've been waiting for you."

"I don't have anything new to tell you since last night. I'm really tired—"

"I found Camden Brewton."

"Damn." Tipsy tried to run her fingers through her wind tangled hair but got no farther than her ears. "At the old Huger House?"

Henry nodded. "I almost gave up. I walked the whole house, including the attic and the cellar. Combed the servants' quarters and the carriage house. Nothing. Then I strolled onto the second floor piazza and there he was. Sitting in a rocking chair like the king surveying his kingdom."

"So you talked to him?" Tipsy was suddenly wide awake.

"Not really, unfortunately."

"Did you try? Where you, like, *nice* about it?"

"Of course. I can be nice when I want to be. I'm not Jack the Ripper."

"So why didn't you talk to him then?"

"He looked at me like we'd seen each other last week. He told me I hadn't aged a bit. When I reminded him that we don't age in this state, he went dotty. Started cackling like the head of a rooster that doesn't realize its decapitated. He said, *Oh, Henry, Henry, what state is that?* Then he disappeared. Clearly, he didn't want to talk."

"Irk! What is it with these avoidant, passive aggressive ghosts? Did you try to, like, grab him? With your mind?"

"I have never grabbed another ghost, thank goodness. I might have throttled Jane when we were stuck here together losing our minds."

"Don't worry about it. I get it. You don't understand how I dragged you out when you were hiding. You're, like, a total novice. A ghost snatching rookie."

"I beg your pardon. If you're such an expert, go grab him yourself!" Henry stood, spun around like an overzealous figure skater, and stormed off through the fireplace.

"Henry! Wait. I'm sorry!" she said, but Henry didn't reappear.

If she wanted to talk to Camden, she would have to figure out how to do it herself. After all, as Pamella had said, she was the boss. Some jobs you just can't delegate.

Chapter 12

Tipsy woke up the next morning to a quiet house and a mild headache, which she blamed on a few gulps of White Claw. She opened one eye and then the other to give herself time to adjust to the light streaming through the window. Once her brain worked, she thought about Camden Brewton. She badly wanted to speak to him. But how? She couldn't walk onto private property and ask to speak with the dead guy on the second floor piazza. She'd have to convince him to come into the yard to talk, as Luisa Bishop had.

But Meeting Street is so much busier than Water Street, she thought. *How can I converse with a ghost without looking sketchy?*

She reached for her phone on the table beside the bed. She read texts from Shelby (Brian had survived his introduction to her cousins, and even gotten some laughs in a raucous game of Cards Against Humanity), and good morning messages from Little Ayers, who had a watch that allowed him to send texts. She swiped on Pamella's name next. DON'T FORGET BRUNCH TODAY! 11:30 AT RED DRUM!

"Ugh." She'd forgotten she'd agreed to have brunch with Pamella and a few other women. At the time, it sounded like a good idea. She should make some new lady friends since she was once again single and her besties were far from it. Besides, given yesterday's failed attempt at a platonic adventure with Clarice, she wanted to avoid men for a while. In the moment, however, it sounded like a lot of work to shower, get ready, and drive a mile down the road to Red Drum, a popular Mount Pleasant restaurant and watering hole.

Tipsy had texted Lindsey before she went to bed, and she got a reply as she weighed her options. Tipsy wanted to be the one to tell Lindsey about her boat day with Clarice, since Lindsey had warned against going out with him. She was also Tipsy's closest divorced friend. Tipsy wanted to talk to her about the weird malaise she'd experienced lately.

LINDSEY: P.D. AND I ARE GOING ON THE BOAT WITH HIS SISTER AND HER HUBS! CAN WE TALK TONIGHT?

Tipsy sighed. Everyone was always on the boat except her. When she did get on the water, drama followed as surely as a big wake in a posted no-wake zone. SURE, NO PROB, HAVE FUN!

I definitely need to keep my friendship options open, she thought, as she put both feet on the floor.

I agree. You need more living friends, said Granna.

Lately the dead are more enjoyable than the living.

She got dressed in a short, strapless gray dress and pulled her hair up in a loose bun. It was too hot for sleeves, long skirts, jeans, or hair on her neck. It was even too hot for a bra, but she had to do something. She tried one of her stick-on adhesive bras—the ones the girls called *Mama's sticky boobs*—but two minutes told her those bad boys would fall off the second she started sweating. The brunch ladies would be offended if one of Mama's sticky boobs landed in their pitcher of mimosas. She switched to a regular strapless and hoped the tight band wouldn't make her sweat through the cotton.

She put on a pair of towering wedges that wrapped around her calf. Another gift from Pamella, who had decided she needed an entire new footwear wardrobe, so she gave a bunch of her old shoes to Tipsy. She looked at herself in the mirror. Will would be about eye level with her nose. *Eat your heart out, Wi-yum,* she thought.

She gave her keys to the valet when she arrived at Red Drum. She strolled through the dark, cozy interior to the outdoor patio. The patio overlooked Coleman Boulevard, but made up for the lack of view with a pretty iron fence, stonework, potted flowers, and a festive outdoor bar. The brunch ladies had secured two round tables with umbrellas.

Pamella waved. "Tipsy! I saved you a seat."

Tipsy scooted the iron chair away from the table and sat down as Pamella introduced her to the six other women around the table. She caught a few names—Jessica and Amy—but the rest ran together like the tasteful blonde highlights on everyone's head. She turned to her right and there was Kim Nowak, the woman she'd met with Pamella at High Thyme. She remembered Pamella's comment about Clarice getting a little something-something from Kim on the side, as well as her own intuition about Kim labeling her as competition.

Good lord, what are the chances I'd kiss a man one day and brunch with a member of his harem the next?

In this town, the chances are pretty good, said Granna.

Should I feel guilty about going out with him?

Tipsy, he's made it pretty clear he's single, no matter what Kim thinks.

I guess so… but ugh. I predict this is going to be awkkkkk-ward!

"Tipsy, hey! Good to see you!" said Kim. She gave Tipsy a bright smile.

"Nice to see you, too."

"Pammy told me all about your painting. She said your work is amazing! I'll have to get a couple of your cards. I know *lots* of interior designers."

"That would be awesome. Thanks." Tipsy smiled back at her. "Your earrings are so cute."

Kim was already talking to the woman across the table, so Tipsy's friendly compliment hung out there unacknowledged. She turned to Pamella. She had a glass of wine and a mimosa, both half-finished.

"We just got here," said Pamella. "We haven't even *order-ed* yet. *Per-fect* timing on your part!"

Tipsy immediately recognized Pamella's precise enunciation as an overcompensation. If they'd just arrived and she was already fighting the slur, she'd been drinking alone this morning. She felt a pang of sadness. It was becoming more apparent that something was not right with Pamella.

"I'm starving," said Tipsy. "What are you having?"

"Oh, I don't know. I had a smoothie this morning. Not hungry."

Pamella's disdain for solid food also alarmed Tipsy. She'd never seen Pamella eat anything more than a cup of yogurt. Even with her own stress and sadness depleted appetite, Tipsy consumed way more solid food than Pamella did. She claimed to be a vegetarian, but Tipsy figured she was more vino-vore than herbivore. "Come on. How about the French toast?"

"Maybe!" Pamella didn't look at the menu.

Kim put a hand on Tipsy's arm. "I heard y'all went to Clarice's house in DeBordieu."

"Yeah. Uh. For one night. We were meeting Pammy's cousin in Murrell's Inlet—"

"Isn't the house lovely? I've stayed there several times." She sipped her mimosa. "Did you notice the countertops?"

"Actually, yes. They're beautiful."

"My idea. His ex-wife put in hideous black granite like ten years ago. He wanted to update the kitchen, so since I have so much experience getting houses ready to go on the market, I helped him out. My guy painted the cabinets and replaced the fixtures but the countertops are the centerpiece. Custom made by a supplier I know *personally*."

"Wow. That's nice of you. It looks great."

"The master bath is next on the list—"

"Y'all." Pamella leaned across Tipsy with her phone in her hand. "Speaking of master bedrooms, Doug will *not* stop texting me. We're trying to decide who keeps the bedroom set. He picked it out, but of course, I bought it." She rolled her eyes. "Like I bought everything."

"Didn't y'all have a pre-nup?" asked Kim.

"Yes, so it's not complicated. Just stuff we accumulated during the marriage. He's in insurance, so he does okay, but he's still paying child support and alimony to his last wife. So now he wants stuff like the sectional sofa and the nice pots and pans."

"I can't imagine going through it twice," said Tipsy.

"Try three times. I should have known better. I was his first relationship after he left his ex. *Everyone* needs a practice relationship after a marriage."

Tipsy thought about Will. He'd dated someone for almost a year before her, but he was her first real relationship. "Why do you say that?" she asked.

"First of all, you can have fun with *almost anyone* for a while if there's attraction and booze involved. Second, even if you think you're in a good place when your marriage ends, *believe me*, you're not. Most people either repeat their old patterns or overcorrect."

Her last statement resonated painfully with Tipsy. She'd already acknowledged that Will and Ayers were polar opposites. Ayers was all excitability and erraticism. Will was so stable sometimes Tipsy wanted to yell into his ear, just to see if he'd jump. She'd gone from one extreme to another. Overcorrection central.

"Shit," she whispered.

"Sound familiar?" Pamella patted Tipsy's knee. "Nothing like a dysfunctional relationship to help put it all in perspective post-divorce. Just don't marry your mistake."

"I don't think there's a danger of that anymore."

"Listen to me with all my *sage advice*, yet here I am dealing with the same old crap. I should have known he'd do this." She typed and hit send. "He's a cheapskate anyway. Moody as hell. Snores. Sometimes I think he's *legit-i-mately* crazy. One day he's an asshole trying to *weasel* me out of my imported *I-tal-ian* bedding, and the next he's begging me to take him back. Maybe he's *bipolar*."

"Everyone says their ex is bipolar," said Tipsy. "If half of marriages end in divorce, can there really be so many bipolar people out there?"

"I don't know, but he's all over the place."

"Maybe he just wasn't ready to get remarried, like you said."

"That could be it," said Kim. "Look at Clarice. He's not even ready to *date* seriously. We had a long talk about it the night of Lucy's birthday." She tapped Tipsy's arm again. "Did I not tell you?"

Tipsy knew what was coming, but she instinctively feigned ignorance. "Tell me what?"

"About me and Clarice, girl! We dated for a while after he and his wife split up. It wasn't the right time, but we're still *such* close friends."

Oh hell, thought Tipsy, *Close friends… I know what* that *means.*

"Y'all must be," said Tipsy, "if you're doing his interior decorating."

"It's so much more than countertops and cabinet door pulls. We have such a deep connection. I've never felt so close to a man. It's something special."

We talking about the same guy? asked Granna. *He struck me as a little too cut and dry to be a romantic poet.*

Henry he is not, Tipsy agreed.

"Sounds like y'all are more than just friends," said Pamella. She subtly tipped one of her acrobatic eyebrows in Tipsy's direction.

"The chemistry is totally there," said Kim. "I know he feels it too, even if he doesn't like to admit it since he's not in the place to get serious. I'm not waiting around or anything. But he'll want to settle down eventually. Don't they all?"

Kim clearly didn't want to hear the message Clarice had been so up front about delivering. Tipsy shifted uncomfortably. Granna was right; she hadn't done anything wrong by going on one date with a famously single guy. Still, Kim seemed nice and Tipsy didn't want to hurt her feelings. Someone was bound to ask her a polite how-was-your-weekend question. She had to decide whether to mention she'd spent the day with Clarice on the boat. She pushed back her chair. "I have to run to the bathroom," she said.

"You haven't even had a drink yet!" said Pamella.

"I have a three kid bladder!"

"I'll order you something."

"No, no. I'm good." Tipsy didn't want to drink any more than she wanted to discuss Clarice Andrews. Kim was obviously in the throes of unrequited love. A love she was grasping for over custom made oyster shell and sea glass countertops.

Tipsy peered into her purse as she walked into the restaurant. Her whole mouth was dry, lips and all, and she needed Chapstick. She bumped into someone as she walked past the hostess stand.

"Oh, uh… hey, Tipsy!" said a vaguely familiar perky voice.

It was Julia, the aesthetician who had been on the boat with Shelby, Lindsey, and Will. She was with a boisterous group of chattering twenty-somethings, women and men. Tipsy forced herself to smile. "Hey, Julia. How are you?"

"I'm great. How are you? The kids?"

She was a short, fair skinned brunette. Her face was bright red. Tipsy wondered if she'd forgot sunscreen on her last boating outing. Bad form for someone who made a living helping other people erase their wrinkles.

"Everyone's great. Thanks for asking."

"Hey—how long is the wait?" A male hand touched Julia's waist.

Tipsy knew those fingers. And the birthmark on his wrist.

She looked into Will's face. He looked back at her with equal surprise. Or up at her, since she was indeed a good three inches taller than him in Pamella's shoes.

For a moment, no one said anything, but Tipsy now understood that Julia's redness had nothing to do with sunburn and everything to do with brunching with Tipsy's recent ex-boyfriend.

"Hey," said Will.

Tipsy said the first thing that came to mind. "You're not in Columbia."

"One-day tournament. Got back last night and the kids went to their mom's."

"Oh."

Julia started chattering. "There's an hour wait for a party of eight. Crazy how busy this place always is, right?"

"Crazy," said Tipsy. "Y'all enjoy your mimosas."

She pushed through the crowd to the bathroom, locked herself in a stall, and leaned against the wall. A sob built up in the back of her throat but she held it in. Her makeup would run and she refused to let Will see her cry in public. She pulled out her phone and texted Pamella.

I HAVE TO LEAVE. SOMETHING CAME UP. I'M SORRY. THANKS FOR INCLUDING ME.

She didn't wait for a reply. She washed her hands and walked into the bar. Will and Julia were deliberating beside the rest of their party.

She figured their conversation was not about whether Will should order a Caesar salad or huevos rancheros. She wished she'd worn shorter shoes. At this height, it was impossible to sneak through the restaurant. She met Will's gaze for a second as he looked over Julia's shoulder.

Tipsy walked outside. She pulled up Will's contact on her phone as she waited for the valet to bring her rental car. Her eyes burned as she looked at the profile photo she'd attached to it. A picture of the two of them from last Halloween, dressed in 1920s flapper and gangster costumes. Of course, Henry had found their attire highly amusing.

She deleted the photo before she talked herself out of it. Then she blocked his number.

She didn't want to hear his excuses, but the saddest part was, even after everything they'd been through, she wasn't sure he'd reach out to offer them.

Tipsy sat on the picnic table behind True Blue a couple hours later. She was waiting for Ivy to come out, but she was also simply waiting. Waiting to feel angry with Will instead of hurt. Waiting to know what to do next, who to call, who she wanted to see. Waiting to understand why her personal life was a disaster and she once again doubted her ability to pay her bills. Unless she figured out what happened to John, or convinced Ivy to move on without him, she wasn't getting her fifty-k, and the rent was literally coming due. Talking with Ivy at least made her feel productive, but she didn't have the energy to yell for the stubborn ghost to come out. She knew Ivy saw her. Tipsy had time before she had to go to the grocery store and the kids got home. So she sat there, waiting for some great revelation about her life, or for Ivy to appear and give her something to do.

It only took about twenty minutes. Ivy walked out from behind the shed and crisscrossed the grass as if patrolling her backyard for mole holes. She finally meandered over to the picnic table.

"Pammy and I went up to Murrell's Inlet and met Saul's son," said Tipsy. She wasn't in the mood for pleasantries. In fact, she was annoyed with Ivy, who was making her life harder. She didn't even know if Ivy's memories would cooperate. What if she found out what happened to John and then it took another six months to figure out Ivy's death? She needed to get started on that mystery, too.

"I didn't know Saul had a child."

"Yup. He was born after you died. He's named after Saul, but he goes by Sandy." Tipsy filled Ivy in on the gist of their conversation with her nephew.

"He sounds like a nice man. Doesn't surprise me. I'm sure Saul made a fine father. He knew what it was like to crave a parent's love. Daddy was always so hard on him and Mama was damn near useless. She cared more about messing around with the little power she had than caring for her son."

"Her supernatural power?"

"Yes. Always dithering around trying to see ghosts. Casting curses on the mailman. Coming up with quack-pot cures for the ague. Any success made her giddy and failure sent her to bed for a week. I worried about her after I married Camden, but there wasn't much I could do. She refused to live with us. Camden wouldn't have tolerated her, anyway. At least Saul could look after her when they all moved to Georgetown."

"Sandy told us Saul and Alma came down to visit right before you died. They were in town when it happened."

"Goodness. I don't remember that. It must be in my—what did you call it?"

"Your blackout zone. The week before your death."

Ivy shivered, as if she were suddenly unaccustomed to her own constant chill. The smell of nutmeg washed over Tipsy, reminding her of Thanksgiving.

"Oh, and Henry found Camden, too."

"My, my. Y'all have been busy."

Tipsy scowled. "Since you won't help us, we have to do what have to do. I looked into John's past again, too." She explained how John tried to convince Camden to help him kill Bubba.

"I can't imagine Johnny wanting to kill anyone, even for me. But now I know more about both our deaths than I ever have." Ivy looked about as sheepish as an itchy wool sweater. "Thank you. I probably should have said that already."

"You're welcome. But can't we start working on the whole story of what happened to you?"

Ivy took a step back. Contrition aside, the sheep still wasn't ready for the shears.

"I wish you'd trust me," said Tipsy.

"Please don't take it too personally. I've never been free with my trust."

"Did you trust your mother?"

"When she was in her right mind. She knew *I* wasn't crazy. Even if it often seemed like she was."

"I had that kind of trust with my Granna. You can't help but feel a kinship with another person who bears this burden."

"That's true. I'm so thankful I had her to explain everything to me. Ghosts. Curses. Potions."

"Curses and potions again? Come on. We don't live in a Harry Potter novel."

"I don't know Harry Potter, but you're talking to a ghost and you don't believe in curses? What do you think all your fancy medicines are, but potions? My mother wasn't very *good* at any of it, but she taught me there's more to the universe than the dead and the living."

"The dead and the living are enough for me. Listen, Ivy. You and I share this strange talent, too. We should understand each other better than most people do. I do want to help you and John. But without your granddaughter's money, I'm moving my three kids out of a place they finally love into an apartment. And believe me, in Mount Pleasant, even apartments aren't cheap."

"I understand, but—"

"Do you? Oh, yes. You're a mother, too. But I've seen pictures of your Bobby. He looked pretty damn miserable to me." As Tipsy talked, the wind around Ivy blew faster, but Tipsy's need to protect her kids overrode her fear of Ivy's power. Let her disappear. Maybe it was time they had a supernatural tug of war. "You might have given him money and good schools and whatever, but you also got yourself killed when he was only twelve. Look at this damn place. Painted haint blue and a garden full of bottle tree weeds. You think Bobby Brewton wasn't fighting his own ghosts?"

The wind stopped. Ivy's skirt went still. Her dark curls drooped.

Her unexpected meekness softened Tipsy's frustration and her voice. "Pamella is your granddaughter. She wants to stay in this house. She wants you to be at peace. If I can help her, I can find a little more stability for my kids, too. A win for everyone."

"Don't you see? I've been missing Johnny for so many years. If I go on without him…"

"I *told* you, you won't— wait." Tipsy decided to send her engine of persuasion down a different track. "How about this? Try to show me something you *do* remember. Henry has done it. So you'll see it's not some magic bullet that's going to send you flying into the afterlife. But maybe… like, try to make it useful. Maybe something about the days after Camden found him?"

Ivy's hair fluttered while she considered Tipsy's offer. Tipsy's hopes rose as it flittered about her head like new ideas. Or old recollections.

"All right. I'll try. Give me a moment." Ivy pressed her fingers into her eyes, as if trying to push a memory to the forefront of her mind. "That's right," she murmured. "Cam found him."

"Yes." Tipsy tried to encourage her. "The papers said Camden found him floating at the edge of the beach in a red and white striped bathing suit."

Ivy laughed and covered her mouth with her fingers.

"What's so funny?"

She offered one shaking hand. Tipsy reciprocated and prayed for a helpful vision. Their palms came together. Ivy flinched, but she pressed on. "It's funny because… well, hopefully I can show you."

———•✕•———

Tipsy is on a dune on one of those random fall afternoons in the Lowcountry that feel like summer's hangover. The tall grass around her is brownish. The remaining yellow and white flowers droop like the tongues of panting dogs. She walks toward the ocean. There's no clear path, but in her current form, she can plow through the shrubs without worrying about burs or thorns or contributing to beach erosion.

She looks around to get her bearings. There is no black and white cow leg of a lighthouse behind her—it won't be built until the 1960s. Across the harbor is a bridge, but it's not the graceful, spacy Ravenel Bridge Tipsy loves. It's old Grace Memorial, the steel and concrete death trap, reaching over the Cooper River in two mountainous humps like an old-fashioned roller coaster.

She's on the south end of Sullivan's Island, near True Blue, but there aren't yet mountains of protective rock jetties and seawalls. It's more like Dewees Island in its quiet beauty. There are a few clapboard houses, but they're tucked behind the dune, children hiding behind their mothers' grassy skirts. The low, squat buildings that make up Fort Moultrie are further down the beach.

Ivy More sits on a blanket to Tipsy's right. She's wearing a pink dress and her hair is pulled up in a ponytail. She's shifting her legs out from under her, as if she's been sitting here for a while and they've fallen asleep. She squints down at a magazine. Black and white photos of glamourous stars—Greta Garbo, Norma Shearer, Clark Gable—stare back, as if they have a secret to tell her. She's singing softly to herself.

A yell makes Tipsy jerk, but Ivy doesn't move. Tipsy sees two figures by the water. One is a man in a Confederate uniform. He's yelling at a black man who wears nothing but a loincloth. The black man's arms are outstretched and he's chanting. He ignores the hysterical white man. Tipsy can just hear what the soldier is saying. "Shut up! Shut up with your darky conjuring! It's driving me mad!" He falls on his knees. "Please make it stop. Please!"

The black man smiles and looks across the ocean, back in the direction where someone ripped him from his family and sent him to this place. He must have died before his captors could further destroy his life. She sees the flash of white teeth in his grin. He's enjoying tormenting the soldier. Tipsy doesn't blame him.

As for Ivy, she sings louder. The soldier runs toward the ocean, as if he can die again and escape the black man's repetitive incantations. He disappears. Once he's gone, the black man lowers his arms. He sits on the beach with his arms wrapped around his knees. Tipsy makes a mental note to try and find this man herself someday. Maybe she can help him.

Tipsy realizes Ivy sings to block out the ghosts. She can't sit on the beach without a way to ignore them. She stops singing her protective tunes once the black man goes silent. She's engrossed in her magazine.

Tipsy raises her head at the sound of crunching sand. A man walks toward Ivy, but he's not dead. He exudes life and vigor as if he's just walked out of the sun itself.

It's John Huger, in all his Viking glory. And by all his glory, Tipsy means all of it. Her mouth falls open. John is naked.

Well, he's not totally naked. He's wearing white 1930's underwear, but they don't leave much to the imagination. Water has darkened his blond hair and its splattered across his forehead. He's still dripping wet. He's not ripped in a modern protein supplements and Cross Fit kind of way. His strength is somehow more real. Not an ounce of fat on him, but every muscle he earned the honest way. Through swimming and playing tennis and probably chopping wood at his rustic island cottage.

He sees Ivy and stops. "Oh. Afternoon, ma'am."

Ivy doesn't notice him. She's too used to ignoring the ghosts that try to talk to her out here. John tries again.

"Ma'am?"

His shadow falls over her. Since ghosts don't cast shadows, she looks up. Her eyes widen and she scoots backward, as if John Huger is far more terrifying

*than dead Confederate soldiers or African slaves. John raises his hands. "Sorry!
I didn't mean to scare you. Your heart's not going to give out on me, is it?"*

*Ivy looks at the ground, her face aflame. "Yes. No. I mean, yes. You
scared me. No. My heart's still beating."*

"I was just out for a swim."

*Ivy's eyebrows are up in arms. They creep up her forehead. "Ah... You
don't say."*

*He looks down at his dripping torso. "I suppose that's obvious. I don't
usually see anyone out here. Y'all live around here?"*

Ivy looks around her, as if John might be seeing her ghosts. "Y'all?"

"You and your husband."

*"Husband?" Ivy looks down at her hands. She's wearing a plain gold
band on her right hand. "This? It was my grandma's. Besides, wrong hand."*

*John turns sideways to get his bearings and smiles again. "It is, isn't it.
Guess I figured a beautiful lady like you would be married."*

*Ivy frowns, as if she senses danger in his pretty compliment. "I'm not
married, but my father don't like me talking to strange men." She stands up.*

"I'm John Huger. There. Now I'm not strange."

*Ivy wipes the sand from her skirt. "I don't mean to be impolite, sir, but
you're standing in front of me near as naked as the day the lord welcomed
you into this world."*

*He laughs. "That is pretty damn strange. Would I be less strange if I
got dressed?"*

"It's a start, but I have to be going."

*"Wait." He jogs toward a pile of clothes and a towel. He runs the towel
over his head and his hair sticks up in salty spikes. He yanks on a light blue
shirt and hops into a pair of tan trousers. Ivy bites her lip to keep from
smiling as he flails around.*

He walks back to her. "Better?"

*"Yes, sir. But why don't you wear a swimming costume? It would make
things a little less strange."*

*"Ach. I hate those things. They look like prison pajamas for elves. They
don't even make them in my size. My daddy bought me one, with red stripes.*

I tried to cram myself into it—" He gives a compelling visual, with his cheeks sucked in and his arms scrunched by his sides. "It went right up my backside."

Ivy bursts out laughing. She covers her mouth. John grins at the sound. Encouraged, he keeps going. "I looked like a giant peppermint stick."

"Stop, please," she says. She wipes her eyes.

"My. You have a wonderful laugh. Why you hiding it?"

She digs her toes into the sand and looks up at him from under her dark lashes. "My father don't think it's ladylike to bray like a donkey."

"It's more like a bleating sheep, really. All around, sort of fluffy."

She giggles again. "Thank you for your kind words, Mr. Huger, but I have to go."

"Wait. What's your name?"

"Ivy More."

His nose wrinkles. "More. Your father's not Bubba, is he?"

"He is."

"I know your house. Right across the Pitt Street Bridge?"

"That's it."

"Ah. I accidentally came onto your father's property on my way to my cottage. My dog busted loose from his leash and chased a squirrel into the yard. Bubba threatened to shoot. Not sure if he was aiming for me or the dog."

"I'm sorry. He's not the friendliest."

"He's a preacher, right?"

"Yes. I should go—"

"Guess he hasn't heard about our lord welcoming strangers and all that. What's the line? I was lost and you gave me food—"

"I was a stranger and you welcomed me. Whatever you did to the least of my brothers—"

"You did to me. Yes. That's right. You're clearly listening to his sermons."

"His whole life is a sermon even if he don't follow his own advice. I don't need to listen to what he says in church."

"So what do you do when you're in church?"

"I think. What do you do?"

"I try to stay awake."

"There are plenty of things you can hear in church if you're quiet that ain't got nothing to do with your preacher." She gestures over the beach. "I hear it out here, too. The ocean. The birds. The wind." Tipsy knows she's thinking about ghosts too, but she's not telling this odd, beautiful man about that. She's not even sure why she's still standing here, much less running her mouth. Her daddy has always said her mouth will get her in trouble someday, but she can't close it. "They all got lots to say."

John watches her as if she's some kind of rare bird he's never seen, even though he thought he knew every creature on this island. "I understand. That's why I swim."

She has to shade her eyes when she looks up at him. He takes a step forward and she takes one back.

He grins again and breaks the silence. "Now I truly can't wear my swimming costume. Those damn colors are so loud, I'd never hear what the ocean is trying to tell me."

She smiles back at him. This time it's wide open and natural. "You really come out here like this, all the time?"

"Yes. Always. Just like this. No hideous peppermint stick sausage casings for me."

Tipsy suddenly sees how this is useful. John has a red and white swimming costume, but it barely fits him and he never wears it. The second Tipsy mentioned he'd been found in it; Ivy knew someone must have put it on him after he died. No small feat, to wrestle John's giant body into a too-small bathing costume. Someone wanted badly to make sure everyone thought he died swimming.

"I'll be here like this tomorrow, if you want to come back and confirm it." He picks up her magazine and her blanket.

She takes them. "Will you now?"

"Yes, ma'am. I promise I'll be here. I'll be here every evening until you come back."

"It's likely to get colder soon." She says as she turns away from him.

"It might, but I'll still be here. You come back and see me, Miss Ivy, and I'll be right here."

She's walking away from him, but she's grinning down at her feet. The grass waves as she passes, although there's no real breeze. The flowers subtly raise their heavy heads to her, as if drinking in her burgeoning excitement. "We'll see, John Huger. Maybe I will."

Chapter 13

On Sunday evening Big Ayers brought his namesake home with an oyster shell cut on his heel. Oyster shells cuts are notoriously prone to infection. Tipsy had to slather the cut with antibiotic cream and wrap it with a bulky bandage. Thankfully it didn't hurt much, but basketball shoes were out, so she couldn't send him to basketball camp on Monday morning. She had to drag him around with her all day. One child was easy and she relished one-on-one time with any of her three munchkins, but she'd spent a couple hundred bucks on a non-refundable week of basketball camp. She could almost see her limited funds disappearing like a poorly aimed airball through a garage window.

She offered to send him over to May Penny and Tripp's to hang out with his grandfather, but since he couldn't get the cut wet in the pool, that didn't appeal to him. She told him he could come with her to Pamella's and ride his skateboard down to the bamboo forest by the Sullivan's Island playground, but she wasn't going to listen to any complaining.

"Your foot better stay wrapped up. Bandage comes off or I hear one *I'm bored* and you're off to Gigi and BopBop's," she said. "You can help BopBop pull weeds."

That was enough to get a promise of complete self-sufficiency out of him.

When they got to True Blue, Little A got going on his skateboard and Tipsy walked into the house. She was lugging a five foot by three foot canvas and had a bag of paints slung over her shoulder, so she had to maneuver through the door sideways and slide down the hallway to the kitchen. When she lowered the canvas, she found Pamella at the kitchen island staring out the back window. For once, she didn't have a Yeti tumbler beside her. The kitchen smelled like coffee.

"Hey!" Tipsy said. "Did you sleep here last night?"

Pamella looked surprised to see her, although Tipsy had made plenty of noise when she came in. "Hey. I did. After brunch we went to Amy's pool to continue the fun." Her voice was unusually flat; her face uncharacteristically still.

"Sunday Funday."

"Yeah. I left my car at her house over by Breach Inlet. I guess someone drove me here. I'm going to call an Uber soon." There were huge bags under her eyes. Her hands trembled as she brought a coffee mug emblazoned with *Bring on the Beans* to her mouth. Tipsy took the seat across from her. She smelled the rank scent of old booze. Pamella didn't seem to notice that her inability to recall who brought her home told Tipsy she'd blacked out.

"You okay?" asked Tipsy. "I know you've been through a lot with the divorce and the issues with this place."

"Me? Of course. Everything is *seriously* fine."

"I can drive you to your car when my son gets back if you want to take a nap."

"No, I'm fine. *Totally.* So, what's your plan today?"

"Now that we chose a final drawing, painting starts."

"Can I see the sketch again?"

Tipsy removed the protective bag and leaned the canvas against the cabinets. The drawing had come together pretty easily. Bobby Brewton sat on the front porch steps with his arms resting on his knees. It was 1970s Bobby, with parted hair and a mustache. He looked out of the canvas with a hint of a smile, like a hippie male Mona Lisa. Pamella traced his chin.

"That's right," she said. "Daddy wasn't one for mugging for the camera."

"Not like this little girl." Tipsy pointed at the figure of Pamella, about eight years old. She grinned so hard that her eyes were slits and her nose had wrinkled up. She was tall and spindly and wore a terry cloth romper. Two pigtails bounced beside her cheeks. She had one hand on a skinny hip and the other thrust into the air like a Broadway actress.

"I've always been the life of the party." Pamella stood and dumped her coffee in the sink. Her phone dinged and she looked at it. "Doug again."

"He's pretty persistent about his pots and pans."

"He likes to cook."

"That's a positive."

"He leaves the kitchen a disaster and I have to clean up."

"I'll trade cleaning up for cooking."

"He's an *asshole*, okay?"

Tipsy was so taken aback she didn't say anything.

"I'm sorry. I have a headache." Pamella opened the wine fridge. Once she saw a few corked soldiers standing at attention awaiting her command, her face softened. She grabbed a Yeti from the other cupboard and filled it with ice. "I'm *really* sorry. Seriously. It was a long day and I didn't sleep well." She pointed at the drawing. "I love it. Thank you. Anything more about Meemaw?"

Tipsy shook her head. "Bits and scraps, but I'm going to go downtown and talk to your grandfather Camden. If I can figure out a way to do it." She explained the conundrum of ghost hunting on private property.

"That's not a problem. The house is empty. It's on the market."

"Oh, wow. Henry didn't mention that."

"The owners live in New York most of the time. So there's still furniture inside but it's, like, empty of *people*. Living people, anyway. I'll ask Kim to take us through."

"Will she want to take the time to do that?"

"We've talked about me buying it back after a few glasses of wine. I'll tell her I'd like to look through it."

"Would you ever buy it back?"

"No. I have a *lot of money*, but that place is probably out of even my price range. Besides, why do I need a ten thousand square foot house? I just want my cottage. Still, when people know you as *rich,* they always overestimate what that *actually* means."

"I suppose it's all relative. I'm going to set up under the big oak if that's okay."

"Of course. Those branches could provide shade in hell."

Tipsy heard the pop of a wine cork and the clink of ice cubes against the shiny side of Pammy's Yeti as she walked into the backyard. She wondered if Pamella was in a hell of her own making. A hell where one drowned in a sea of sauvignon blanc instead of burning.

Tipsy didn't need to look at True Blue to paint it, but being on the property gave her a sense of intimacy with her subjects, both animate and non. Since the painting would be set in the 1970s, the cottage would be white. Photos from that decade also included a few haint blue bottle trees dotting the yard. The oldest trees were works of art in themselves. Bobby Brewton had made them himself, from driftwood and the bottles he accumulated via consumption of their contents or recovery from secondhand stores. Bobby had moved his creations around in the yard over the years. Pamella wasn't sure why. Perhaps aesthetics or to make room for new pieces. Maybe he hoped Ivy would be blown into a bottle if he caught the marsh breeze at the right angle.

Tipsy examined the bottle trees and chose the most ornamental and elaborate to include in the painting. Her pencils and paintbrushes meticulously followed the twisting lines of the branches. The trees were a company of dancers, and she used her mental Polaroid camera to capture their arms frozen in impossible positions. She recalled the precise tone for each piece of glass. Navy blue wine bottles, cobalt medicinal bottles, and bluish green vintage Coca-Cola bottles.

Although none of the ghosts she'd seen over the years were in danger of true entrapment inside a bottle, the desire to capture them struck

Tipsy as harsh. As if ghosts didn't have it bad enough, the living wanted to make them into genies. It took a lot of nerve to try to manipulate the dead, whether with bottles or painted ceilings or whatever.

The need to control everything comes from fear, said Granna. *But then trying to control things is scary itself. Which came first? Who knows?*

A psychological chicken and egg, Tipsy smiled to herself. *If the Piggly Wiggly hadn't worked out, you should have been a therapist.*

Pee-shaw. In my day no one saw a therapist, and we were just fine.

Tipsy thought of Bobby Brewton. He was probably about Granna's age, and surely could have used some therapy, but she didn't say anything.

Little Ayers hobbled around the side of the house in his flip flops with his skateboard under his arm. The bandage had held but he looked pretty darn annoyed with his lot.

"This stinks," he said. "It's so hot. I can't be at basketball camp in the air conditioning and I can't be in Gigi and BopBop's pool, either."

She sat on the picnic table and patted the spot beside her. "You are much put upon, buddy."

"What's that mean?"

"It means you, like, have Mount Pleasant kid problems."

"Yeah. To be worried about camp and swimming pools. Especially when I hurt myself boating."

She smiled at his observation. Even though she herself struggled mightily with her finances, she'd been upfront about teaching her kids about their own privileged position, given Ayers's family. Still, Little A had never brought up the topic himself. While he had as much rambunctious energy as the next almost ten-year-old boy, he was always an old soul. "Next time watch out for those oysters." She fiddled with the bandage. "I think this will hold until we get home."

He looked at the canvas. "Your drawing is nice. Aren't those the statues in the front yard? They're pretty weird. What are they?"

She gave him a succinct version of the story behind the bottle trees. She explained about the haint blue ceiling paint while she was at it.

"Wow," he said. "Those olden days people were really scared of ghosts to do all that. How would the ghosts get in the bottles? Do they get, like, sucked up?"

"I don't know. I guess we'd have to ask someone who has trapped a ghost in a bottle."

"It's kind of sad to think about ghosts stuck in bottles. Makes me want to break them and set them free."

"Let's not do that, please. The bottle trees belong to Miss Pamella and her father made them. But don't worry. I promise there are no ghosts in those bottles." She was the rare mother who could assure her children about such supernatural fears with absolute confidence.

"Is Dad going to marry Miss Kate?"

The abrupt change in topic surprised her. "I'm not sure. Why do you ask?"

"They're kind of like married now. I mean, you always hung out with Mr. Will, but not like Dad and Miss Kate."

"Are you okay with it?"

"I like her and I like her kids. So I guess so. But I worry about where we would live. Dad asked me the other day if I wanted to live in a bigger house with a bigger yard. I said I don't know. I don't want to leave my friends. But he said we'll stay in our neighborhood. And he'll get a trampoline and a zip line. That would be pretty cool, I guess."

It was a lot of guessing, but Little A was old enough to read the writing on the wall.

"I really can't say what your dad will do."

"I heard them arguing the other day. Dad and Miss Kate."

Again, Tipsy trod lightly. "How did that make you feel?"

"Sort of weird. Y'all never fought. Dad gets mad a lot, but y'all didn't like, yell at each other." He smiled. "Just at us when we're being pains in y'all's butts."

She poked him in his side. "I try not to yell, buddy."

"Mom, if I had three kids who are as loud as us, I'd yell too."

She laughed and then said, "Fighting isn't always wrong. Or arguing, anyway. If someone upsets you, you should be able to talk about it. Dad and I didn't talk when we should have sometimes. But you have to fight fair, and respectfully."

"You and Mr. Will don't fight either."

"We have. But not around y'all." It was time to say it. "Actually, Ayers, Mr. Will and I are not dating anymore. We've broken up."

"Oh. So you're not marrying him?"

"No. Mr. Will and I aren't getting married." She wanted to cry, explaining to her son that she'd failed again.

"Why?"

"It's nothing for you to worry about, sweetheart. We're still friends." A fib, since she had no more love for Will than she had for Big Ayers at the moment. "But we won't be seeing him and the girls as much."

"Okay."

"Does that bother you?"

"Not really. He's nice, but sometimes he's kind of boring. Dad might be louder but he's more fun." He looked up at her. "Sorry, Mom. Maybe that was, like, mean to you."

"No, honey. You're probably right." Even her kid knew she'd overcorrected.

"M.P. and O-liv will be bummed out though."

"Hopefully we'll be able to get them together with Rosie and Ella sometime soon." She left it vague, as she planned to do when she told the girls. Now that she'd told Little A about the breakup and gotten past the initial sadness and embarrassment, she felt better. She decided to talk to the girls about it as soon as possible.

Little Ayers rubbed his arms. "It's so hot today but it's chilly under this tree."

Tipsy looked over her shoulder. Ivy stood behind them. She watched Little Ayers with those glimmering ghost tears in her eyes.

"Listen, buddy, if you want to talk to me about anything that's going on with your dad, or me, or anyone—"

"Even BopBop's bald head that's getting balder?"

"Yup. Even sweet BopBop's bald head. Just say, *hey, mom, let's talk,* and I'm talking. Okay?"

He nodded.

"Why don't you go inside and play on your Switch? It's in my purse in the kitchen. You've been outside sweating long enough."

"Awesome." Ayers loved to carry that Nintendo portable game player around. Truth be told, there were times Tipsy was damn grateful for it.

He jumped off the table and hop-skipped into the house. Ivy walked around to Tipsy's side of the table.

"What a beautiful child," she said.

"Thank you. I'm blessed to have three of them."

"I should have asked you about your family. How rude of me."

"No worries. I have Little Ayers—he's named after his dad and granddad—and twins. Mary Pratt and Olivia Grace. They're seven."

"Goodness. You are a busy lady. Raising children. Painting pictures. Releasing ghosts and solving old mysteries. The boy looks like you. Do the girls look like your husband?"

"They do look like him, but we're divorced." She waited a beat for Ivy to look offended, but she merely nodded.

"Wow. The idea of divorce thoroughly scandalized Jane."

"My family would have been the same. But not me. Honestly, sometimes I prayed South Carolina would allow divorce so Camden would leave me for another woman."

"If you had lived until 1949 you could have been rid of each other through divorce instead of death. That's when South Carolina finally caught up to the rest of the country and legalized it."

Ivy smiled. "If I'd known that, maybe I would have watched my step on the dock."

"Haha. You ready to show me another memory? Since we're being friendly again."

"Have you talked to Camden yet?"

"No. Hopefully in the next few days. Once Pamella can get me into the Huger House. We're going to sneak in with a real estate agent—someone who wants to sell the house for the owners. Then I have to find him in that giant house and see if I can get some answers out of him without the agent thinking I'm a lunatic. Or being caught on the security cameras talking to myself. Or—"

"I'll let you look into my mind once you talk to him."

"Why?"

"If you're willing to risk all that, you're serious about finding out what happened to John."

Tipsy pointed after Little Ayers. "That kid might be moving with his dad. If it means I can get the money to stay where I am, and my kids can stay put, I'll risk pretty much anything."

Tipsy had to work at the GQB the next day. Whether Little Ayers liked it or not, he was going to May Penny and Tripp's. Tipsy dropped him off at their house on Sullivan's with extra bandages and the tube of antibiotic cream. On the way to camp, she bit the bullet and told the girls about her breakup with Will. To her relief, they took it well. They expressed the expected disappointment in not seeing Ella and Rosie, but as planned, Tipsy told them it wouldn't be forever. They seemed satisfied with her answer, even if Tipsy herself was not sure of its truthfulness. They were young. Hopefully time would be kind, and help them forget the loss faster than Tipsy would forget it. Her load felt lighter with the breakup out in the open. At least if they asked questions, the background tableau was complete. She'd just have to work in the human element as best she could.

She dropped the girls at volleyball camp at the recreation center off Long Point Road. After taking such a wide tour around her ass to get to her elbow, she raced over the Ravenel Bridge to the GQB. She got a text from Pamella as she sat in traffic on East Bay Street.

PAMELLA: HEY LADY. KIM CAN TAKE US THROUGH THE HOUSE ON THURSDAY EVENING.

TIPSY: OK GOOD. I'LL GET A SITTER. OR MAYBE TRIPP CAN WATCH THEM.

Tipsy wanted to get in sooner, but given her busy week, it was for the best. Shelby needed her to work at the GQB on Tuesday, Wednesday, and Thursday, and she still had to work on Pamella's painting, sketch other paintings, and manage the kids.

It's a lot easier solving a ghostly mystery when the ghosts live with you, said Granna.

Right. Paying a sitter to watch my kids while I stalk ghosts is not in my budget. She willed the lights to stay green as she zipped through them. *I'll miss them, but this trip to Florida is a blessing in disguise.*

Tipsy parked in the garage and pulled her hair up in a ponytail before speed walking to the GQB. She pulled out her key, but then she saw Shelby through the window. She opened the door. The bell greeted her with a pleasant *ding-dong*. Nothing like the *gong-gong-gong-gong* it always hysterically let off when Shelby blasted in and out of the gallery.

"Hey," Shelby said. "I got everything prepped already, if you can restock the toilet paper."

"Yeah. Sure. Where are you heading today?"

"Brian's sister and brother-in-law are staying on Kiawah. We're going out there for a couple days."

"Ah. You didn't mention that." Come to think of it, Tipsy and Shelby hadn't been texting as much as usual. Tipsy hadn't thought to text her about the weekend's events. A weird feeling.

"Oh. I guess I didn't think about it. It's stressful meeting her. They have four kids and are supposedly, like, the perfect family."

"Sisters are only a little less intimidating than mothers. Meeting Mimi scared me back in the day, but I adore her. Maybe it will be the same for y'all."

"I hope so." Shelby's phone dinged. "Hold on—it's Brian. He wants me to make something to take out there. Damnit. His family are all health food nuts. I don't think my Gram's mayonnaise laden potato salad will go over well."

"What about a corn and tomato salad? I have a recipe saved on my phone. It's pretty healthy."

"Will you send it to me? That would be a lifesaver." Shelby started toward the door. "By the way, how was your weekend?"

Tipsy didn't feel like talking about any of it—Clarice, Will, Pamella's drinking, Little A's injury or his questions about Ayers getting remarried. Another peculiar development. Usually she told Shelby everything. "Okay, I guess."

"Did you go to Capers with Clarice Andrews?"

"Uh, yeah. Who told you?"

"You remember Andrea, my neighbor down the hall?"

"Sort of." Shelby lived in one of the swanky condos at the foot of the Ravenel Bridge. She'd hosted a few parties for the neighbors on her floor. The name Andrea called to mind a picture of a blonde woman who had stood out from the other blondes because she wore her hair in an unusually short, spiky style. She was nice and chatty, and sexy in a Billy Idol sort of way. "Is she the yoga instructor? Whose husband left her for another man?"

"Right. She passed y'all on the boat somewhere. She said y'all looked pretty cozy."

"I don't know about that. I sat beside him. She must have the eagle eye to be able to tell how cozy we were. Why does she care?"

"She's gone out with him a bunch of times."

"Right. He's got a few of those. Poor thing. I hope she realizes she's one among many."

"She sent me a bunch of texts asking if y'all are dating. I couldn't tell her anything since I didn't *know* anything. She said she mentioned going out with him when y'all talked at my wine tasting."

"If she did, I don't remember. That was like four months ago. I didn't even know him. I barely know her. If she thinks she's got something going on with him, she'd better talk to him about it. Not gossip about what I may or may not be doing."

"Don't get all mad."

"Look, I'm sorry she's fallen under his spell, but I still think it's bizarre she'd text you and ask about it. Good lord."

"Whatever his deal is, apparently she's into him. She wants to know." Shelby set down her purse. "You know what I think is odd, though? You didn't tell me you were going out with him. In fact, I looked at my texts and I've barely heard from you all week. My messages about our lake house trip got one thumbs up emoji, a couple ha-ha's, and a freaking LOL."

"Sorry. I've been busy."

"Kind of hurt my feelings you didn't say anything about Clarice."

"Like you didn't say anything to me about taking the boat out for Julia's birthday and taking Will?"

"Huh? Lindsey and I wanted to take her out since she gives us discounts all the time. You were working that day. We took P.D.'s boat and he invited Will."

"You didn't think it might hurt *my* feelings if you went on the boat without me and took Will along with a bunch of twenty-something single women?"

"I guess. I'm sorry. But it was harmless. I don't remember him even talking to any of them."

"Now you sound like Lindsey. He didn't flirt with anyone at Hall's… big freaking deal. We all know Will is pretty reserved. He's not going to throw himself at anyone. But he apparently flirted with Julia enough to have brunch with her at Red Drum yesterday."

"No way. They did? She told me she wasn't interested in him."

"Wait. What?"

Shelby shifted uncomfortably. "She texted me after her birthday asking questions about Will. If y'all were still dating. I said y'all just broke up and it's kind of weird right now."

"*Right.* I get it. Everyone's a text warrior in this town."

"It did cross my mind that she was fishing for info, so I asked if she was into him. She said, *no, no, he's too old for me. I'm just being nosy, haha.*"

"Nosy. Sure. She's a regular Pinocchio. If it makes it any better, he told me he wasn't interested in her, either. So their long ass noses will get in the way when they make out."

"I'm sorry—"

"So now they're dating?"

"I don't know. I can text Brian—"

"Do *not* do that. Don't. I'm not going to be like Andrea. Creeping around for text information. *Eyes without a fa-ace.*" She burst out laughing at her own Billy Idol reference, but Shelby looked at her like she'd lost it.

"Are you okay?"

"No, Shelby. Actually, I'm not." She giggled again, and there was a hint of hysteria in it. "Jimmy asked me to start paying rent, so I may have to move."

"Oh, damn."

"And my heart has been broken into a million pieces! But thanks for *finally* asking if I'm okay."

"What's that supposed to mean?"

"Nothing. Forget it."

"Tipsy, don't give me that bullshit. If you want to say something to me, say it."

"Okay, fine. I will. It's kind of shitty of you and Linds to carry on all the time with P.D. and Brian without me and include Will all the time."

"We're not carrying on all the time. Lindsey and P.D. are married and Brian and I are still dating. Will is their best friend, so he's been around a few times."

"Y'all haven't asked *me* to do anything without *him*." It sounded childish, but Tipsy didn't care.

"It's not like we planned it. It just happened. You've been working a ton and you always have the kids—"

"Ayers had them two weekends in a row!"

"You didn't tell me that! I didn't even know you were kid free until freaking Andrea texted me about your romantic cruise with Clarice!"

"It was not a romantic cruise—"

"Whatever! If you want to shack up with Clarice to revenge screw Will, have at it!"

"Oh good lord, Shelby."

"Don't complain when you get your heart broken. Lindsey told you he's bad news."

"Really? Really?" The painting behind Shelby's head featured a flock of seagulls lifting from the sand, as if frightened off by Tipsy's increasingly shrill voice. "You're going to tell me you don't want to listen to me complain, after all the years I listened to your dysfunctional crap? Now you're finally in a decent relationship and you're all high and mighty?"

Shelby's hands balled into fists at her side. "You made plenty of your own screwed up relationship decisions. Hello! You married Ayers!"

"Oh, yeah? Well—well—"

"You're pissed because Lindsey and I are both happy right now, and you're miserable. How do you think I felt all those years? Huh? Watching you have your babies and play Supermom with Ayers's postcard perfect family? Happy holidays on Sullivan's Island? Cute house with double decker front porches? Birthday parties and trick or treat and Elf on the goddamn Shelf? You think I didn't want to tell you to get over yourself when you were depressed after the girls were born? Or when you claimed you couldn't paint?"

"Screw you, Shelby. How dare you talk to me about perfect families or tough lives with your livin' in a bubble, Pinegrounds School, downtown money ass and your two doting parents who have given you everything your whole damn life. *Grow up.*"

They both went silent, as if stunned by the exchange. The figures in the paintings were suddenly embarrassed, like neighbors who had overheard way too much of a backyard argument.

"I have to go." Shelby wiped her eyes.

Tipsy's own lip trembled. "Okay. Go. I'll handle things here."

"Yeah. Thanks. Don't forget the toilet paper."

"Right." Tipsy turned toward the desk. For once, when Shelby left, the bell barely made a sound.

Breakfast for dinner was Tipsy's go-to option on nights she was too tired to do anything else. She usually made it further into the week before resorting to breakfast, but after the draining fight with Shelby, she couldn't manage anything more than eggs, bacon, and Pillsbury biscuits. The GQB had been unusually busy and she'd barely gotten anything done. At least she didn't have to run to Sullivan's. Big Ayers had gone over to his parents' house to fish off the dock with Little A and was bringing him home. A small blessing, as she hoped to set up the easel on the front porch later and work on a sketch for a new painting of the guitarist from DeBordieu. Quick, easy dinner was a necessity.

She stood at the kitchen and cut up a pineapple as the girls thundered down the stairs. M.P. took in the carton of eggs on the counter. "Yay! Breakfast—" She pointed at Tipsy to finish the sentence.

"It's what's for dinner!" said Tipsy. "What are y'all up to?"

"We're going to watch a show. We're sooooo tired." O-liv hung her arms at her sides and dragged her feet through the kitchen like a small, female Jacob Marley.

"Volleyball was really hard," said M.P. "And it's like, sooooo hot outside."

Tipsy smiled at their pre-tween drama. "Go ahead. Y'all earned it."

"Are you making pancakes, Mama?" asked Olivia Grace.

"Not tonight, honey. Biscuits are our bready breakfast product of choice."

"Darn. I miss Miss Kate's pancakes. Yum."

Tipsy's smile froze on her face like an early spring caterpillar in an unexpected frost. "Y'all like biscuits, too."

"Yuppers! M.P., I want to watch Disney."

"But Nick Junior has better shows—"

"One of each," said Tipsy. She wiggled her lips until her expression thawed. "That's it."

"We'll have pancakes all the time when we move into the new house," said O-liv.

"I might get sick of them though. Like I get sick of peanut butter and jelly for lunch every day at camp."

"Hey. Who's moving into a new house?" asked Tipsy.

"Daddy says we'll move when he and Miss Kate get married."

"Ah. I see. When did y'all talk about that?"

"When me and O-liv were riding with Daddy to Lowe's."

"Was Ayers with y'all?"

"No. Just us." Mary Pratt grinned. "We get to be flower girls! I can't wait—"

O-liv took her arm. "M.P., let's go watch the show now."

Tipsy walked toward them. "It's okay O-liv. Y'all can talk to me about it. Being flower girls will definitely be cool."

"But does it make you upset if Daddy marries Miss Kate?" O-liv asked.

"No! I just wanted to make sure y'all all know what's going on. I don't think Ayers has heard about this yet. So why don't y'all let Daddy tell him, okay?"

"Sure, Mama. I'm sorry I'm talking about it," said M.P.

"No, honey. Please. Don't be sorry. You didn't do anything wrong. Y'all go watch your show."

Tipsy grabbed the container of biscuits from the fridge. She pulled at the tab until the cannister exploded in her hand. Sort of like the resentment between her and Shelby, or the anger toward Ayers that swelled by the second.

You going to reach out to her? asked Granna.

No. I can't deal with her drama right now.

I'd say the drama was mutual, sugar. What about Ayers?

His drama has to be addressed.

She thought about what she wanted to say to Ayers as she slapped the biscuits on the tray. She got more annoyed with each splat of dough. If Ayers truly planned to get married, she wished he'd discuss those plans with her so she knew what to tell the kids. Tipsy breaking up with Will, who they basically saw every other weekend for playdates, paled in comparison to Ayers getting married and them moving into a new house. One would think he'd talk to all of them at the same time so they fully understood the situation. Nope. It was all about Ayers and his convenience.

Pamella's warning about backing him into the corner and shotgun weddings started creeping in, but the front door slammed and cut off those thoughts. Little A walked into the house. He was sweaty and red in the face. She approached him. "Hey, buddy. Did you wear a hat while you were fishing?"

"No."

She tilted his chin up. "You're sunburnt."

"Dad and I forgot sunscreen."

"Okay. Go get some water. You look like a rung out sponge." She walked to the front door. Ayers was still in the driveway, on his phone as usual. Tipsy opened the door and jogged toward his truck, waving. Bass blasted through the closed truck doors. Not his usual country music. Ayers was in a festive mood.

He saw her and rolled down the window. Lady Gaga's boisterous voice leapt out of the cab. She caterwauled about how God made no mistakes. As for Gaga, she was on the right track, baby. Under other circumstances, Tipsy might have laughed at the idea of subtly homophobic Ayers be-bopping away to an LGBTQ anthem in a truck purchased by his conservative Southern father's company. He was typically atypical, as always.

"Hey. Sorry about Little A's nose," he said, as Gaga howled. "I spaced sunscreen."

"Right. I'll put aloe on it."

"Great, thanks." He went back to his phone, but her lingering presence cut through his texting. "What's up—you need something?"

For a second, Tipsy paused. She still got anxious when she confronted Ayers about anything. Then she remembered Shelby's accusation—*Hello! You married Ayers!* That she had. Pamella's advice aside, she had to deal with him.

"The kids all talked to me about moving and you getting married. What's the deal?"

"I already told you. Kate and I are getting married."

"Don't you think it's a little soon for that?"

"I'm forty, Tipsy. I know what I want."

"Are y'all engaged?"

His face reddened. "Not officially. Yet. Still working on some stuff."

"For the kids' sake, maybe work on your stuff before you talk to them."

"It's none of your business."

"They're my kids, Ayers. It is my business. I got Little Ayers asking me nebulous questions about what you might be planning while the girls are talking about it all like it's cold concrete. Have you even told them the same thing?"

"I haven't had a chance to talk to Ayers yet—"

"What about fishing tonight?"

"Never came up."

"He's nine. It's not going to *come up. You* have to bring it up and talk to him about it. Like you did with the girls on the way to Lowe's, apparently. Sparkly flower girl dresses and all."

"I'll talk to him soon."

"Moving is a huge deal to them. They've lived in that house their whole lives. You can't toss that kind of thing out there without any context—"

"The girls are excited about us getting married!"

"They don't even know what it means beyond flower girl dresses and pancakes!"

"What's the *real* problem here? You broke up with your man and now you're pissed I'm in a relationship."

"Why does everyone think I'm pissed they're in a relationship? I'm glad you're happy. I just want what's best for the kids."

"Of course you know what that is."

"I know that according to the judge, it's not living with someone you're not married to—"

"You gonna file an action in the court? Go ahead. Try it!"

"And common sense says it's not marrying someone you barely know. Y'all just met, Ayers. Come on. You know it's too soon to know if y'all are right for each other."

"You and I dated for five years before we got married! Clearly, time doesn't mean much."

"We were just kids ourselves—"

Ayers opened the car door and got out. He was so big. Not as tall as John, but wider. "Why can't you be happy for me, huh? You're the one who left me. You ruined my life. You wouldn't even try to work it out. Now I'm trying to create a family again and you're intent on ruining that, too."

"That is not what I'm doing—"

"I loved you, Tipsy."

"You didn't love me for years. You only decided you loved me when I asked you to move out."

"Maybe I didn't show it very well, but I did."

"I don't want to rehash this stuff. Jeez. I just want you to make good decisions for the kids."

"I've tried to do that from the beginning of all this bullshit! I'm not perfect, but why do you always have to make me the bad guy?"

Gaga yelled over their arguing. "*Baby, I was born this waaaaaay...*"

Tipsy opened her mouth but Ayers held up both hands. "Screw this." His lapse into warped nostalgia or regret or whatever it was disappeared. The expression she knew all too well replaced it. This Ayers wasn't worried about being the bad guy. He'd do whatever it took to win, as he always had. He was, to quote Gaga, born this way.

He got back in the truck, slammed the door, and poked one thick finger in her direction. "You want to mess with me, bring it on. I dare you."

Gaga had moved on to *Bad Romance*, which seemed more apropos. Tipsy ignored his taunt. Instead, she said, "You really have a Lady Gaga playlist?"

"I *love* Gaga," he said. "I don't know how you were married to me for all that time and don't know that. Thank God we're divorced."

He rolled up the window, put the truck in reverse, and peeled wheels backward down the driveway. If someone had been walking down the sidewalk, that someone would be as flat as Miss Kate's famous pancakes. Fortunately he took off down Bennett Street without killing anyone.

Tipsy walked back into the house. The kids lounged on the sofa in the den. The fan whirred overhead. Tipsy squinted up at it. She didn't remember turning it on.

"I did it," Henry said from over her shoulder. "I thought it would help drown out their father's noise."

She nodded her thanks. Henry walked toward the television and sat primly on one of the club chairs. She took a moment to observe her children and her dead roommate watching television together before dragging herself into the kitchen.

Her biscuits sat in starchy blobs on the tray. They mocked her with their quasi-homemade blandness. She stuck the baking sheet in the oven. She cracked eggs like broken hearts, broken families, broken friendships. Will, Ayers, Shelby. She thought of Henry and Jane, and John and Ivy. She banged a few more eggs on the edge of her stainless steel bowl.

She beat the eggs like they'd done her a personal wrong. They were fixing to be the fluffiest eggs she'd ever made. Strips of bacon sizzled in the pan as she removed the biscuits from the oven. She stuck them on a plate and only burnt her fingers once. She called the kids in for dinner once she had everything on the table. She stood by the counter and added pineapple chunks to plates or topped off orange juice. She still didn't feel like eating. Not even bacon tempted her. They finished and brought their plates to the sink, so she sent them upstairs to shower and get ready for bed. The lonely remaining biscuit slightly mollified her. The kids had scarfed up the rest. Miss Kate's pancakes had some competition from the explosive cannister of dough. She cleaned up, wiped down the table, and turned to her phone. She had a text from Lindsey.

HEY HONEY. I HEARD ABOUT WILL AND JULIA. I KNOW YOU'RE HURTING SO BAD. I'M AS SURPRISED AS YOU ARE. ALL I HAVE TO SAY IS HE BETTER BE CAREFUL DATING A MUCH YOUNGER WOMAN. WAIT TILL SHE WANTS KIDS! CALL ME IF YOU WANT TO TALK. LOVE YOU!

Tipsy sat at the table and reread the message. She knew Will didn't want any more kids. Yet he was getting involved with a woman who wasn't even thirty. Of course they just started dating, but if he kept going with it and Julia did want her own children, it was actually selfish on his part to waste her time.

She'd always thought of Will as Mister Nice Guy. But maybe he was as egocentric as Ayers, who apparently considered her an emotionally abusive spouse because she hadn't recognized his dedication to Lady Gaga. Never mind that she'd managed and tolerated his moods and temper for sixteen years without complaint. Will was a different version of the same self-centeredness, the Mac to Ayers's PC. More user friendly but still prone to viruses. She grabbed her phone.

"Who are you sending texters to?" Henry stood on the other side of the kitchen.

"Texts. Not texters. I've told you a thousand times." She scrolled through her contacts and found Will's name. No picture anymore but the contact remained. No point in deleting it since his was one of the few numbers she'd memorized in the past five years. She unblocked him.

"You look very upset," said Henry.

"I am upset. I got in a fight with Shelby today. Then I got in a fight with Ayers."

"Are you about to get in a fight with someone else?"

Tipsy hit *send message* on Will's contact. The text box opened up, a blank expanse waiting for her to fill it with her vitriol.

There's something about texting. It allows the sender to say all manner of things she would never say in person. The urge to communicate all her hurt and her frustration in this simple, convenient way consumed her. She didn't have to call Will or go to his house. She didn't have to look him in the face or hear his side. She didn't have to be embarrassed by her own tears or her gasping, cracking voice or her blotchy face and swollen eyes. Distance and a wall of technology protected her. She started typing. Her fingers flew over the letters like a piano virtuoso playing Stravinsky at the Vienna Opera House.

YOU REALLY ARE THE WORST. Send.

OR MAYBE I'M NAIVELY OPTIMISTIC. Send.

ALL THIS TIME I THOUGHT YOU COULD BE MORE THAN YOU ARE, BUT YOU'RE A SMALL-MINDED PERSON WHO CAN'T STAND ANYTHING THAT ROCKS YOUR BOAT. YOU HAVE THE EMOTIONAL DEPTH OF A SHALLOW CREEK AND YOU STILL SUCKED ME IN. YOU'RE PSYCHOLOGICAL PLUFF MUD. Send.

I HOPE YOU HAVE A FABULOUS TIME BRUNCHING AND BOATING AND BARHOPPING WITH MISS JULIA. SHE'S IN FOR IT ANYWAY, SINCE YOU'LL SEEM LIKE THE NICEST GUY SHE'S EVER MET BUT IN REALITY YOU DON'T HAVE ANY STRONG FEELINGS GOOD OR BAD ABOUT ANYTHING. DO YOU EVEN HAVE A PULSE? Send.

More kept coming to her as she typed and sent and typed and sent.

HOW DARE YOU TELL ME YOU WANT TO BE MY FRIEND AND ASK ME TO SPEND TIME TOGETHER WITH THE KIDS. YOU THINK I'LL BE YOUR FAKE FAMILY WHEN IT SUITS YOU. MEANTIME YOU'RE CHASING SOME CUTE YOUNG THING LIKE YOU CAN HAVE YOUR JUICE BOXES AND YOUR JELLO SHOTS AND SLURP THEM ALL DOWN, TOO.

Suddenly, Will replied. I GUESS YOU NEED TO GET SOME THINGS OFF YOUR CHEST.

TIPSY: SCREW YOU, WILL. YOU INFILTRATED MY ENTIRE LIFE. IF YOU DIDN'T WANT EVERYTHING THAT CAME ALONG WITH IT, YOU SHOULD HAVE BACKED OUT LAST SUMMER. YOU KNEW EXACTLY WHAT YOU WERE GETTING INTO. I HATE YOU.

WILL: JUST STOP TIPSY. I DON'T NEED THIS CRAZY DRAMA.

TIPSY: YOU BROUGHT IT ON YOURSELF. AFTER THE WAY YOU'VE JERKED ME AROUND WHILE I'VE BEEN SO STUPIDLY NICE ABOUT IT YOU CAN LISTEN TO MY CRAZY DRAMA. THEN YOU CAN GO GOSSIP TO YOUR SIMPERING LITTLE GIRLFRIEND ABOUT HOW TERRIBLE I AM AND I WON'T GIVE A SHIT.

WILL: NOW YOU'RE INSULTING JULIA. DON'T MAKE ME DISLIKE THE PERSON YOU ARE.

Tipsy stared at the phone as if Will had screamed out of it into her face.

"Tipsy. You're very pale. Maybe put down the phone."

She held up one hand. "No, Henry. I'm almost done."

THE PERSON I AM IS THE PERSON YOU'RE TOO MUCH OF A COWARD TO BE WITH. AS FOR JULIA, I FEEL SORRY FOR HER. HAVE A NICE LIFE, WILL GARRISON.

Before he replied, she blocked him again. She dropped the phone into a box of palmetto flag cocktail napkins.

Henry waved a hand over the chair beside her and it scooted away from the table. He sat down. "That seemed like quite the violent, silent row."

"That's a good way to put it." Tipsy's heartbeat slowed as if she'd come to the end of a long run and started her cooldown walk.

"Do you feel better? I sometimes did after I lost my temper. But that relief was often fleeting."

"I feel better for the moment. That's all I can handle right now."

"All this fighting is unlike you."

"Yeah. But some of it probably needed to be said." She reread her messages to Will. Less than five minutes later, some of them already surprised her. The first hints of embarrassment crept from her tingly fingertips toward her heart. She liked to think of herself as above such hysterical ranting, but she'd gone all text warrior in her own right. "Wow. Bitch-o-rama."

"Wi-yum has been leading you in circles for months. I don't know what exactly you said—"

"I called him psychological pluff mud."

"Ah. That's rather poetic. Anyway, you've been very patient with him. This man owes you a good rant."

"Maybe." She stood. "I'm going to get the kids tucked in."

"Why not leave your phone down here tonight?"

"That's an excellent idea." Tipsy walked up the stairs. She tucked the kids in, got ready for bed, and slid between the sheets. For a second, she reached for the bedside stand. She opened her eyes. The empty charger was oddly comforting. It reminded her of the days when cell phones were not as important, and her problems seemed less important, too.

———※———

Tipsy and Ayers's new apartment isn't really new, but that doesn't make it any less novel to her. It's in an old house in downtown Charleston's Ansonborough neighborhood, on Society Street. Given her humble roots, it amuses Tipsy that she lives on a street whose very name insinuates class distinctions. She is twenty-three years old, and she and Ayers have been married for two months.

Her new mother-in-law, May Penny, gave them some hand-me-down furniture, and Tipsy is proud of how she made it work. Tipsy's own art is all over the place, including her beloved charcoal drawing of two appaloosa horses hanging over the fireplace. The self-portrait from her high school freshman year is in an alcove by the front door. A cute sitting room is separated from the skinny kitchen by May Penny's old dining table and chairs. Their one bedroom has a real bed in it, not just a mattress on box springs. Tipsy hung curtains across the French doors that open onto the second floor piazza. A lovely painting spot in decent weather.

The best thing about the whole place, however, is the walled-in section of the piazza off the kitchen. The perfect little studio. She keeps all her paints and supplies in there. When it's too hot or rainy she works in the studio, in the air conditioning with the rain pattering on the roof. The murky paned windows enclose a lovely view of thick live oak branches and dangling Spanish moss.

I finally have a grown up place, she said to Granna.

Granna's silent approval surrounds her like a hug. On this fine morning, she'd already been painting on the piazza for two hours, but Ayers was still asleep. He finally emerges in his boxer shorts and a tee-shirt with his hair a mess and a cup of coffee in one hand.

"Morning, sleepyhead," Tipsy says. "Y'all were out late, huh?"

"Yeah. Too late." *He walks up behind her and puts his arms around her. She giggles when he nibbles the back of her neck.* "But I think I made some good connections."

Ayers has recently taken a pharmaceutical sales job. Tipsy is tentatively hopeful the new gig will stick. He'd worked for his dad since he got back from New York. She knows his pride doesn't love the family business arrangement. So she's glad he's out making connections, but she's confused about who he's making them with. "Where did y'all go?"

"Uh, let's see. The Griffin. And then A.C.'s."

"Those are dive bars. Are there a lot of GI docs hanging out there?"

He stiffens and his voice becomes defensive. "No. But you know how it is in this town. Everyone knows everyone."

"What about that guy your dad said he'd introduce you to—"

"What are you working on?" *Ayers peeks over her shoulder. She isn't sure if he's genuinely interested or he wants to change the subject. She hopes it's the former. Ayers used to be fascinated by her work, but she can't remember the last time he asked her about it. They'd even gotten into a fight when she mentioned taking a weekend trip to New York City with Shelby and Mrs. Patterson to meet art dealers. Unless Mrs. Patterson paid for it, he didn't think they could afford it. He always had money for whatever he wanted to do, like his hunt club membership, but somehow that seemed irrelevant.*

All this flashes through her mind in about two seconds, and she decides to stick with the positive. He's asking her about it now. "It's going to be a woman in a red robe. Or like, a blanket."

"Doesn't look like she'll be wearing much else." *He presses against her with his head beside her ear.*

"She won't. It's really about the shape of her body and how it influences the folds in the fabric."

"It's pretty sexy when you talk like that."

She turns around in his arms. He's so good looking, with his big brown puppy dog eyes and straight nose. The nose she hopes he'll pass on to their children someday. "Ayers. I'm working. Aren't you heading to work soon, too?"

He scowls, but he kisses her forehead. "Why you gotta ruin my good mood?"

His expression and the kiss are at odds with each other, so she's not quite sure how to react. Is he joking or serious? Sometimes it's so hard to tell. The longer they live together, the more she finds herself trying to read his moods. Two nights ago, when they were attempting to rearrange the living room to fit in an armoire May Penny dropped off, she'd thought they were getting along fine. Even had a few laughs. Then all the sudden, when she asked him to move the armoire to the right, he'd looked up at her with sweat dripping in his eyes.

"Why don't you go your way and I'll go mine, and maybe we'll get through this goddamn evening?"

She'd been shocked and wondered if he'd dropped something on his foot, but she couldn't figure out anything she or the armoire had done to make him angry. She wasn't sure what to say, so she went into the kitchen and started cutting up salad fixings. She heard him in the shower thirty minutes later, and he'd grilled chicken breasts like they planned as if nothing had happened.

The more such experiences they have, the more Tipsy feels like she's on alert. So today, when he asks her why she had to ruin his morning, she doesn't reply. She gives him a half-assed chuckle and turns back to her art.

"I'm gonna take a shower," he says. "Then I'll go see some doctors. Damn. I hate putting on a suit in this weather. I don't know if I can keep this up."

He's only been at it for a month, so his negativity brings up more trepidation in Tipsy. She's doing well with her paintings, but they need Ayers's steady salary if they're going to have a cushion apart from his parents.

She decides not to play into his grousing, one way or another. Granna speaks up inside her head. It's always an emotional negotiation with him, and you're always the one doing the bartering and bargaining.

Tipsy dabs red paint on her canvas. We're getting used to living together. I'm sure he gets frustrated with me, too.

I don't know about that. He seems pretty content to do and say whatever he wants.

Movement on the street below catches Tipsy's eye. She's seen the pallid woman in the full skirt standing on the corner a few times since they moved in. She wears a red bonnet. She walks up and down the sidewalk talking to herself and waving her hands. Every so often, she steps into the street and then jumps back.

What an awful place to haunt, *Tipsy says to Granna.* Remember when you reminded me to have pity for the dead during my own middle school pity party? That woman deserves it.

The ghost looks up at the trees around her. Tipsy looks away before they make eye contact, but she sees most of the woman's face. She's pretty, with dark hair and eyes and cleavage pushed up toward her nose by her tight corset. Tipsy's mental camera clicks, and she decides to change the figure in her painting. She's been thinking of the woman as blonde, but now she knows the woman in the painting must have the ghost's dark hair and her beseeching expression.

She goes inside to grab brown paint. She'll need to add red and yellow to get just the right shade.

"Hey," says Ayers as he walks out of the bedroom in a suit and tie. "Sorry I kind of bit your head off."

His rare apology pleases her. "It's okay. I wasn't sure if you were mad or not, honestly."

"It's this job. I don't know. I always thought I'd do something more original than walk around MUSC selling colon drugs."

"Baby, I know it's not what you planned, but it's a great opportunity—"

"Baxter is thinking about starting his own investment company. Hotels. B&B's. We talked about it last night. I might want to get involved."

"Really?" Tipsy's heart sinks. Ayers knows nothing about hotels. Even less than he knows about colonic health.

"*But I won't have time to peddle this crap and really dive into that, you know?*" He wraps his arms around her. "*I'm going to call Baxter today and let him know I'm interested. I know you'll support me, whatever I decide.*"

"*Uh, of course. But maybe—*"

"*That's one of the things I love about you, Tipsy. You're not selfish at all.*"

Tipsy hugs him back, because it seems like a nice compliment, and after all, they're married. Of course she'll support him.

The supportiveness is pretty one-sided in this marriage, *says Granna.*

It's okay, *says Tipsy, as Ayers grumblingly kisses her goodbye and heads out the door for what will prove to be his last day as a colon medication salesman.* He supports me, too, in his own way. *Before Granna can reply, Tipsy says,* I think the ghost will be lovely in the new painting, don't you?

She will, but you're right. What a sad place to be stuck.

Tipsy gets to work on her painting. In the rush of creativity, for a while she forgets that she, too, is starting to feel a little stuck.

Chapter 14

O n Thursday evening, Tipsy and Pamella stood outside the ten foot stone wall surrounding the Joseph George Huger House. She'd seen bits and pieces of it in John's memories, inside and out. None of those visions did justice to the four-story brown brick behemoth with Charleston green shutters and bright white columns. While the address and the main entrance were on Meeting Street, the property took up several acres at the corner of Meeting and South Battery. The traditional piazzas on the side of the building overlooked Whitehall Gardens, the public park that in turn overlooked the harbor. The piazzas' purposeful slant for rainwater run-off made the building seem lopsided until the perspective made sense. The house almost dared one to notice its flaws; a grand dame dressed in outdated clothing but still the most beautiful guest at the party. Tipsy peeked through the iron gate at the manicured gardens and the two intertwining live oaks.

"It's a Phillip Simmons," said Pamella, as she ran her fingers over the gate.

The late Phillip Simmons, a celebrated African American craftsman, was one of Charleston's most beloved artisans. Over his near century of life he gained well-deserved fame for twisting burning iron into intricate, practical art. Mr. Simmons had woven a palmetto tree into the loops and swirls of this piece. A man who played with fire had taken a bit of unyielding earth and wrestled it into pleasing submission.

Paint was pleasantly malleable. Canvas had no permanence. The gate seemed like an art form beyond anything Tipsy contributed to the world. "It's lovely," she said. "You really grew up here?"

"Sort of. We lived here until I was about eight, then moved to Atlanta. We'd come back and stay here sometimes when it wasn't rented. It's funny, when I went into the house right before Daddy sold it in the eighties, it seemed *small*."

"This place, small?"

"I remembered it from my little girl's perspective. It seemed beyond huge to me. Endless. I literally got lost a few times. Back then it was full of clunky antique furniture and creepy paintings. There were even old clothes in the closets. The closets in these houses were put in with the indoor plumbing. They're *tiny*. Once I got locked in one during a game of hide and seek. There were these dusty men's shirts hanging around me. When I banged on the door to be let out, a shoe fell off the shelf and hit my head. If a four year old can have a heart attack, I nearly did."

"Your description makes True Blue sound downright homey, even with Ivy blowing out the windows."

"I can't believe my father lived here alone all those years. Or mostly alone. His first wife cheated on him with one of his golf buddies. Then my mother left us when I was almost one."

"What happened to her?"

"We didn't know for a long time. About twenty years ago I hired a private investigator to search for her. She died of cancer in prison in Alabama in the seventies."

"What was she in prison for?"

"Murder. She poisoned a man she lived with in Mobile. She was in and out of psychiatric facilities for years." Pamella chuckled. "I know I have my issues, but between my mother and what I now know about my great-grandmother Alma, I should be *seriously* nuts."

"Oh, Pammy. I'm sorry. My mother is flaky and weird, but she stuck around until I was fourteen and she never poisoned anyone."

"I never knew her, so it's not like I *missed* her. I mostly remember feeling angry with her for leaving my father. He was so sad all the time. I think that's why I became so—you know. The girl in the painting."

She replicated her childhood self's sassy pose with one hand in the air and one on her hip.

"Vivacious? Entertaining? Full of personality?"

"I was thinking *over the top*, but your way sounds nicer. I remember being so happy whenever I made Daddy smile."

"I understand trying to make people happy. I went about it in other ways, but same idea. Didn't he remarry?"

"Yeah. My step-mother. She was nice and we were close for a while, but she got sick of his melancholy. They had a pre-nup so it was no biggie when she peaced out."

Once again, Tipsy didn't agree that the loss of a maternal figure was no biggie, but Pamella pointed through the gate and changed the subject. "I love how they turned the carriage house into a pool house."

Tipsy squinted to pick out the blue glow of the pool hidden behind tasteful shrubbery. A white Lexus pulled into the driveway. Kim got out of her car in a Lily Pulitzer dress and hot pink pumps. "Hey, y'all! Sorry I'm late! A client decided she had to see a house and business is business!" She beamed at them. "Home sweet home, Pammy! Y'all ready? I'm so excited to go through this place. One of the perks of the job, right?"

They walked up the brick and iron staircase to the piazza door. Kim opened the lockbox with a code and they stepped onto the piazza. Tipsy had been in a couple of these old houses over the years, but the piazza of the Huger House was something else, even by Charleston standards. It was over twenty feet wide and the pillars were like young sequoia trees. Floor and pillars were freshly painted a blinding white. The sitting area overlooking the garden showcased a full bar carved from a hunk of dark wood and surrounded by tall iron chairs with white beaded cushions. The scene gave off conflicting vibes, like a boutique Caribbean hotel crossed with The Overlook from *The Shining*.

Tipsy had thought of that famous story about the psychotic writer and the possessed hotel when she first visited this place, in Henry's memory last summer. Back then, she'd compared John's lavish birthday party to the famous ballroom scene.

A dark figure stood behind the bar. For a second, anxiety identified him as the creepy bartender who pushed Jack Torrance further down his predestined literary path to insanity.

What will it be, Miss Collins? Or is it Miss Denning these days? Bourbon on the rocks? A mint julep? How about a tasty White Claw?

The man behind the bar moved out of a pillar's shadow. Light struck him. He wasn't dark and swarthy like Lloyd of the Overlook Hotel. He was pale and had thinning, graying blond hair. He turned sideways and revealed dark horn rimmed glasses.

Tipsy took two quick breaths. Her heart forced the adrenaline to dissipate through her veins. Once she got a hold of herself, she appreciated the man's appearance as an unexpected score. For once, her mystery solving might be simple. Or at least easier than Henry's multiday hunt for Ivy's late husband. "Jackpot," she whispered. "Camden."

"… the bar is made from the hull of a shrimp boat. The artist is based on Daufuskie Island, below Hilton Head—"

Pamella put a hand on Kim's shoulder to shut her up. "Sorry. What was that, Tipsy?"

"Uh—call came in." Tipsy held her phone to her ear. "Yes. I have a few minutes." She dropped her voice to a whisper. "New commission. Have to take it."

Pamella pushed Kim toward the front door. "Sure. We'll meet you inside."

"Be careful on the cushions," said Kim.

Tipsy nodded. Once they were inside, she lowered the phone. She squared up and walked across the piazza toward the ghost of Camden Brewton. She reminded herself that he wasn't a manifestation of the house's inherent evil disguised as a cocktail mixologist. He was just the sad vestige of a middle-aged man who, unlike the familicidal maniacs of The Overlook, had only taken himself out. Nothing to be scared of here, and he better be prepared to talk. This guy might hold the key to helping three of the most tragic people she knew—John, Ivy, and Pamella, who grew up trying to make her depressed father smile in a giant haunted mansion while her mother roamed anonymously around the Southeast, poisoning people and dying of cancer. Tipsy was determined to get her mystery solve on, and unlike Henry, she was no longer a ghost wrangling greenhorn.

Tipsy slid into one of the stools and set her phone on the bar. Camden paid her no attention.

"What's on tap?" she asked.

He continued to watch the garden. Tipsy peered down there herself. They were above the pool. The pool liner darkened the water to the cobalt shade of the wine bottles on Bobby's trees. She wondered if Camden had thought about jumping in there. Trying to drown himself like the Confederate soldier on Ivy's beach. Maybe he'd wake up somewhere else. Or maybe a second death would merely trap him in a smaller place. The pool would become a true blue bottle.

"I said, what are you serving? Camden, right?"

She scared him as much as he'd scared her two minutes ago. He jumped in place and backed away from her, but there wasn't anywhere to go in the small space between the bar and the railing. Surprised ghosts sometimes forgot they could disappear or walk through solid wood. He pressed against the railing like Tipsy was on fire and kicking off too much heat.

"Hey, don't freak out. Listen, I know Henry Mott came to see you the other day." Tipsy started chatting like they were guests at a wedding. They didn't know each other, but knowing someone in common should make the conversation easier. "You didn't want to talk to him, but we need your help, so—"

"How on earth can you see me?" He had the scratchy voice of a long-time smoker. Lung cancer didn't care if one was rich or poor. Maybe if Camden hadn't killed himself, the Marlboro Man would have taken him out, the same way he paid a banshee-like visit to Alma, Bubba, and Granna.

"That's a long story, and I don't have much time. So let's cut to the chase, okay?"

Camden turned toward the garden. He started to fade. Tipsy saw crooked oak branches through his green plaid shirt, as if the straight lines of the pattern had gone haywire.

"Whoa. Don't try that, dude. Henry isn't as experienced with this kind of stuff as I am. You can't just disappear on me."

"Why not?"

"Because I can make you come out if I want to."

"I don't believe you, ma'am. You're alive, and I'm—I'm something else—"

"You're dead, and you're a ghost. But I can see you, right? Anyone else seen you since you died?"

He watched her silently through his Buddy Holly glasses.

"Besides Henry. And he's, like, also dead."

A tiny shake of his head.

"Exactly. So you don't know what I can do, do you? Do you want to find out?" Tipsy was bluffing some, but she'd rather intimidate Camden into sticking around than drag him back if he disappeared.

Camden didn't reply, but he crossed his arms over his chest.

"Great," said Tipsy. "I need your help. More than that, Ivy needs your help. And so does your cousin John."

"What do you know of John, or Ivy?"

"I know they're both ghosts, like you. Y'all have a lot of ghosts for one family. So I also know all of y'all had serious issues. Peaceful, legit deaths don't lead to hauntings."

"You speak as if all of this is commonplace." He karate-chopped a bottle of expensive bourbon; Angel's Envy, how apropos. He wanted to touch it, so unlike his unintentional lean on the railing, he got nowhere. His hands passed through the bottle. "None of it is normal," he said. "No matter how one dies."

"It's normal to me. I've been dealing with dead people since childhood. From what I've seen, ghosts are a rare but natural part of life and death."

"Nothing in my life or my death turned out like it was supposed to."

"I often feel the same way about my life." She wrapped her knuckles on the bar. "I can still knock on wood, so I can't speak to my death yet."

"Did you marry someone wholly unsuitable when your life fell apart?"

"Uh, no. I married someone unsuitable, but it was more of an effort to put my life together."

"When John died, it was like I lost a limb, or one chamber of my heart."

"So you married Ivy to, like, be close to him? Or because—"

"Marrying Ivy ruined my life. I did it on a whim. I wasn't in my right mind."

"You got your son out of the marriage."

"That was the only good thing to come from it." He walked back and forth in the small space behind the bar, reminding Tipsy of one of the little figures that ice skated in circles on May Penny's holiday music boxes. "I tried to do the right thing. I always tried."

"Right, like when you apologized to Henry for bullying him! That was thoughtful of you."

"Thank you—wait, how does Henry play into this?"

"Right now I want to talk about John. He's stuck in the old soldier's barracks on Sullivan's, haunting it."

"So we both ended up this way. You're right. What are the chances, in one family?"

"Slim for sure, but it gets more complicated. John's haunting doesn't make sense, since everyone said he drowned and you found him floating in the ocean. That's right, isn't it? You found him in the ocean?"

A nod.

"But he must have died somewhere else. I know you were with him the day before he died. He showed me, in his memories—wait. Let me back up and give you the basics." Tipsy briefly explained her own ability to help ghosts move on, as well as Ivy's refusal to do so without John.

"She still loves him so much?"

"Yeah. She does. Maybe that's hard to hear since you're her husband."

"No. It's not surprising. Neither of us ever got over John. He's not trapped in this house with me, but he haunts me nonetheless."

"So do you know anything about what happened to him? Or can you give me some information about Ivy's death? Bobby's daughter told me you found Ivy after she died, too." She strummed her fingers on the bar. It was a lot for one person to find the bodies of his best friend and his wife. Maybe the trauma ultimately became too much for Camden to bear. Curiosity got the better of her, tight schedule or not. "What about you? Do you know how you died?"

"Are you referring to my suicide? My son spoke of it. So did the new owners. The story became part of the long history of this house."

"Wait. If you know how you died, you should be able to move on. Unless you don't know why?"

He smiled for the first time. "Tell me about my Bobby and his daughter."

"I got off track for a second. I really don't have time, but…" His hopeful expression pulled at her. "That tall woman with me? That's his daughter—"

"Is it? I would like to see her face—"

"Later! Once they come back, I have to leave. Hold your hand to mine, and think about whatever you can tell me about John's death—"

"I can tell you everything about John's death."

"You were there? Did Bubba kill him? How did it—"

"Now you're asking me questions, when you keep saying time is of the essence."

"Right. Okay." Tipsy scooted the stool in closer to the bar. She gripped the edge of the thick wood along the curve of the old shrimp boat's hull. She thought of Bubba More's bible verse. *Into your hands they are delivered.*

"I have to hold on," she said. "But, just… touch me."

"Anywhere?"

"Anywhere appropriate."

"Is your face appropriate?"

Tipsy nodded.

"Very well. I'll touch your cheek. I might have touched my granddaughter's cheek like so, if my sins hadn't led me to end it all."

"Wait. What? Why *did* you kill yourself, seriously? Why are you still here if you know what happened?"

"Shhhh. You asked me to see John's death." His pale hand drifted toward her face like a hypnotist's pendant.

———✦✕✦———

The old barracks has only been abandoned for a few years. In Tipsy's twenty-first century mindset, the interior reminds her of a place where people go to covertly poison themselves with meth or heroine. She's in a rectangular room lined with broken iron bunk beds. Flat mattresses molder in the corners. Some of them have vomited their stuffing. As the Great Depression unfolded, desperate hobos found even this remote place. There are a few piles of clothes, discarded cans and bottles, and the remnants of a cooking fire. One of the interior walls has collapsed, revealing a line of stained white bathtubs.

For a moment, the tableau remains frozen before the camera starts rolling. John stands at the far end of the room, fidgeting like a misplaced bridegroom. Camden's back faces Tipsy. He's striding toward his cousin. Tipsy takes two jogging steps to catch up and then settles in behind him, an unseen member of a strange wedding party.

John is wearing his death outfit, a navy blue shirt and tan trousers. He waits until Camden is close enough for him to whisper-yell. "Did you see Bubba?"

"I did. I went to his church. He was getting ready for bible study."

"Did you talk to him? Is he coming?" John runs a frazzled hand through his hair. His eyes burn like azure fire. Tipsy's high school chemistry teacher told her blue flames are the most efficient, but also the hottest. "I filled the tub. The closest one—there." He points vaguely into the washroom. "When will he be here? My nerves are in a state. I'd rather get on with it."

"I told him you wanted to talk and there'd be money involved. He's coming."

"Good. All right. I can do this. I can—"

"He'll be here soon, but I won't be here when he arrives."

John glowers at him. "You said you'd help me."

"I did! I got him here, right?" Camden shoves his hands into his pockets. "I told you I wouldn't do anything more than that. I can't, John. And you shouldn't. You don't have to do this." He paces in a small circle, like his ghost did behind the bar at the Huger House. "I've been thinking. There's still a way to salvage it. I have some money saved up. I'll gladly loan you whatever you need. If you insist on keeping up this business with Ivy, pay Bubba and set her up somewhere you can visit her. Until it blows over."

"What blows over?"

"This infatuation of yours. Get her an apartment for a while. Maybe a better job. She seems bright. She'd probably make a good secretary, if you vouch for her. You'll be doing her right in the long run."

"So not only will you not help me, you're making other plans for us." John huffs and puffs like he's got emphysema and can't get enough air. "You're right. You might as well leave. Go on. Get."

"Hear me out, cousin." Camden beseeches him, like a preacher trying to reach an indifferent member of the congregation. "I understand. You're caught up in the romance of this beautiful girl. She's different from the women we know. It's exciting. But have you ever thought about what she's really all about? You say her father hits her, but how do you know she's not putting you on?"

"I've seen the bruises!"

"You said she doesn't care who you are, but everyone knows who you are. The family name. The family money. You think she's ignorant of all that? You'll be taking care of her loony mama, too, when Bubba's gone. Quite a convenient and cushy escape for mother and daughter."

"You don't know her! You don't know one thing about her, or us, or the plans we have."

"You want to kill someone, and make me an accomplice, over a girl you've known less than a year. No woman has ever kept your attention for more than a few months. This will pass!"

John's eyes are wild, raging. Sweat runs down his face in lines like premature wrinkles. "Get out of here before I put a boot in your cowardly ass."

"I'm trying to help you. You're an arrogant asshole!" Camden closes the space between them. "You always have been!"

John punches Camden. His nose explodes. He reels away from John.

"I said get out of here, Camden. You're not my family."

Camden reaches for something to staunch the flow of blood from his nose. He lunges for a navy blue army issue blanket draped over the edge of a bunk bed. Once his face is half covered, he turns on John. "I am your family, you lovestruck idiot. I'll tell you the truth, even if you refuse to hear it. Always, you think you know best."

"This is my whole life you're talking about, and Ivy's. Now you're meddling in it!"

"It's my life too, since you want me to help you kill Bubba!"

"Shut up! Bubba could be outside the door listening right now. You'll be dead if you don't shut your mouth!"

Camden looks like he might cry. "Really, Johnny? You're threatening to kill me now? Have you lost your mind?"

"Leave, Cam. Please leave. You're breaking my heart."

Camden turns and walks right out the door. Tipsy gets out of his way. Don't leave yet, Camden! What the hell. I need to see what happens when Bubba gets here. *She stands in the empty space between John and Camden like a buoy on rough water. John walks into the bathing room. Tipsy follows him.*

He places both hands on the side of a tub filled with water that's too clean to have been there long. The tub is deep, almost like a horse trough. Big enough for a large man to take a bath. Or be drowned.

John stares down into the water. He's talking to himself. His lips curl and uncurl. "Kill Bubba More. That's what I have to do. But now Camden knows." *His eyes narrow, and Tipsy is afraid of the dirty blue-black water that's boiling behind them.*

Oh, lord. John is going to go after Camden, before Bubba even gets here!

"Camden. Knows. I'm. Going to kill. Bubba. More. Camden knows." *Something is wrong in John Huger's brain. He wants to strangle his closest friend, and his head is dangerously close to the water in the tub. Bubba More is on the way.*

She turns at the sound of footsteps, expecting to see Bubba. But to her shock, it's Camden. His own face is contorted with rage. The emotions coming off him—love, hurt, jealousy, years of resentment and desperation for approval—are too much to handle.

Camden shoves John, and he falls into the bathtub.

Camden, stop it! Stop! *Tipsy screams, but as always, no one hears her. She flutters helplessly as the two men flail in the tub. Camden's nose opens up, and more blood drops into the dingy water.*

"Goddamn you, John," *says Camden.* "You won't listen. You never, ever listen to me."

Tipsy runs toward the door, with the vague hope Bubba More will actually show up and stop this, although she knows he didn't. She turns around and Camden is still on top of John. One of John's legs hangs out of the bathtub. She runs back to them. Camden has his hands on John's shoulders. John is face down in the tub.

He never saw who killed him. He last saw Camden walking out the door. He couldn't show Tipsy something he had not even a vague memory of, so she had to see it from Camden's perspective.

Camden murdered John. The cousin he'd adored and worshipped all his life, because John wouldn't listen to Camden's plan to save him from his own unhinged plotting. Two men who had tried to force life to bend to their wills, and instead, it snapped in all the wrong places.

John stops moving but Camden holds him down. He whispers about the unfairness of it all. John always has everything. Everyone loves him more. He won't listen when Camden knows what's best this time.

"I'm trying to save you from yourself!" Camden says as he pushes on the back of John's neck. "Save you—"

He freezes. His eyes race over the pinkish water. He jumps out of the tub. John floats to the top. His left leg still sticks out of the tub like a chicken that's too big for the pot.

Camden shoves a fist into his mouth. His eyes widen in horror. "Johnny? John? Cousin?"

He repeats himself again and again. He falls to his knees and starts rhythmically slapping the side of his own face. Fear and anguish roll off him.

Tipsy presses her hands to her temples and stomps her feet. She's afraid her own heart is going to burst. Oh god please let me wake up I need to wake up now it's too much please-please!

Camden shifts and the floorboards creak below him.

He flinches at the sound, as if it reminds him that others might soon be walking across this floor. He looks at his wet wristwatch. "Bubba."

He jumps to his feet. Tipsy feels him shove his grief and confusion to the side as fear takes over. He has to hide what he just did. She catches bits of his thoughts as his conscience tries to make sense of what happened. How could he have done it?

Then he tugs on John's broad shoulders, and the memory mercifully fades.

Tipsy woke up to Camden staring at her like a helpless husband watching his wife give birth. A line of spittle hung from her lower lip. It dangled over her hand as she gripped the edge of the bar. The teardrop at the end of the string of saliva hit her skin with a cold plop. She thought of Camden's blood dripping into the bathtub. How the drops had spread out and turned the water pinkish.

"I'm going to throw up." She lunged out of the stool. Her hands went from gripping the bar to gripping the piazza railing. She retched into the fading hydrangeas.

Kim's sharp voice behind her made her jump. "Tipsy! No! Is there puke all over the flowers?"

"Lady, are you okay?" Pamella touched her back.

Kim yanked off her pink pumps. She ran down the piazza stairs and across the garden. She hopped over a few shrubs. Her frantic dash reminded Tipsy of the principal running from the rottweiler on Ferris Bueller's famous day off.

"I'm okay," whispered Tipsy. "I haven't had a reaction like this in a long time. It must be seeing John's murder."

"You saw it? Was it Bubba?"

Tipsy turned and leaned on the railing. Camden still stood there, unseen by Pamella. "No. It wasn't Bubba. It was Camden."

"What? Camden, my grandfather?"

"Yes. And he's right here. Looking at me. Murdering asshole!"

"Y'all! Hey!" Kim called up to them from the garden. "It's not too bad, but I'm going to spray the hedges anyway. I don't want to be *that agent,* who gets puke on the landscaping."

"That woman is unpleasant," said Camden. "She hasn't even asked if you're ill."

"It's pretty obvious I'm ill. Pammy, go help Kim with the sanitizing. Keep her down there for a minute if you can."

Pamella nodded and walked down the stairs into the garden. Tipsy sat on the stool again. "What happened after you killed him?"

"I dragged him out of the tub. Covered him with blankets in the corner and hid outside. I watched from one of the windows. Bubba came. He stayed for a while, but he stormed off when it was clear no one was meeting him. Then I went back to the cabin. Found his old bathing costume—the red striped one his father gave him he never wore. Brought it back and squeezed him into it. That night, I… I… put him out to sea, so to speak. I took his clothes back to the cabin. Washed the blood out of them and hung them on the line. It looked to everyone like he'd just gone for a swim. Only Ivy and I knew he never wore that swimming suit. He called it the candy cane costume."

"I heard him say something like that in Ivy's memories."

"I simply couldn't let John be found dead in only his underpants. The bathing costume provided a little more dignity."

"How kind of you to make the decision for him, but I think he would have rather been naked than in that stupid suit. You're a sick bastard. I thought you loved him."

"I did. I do. I don't know what came over me that night. I've spent decades thinking about it."

"At least one thing makes sense. You and Ivy. It seemed so unlikely, given how you tried to talk John out of marrying her. You felt so guilty about killing him, you married her yourself."

"I hoped to make amends in some way. Take care of her for him."

"I have to tell John you did it."

"At least I'll know I helped get him out of where I put him."

"Now I have to figure out what happened to Ivy."

"I can help you there, too."

"Y'all, we should go." Kim walked up the piazza stairs. "Sorry, Tipsy, but I can't, like, take you inside and have you yack on anything."

Camden had a point about Kim. She still hadn't asked if Tipsy was okay or needed anything.

"I need just a couple minutes before I get in the car," said Tipsy.

"Okay, but if you need to throw up, please run out to the sidewalk. Pammy, do you want to see the pool?"

"Uh, sure?"

"Go ahead," said Tipsy.

They walked into the garden.

"What you do you mean?" she hissed at Camden. "You know something more about Ivy's death?"

"I killed her."

"Good lord almighty! What?"

"It was an accident. Do you want to see?" He held up his hand.

"I can't right now. My stomach can't handle it and we don't have time." Her mind raced. She hadn't actually seen Luisa Bishop's death, but she knew enough to explain it to her. "Tell me what happened. If you explain it to me, I can tell Ivy. Hopefully it will be enough to set her free. But hurry up! I have to leave."

"We were on the dock. We were arguing—"

"About what?"

"She was ranting and raving about John's ghost. Of course, I didn't believe her about any of it. She'd been acting odd for weeks. Drinking all day. I thought she'd lost her mind."

"You called her family to come help out, right?"

"Yes. I didn't know what else to do. They stayed at the cottage because Ivy refused to leave Sullivan's Island. I left Bobby here with the housekeeper and met them out there. I hoped we might talk sense into her."

"Sounds like what we'd call a family intervention."

"Perhaps. But it was a disaster. Ivy was stone drunk, and I… I admit, I had too much to drink myself. She followed me onto the dock, talking all manner of supernatural nonsense. She accused me of killing John and said she'd go to the police. It's all a bit of a bourbon blur, honestly. Ivy kept saying, *you did it, Cam, you did it.* And I saw red. I grabbed her and pushed. She fell off the dock, headfirst."

"Whoa. So you killed them both. No wonder you killed yourself. But—you know you killed yourself, and it seems pretty obvious why."

"I have no doubt why. I planned it for months before shooting myself. Living with the guilt became too much for me. Bobby was grown. I had no other reason to keep living."

"So why don't you go on?"

"Go on where?"

"Good lord. Why does every ghost ask me that? I don't know. Just like… *move on.* To the next plane or world or whatever."

"I can't go anywhere. Why would I linger here if I could? I killed myself to get away from my remorse and sadness. I don't know anything about other worlds or heaven or hell, but I'd welcome oblivion itself if I didn't have to think anymore."

Pamella poked her head around the corner. "Kim really wants to go."

"I'm coming." Tipsy closed her eyes in the hope of regaining her equilibrium, but the world refused to stay wholly in place. "You should be able to move on, given how much you know. Maybe you—"

She opened her eyes, but Camden had already disappeared.

Tipsy stood and walked gingerly toward the steps.

If that ain't something, said Granna. *Turns out Bubba More was a stinky ol' red herring, and you got an answer about Ivy, to boot! Nice work, Paranormal Investigator Numero Uno. Now you'll be able to set John and Ivy free, and have your fifty-k.*

I sure hope so. But why can't Camden leave?

Why can Henry move from place to place, but Ivy can't? It's not the same for everyone.

Right. Still, Camden's inertia bothered her.

By the time Tipsy got downstairs, Kim was gone. "You sure you can drive?" asked Pamella.

"Yeah. Camden killed Ivy, too."

"What in the holy hell? I knew my family was messed up, but this is more than I bargained for."

Tipsy got into her rental car. "I feel terrible and I have to get the kids from Tripp. Can I call you later and tell you about it?"

"Sure. That sordid tale will go great with a glass of wine."

Tipsy waved and smiled, but the thought of wine made her want to puke again. She blessed Tripp for agreeing to keep the kids for a few hours. He always ordered pizza, so she was off the cooking hook this evening. Normally she'd be crossing her fingers for a few leftover slices, but pizza sounded as unappealing as wine.

She pulled up to the stoplight at Meeting and Market Streets beside Pamella's car. Pammy waved and slurped from her Yeti. Not the best decision. Police swarmed around Market Street looking to hand out DUIs along with underage drinking citations.

She's going to get busted eventually, Tipsy said to Granna.

Not sure she cares, sugar. She's used to getting her way, like John Huger.

That attitude certainly didn't do him right. Tipsy waved to Pamella, but the light changed and the blue BMW zipped down Meeting Street.

Granna sniffed. *Pamella might have it worse than John does.*

How so? He's stuck haunting the old barracks and hobnobbing with the local vermin.

John Huger might be a ghost, but Pamella Brewton is the one stuck in a bottle.

Chapter 15

T he next morning, after dropping the kids at camp, Tipsy stood on the front porch of the old soldier's barracks with Henry and John. She wanted to go inside. The surroundings might jog John's memory, but she also feared he might go ballistic. She preferred prudently remaining out of sight over managing an unhinged spirit in broad daylight.

She pictured herself standing on the barracks lawn while talking a hysterical John Huger off the spectral ledge. She'd yell and argue and plead with empty air. She'd jockey for position while John stomped and fumed and commiserated with his animal confidants, unseen to the average human eye. From a distance she might appear to be battling a swarm of bees, but better safe than sorry. She imagined the 911 emergency recording.

911, what's your emergency?

Concerned citizen here. We're on the boat passing Sullivan's and some crackhead woman is having a psychotic break behind the old barracks.

Thanks for the call. We'll send an officer out with a taser and a straightjacket.

Henry and John hovered beside her as she examined the haphazardly boarded up entrance. She pushed and it gave some. Eventually teenagers looking for a party spot would take an ax to the flimsy drywall or throw a keg through it.

She walked the length of the porch, squatted, and tugged at a broken porch railing. "Maybe if I hit it with this—"

Wood creaked behind her. She looked over her shoulder. Henry stood before the door as if in a staring contest with someone on the other side. The drywall bent inward, away from the pressure of Henry's gaze. Rusty nails landed on the porch. The barrier collapsed with an exhausted sigh like a tired soldier told to stand at ease.

Henry exhaled and stepped away from the entrance. "Ladies first."

"Thanks." Tipsy rejoined them and peered inside the barracks. Stripes of light crisscrossed the dimly lit, cavernous space. It reminded her of a jewel heist movie, where the thief has to climb around the laser beams to avoid setting off alarms. She turned on her phone's flashlight. Henry followed the light like a cat chasing a dangling string. Tipsy stepped inside herself and called over her shoulder. "Hey, John, are you coming?"

"I'm here."

Tipsy raised her phone. She jumped when the light hit John's glowing, bluish green face. Dark caverns under his eyes. His cheekbones stood out in harsh relief.

"Jeez. Warn me next time, Bela Lugosi," she said as she looked around. The barracks was empty. No bunk beds or bathtubs. The wall between the sleeping area and bathing room had been knocked down to create a simple rectangle. "This place is cleared out."

"Nothing in here but the rats and bugs. I *talked* to them until y'all started visiting me." John looked like he'd figured out the answer to a difficult math problem. "But now ... I don't think they truly talk back to me."

"Good, John. That's very good," Tipsy said, as if John were a puppy learning a new trick. John's return to rationality pleased her, but she wished he hadn't reminded her about the creeping occupants of the barracks. She chided herself for wearing flip flops instead of running shoes. An amateurish ghost wrangling move, considering she'd planned to enter an abandoned building. If a giant palmetto bug scurried over her toes it would be her own fault.

Tipsy shone the flashlight toward the ceiling. She felt like a camp counselor about to tell a scary story at a bonfire.

"I can't show you what I saw, but I'm going to tell you. Listen closely." Tipsy explained what she'd seen in Camden's memory. She included the sounds and smells and the feelings she'd gleaned from

Camden himself. She spoke of the blood in the bathtub, although it made her sick to her stomach again. Dramatic expressions vacillated across John's face like the cartoon panels in a noir comic strip.

He eventually walked away from her with his hands in his hair. He rested his forehead against a wall he could walk through, in the strange way ghosts sometimes obeyed the laws of physics while simultaneously being able to avoid them or unable to take advantage of them. John could mimic leaning on the wall and he could also move through it as if it weren't there. His fist would pass right through it if he struck it in anguish. The wall might be a source of support or frustration, or a non-issue to be ignored. Sort of like a longtime spouse.

"So that's how they found you," said Tipsy. "In the ocean."

"Wearing the candy cane costume." John turned around. "Looking like a damn rigor mortis peppermint stick. Jesus wept."

Henry spoke up. "At least your… *ahem*… was safely covered."

John's mouth twitched. "I don't care if my *ahem* was floating beside me for all the world to see. Nothing to be ashamed of there."

"Maybe that's why Camden wanted you covered up in that suit. You'd set unreasonable expectations of what ran in the family."

"He might have ended up with all my money, but my daddy's will couldn't bequeath those family jewels."

Their laughter burst like a shiny soap bubble. John leaned against the wall with his arms crossed over his chest and cackled at the ceiling. Henry stomped his foot and clapped. Shiny tears down his cheeks.

"Okay." Tipsy toggled the flashlight between the two of them. "Enough locker room talk, y'all. Jeez, I thought y'all were too gentile for that."

"Oh, Tipsy," said Henry. "Throughout history, and regardless of social status, men are united by our love of phallic humor."

"Nowadays, you talk like that in front of a woman and she'll go all Me Too on your ass. Luckily for y'all, you're dead so I can't sue you for sexual harassment. Besides, infantile as it is, it's nice to hear you both laughing."

"It feels nice, too," said John.

"Rather bizarre, old man," said Henry, "since we're laughing about how your cousin killed you and ended up with your expansive inheritance."

"It is bizarre. So it was Camden. My dearest friend."

"You remember what happened now?" asked Tipsy.

"I remember staring into the bathtub, thinking about how to kill Camden." John shook his head. "I would never have believed myself capable of such thoughts. But they were cut off when someone pushed me from behind. When I thrashed, it stirred up the dirt on the bottom of the tub. Murky water. Bubbles from my screaming. The noise was muffled, like I was yelling into my pillow to wake myself up from a nightmare."

"It might be weird to think you wanted to kill Camden then, but you must hate him now," said Tipsy. She waited for John to realize the magnitude of what she'd told him and explode like her can of biscuits.

"I don't know how I feel about Camden."

"Do you feel like you can move on?"

"What does it feel like, exactly?"

"Warmth," said Henry. "Like my senses opened up again. Do you feel any of that?"

John rubbed his fingers together. "I don't think so."

"Ugh," said Tipsy. "You're sure? But Camden's story sounds right to you?"

"Yes. I remember everything that's possible for me to remember. It's as if you're reminding me of a forgotten dream."

"That's kind of how Jane described it. And you feel, like, at peace about it?"

"It's food for thought, certainly, but yes." John smiled. "I'd say I do. Damn peaceful, indeed."

"Then why can't you move on?" If he felt so content, Tipsy was pleased for him, but she wanted to scream for herself. She hopped in place in agitation. The beam of light from her phone bounced across the barracks walls. Teenagers had indeed breached the drywall gate at some point. Some of their old graffiti was mundane: *SAM LOVES JENN. ELLIOTT B. IS GAY. WANDO HS C/O '07.* Then there was the philosophical: an anarchy symbol, a giant peace sign, *DEUS EX MACHINA.*

God in the machine. She could really use one of those endings right about now, but it looked like she would get no simple resolution. "I don't understand what the problem is. Camden knows how he died, and he can't go on either!"

"Me and Jane. Luisa Bishop. Proctor James," said Henry. "Knowing what happened worked for all of us. But something must be different for Camden and John."

"Oh, lord. What if Ivy's death is the same?" Tipsy felt growing despair. It seemed she would never sort out all this death drama.

John didn't share her pessimistic view. He was eerily calm. "I'm certain you'll resolve it, Tipsy. I'll have time to sort out my feelings about Camden while I wait."

Tipsy decided not to ruin John's thoughtful, post-death revelation vibe by telling him Camden had also killed Ivy.

It's not the time or the place, said Granna. *Not when he's acting like he's taken an emotional horse tranquilizer.*

Existential peace is apparently a pretty strong sedative, Tipsy replied. *Damn, I could use some of that juice.*

John whistled as he walked toward the door. He passed into the sunlight and disappeared. Tipsy lowered the phone and the flashlight beam struck the floor. A dozen black cylinders scurried into the darkness like six-legged matchbox cars.

Tipsy jumped in place. Panic seized her. "Henry, the roaches, oh lord— Henry—"

Henry pointed his fingers and raised his thumbs like a little boy playing cowboy. He fired into the darkness. The bugs popped like corn kernels. One raced past Tipsy's foot. Henry picked it off, an insect sniper. It exploded and shot across the cement.

Tipsy squealed and ran out of the barracks into the sunshine. She stood panting in the grass with her hands on her knees. Henry appeared beside her. "Tipsy. You cannot live in Charleston and be a prisoner of your fear of these bugs."

She straightened and rested a hand on her chest until she caught her breath. "You're probably right. But for now I have you, Doc Holliday."

Henry held his imaginary gun to his lips and blew away the pretend smoke from his six-shooter. He winced and pressed his trigger finger into his temples. "The house is calling me."

"Go on. I'll see you at home."

He disappeared. Tipsy stood alone beside Cove Creek. No John. He was off pondering his feelings about being murdered by his cousin. No Henry. He was recuperating from playing roach assassin in her honor. She thought of the two men, so grand and glamorous in their very different ways, laughing hysterically over penis jokes like middle school boys. Henry still hadn't admitted it, but his frosty century-old disdain for John was clearly melting as he realized John wasn't just a one-dimensional fop. Such interesting people, both of them.

Some of the coolest people I know these days are dead. Tipsy thought of Shelby. She'd go gaga for Henry and John. She smiled as she pictured Shelby swooning over them both. Fretting over who was hotter, the brooding tortured artist or Mr. All-American.

Then Tipsy remembered their argument.

Don't give up on Shelby's goofy ass, said Granna. *Y'all have been friends for too long.*

What am I going to do about this mystery? It should be halfway solved, but it's back to the drawing board.

Nothing to do but keep at it. What choice do you have?

Male voices drew her attention to the water. A boat eased past the barracks. The two men onboard watched Tipsy like she was doing cartwheels in her underwear. One had his phone in his hand. *Uh oh. 911 call.*

Better look normal, quick, said Granna.

Tipsy smiled and waved. She held up her phone as if talking to someone on Facetime. The first boat guy lowered his own phone and the other guy waved back.

Involuntary commitment averted.

Not by much, said Granna.

Tipsy gave her phone duck lips in an imaginary selfie, and then she got out of there. She thought about Granna's words as she got into her car. *Nothing to do but keep at it* was setting up to be the story of her life.

The next morning, Tipsy dropped off the kids with Tripp for their Boca vacation. She had all their stuff packed, for as usual, that task had fallen to her, not Big Ayers. They were wildly excited and didn't pay much attention to her leaving. She kept her goodbyes short and sweet. Ayers would arrive soon and she had no interest in running into him. Or Kate, should he decide she needed to be part of the family send off.

Since experience had taught her it was indeed easier to solve a murder mystery when one lived with the ghosts involved, she had her own bag packed for an extended stay at True Blue. Pamella had set up one of the three guestrooms for her. It had a double bed with a cute blue and white striped quilt, a white antique dresser, and two blue and white china lamps on the bedside tables. A pale blue candle sat on the dresser with a pack of matches beside it.

Tipsy lit the candle and the scent of something clean and soft wafted over the room. It relaxed her. She looked forward to spending time at True Blue. It felt like her own vacation.

She unpacked her bag, checked her phone, and walked onto the screened back porch. Henry appeared in front of her.

"Hey. Did you have any trouble finding the place?" she asked. Such a mundane question, but Henry's directions had nothing to do with Google maps.

"Your description sufficed. Where is Miss Ivy? My time is limited. And what exactly do you want me to do?"

"I thought another ghost might, like, ease the weirdness of learning about her death…"

"Hmm."

"She also might blow something up. I could use some backup."

"I'll do what I can, but it sounds like Ivy is more powerful than me. Besides, remember, you managed to put me off a few times when I had a hissy fit."

"But I was protecting someone else. Will, and then Jane."

"Don't you think you should practice protecting yourself?"

"I guess, but I'd rather not start with Ivy. She might toss me right through the screen—"

"Henry?" Ivy's tentative greeting cut through their bickering. She was on the far end of the porch. She wrung her hands and smiled nervously.

Henry stood. "Ivy! Hello there. It's been some time, hasn't it? Come, come. Sit with us."

Ivy glided across the porch. She stopped beside Pamella's sleekly modern porch furniture like a classical statue in the wrong museum.

Henry waved her toward one of the chairs. He sat in the other. Tipsy sat across from them on the sofa.

"So," said Henry. "Ivy! You're looking… ah, nice."

"I'm *deceased,* Henry." Ivy gave him a quizzical look. "Did you kill Jane? John told me you did, but Tipsy says you didn't."

"I'm rather tired of answering that question from other ghosts who have their own complicated death stories. But no. I did not. Now enough about me. You were barely grown when last I saw you! I hope the next couple decades treated you well? Wait— I'm sorry. That sounded… what I meant is…" Henry threw up his hands. "Hell. This is silly. We're both dead and still here. Our lives were clearly disastrous."

Tipsy stepped in. "We spoke to Camden, Ivy. This might be hard to hear, so I asked Henry to join us. He can provide some, like, moral support."

"Camden knows what happened to John?"

"Yes." Tipsy told Ivy about Camden's memory.

Her face darkened as Tipsy reached the end of the vision. She spoke through clenched teeth. "Camden killed Johnny. Evil. *Bastard.*" She got to her feet. Beaded throw pillows levitated and spun slowly, planets about to be knocked out of orbit by the incoming comet of her anger. Tipsy tried not to panic as Ivy herself floated toward the ceiling. Her black shoes hovered over the coffee table.

Tipsy turned to Henry. "A little help here?"

Henry scooted to the edge of his seat. "Ivy? Now listen—"

The pillows exploded. Balls of cotton and plastic beads spun around the room in a tornado of Ivy's emotions. Plastic beads stung Tipsy's skin like artificial hail. The couch vibrated under her butt. The ceiling fan whizzed above her head with a power beyond anything the house's electrical circuits could provide. The fan howled as if Ivy were wrenching its wooden arms from their sockets. It was a giant mechanical cicada, screeching as she ripped off its wings. It couldn't take much more.

Tipsy stood with her arms covering her face and peered out from behind her elbows. She smelled burnt apple pie. She coughed, inhaled a few plastic beads, and spit them out. Henry stood before Ivy with his own arms outstretched. He mumbled to himself. Cotton and beads and ripped fabric passed through him like bullets.

Tipsy lowered her own arms from her face. She didn't share Henry's convenient transparency, so she'd have to act fast. Anything Ivy threw at her would make its mark.

What do I do, Granna?

Not sure honey, but you've protected others. You're just as worthy of protection.

Tipsy had a brief image of her twelve-year-old face in Granna's bathroom mirror. That girl had been frightened but fierce. She'd decided she wouldn't take any grief from the mean girls, and she kept her promise to get out of Martinville. Tipsy loved her, in all her self-conscious preteen glory.

This ghost wasn't going to hurt her. The time had indeed come to flex her own supernatural muscles. She was strong, and she suddenly knew what to do. Like her brain knew how to tell her legs to walk. She didn't have to think about it. She just did it.

Her own power rose inside her. A building clairvoyant sneeze she couldn't hold back.

ENOUGH, IVY! she shouted.

Tipsy's trembling hands steadied into tight fists. Henry snarled beside her. Tipsy's power met Henry's in a combined force like the confluence of two rivers, where the most dangerous currents churn.

We are tributaries of a greater body of water, she thought.

Beads pinged off the floorboards. Cotton had stuck in the ceiling fan and the screen. White blobs like wet toilet paper congealed in spilled water around the shards of a broken vase and scattered sunflowers.

Ivy's hair stood straight out from her head in dark spikes. Perhaps a shock reflex. She'd spend the past eighty years having supernatural tantrums and no one had ever intervened.

"That's indeed enough of that," said Henry. He had a tick under his eye.

Ivy glared at them from her spot near the haint blue ceiling. She looked like a sullen teenager who had been put in her place, but was stubbornly hanging onto rebellion.

"Come down, Ivy," said Henry. "This is all very disturbing, but let's try to remain calm."

Ivy sunk into the chair. Tipsy sat on the sofa herself. Her heart was beating like mad, but it wasn't unpleasant. She felt as if she'd finished a Crossfit class and lifted much heavier weight than expected. Maybe she'd be sore tomorrow, but for the moment, she was proud and exhilarated.

Tipsy's successful self-defense buoyed her. She didn't need to fear Ivy and had no more time for nonsense. "You need to be prepared. You're not going to like what happened to *you*, either."

"You must remember that what's done is done," said Henry. "If you blow up this house, you will still have spent the past eighty years trapped here. You will still have spent your last twelve living years without John. Nothing will change any of that. But you can celebrate the chance to see him again."

Some of the tension drained out of Ivy's shoulders. Her preternaturally beautiful face had frozen at an age where she'd never develop another wrinkle and nothing would ever sag, but she was suddenly a paradoxical mix of exhausted old woman and frightened child. Ivy had almost suffocated Tipsy with flying pillow entrails, but Tipsy still felt intense compassion for her.

"All right then." Ivy squeezed her handfuls of her skirt, as if in an effort to hold herself in place. "Tell me. Hurry though, before I change my mind. Or lose it."

"I only got the basics, but it seems relatively straightforward. It should be enough to help you remember." Tipsy leaned toward her. "You and Camden were arguing. You brought up John's ghost. You thought Camden killed him—"

"Why would I think Camden killed him?"

"We didn't have enough time for me to ask him. But you thought Camden did it, and he said he didn't. So then Camden grabbed you when you yelled in his face about killing John."

Tipsy waited for recognition to dawn on Ivy's face, as it had on John's, but she remained as blank as one of Tipsy's new canvases.

"So Camden *grabbed you*. He *pushed you*."

Still nothing.

"You fell off the dock. So Camden killed John, but he also killed *you*."

Ivy rested one elbow on the chair's armrest and the other on her chin. "Really?"

Tipsy exchanged glances with Henry, who was tensed to intervene in another supernatural explosion. "Uh, yeah. Does any of that ring a bell?"

Ivy shook her head.

"You don't remember any of it? The argument? Camden pushing you?"

"No. I don't. In fact, it strikes me as odd. Camden and I rarely fought. We mostly ignored each other."

Tipsy sat back. "What the actual?"

"Perhaps he lied?" For someone always on the edge of a conniption, she was remarkably calm. As if the story of her death were a mildly unpleasant fairy tale, or a piece of gossip that didn't involve her personally.

"He didn't lie about John," said Tipsy.

"John can leave now?" Ivy looked alarmed again.

"No. He can't, but he at least remembered what happened. We're not even getting that much with you." Tipsy stood. She yelped when she stepped on the beads from the destroyed cushions. "Argh! Maybe it's not straightforward at all. Maybe your mystery is the most convoluted one yet."

She wanted to pace around the porch to add fluidity to her pondering, but she winced and hopped with each step. Ivy leaned over and blew as if she was snuffing the candles on her one hundred and fifteenth birthday cake. The beads rolled like a stampede of roly-poly bugs and congregated in a neat pile beside the door.

"Damn these complicated deaths. If explaining yours won't get us anywhere, we have to look into your memories." Tipsy sat again and wiped a few beads from the bottoms of her feet. "You down?"

Ivy frowned. "Down where?"

"She means are you in agreement," said Henry. "They use directions in the oddest ways. Break up, you down, hang out."

"Yes. I'm down."

"Okay." Tipsy scooted to the end of the sofa. "Ivy, you sit in the middle. Henry, there."

They did as she asked.

"When I count to three, Henry and I are going to take your hands. You ready?"

Ivy closed her eyes and nodded. Tipsy started counting.

———•✕•———

Tipsy opens her eyes and she and Henry are standing at the head of a sandy path. The overhanging shaggy trees have created a tunnel to the beach. Brush opens up to dunes about a hundred yards ahead. The setting sun will soon melt away in the cold sea as it has done every evening since time immemorable. Like it will each night over the many years that separate Tipsy's when from this memory. It will continue to do so long after Tipsy's present becomes her own past.

The sunset is nothing special by Sullivan's standards, just a pinkish glow on the horizon, but the dark comes on fast. It's doubly murky under the maritime forest's canopy. A squirrel and a crow are arguing on the path. Tipsy feels like she's walking through a passageway to Wonderland. This time there's no grouchy caterpillar in her nonsensical allusion, but maybe the crow will suggest a caucus race. She and Henry and the squirrel will chase each other in haphazard circles. A race toward nowhere, seeking answers that elude them.

Ivy walks toward them from the beach. She's wearing her blue and white floral dress. This must be the day of her death. She's barefoot and her legs are covered in sand and water droplets. She stops to pick up her black, low-heeled shoes but she doesn't put them on. As she passes, Tipsy notices dark circles under her swollen eyes.

"She's been crying," whispers Henry.

"You don't have to whisper." Tipsy turns to follow Ivy and sees Camden approaching from the road. He's wearing a short-sleeved striped tee-shirt tucked into high-waisted brown trousers. He's barefoot too, and his pants are rolled up to reveal pale calves. He's still a handsome man in his mid-forties, but his fine blond hair is starting to go.

"Ivy," he says. "Where have you been? You've been gone three hours."

"Walking."

"You're always walking, but you're not eating. You're so thin you're going to disappear. Come on back to the cottage. Your family is expecting supper."

"I'll start supper when I'm done walking."

He takes her arm. "You can't expect me to entertain them."

"You're the one who invited them."

"You been crying?" He sniffs her. "Drinking?"

"No," she says, but she wipes her eyes and tries to put some distance between herself and Camden's nose.

"See here now. I know you and me don't talk a lot these days but I'm worried about you. That's why I called Saul. Bobby keeps asking me what's wrong with you."

"You won't believe me. You'll try to lock me up in the state hospital."

"Bobby needs you," Camden says, but he licks his lips like a man trying to get rid of a bad taste in his mouth. "I wouldn't do that."

Tipsy can feel her emotions—grief and longing and frightened hope—but her thoughts are scattered. She's been trapped in a mental loop for days. Asking herself the same questions over and over and coming up with faulty solutions. Impossible riddles drone behind her forehead. Between her vibrating head and her moonshine buzz, she's not thinking straight.

She abruptly decides to commiserate. Maybe Camden will understand. He loved John, too.

"It's Johnny," says Ivy.

Tipsy's eyes switch to Camden so fast she gets ocular whiplash. He pales under his ruddy farmer's tan. "What about him?"

"Not the true him. His ghost."

Camden chuckles. There's relieved disbelief in his voice. "What are you talking about?"

"My mother saw John's ghost."

"Damn, Ivy. We all know Alma is eccentric, but that's some story, even for her."

"It's not a story. I never told you, because—because… please believe me, Camden."

"All right now. Be serious."

"I'm as serious as a preacher on Good Friday. People in my family can see spirits. I've been looking for him because—"

Ivy comes a few words from telling Camden that she, too, sees ghosts, but the skepticism on his face and the thought of the straightjacket stop her. "Anyway, Mama saw him. John."

"That's what you've been doing the past few weeks? Walking around, looking for John's ghost?"

"I thought I might sense him. Might feel something from him." The truth is she's been desperate to find him and speak to him and look into his eyes. Even if they are the eyes of a dead man, a shadow. It's more than she has now, with the shadow of him across her heart every waking moment.

"Ivy, John is not a ghost. There's no such thing. He's—he's in heaven. He's playing poker with the angels and drinking the lord's whiskey."

"Why is that any more likely than him being a ghost?" She wrung her hands and the breeze picked up. "Maybe he is here. In some way. Since he drowned on the beach."

"John is dead. He's been gone twelve years."

"Wouldn't you want to see him if you could? We both loved him. It's the reason we're both standing here, miserable with each other. Because we loved him!"

"Just go home," says Camden.

She scowls. "John would have believed me. But you're not John."

"No. I'm not, but you're not what I wanted you to be, either. Go back to the cottage."

"No, I want to walk to—"

"Your damn family is in my house," snaps Camden. "A good, sane wife would feed them."

She backs away from him. Bitterness washes over her with a spurt of tears. Her indignation flows down her arms and into the sand below her. Those emotions creep up Tipsy's legs to her chilly heart like she's standing in a winter ocean. Ivy and Camden glare at each other until the crow returns to heckling the irritable squirrel.

"I'll see you at home," Ivy finally says.

Camden turns and walks toward the beach.

"Where are you going?" she asks.

He speaks over his shoulder. "Now it's my turn to find some peace. I surely won't get any in my own home tonight."

Tipsy senses different thoughts flitting through Ivy's befuddled mind. They solidify and then retreat back into the haze. Tipsy gets bits of insight into how Camden feels about the beach. He hates it. He refuses to go down there ever since he found John.

Ivy watches until he disappears in the gloom, then she follows him. She walks to the edge of the sandy path and crouches. She hunkers down until she's almost crawling along the beach. She scoots between one clump of tall grass and another like a ghost crab hiding from a hungry seagull. Henry motions to Tipsy and they go after her.

Camden stops walking. Tipsy and Henry jog toward him. Ivy huddles behind the nearest clump of grass and peeks through.

Camden's hands are in his pockets. He pulls out a handkerchief and presses it to his eyes.

"John? You here?" He takes a step toward the ocean. "Johnny!"

He gets no reply. There's no sound but the distant slosh of small waves against the shoreline. Camden sniffs. "It was low tide when I found you."

He sits on the beach in a heap. He slaps his cheek like he did in the barracks on the night he killed his cousin. "John. If you're out here anywhere, give me a sign. If you're in heaven or on this beach, please forgive me. I'm so sorry."

Ivy leans around the grass.

"Why?" Camden looks up at the stars. "What happened that night? Why did I do it? I don't know. I'm so sorry, Johnny. I miss you so much."

The whites of Ivy's eyes glow in the moonlight. She clenches fistfuls of sand.

Camden wipes his face. He snorts. "Now who's as crazy as Alma More. Nothing out here." He looks up at the sky. "I hope there's good whiskey in heaven, cousin."

Ivy's lips pull back in a snarl. The wind gusts, and Camden looks over his shoulder. Ivy hides again. Camden pulls a flask from his other pocket. He takes a long swig, and coughs. "Cheers," he says to the ocean.

Ivy backs away. Now she's a scorpion about to strike, not a skulking crab. For a moment, Tipsy is unsure if they should stay and try to watch Camden, or follow Ivy. It doesn't really matter, because as Ivy retreats into the darkness and Camden takes another drink, the memory fades.

◆⟩⟨◆

"No, no, no, no." Tipsy woke to the sound of her own voice protesting the end of the memory. The porch spun as she raised her head from the cushion. Henry had slid to the floor in a heap. Ivy was on her feet. She leaned over them.

"Did you see my death?" she asked.

Henry opened his eyes. "No. No death."

"We're so close." Tipsy's stomach turned, but she pulled the hairband from her wrist. She yanked her hair up into a ponytail. "Henry. Wake up. We have to go back."

"Yes. Back to Bennett Street." His head rolled on his neck like an apple with a loose stem.

"No. Back to Ivy's memories."

"I can't, Tipsy. It's too soon for me."

"Me too. I'll probably puke." She got up and retrieved the small trashcan from beside the screen door. She set it beside her and sat on the sofa again. "Now I'm ready."

Henry looked at her with exhausted eyes. "I'll try."

"Ivy. Sit, sit." Tipsy waved to the sofa. Ivy walked through the low coffee table as if it wasn't there, and sat between Tipsy and Henry again.

"I'm staying down here," said Henry. He held up one hand.

"Right. Ivy, I'll take your hand. You get Henry's. Ready? One... two... three..."

Ivy grabbed for Henry's misty fingers, and Tipsy's hand passed through hers. Unfortunately, as seemed to be becoming a trend, nothing happened.

◆⟩⟨◆

Henry's edges were starting to blur so he went home. Tipsy agreeably sent him on his way. He was usually a crisp lines kind of ghost, so it was not a good sign when he went from DaVinci to Monet.

Tipsy tried for another hour and got nowhere. She went to the gym to dispel some frustration and returned to True Blue to paint for the rest of the afternoon. By dinnertime, she rejoined Ivy on the back porch. She made a frozen pizza and forced down a piece. Another slice lay congealing on the plate on the coffee table.

"Why isn't it working?" Tipsy strode from one side of the porch to the other.

Ivy sat on the sofa and watched her go back and forth. For once, Ivy had to soothe Tipsy's agitation. "Maybe Camden thought he pushed me because we were fighting, but I just tripped and fell off the dock myself."

"Okay. So. Ivy. Y'all were fighting. You tripped and fell off the dock yourself. Any great revelation?"

Ivy sighed. "Nothing."

Tipsy stomped back to the chair and flopped into it. "What about Alma? Sandy said she came to town with Saul. She was there."

"What about her?"

"I mean—could she have killed you?"

Ivy looked as if Tipsy had told her Curly from the Three Stooges became President of the United States. "My own mother?"

"After Jane and Henry, and then Camden killing John, I've learned anyone can kill anyone."

"Could your Granna have killed you?"

Oh for heaven's sake!

"It's a legitimate question, Granna." Tipsy said it out loud, since she didn't need to hide her spectral communication from Ivy.

I'm offended.

"Granna is offended," said Tipsy.

"Mama would have been offended, too. She may have been a crackpot, but she loved me and Saul. After my daddy disowned me, they were all the family I had. She came to help me, not—" Ivy chuckled. "—*kill* me."

"We're never going to get anywhere muddling around like this. We need to see what happened." Tipsy rested her head on the back of the chair and stared up at the haint blue ceiling. "We're still missing something. Or someone. I needed Camden's view of John's death. With Jane and Henry, I had to see into both of their memories at once to get the whole story."

"Touch them both?"

"In a way, yes. Camden was there when you died. I want to touch you both and see what that reveals. But Jane and Henry haunted the same location. How can I get you, me, and Camden in the same place?"

"That is a conundrum," said a smooth male voice.

Henry was suddenly sitting in the chair to Tipsy's right as if he'd never left the porch. "Sorry for the abrupt entrance, ladies."

"You're a DaVinci again," said Tipsy.

"Ah. I'd prefer to be a Raphael. More romantic." He soundlessly strummed his fingers on the chair's arm. "If Camden and Ivy need to be in the same place, it makes sense that she goes to him."

"But I can't leave this cottage the way you leave your house," said Ivy.

"Maybe you don't know how. You're mighty powerful. Throwing tree limbs and what not. If I manage to travel in fit and spurts, surely you could master it."

"But I've tried a million times. I wanted to keep looking for John. I figured if we were both ghosts, at least we'd be ghosts together."

"I said that to Jane!" said Tipsy. "Like, a couple's haunting! It's ideal, when you think about it."

"Not if your wife thinks you killed her," replied Henry.

"It never worked," said Ivy. "I walked to the edges of the yard. I pushed and pushed, but nothing happened. I ran toward the water and tried to dive in. I jumped off the roof. I climbed the trees—"

"I see the problem." Henry stood. "You're treating the boundaries of your haunting as if they are physical barriers. As if they exist like a door or a fence. You're trapped in the mindset of the living."

Ivy scowled. "I'm offended by that comment."

"Perhaps it's been easier for me, since I'm a writer of fiction. I have always existed in the imaginary places in my head. They are as real to me as this porch is right now. Smells, sounds, colors."

Tipsy nodded. "It's the same with my paintings. They're more real to me than reality, sometimes. It's sometimes a relief. I have a place to escape."

"Do you have any such creative talents?"

Ivy shook her head.

"What about music," said Tipsy. "You sing."

"That's merely repeating the words. There's not much creativity in it," said Henry.

"Said like a true creativity snob. There's a lot of creativity in it. Everyone sings a song in their own way. It's your personal interpretation of the story in the words. Like *Somewhere Over the Rainbow*. I loved your version. You made it your own." Tipsy turned to Henry. "You remember that song, right? From when you watched *The Wizard of Oz* with me and the kids last winter."

"Ah, yes!" said Henry. "A splendid film. And a lovely tune."

"When I sing," said Ivy. "I do sometimes imagine myself leaving this place. Blown away by one of my own tornadoes and ending up in Oz, where I can walk right on down the Yellow Brick Road for hours if I want. No imaginary walls stopping me." She squirmed. "It sounds silly when I say it."

Henry rested his elbows on his knees. "It's not silly at all. That's what I mean. Can you see the lines between the yellow bricks? Hear the munchkins singing lullabies? Smell the flying monkey shit?"

"Yuck, Henry," said Tipsy.

"Sorry to offend, but that's the kind of vision she must harness."

Ivy stood. "Camden and I took Bobby to the theater to watch the movie for his birthday. I'd never seen anything like it. I remember how

Dorothy's red slippers sparkled. How the witch's skin was the color of spring grass. When I imagine going to Oz, I see those colors as clear as they were on the screen at the Riviera on King Street."

"Yes. That's what you need," said Henry. "You visit those places in your daydreams. You must bring the same clarity of thought to the places you want to visit outside of this house. Don't try to walk or run or even fly there, just *be there*."

"Of course I'd like to be with John… but I can't imagine it will really happen—"

"No, no. You must imagine. *You must imagine all things.* You must believe you can travel to John as easily as you travel to Oz in your fantasies."

Ivy closed her eyes.

"Wait, Ivy. Be careful," said Tipsy. "What if something goes wrong?"

"She'll have no choice but to come back." Henry lowered his voice. "See the place, Ivy, but also smell it, and listen to it, and feel it."

Ivy whispered to herself. Once again, she floated toward the ceiling with her feet hanging limply below her. Her hair and skirt fluttered like the wings of a thousand bluebirds. "Johnny," she said. And with that, over the rainbow she went.

Tipsy jumped to her feet. She grabbed her keys and hustled through the house. "I'll meet you there, Henry!"

She drove down Thompson Street like a restrained bat out of hell concerned about a speeding ticket from the devil. She parked in front of the old barracks. Henry stood beside the barracks looking out toward the Ravenel Bridge. Tipsy ran toward him. "Do you see them?"

"Shhh." He peeked around the building. "Give them some privacy, Tipsy. It's been ninety years."

"Right." Tipsy crouched and peered around the corner herself. The sun was setting. Ivy walked across the dock. John stood on the end of the dilapidated structure. He watched the water, as he had done on an immemorable number of late summer evenings.

Ivy must have said John's name, because he spun around. Ivy stopped and placed a hand over her heart. They both stood still with the light dancing on their shimmery outlines. They were ghosts seeing ghosts.

John strode across the dock. His arms wrapped around Ivy's waist. Hers went around his neck and they came together. Tipsy wasn't quite sure what was happening, but the light shining from them was like a second sunset.

Chapter 16

At first Ivy could only stay with John for short bursts of time, but she quickly learned to manage the stress of her comings and goings. She'd return to True Blue, hibernate in her invisible state for a while, and reappear at his side for an hour or two. Henry was impressed, as he turned into a proverbial pumpkin much faster himself.

The change in Ivy was nothing short of amazing. She glowed like a Fourth of July sparkler. Between Tipsy's newfound confidence in her ability to protect herself and Ivy's change of mood, she no longer feared the ghost at all. A relief, since they were temporarily existing under the same roof.

Ivy laughed and chatted and asked Tipsy questions about her own life. A little distracting when Tipsy was working, but she'd almost finished Pamella's painting. She'd never had the chance to talk to a friend about seeing ghosts, so the two of them enjoyed trading war stories.

"I wish I'd known my grandfather," Ivy said, as they sat on the back porch. "He was mighty powerful with all things, worldly and otherworldly."

"In our family it skips a generation," said Tipsy. "Granna's grandmother passed it to her. She passed it to me. All women in my family."

"Mama told me it's more common in women. But when it comes through in men, it comes strong, like my grandfather."

"Yeah. Look at Henry. He's no half-assed male clairvoyant. He's an unusual guy in general. Pretty intense."

"Abundance Chapman was the same. He was a powerful preacher. People came from all over to hear his sermons. They would faint on the regular from the power of his words. Or from his true power acting on them in other ways," said Ivy. "I wish I'd known Henry and I shared this talent. It would have been nice to know someone who truly saw spirits like I did. Not like Mama's wishy-washiness."

Tipsy set down her paintbrush. "Were you afraid you'd end up a ghost?"

Ivy nodded. "I had nightmares of being trapped in Bubba's house, and then in the Huger House. I never felt trapped at this cottage in life, yet this is where I ended up."

"Funny how for us, the fear is about *becoming* a ghost. Most ghosts themselves aren't very scary. Just sad." Tipsy's phone dinged. "Ugh. It's Ayers."

"Large or small?"

"Big Ayers. I never *ugh* over a message from Little A. The question is, since he doesn't have the kids, do I have to read his message?"

"I think I'd be too curious to ignore it."

Tipsy nodded her agreement and opened the message.

AYERS: WE SET A DATE 4 WEDDING. SATURDAY OF LABOR DAY WEEKEND AT MOM AND DAD'S. KATE'S PARENTS, SISTER AND BROTHER NEED THE 3 DAY WEEKEND TO COME IN FROM TN AND MIMI AND JIMMY WILL BE BACK. SINCE THAT'S YOUR KID WEEKEND, I NEED U TO SWITCH WITH ME. THX

TIPSY: CONGRATULATIONS. HAVE YOU DISCUSSED WITH THE CHILDREN?

AYERS: FACETIMING THEM TONIGHT. THEY WILL BE EXCITED. THEY LOVE KATE AND HER KIDS

TIPSY: I WISH YOU ALL THE BEST.

AYERS: DON'T BE AN ASSHOLE TIPSY

I'M NOT BEING AN ASSHOLE. I TRULY HOPE IT WORKS OUT, FOR THE KIDS' SAKE. Tipsy paused, and then added another message. AND FOR YOUR SAKE, TOO. I HOPE YOU'LL BE HAPPY.

THX.

"What did he say?" asked Ivy.

Tipsy told her, and then said, "I do want him to be happy. And I feel a little guilty. Pammy warned me if I pushed him, he'd rush into marriage. That's exactly what I did. I'm always trying to fix things. It's about fifty-fifty as to whether my efforts help or screw things up. But I'm not good at waiting it out."

"Being dead and trapped in a house teaches you nothing if not how to wait."

"That makes me really hope I don't end up a ghost."

"I learned to exist with it and not go completely insane."

"Partial insanity is not terribly reassuring."

"I know, but when you take action, there will always be result. It might not be the one you want. You must be willing to accept the outcome, or learn to pause for a moment and see what happens naturally."

Tipsy thought of her struggles with painter's block in the past. Several months of waiting on Jane and Henry to inspire her had ultimately helped her remember how to let her ideas flow naturally. "The paintings that come together on their own are better than the ones I force onto the canvas."

"Weigh the scales between action and patience. All things require balance."

"Lately I've been pondering the balance between settling for less and expecting perfection. Granna and I were talking about fear and control, too. I'll add action versus patience to my weigh-ins. I'm, like, on an emotional tightrope that's strung across a river of theoretical conundrums." She chuckled and picked up her paintbrush. "I'm living in a Henry Mott novel."

"I remember Henry used to talk about his stories, but I don't know if I ever actually *saw* a book he'd written. We certainly didn't stock them at Patjen's with the flour and lye soap."

"Henry's still hammering away at his literary masterpiece."

"I'd like to hear the moral of his story."

"I don't know how Mr. Mott's grand fable turns out, but living with someone like him sure gets you thinking in useful metaphors." Tipsy picked up one of her kneaded erasers. "Like, blue paint doesn't keep ghosts at bay. Forcing them into bottles doesn't work either. Getting to know your ghosts takes longer but ultimately gets them moving on their way."

"I'm certainly glad you persevered with me."

"Me too. So I'll give patience a try. Or I'll *try* to give it a try. I have a lifetime of impatience to overcome." Tipsy smushed the eraser between her palms like a stress relief ball. As if the thought of practicing serene forbearance already gave her anxiety. "Do you think you're ready to go downtown and see Camden?"

Ivy shivered at the thought, but she nodded.

"Now I have to figure out how I'm going to get back into the Huger House," said Tipsy, "so I can be there with y'all."

"Will your house selling friend take you inside again?"

"I doubt it. Last time I threw up in the shrubbery."

"Ah. Well, this might be a situation where it's best to push rather than wait and see what happens."

"Right. No one is going to let me in, so I might have to bust open the doors. I'll talk to Pamella tonight. She might have ideas. We're going to the Windjammer to see a Michael Jackson cover band."

"Pardon?"

"A place on the Isle of Palms where people go to watch musicians play. It's a band that only plays songs by this famous musician who died a few years ago. Sort of like a memorial to him. Funny, he wrote a super famous song about dead people."

"Ghosts?"

"More like zombies. Walking corpses."

"Distasteful."

"People are into zombies these days. Ghosts too, even if they don't understand them."

"I'm glad there are people like you who *do* understand us."

Tipsy blew an air kiss in Ivy's direction and went to her room to get ready for a night at the Windjammer. As she slathered mascara over her eyelashes, she mulled over her previously sound theories about ghosts and hauntings.

Can anyone ever truly understand ghosts?

Can anyone ever truly understand the living? retorted Granna.

Touché, Granna. Touché.

Tipsy stood on the Windjammers' sprawling back deck. She and Pamella had maneuvered past the indoor bar and stage to find fresh air and a shorter line at the outdoor bar. The deck overlooked a beach volleyball court that doubled as a venue for the Windjammer's famous weekly bikini contests. Even outside, the smells of beer foam and fry grease hung in the warm air like trailer park perfume. The Jammer always teemed with a mix of tourists and hard partying locals. Regional bands attracted diehard fans who clustered around the stage, screaming out their favorite college jams and Southern rock covers. Tribute bands also drew large crowds. Tipsy had seen it all in this place over the years. Disco nights. Eighties cover bands who came dressed in neon legwarmers and hair band kitsch. A Zach Brown imposter for those who might not be able to afford tickets to see the real thing.

This MJ cover band, Bad Attitude, had quite a following. Pamella had bought tickets months before. Since she no longer needed one for her estranged husband, she'd offered it to Tipsy. Tipsy had always had a soft spot for the King of Pop, so she accepted. She'd pulled out her white shorts and mixed it up with a flowy, flowery red top. She wore wedges to lift her feet out of the beer residue. Pamella wore spandex bike shorts, a retro MTV tee-shirt with the sleeves ripped off, huge hoop earrings, and designer tennis shoes with gold laces and stars on the toes.

"MJ would approve of this outfit," said Tipsy, after they got their drinks.

"I wear it in his honor. Would have sported it in high school in his heyday, but my hair would have been bigger."

Tipsy scanned the assembled MJ fans. As she scrolled over the people clustered around the outside bar, she locked eyes with Kim Nowak.

She started to wave, but Kim tossed her hair and returned to resting her boobs on the bar to entice the tattooed bartender. "There's Kim," said Tipsy.

Pamella rolled her eyes. "Whatever. I forgot to tell you. She's *annoyed with me* for giving Clarice your number. I guess someone told her y'all went out."

"Is she mad at me?"

"Probably."

"Oh, lord. I sensed she was into him, but they're not dating. I mean, he's pretty adamant he's not dating *anyone*. Like, ever. But now I feel bad about it! She seems nice and I—"

"Yeah, she's nice. I've known Kim for years." Pamella sniffed, and Tipsy detected contempt in that quick intake of air. "She is the nicest person ever, but *only* as long as she gets her way."

Tipsy's stomach flipped. "Crap. What happens when she *doesn't* get her way?"

"*Seriously*, don't worry about it. It's obvious to everyone but her they're not a couple. She's obsessed with him. It's not healthy, bless her heart."

Tipsy thought of her conversation with Shelby, before it disintegrated into the BFF Battle of the Century. About her female Billy Idol neighbor's equally angsty curiosity. "Apparently a lot of women are obsessed with him."

"Are you?"

"No! I've barely talked to him since we went on the boat. A couple texts. Ugh!" Tipsy added *Date with Clarice Andrews* to her list of recent questionable decisions. How had she thought going out with the most desirable yet emotionally unavailable bachelor in town would be uncomplicated? "Lindsey was right. I should have stayed away from him. Now all these women are pissed at me. And how are we going to get into the Huger House without Kim?"

"I've been thinking about that. There's a gate on the side of the house. From what they did with the landscaping, it's probably covered up with trees. I bet no one uses it anymore. At least it's more private than the Philip Simmons on Meeting."

The familiar beat of *Billy Jean* pulsed through the walls. The buzzed masses, including Kim, shuffled toward the door.

"... *not my lov-a... she's just a girl*—you wanna go in and dance?" asked Pamella.

"In a minute. I'm going to get water out here so I don't have to wait in the line inside."

"I'll meet you in there!" Pamella moonwalked backward with her plastic cup of wine held over her head.

Tipsy bellied up to the cleared out bar. The bartenders were doing shots, so she fished through her purse for her lip gloss.

"Can I get this one?"

No mistaking that voice. She looked up at Clarice Andrews. "Oh, lord. Look who it is. The man who loves to buy my drinks. Why do I see you everywhere now?"

"Maybe it's fate."

"Doubtful. I know something about fate. You're not part of mine."

"Ouch. So can I get you a beer? Bud Light, right?"

"I have a beer." She tapped her beer can. "Getting water. So thanks, but no thanks."

"Why are you so testy with me?"

She leaned on the bar. "I'm not. I just don't want any complications. You're already turning into a big one."

"How so? To the contrary, I'm the easiest man you'll ever deal with."

Tipsy laughed. "That's what you don't get. Your male version of simple is actually a woman's version of complex."

He tucked a stray piece of hair behind her ear. "When you want to consider my version, you let me know, and I'm there."

She gently pushed his hand away. "I won't want to consider it. Ever."

"What if I want to consider *your* version?"

"*You* won't."

"But maybe I will. Maybe I'll—"

"Clarice, listen. You're nice and I had fun on the boat, but I don't think it's a good idea—"

"Don't *y'all* look cozy!"

Tipsy turned toward a shrill voice that carried over MJ's classic bass beat. Kim Nowak stood a few feet away from them with her arms crossed over her breasts, a beer can in one hand, and a plastic shot cup in the other.

Tipsy hadn't gotten her water, but she backed away. "I told Pamella I'd meet her inside."

"Yeah. Why don't you do that, *Tipsy*," said Kim. "I think Clarice owes me a private conversation."

Tipsy tried to scoot by Kim. As she passed, Kim whispered under her breath. "*Whore*."

Tipsy navigated the crowd and found Pamella dancing near the stage. "Kim just called me a whore!" she yelled, as Pamella swayed and shimmied.

"Who cares?"

"Maybe I should go home. Plus Ayers told me he's getting married—"

"Screw her! Screw Ayers, too! Whooo! *Mama-say-mama-sa-mama-poo-saw!*"

"Yeah, pretty girl! Screw them!" A guy in his twenties busted into their conversation. "Y'all want a shot?"

One of his friends magically seemed to have Fireball shots in his pocket. He handed one to Tipsy. She shook her head. "No thanks. I haven't eaten much—"

"Hell, Tipsy! *Lighten up!*" Pamella slurped a shot. "You going to let Kim get under your skin and ruin your night?"

Tipsy scowled. She had come to have fun. "You know what? You're right. Screw her." She grabbed the shot and threw it back. Her gorge rose, but she kept it down.

"Hell, yeah!" The young dudes high-fived her.

Tipsy started dancing. For the next two hours, she almost felt twenty-something, with no responsibilities. She sang along. She yelled out

"*Who's bad?*" She did the thriller zombie dance and wished Ivy could see her. She threw back two more shots and someone got her a vodka tonic. Sweat darkened her chocolatey brownish hair to true brunette. Her thighs would surely hurt tomorrow from gettin' so low.

The band finished off with *Beat It*. Tipsy screamed along with everyone else. The music stopped and she realized she hadn't yet broken the seal. She stood still but the room kept spinning.

"I don't feel great," she said to Pamella. "I never got my water but I need to pee."

She fought her way through the revelers to the bathroom. The women's line was twice as long as the men's line, but she finally made it into a stall. She hunched over the toilet to pee without touching the seat.

She opened the door and walked to the sink to wash her hands. Her sweaty reflection stared back at her. Her eyes were bloodshot. She desired a cold Coke above all things.

"Can I talk to you?"

Tipsy kept washing her hands.

"Umm... hello! Can I *talk to you?*"

She turned. Kim leaned around the women in front of her in line. If looks could kill, Tipsy would have been just as dead as any of her ghostly pals.

"Kim, I'm sorry you're upset but I'm going home—"

"That wasn't really a question. I want to talk to you. Now."

The women around them glanced at each other and grimaced. A few giggled.

"We're in a public bathroom," said Tipsy.

Kim stepped into the fluorescent lighting. "I don't care. I have nothing to hide!"

"Whatever is going on between you and Clarice is between y'all. Leave me out of it." Tipsy tried to scoot past Kim, but Kim moved into her path. Tipsy blinked down at her as the bathroom spun.

"I thought we were friends!" said Kim. "Then you go screwing Clarice behind my back!"

The women in line twittered and turned away. Frustration shone through Tipsy's Fireball fog. "I did *not* screw Clarice."

"Sure! Like I believe you after you sat beside me and didn't even mention you were seeing him!"

"I'm not seeing him, either!"

"That's right. You're *not* seeing him. Because he's just using you for a booty call." She guffawed. "I don't even see what the appeal is. You're not even that cute."

"You make no sense. Please move."

"You wait. He'll be sick of you soon and screw you over. Don't come crying to me."

"Whoa. First of all, I'm not crying to you about anything. Second of all, if anyone is a booty call, it's you."

"You bitch!" Kim's voice carried over the flushing toilets and blasting hand dryers. "I knew you were a snob as soon as I met you."

"What the hell—I liked you. I even felt sorry for you!"

"Did you like me? Did you *really*? Or were you just trying to get to him?"

"You're insane. Get out of my way."

"Stay away from him!"

"I don't want him! But guess what—you're delusional, because he doesn't want you! You look like a fool talking about how y'all have this *big loooove connection* when you're number one on his hook up short list! Wake up, Kim!"

Kim looked as if Tipsy had slapped her in the face. The women around them were shocked into wide eyed silence.

Kim started babbling. Tipsy heard some of it—a myriad of ways to describe a prostitute—as she fled into the crowd. She fumbled her way down the step front steps to the sidewalk. People were milling around while waiting for Ubers and singing about *rocking with you… all night*. She looked for Pamella's dark hair towering above everyone else, but for once, Pammy hadn't been wearing heels.

Sugar, get it together.

Okay, Granna. Okay. Tipsy opened her eyes as wide as possible, as if bug eyes would fix her wobbly vision. She crossed the street near The Dinghy, a dive bar where the party would continue. She needed a spot to call her own Uber. She absolutely could not drive.

Spit built up in the back of her throat as she walked.

Are you going to be sick? asked Granna. *Oh lord, Tipsy—*

Tipsy darted into a condo parking lot and retched into a bush.

That's two shrubs I've puked on in the past week. She grabbed for her phone. *Uber. Uber.* Her keys jangled in her purse.

"Hey! Tipsy!"

She spun around at the male voice. She brandished her car key, ready to stab a potential rapist in the eye, but it was Clarice.

"What the hell do you want?" she asked. "Leave me alone!"

"Whoa. Are you okay?"

"Stop asking me that! No! I'm puking in a damn bush and Kim Nowak called me a whore in front of about twenty people!" She screwed up her face in an effort to replicate Kim's disdainful scowl. "And she was all, *you're not even that cute.*"

Clarice chuckled. "She's jealous, because you're not cute, you're beautiful. I'll deal with her. She went off on me too. Don't worry about her. She'll get over it."

"That's easy for you to say! God knows what she's going to say about me to other people."

"No one will pay attention to her. Everyone knows she's nuts."

Tipsy balled her hands into fists to keep from shoving him. "If she's so nuts, why are you still sleeping with her? You are, aren't you?"

"Uh—well…"

"And it's not just her! What about Andrea who looks like Billy Idol?"

He laughed out loud this time. "She kind of does. I hadn't thought of that. But she's nice, and harmless, too."

"Neither of them is harmless to me when they're clearly infatuated with you. If you like me, why are you dragging me into this crap? You say you want to be my friend, but I don't want a friend who alienates me from half the female population of Charleston. Plus if you really want to be friends, why can't you just be my *friend*? Why touch my face and be all coy and—"

"Because I guess I don't just want to be your friend. But I'm still not looking for a girlfriend."

"So leave me alone, Clarice!" She sniffed and wiped her eyes.

He held up his hands and crept toward her as if approaching a skittish horse. "I swear this time. Just a hug, okay? You need one."

She stiffened when he put his arms around her, but she felt too awful to push him away. "I don't want my life to be like this. I only want my family and home and peace."

"I wish I wanted those things too," he said. He rubbed her back.

"I'm going to throw up again." She lunged away from him toward the bush.

"Can I help?" he asked, as she yacked.

She shook her head.

"I'm driving you home," he said.

"I'll take an Uber."

"There's no way in hell I'm letting you get in the car with a strange guy, Uber or not. Let me drive you home."

Let him drive you, sugar, please. I'll worry if you're in one of those strange cars.

Tipsy wiped her mouth. "Fine. You can take me back to True Blue. But that's it. Do you promise?"

"Promise."

"If you come in the house, I'll start screaming." Tipsy thought of Ivy. "If I yell bad stuff will happen. Like crazy stuff. Ceiling fan might fall on your head. Rug pulled out from under you."

He patted her shoulder. "Okay. What exactly did you have to drink?"

"I won't be held responsible if an unseen hand pushes you down the steps."

He turned on his phone and shone his flashlight into her eyes. "Your pupils look alright."

"You think someone roofied me?"

"It's possible."

"Or maybe I'm crazier than Kim." She giggled. "Maybe I am, to quote a friend of mine, partially insane." She stumbled and Clarice caught her.

"No. You're not crazy. But you're obviously a lightweight." He put an arm around her waist. She leaned on him as they walked toward his car.

He opened the door and helped her into the passenger seat. "You're going to feel this tomorrow."

She rested her head against the window. "I've lived with nausea and headaches before. I'm a pro."

He got into the driver's seat. "When you were pregnant?"

"No," she mumbled. "Ghosts make me sick."

"Okay. Close your eyes."

She did as he asked.

◆✕◆

Tipsy had not had a hangover like this in years. She got up and slept on the bathroom floor for a couple hours, for toilet proximity and the soothing coolness of the tile beneath her face. She crept into bed before dawn, but when she woke a little after eight, nausea gripped her and the room still spun when she moved. Over the next four hours, she threw up twice more. The last time she had nothing left in her stomach, so she weathered the terrible gut-clenching, eye-bulging torture of the dry heaves.

Ivy had appeared in the living room when Tipsy stumbled inside and slammed the door. Now that they were friends, Ivy was always up for girl talk, but Tipsy had shooed her away with her hand over her mouth and plowed toward the bedroom.

"Goodness," Ivy said, as she passed. "You look saucy."

"Understatement." Tipsy couldn't get anything else out and Ivy left her alone to hurl up her guts in private. When Tipsy woke a glass of water sat on the bedside table, courtesy of her new friend's telekinetic power. Granna stayed silent, but Tipsy sensed her concern.

By noon, she'd recovered enough to look at her phone, although her eyeballs pulsed in time to the rhythm of the words. Pamella and Clarice had both texted well after midnight, asking her to confirm she was still alive.

She sent a reply to Pamella (YUP STILL HERE FEELING LIKE CRAP NEAR DEATH EXPERIENCE TEXT YOU LATER XO). She copied the same message to Clarice but modified it slightly (YUP STILL HERE FEELING LIKE CRAP NEAR DEATH EXPERIENCE THANKS SO MUCH FOR THE RIDE).

Granna finally spoke up. *I know you're feeling bad when you leave out the punctuation.*

I'm so sorry, Granna. I feel like I've made one mistake after another lately and last night was the disaster to top it all off. The cherry on my chocolate sundae of bad decisions.

Everyone makes mistakes! I'm just glad you're safe.

Tipsy read the next message, from Lindsey. As she squinted at the tiny text, her stomach turned again.

LINDSEY: HEY HONEY YOU OKAY? MY NEIGHBOR TOLD ME SHE SAW YOU AT THE WJ LAST NIGHT AND YOU WERE STUMBLING… SHE WAS AFRAID YOU'D FALL DOWN THE STAIRS. SHE ALSO HEARD SOME CHICK WENT ALL MIDDLE SCHOOL DRAMA ON YOU IN THE BATHROOM?!? WTH. CALL ME.

Tipsy huddled against the pillows. Word of her catfight had already gotten out. Mortification leaked from every pore. What if Ayers found out about the drama? Or Will?

Ivy materialized at the foot of the bed. "Can I get you anything?" asked the ghost.

"A new reputation? If that's not possible, a Coke would be amazing."

Ivy disappeared, and a few minutes later, the bedroom door creaked open. Ivy slid through it with a Coke floating before her. The shine of frosty condensation on the crimson and white can about made Tipsy drool. "Oh, lord. Bless you."

The can floated across the bed. Ivy popped the top as Tipsy took hold of it. Soda struck Tipsy's wrist, as refreshing as the salt spray hitting her shoulders on a hot boat day. The fizzing and popping bubbles were whispers of reassurance. She would not join Ivy in haunting this house via alcohol poisoning.

She took a tentative sip. "Why is this stuff so delicious?"

"Always has been. I kept a few bottles in the icebox after I married Camden. We couldn't afford it when I was a child. Besides, my Daddy only liked ginger ale."

"Blech. Granna made me drink ginger ale when I was sick."

Don't hate on ginger ale, said Granna. *It's the great cure all.*

"Granna says it's the great cure all, but I prefer Coke. Nectar of the gods."

"I made my Bobby drink ginger ale when he had an upset belly."

Thank you!

"Granna appreciates your support for her homegrown remedies." Tipsy rolled onto her side. "Now if only y'all had a remedy for humiliation."

"What happened?"

Tipsy explained the night to Ivy. Shelby would have been proud of her rendition, which included as many exaggerated facial expressions and hand gestures as she could manage from her Bed of Shame.

"So she was all, *why don't you do that, Tip-seeeeeee!*"

"We danced our asses off for, like, two hours." Bedridden zombie dance hands.

"And I was all, *you're just a booty call, get over it!* And everyone was like—" Staring wide eyes. Mouth hanging open.

"Then I go galumphing down the stairs like confused salmon swimming downstream—"

"All the sudden I realize I'm going to puke—" Cue impression of ralphing cat.

"And Clarice is all, *let me drive you home* and I'm all, *no, no, leave me alone,* and Granna's like, *sugar, get your ass in that car before you get raped—*"

Uh, not exactly.

Shelby-like dramatic effect, Granna!

"And so that's it. Now I'm sitting here like a shriveled prune. I feel like a hundred zombies are moonwalking in my head. I'm already getting texts that word of my performance is making the gossip rounds. Coca-Cola and conversation with my ghostly AirBnB host are my only comfort." Tipsy's body somehow found enough moisture for her eyes to tear up. "I'm seriously so embarrassed, Ivy. That is not me. I don't really like to drink much. I haven't gotten sick in years. No one will remember all the times I *haven't* made a fool of myself."

"I got so used to drinking that I never made a fool of myself. If you did this one time, that's more likely a sign that you *don't* drink too much. You're no good at it."

"But people in this town are unforgiving."

"Nothing has changed, then."

"I can't think about it. Let's deal with your problems." She mentioned the hidden gate. "I suppose it's our best shot, for now. But I'm going to need at least a day to recover from this."

"Why don't you rest? I think I'll go see Johnny." Ivy smiled. "It is amazing to be able to talk to him once more. I feel… dare I say it… I almost feel alive again."

Once Ivy disappeared, Tipsy picked up her phone again. She opened Lindsey's message and typed a reply.

TIPSY: HEY. I'M ALL RIGHT. WORST HANGOVER IN YEARS BUT IT'S MY PRIDE THAT'S HURTING THE MOST. I'M SOOOOO EMBARRASSED. I THOUGHT I WAS ABOVE ALL THE BOOZY BS AROUND HERE, BUT I GUESS NOT.

LINDSEY: DON'T WORRY ABOUT IT! IT HAPPENS TO ALL OF US SOONER OR LATER. CAN'T LIVE IN CHARLESTON WITHOUT AT LEAST ONE GOOD PUKING HANGOVER PER DECADE.

TIPSY: PLEASE DON'T SAY ANYTHING TO P.D.. HE'LL TELL WILL.

LINDSEY: OF COURSE NOT! BUT THEY MIGHT HEAR ANYWAY. ☹

TIPSY: I KNOW. BUT I CAN HOPE THE GOSSIP GODS WILL BE MERCIFUL. GOING TO GET SOME SLEEP. TALK LATER. LOVE YA.

LINDSEY: XOXO

Before Tipsy closed the window on her phone, Shelby's name appeared across the top. YOU OKAY?

Tipsy's eyes watered again. Lindsey probably told her, but Tipsy wasn't annoyed. Shelby would have been her first text under normal circumstances. YES. I'M OKAY. THANKS.

SHELBY: K.

TIPSY: YOU?

SHELBY: GOOD.

TIPSY: THAT'S GOOD.

SHELBY: K.

So Shelby wasn't ready to talk it out yet. Tipsy wasn't really ready either, but it was a start.

◆—————◆✕◆—————◆

That evening, Tipsy sat on the back porch with her third Coke. She'd heated up another frozen pizza. Her headache was slowly dissipating under the weight of sugar and cheese, but she wasn't herself. Every thought took a little longer than it should. Even feeling dusty, she couldn't block out last night's drama. She winced whenever a snippet of her inebriated spectacle popped into her mind.

Never again, Granna.

Famous last words, sugar. Try not to think about it. Remember the Beatles' advice.

Let it be. I should teach Ivy that song. She can sing me to sleep with Mother Mary's words of wisdom.

Her phone rang as she watched a pair of crows bickering along the edge of the marsh. A Facetime call from May Penny. The kids usually called her on their grandmother's phone. She rubbed her eyes and tightened her ponytail for a Pamella-style facelift and accepted the call.

Their three little faces crammed into the screen. They all had wet hair and additional freckles from the Florida sun. She waved. "Hey, buddies!"

They returned her greeting with a dictionary entry for matriarchal synonyms. "Hey, Mom-Mama-Mommy!"

"What are y'all up to?"

"We went fishing on some rich guy's boat!" said Mary Pratt. "It was, like, so amazing."

"It totally was, Mama," said O-liv. "It has, like, beds and a kitchen and a hot tub."

"Wow."

"One of Uncle Jimmy's law firm guys," said Little A, sagely. "If you want to be rich, go into the law. That's what Dad says."

"It's a good job, but not all lawyers are super rich, honey. Some help poor people, too."

"So you're poor if you help the poor, and rich if you help the rich?" Ayers's brow wrinkled. "That seems screwed up."

"It's more complicated than that, but sometimes life is screwed up. Anyway, Mary Pratt, I've always thought you would make an excellent lawyer."

"Because she always has to be right," said Ayers.

"Hey!" said M.P. "But, most of the time... I am right."

Tipsy laughed again and listened to their chatter for a while. They were clearly having a blast with their cousins and their grandparents. Gratitude for their good fortune washed over her. It might seem she'd made a mistake in marrying Ayers, but she got her kids out of it. She'd do it all again and wouldn't change a thing. As for the kids' welfare, being the grandchildren of May Penny and Tripp Collins certainly had its benefits. As long as they stayed grounded, she thanked the lord for the experiences they would have and the safety net below them. Two things she'd never experienced as a child.

"Mama," said M.P., almost shyly. "Can we show you something?"

"Sure, honey. What's up?"

O-liv and M.P. scrambled around in the background. O-liv held a magazine up to the phone and pointed at a photo of a little girl in a long, pale blue dress. "This is our flower girl dress."

Tipsy smiled. "Wow, girls. Those are lovely."

"Do you really like it?" Tipsy sensed a need for approval in O-liv's question.

"I love it! I'm so happy y'all get to wear those. You will be gorgeous."

"Daddy said we can get our hair done and our nails done," said M.P. "So fun!"

"Will you be there?" O-liv asked.

"Liv, of course Mom isn't going to be there," said Ayers. "That would be so weird."

"It's okay, A. No, honey. I won't be there. But it's aaaaallll good. Seriously. Y'all will have a great time and I want you to send me lots of pics!"

"Okay." M.P. smiled down at the picture. "I think everything will be *all good*. Right, Mama?"

Again, there were all kinds of loaded questions in that simple statement, and many potential answers. Tipsy gave M.P. the reassurance she needed, even as she wondered how Ayers's marriage would turn out.

"I think so, buddies. A wedding is always an exciting time. It's a new start."

"A lot of new stuff," said Ayers.

"Yes. Y'all have had lots of new stuff over the past couple years. And you've handled it like champs because I know it's not always easy. The one thing that won't ever change is how much I love you and how much your dad loves you. We'll both always do what we believe is the right thing for y'all. Okay?"

"Yes, Mama," said M.P. She looked over her shoulder. "What?"

"M.P., say *yes ma'am*! Gigi will get mad at both of us because she can't tell our voices apart!" O-liv said. Tipsy heard chatter in the background.

"Yes, ma'am! We're coming!" M.P. yelled. "Gigi wants us to help her shuck corn."

"Okay buddies. Love y'all and miss y'all so much."

The girls returned her declarations of affection and scampered off, but Little A lingered.

"You better get shuckin', buddy."

"Yeah. I will."

"You okay?"

"Yup. I thought about the ghosts in the blue bottles when I saw the girls' dresses. They're the same color as the blue ceilings. What's that color called again?"

"Haint blue."

"Yeah. That's it. I thought of it because…" She saw the wheels turning in his mind like go-cart tires on a slick track. "Miss Kate is nice. Chloe is nice too and Tristan is really cool. But if I don't like living with them, I won't be able to do anything about it."

"Let me think for a minute." Tipsy bit her lip. "First, you spend more time with me than with Dad, right?"

"That's right."

"And you're basically living with them now, and it's good?"

"Yeah. But you know how Dad is, Mom."

"What do you mean?"

"One day he likes something and the next day he doesn't. I hope he doesn't stop liking Miss Kate. Then I'm like a ghost in a bottle that doesn't fit. Stuck in a new house with them."

"Wow. Ayers. Okay." Her son's maturity once again surprised her. "I cannot promise you everything will work out with Dad and Miss Kate. Since I won't break a promise, I won't make a promise."

"I know." He shrugged. "I think Dad thinks he and Miss Kate are going to be, like, happily ever after."

"Happily ever after can be kind of confusing for real grownups. You're smart enough to realize that, but whatever happens with Dad and Miss Kate, you will not be a ghost stuck in a bottle. I don't let things stay stuck. That's not how I roll. Sometimes it takes me a while to figure it out, because complicated situations usually have complicated solutions." She thought about her conversation with Ivy about patience. "If we can ride out the tough stuff, it will be okay."

"Okay, Mom. Thanks."

"Do you feel any better?"

He smiled. "Yeah. I do. Aaaaallll good."

"Doesn't have to be all good, love. Sort of good works, too." The cottage's front door slammed behind her. "I think Miss Pamella is here and Gigi needs you to shuck."

"Okay. I'll text you later."

"Love you, buddy."

"Love you, too." He waved, and the picture froze for a second. Tipsy took in his big eyes and long eyelashes. Her heart about burst with love for her three little peeps.

She'd do it all again without question. Big Ayers and his wackiness; divorce and its detritus. Little A, M.P., O-liv. She wouldn't change a thing.

Little Ayers's face disappeared as Pamella walked onto the back porch. She didn't seem to notice Tipsy sitting on the sofa in the corner with her Coke cans and the remains of her frozen pizza. She stood with her arms crossed over her chest and watched the egrets.

"Hey," said Tipsy.

Pamella jumped in place. She whirled around with her hand over her heart. "You scared me. I forgot you were here."

"Here I am, hangover and all. Want some pizza?"

Pamella shook her head.

"Did you stay downtown last night?"

She shook her head again.

"You weren't here, were you? I hope my hurling didn't keep you up—"

Pamella burst into tears.

"Whoa!" Tipsy stood. She paused to let her headrush dissipate and then walked across the porch. She put a hand on Pamella's shoulder. "What happened?"

"I can't—how did this—so embarrassed—"

"Come sit down. I'm embarrassed too, so lay it on me." She steered Pamella to the sofa. "First let me get you some of Mama Tipsy's medicine."

Tipsy went into the kitchen. She got a soft kitchen towel and grabbed a Coke out of the fridge. She found a Home Team Barbeque koozie in a kitchen drawer and stuck the can inside. She returned to the porch with her hangover cure. To her surprise, Ivy sat on the couch beside Pamella. She leaned toward her sniffling granddaughter.

Tipsy gave Pamella the drink and the towel. Pamella wiped her face. "It's freezing out here. Or maybe I have the chills."

"I'll move," said Ivy.

"Stay where you are." Tipsy said it to both of them, even though Pamella couldn't see her Meemaw beside her. Tipsy grabbed a blanket and draped it over Pamella's thin shoulders. She sat in the chair across from her. "Now tell me what happened."

"I didn't stay here last night, but I didn't stay downtown, either."

"Did you stay with a friend?"

She shook her head and then burst into tears again. "I stayed in the IOP police station. I got a DUI."

As Tipsy had feared and predicted, Pamella's luck with the cops had run out. "Yikes. Did you get in an accident?" asked Tipsy.

"No accident, thank goodness. I went to The Dinghy after the concert. I thought I could drive... but I must have run a stop sign."

"The cops on IOP don't put up with that during the day, much less at two in the morning. How did you get out of jail?"

"Doug drove here in the middle of the night from Atlanta." Pamella cried harder. "I called him and he didn't even flinch. Got in the car and drove six hours to bail me out."

"Where is he now?"

"He dropped me off. I told him I have to make some calls. Lawyer. My daughters. He's staying with a friend in Mount Pleasant. He said he's not leaving town until he knows I'm okay."

"Jeez. That's nice of him." Tipsy couldn't imagine Ayers doing the same for her.

"I know! It's so... *nice!*" Pamella sobbed into the towel.

Tipsy sensed she had to dig a little deeper. "Pammy, what's really going on with you and Doug? He doesn't seem like such a bad guy. I'm the first one to say my ex is a jerk, but—"

"You want to know? Okay. I'll tell you. Last year, Doug started going to AA. He's been sober for almost eighteen months." She sipped her Coke. "He wanted me to admit I had a problem, too. He begged me to attend a meeting with him, so I went to one. All those people looked so normal, but they're sitting there announcing *I'm an alcoholic* to the world and I just couldn't. I told him I'd cut back. Not drink in front of him. Maybe I did cut back for a while, but it made me sneak around more. And then I got a DUI in Georgia."

"Two DUIs?"

"What's a DUI?" Ivy whispered.

"Hold on. Meemaw is here. I need to explain to her what a DUI is." Pamella blinked and looked around. "She's here? Where?"

"Right beside you."

"Meemaw?" Pamella's lip trembled.

"I'm here, child," said Ivy. "Tell her I'm here, Tipsy."

"She said she's here."

Pamella took a deep breath. "A DUI is when you get arrested for driving while drunk. Driving Under the Influence of alcohol. It's illegal because you can kill yourself, or someone else."

"So you got a DUI in Georgia," said Tipsy. "Then what?"

"Doug told me we had to separate. He couldn't keep watching me kill myself, and my drinking made it much harder for him to stay sober. The truth is, he left me. I didn't leave him."

"But he still came to help you."

"I know! I don't deserve him. What is *wrong* with me, Tipsy? Meemaw? Can *someone* tell me? Why can't I drink like a normal person? Why are all my marriages failures? Why am I so *miserable* all the time when I have all this money and my children are healthy and I finally have a man who truly loves me? I should be the *happiest* woman on earth."

Tipsy took her hands. "I can't answer those questions for you, but I can tell you that by asking them, you're on the right path."

"Tell her I had the same problem with the drink," said Ivy. "Tell her."

"Alcoholism can run in families. Meemaw drank too much. My daddy is a drunk, and Granna told me his daddy and grandfather were notorious town lushes. The Drunk Dennings of Martinville. A family tradition."

"But you're not a drunk—"

"I made a conscious decision not to drink much, but I also inherited my piss poor alcohol tolerance from Granna's side of the family. Hence my puking all night last night."

"I've always been able to drink everyone under the table. At UGA, I was famous for out drinking the football linemen."

"I could drink a fifth of moonshine by age sixteen with no ill effects," said Ivy. "I'm sorry I passed it on."

"It's a combination of nature and nurture," said Tipsy. "Meemaw lived with Bubba More all those years and then she lost John. You lived with your depressed father and your mother left you. That's a lot of trauma. I always had Granna to keep me on the straight and narrow. Y'all didn't have that."

"I don't know what to do," said Pamella. "Do I have to *stop drinking* all together? What about having fun? What about my friends? What will I *tell* them?"

"Don't get ahead of yourself."

"It's not only *that*. What do I do when I feel sad? Everyone else can handle life, why can't I? I'm so ashamed." She cried into her hands.

"Don't be ashamed, baby girl," said Ivy. "Don't—Oh, Tipsy. Can you tell her I wish I could hug her? I wish I'd been there to take care of her and her daddy. Tell her I love her."

Tipsy's heart caught in her throat as she relayed the message. As she talked, Pamella's tears slowed and her breathing evened out. "She said all that?"

Tipsy nodded. If she spoke, she'd start crying and she didn't have any extra tears.

"Thank you, Meemaw," said Pamella. "Can you tell her something for me?"

"She can hear you."

"Okay." She blushed. "Meemaw, I'm tired. Can you, like, sit with me in my room? I used to be scared of you, but I don't feel scared now."

Ivy nodded and disappeared.

"She's on her way," said Tipsy. "Come on. Let's get you tucked in."

Pamella walked into the house while Tipsy gathered the rest of the pizza and the empty Coke cans. She washed a few dishes, wiped down the countertops, and filled a glass with water. She walked to Pamella's room.

Pamella was already in bed, asleep. Ivy sat in the chair in the corner and hummed *Somewhere Over the Rainbow*. Tipsy looked down at Pamella as she set the glass on the bedside table. She looked peaceful, even if she couldn't hear her Meemaw's singing.

Chapter 17

The next morning found Tipsy on the wide stairway leading to the porch of the old barracks with the recently reunited couple. John sat one step above Ivy. She rested between his knees. He'd wrapped his arms around her. She peeked over his muscular forearms like a prairie dog emerging from the safety of her burrow.

Tipsy had never seen ghosts interact like this. Their blurred lines fascinated her. The navy blue of John's shirt bled into the azure flowers on Ivy's dress like homemade tie-dye. Their pale skin blended together so she struggled to discern where one stopped and the other began. Their combined energy set off a constant subtle motion, like the gentle movement of glassy creek water in the morning. The screwed up perspective should have been off putting to Tipsy's artist's eye, but she found it peculiarly compelling. Her mental camera clicked over their gently morphing forms.

"Where's Henry?" John asked, as he twisted a misty lock of Ivy's hair around his fingers.

"He wanted to rest up for the trip downtown," said Tipsy. Better that Henry wasn't here to see this intimate, comfortable moment between John and Ivy. It might pain him to know how he and Jane might have spent those ninety-something lonely years in Miss Callie's house.

"The last time he visited, he finally told Ivy and me the tale of his death. And Jane's."

"I hardly believed it!" said Ivy. "Who would have thought?"

"Yeah," said Tipsy. "It's a humdinger, as my Granna would have said."

"Knowing the truth makes Henry's visits that much more pleasant." John smiled. "It's amazing, having company again! Every day, I feel more… real."

"So you, like, know what's true and what's not?" Tipsy didn't want to upset John, but she hoped he no longer believed the palmetto bugs were his six-legged confidants.

"If you mean my conversations with the local vermin, I've put that all behind me." He said it with pride, as if he'd finally kicked his smoking habit. "Having y'all to talk to reminded me of so many things, not merely the gruesome details of my death. The simple joy of having a human being respond when you speak."

Ivy looked up at him. "I hate that you've been so alone, Johnny. I wish I'd known how to visit you."

"You're here now, sweetheart." He tapped her nose and kissed her cheek.

"John," said Tipsy. "You seem so like, chill—"

"I'm always chilled, being a ghost and all."

"No, that's not what I meant. I'm actually hoping for the opposite of chilled. Do you feel any warmth? Any sense you can move on now that you've thought about your death for a while?"

"Sorry, Tipsy. I have no such feelings. I am still very chilled."

"Irk. That's what I figured, but I wanted to talk to you before we see Camden, anyway. If he asks how you feel about him killing you…."

"You want to be able to tell him I forgive him?"

"It might make him more cooperative. But in the end, it's your death. You have to decide whether you forgive him or not."

"I do," John said, and Ivy nodded her agreement.

"Just like that? That's big of you."

"While I certainly wish things had turned out different, a lot of living happened between my death and his. Camden did his best to redeem himself."

"But don't you wonder *why* he killed you?" So much of what had happened between John, Ivy, and Camden didn't mesh with the people they seemed to have been in life. "It just seems so…. extreme."

"I did try to convince him to participate in a murder conspiracy that might have gotten him jailed for life."

"True, but—"

"It doesn't really matter," said Ivy. "In the end, he did the right thing."

"You're both in a damn forgiving mood." Their lenient pardon struck Tipsy as odd, but her anxiety about the big, tenuous picture didn't let her dwell on it. Despite their carefully constructed plan, whatever they learned from Camden might be meaningless. Even if Tipsy witnessed Ivy's tumble off the dock from every angle and Ivy herself could move on, she wouldn't go without John.

Maybe the two of them would spend eternity with Ivy popping back and forth between True Blue and the barracks like a neighbor who never has enough sugar. No fifty-k for Tipsy under those circumstances.

Crossing bridges and what not, Tipsy, said Granna.

What if I start to cross and the drawbridge is up?

Don't go adding drawbridges where they aren't needed. Most bridges go straight on across the water.

Tipsy's phone dinged and she answered a few texts. As she typed, she glanced at John and Ivy's intertwining limbs and listened to their quiet consulting and whispered endearments. Even after all these years apart they were perfectly in sync, down to their mutual nose-bopping.

Maybe they're too happy now to be angry at Camden for what happened so long ago, suggested Granna as Tipsy tucked her phone into her purse.

Tipsy shrugged. The idea had some merit, but still, there had to be more to it.

"Okay, y'all," she said, as she stood. "I'm gonna get going." She cleared her throat. "Hey. I'll see y'all later. Hello?"

Ivy laughed and sat up from John's embrace. "I'm sorry, Tipsy."

"We get rather carried away," said John.

"Tomorrow evening at the Huger House, yes?" Ivy said with a smile. "I'll see you there."

"Right, we can talk more about it tonight at True Blue…" Tipsy trailed off as she realized they were paying no attention to her. Ivy had leaned back into John's arms. Her chin tilted toward him and their faces were inches apart. Tipsy knew she was anticipating a kiss. Her hand on his knee. His hand covering hers. His hair hung down over his forehead. Hers curled over her shoulder in gossamer waves.

The image froze in Tipsy's mind. Captured like the photos of a young, gloriously happy Ivy flirting with John through the camera lens on the beach in 1932. This was a color picture, however, and that's how Tipsy planned to paint it.

Tipsy drove downtown to meet Ivy and Henry at the Joseph George Huger House on Wednesday evening. She wore black leggings, a tight black long sleeved workout top, and black tennis shoes, like a yoga ninja. She planned to linger at the hidden gate and call to Camden. Should anyone question her, she would claim to be a nosy tourist on an evening run. Henry and Ivy had promised to distract any interlopers with falling tree branches and small tornadoes.

She parked on Atlantic Street and jogged across Meeting. Just as Pamella said, a skinny pathway between the two brick walls separated the Huger House from its neighbor. Overgrown shrubs and creeping vines crisscrossed the narrow space, creating a ceiling of wily vegetation that blocked the setting sun. The path was darkening fast. Tipsy hesitated before stepping into the gloom. She once again thought of strange tunnels to other worlds, a la *Alice in Wonderland*.

Don't start clucking now, chicken, said Granna.

Tipsy nodded and stepped onto the uneven cobblestones. She tiptoed along as if she were in a subdued game of hopscotch. She came upon the old gate about halfway down the corridor. If she hadn't been looking for it, she may not have noticed it. She peered through a tangle of thick vines at a patch of grass and weeds between the brick wall and the carriage house. An old bicycle and a broken ladder had sat in landscaping no man's land long enough to develop their own greenery. Grass grew in the bike's ratty basket and misplaced daisies sprouted between the ladder's rungs.

Ivy and Henry stood inside the gate. The foliage rustled as the ghosts wielded telekinesis like spectral pruning shears. The vines clung to the rusty iron with their leafy fingers, but they were no match for Henry and Ivy's combined power. Branches snapped with the *bang-bang-bang* of a Little League pitcher hurling a handful of paper pop rockets onto hot concrete.

Ivy rubbed her chin. "If we want Camden to cooperate, this should be an intimate discussion. Not Tipsy on the other side of the wall like a judge lording over a courtroom."

"I don't know if that's a good idea," said Tipsy. "What about security?"

"I don't see any of those little recording machines people hide in corners," said Henry. "Not back here behind the carriage house."

"Ugh." Indecision closed around Tipsy like a suffocating blue bottle. "I don't know. It's trespassing."

Ivy raised one hand. The metal gate creaked toward her. Never one to be outshone, Henry followed suit. Between the two of them, the gate sprung off its hinges and landed with a soft clunk in the grass.

"There," said Ivy. "Now you were wandering by and poked your head in."

"There isn't a no trespassing sign." Tipsy realized she'd been holding her breath. She sucked in a solid helping of oxygen and crossed the threshold. To her relief, no floodlights shone down on her. No sirens wailed. Nothing but the usual hum of cicadas and the sound of cars passing on Meeting Street.

"I can't turn on my flashlight, but y'all provide a bit of effervescence." She looked around. "Now we need Camden."

"I'll call for him," said Henry. "You should, too. You are terribly loud."

"I'll stay back. He may not be happy to see me." Ivy faded until the blue and white flowers of her dress were elements of the old landscaping.

Tipsy started chanting in her head. *Camden? Camden? Camden?*

Henry called out as if he were yelling after a prized hunting dog. "Camden! Hey there, Camden Brewton! Right here!"

After ten minutes, Camden had not appeared. Tipsy sensed him hovering just out of sight. She'd had the same feeling about Henry when he refused to make himself seen in the days before Tipsy solved his mystery.

"This is BS," Tipsy finally said. "I have to make him come out."

"Can you really do that?" asked Ivy. "You told me you could, but…"

"Oh, ye of little faith. Henry, can I grab a ghost by the throat or what?"

"That's a rather disturbing way to think about it," said Henry. "But yes. I've personally been dragged into the here and now by Ms. Collins."

Tipsy rotated her head and shook out her arms like a weightlifter about to do a challenging deadlift. "Deadlift," she muttered, with a chuckle.

"What? What's she doing?" Ivy whispered to Henry. "What should *we* do?"

Henry hushed her.

Tipsy held out her hands as if she were inviting them to play Ring-Around-the-Rosie. "When I say now, y'all have to grab my hands. Got it?"

They nodded, and Tipsy closed her eyes. She remembered her efforts to grab Henry from the in-between place where ghosts hid when Tipsy couldn't see them. On one hand, she didn't understand it. On the other, she knew it like her own bedroom. It was as familiar as the space between sleeping and waking in her own mind. Where dreams met reality and for a second anything was possible.

Camden had convinced himself that he was out of reach. She felt his shock and fear when he realized she was coming for him. She tried to talk to him.

I'm not going to hurt you, Camden, but you must come out. We need more information about Ivy's death.

I have none. I tried to help you. I told you everything I know!

What you told us wasn't enough.

Please leave me alone. Why is this happening? Why? He started gibbering. *I'm sleeping I have to wake up and you'll all go away wake up Camden wake up!*

Tipsy had almost reached him, but he slipped away again.

Maybe we need to remember together, Cam. Ivy spoke up in Tipsy's mind. Tipsy smelled cinnamon and nutmeg. She hoped those comforting scents would help Camden relax, but he panicked.

Ivy? Is that you?

That's all you can say after almost eighty years? Shoot. And from what Tipsy told me, the last time you saw me, I was taking a high dive into your jon boat.

How did you get here, Ivy? How are any of you here, talking to me? It's a dream. All of you coming and going lately is one long dream. Wake up now, Camden. Wake up—

"We don't have time for this," said Tipsy, out loud. She sat cross legged on the grass. Ivy and Henry joined her on the ground. Henry, pale and solid. Ivy, wispy on the edges, but the angles of her face in stark relief. It was like a morbid slumber party. They were about to play Ouija board, but had no need to summon the dead. They were already there.

No more screwing around, Camden, she thought. He wiggled like a fish on a hook, but Tipsy did what she'd done last summer. She thought of the people she wanted to help. She thought of pretty young Ivy More, sitting on a blanket on the beach, singing songs to drown out unwelcome spirits and fantasizing about movie stars. She thought of John Huger's silly impression of himself in the candy cane costume and his delight at Ivy's laughter. She remembered John begging Ivy to never doubt him, his promise that everything would be okay, and Ivy's deep belief in his ability to fix it all. Lastly, she remembered the two of them sitting on the steps of the old barracks, just as in love as they'd been almost a century ago, tapping each other's noses and whispering like two kids plotting innocent mischief.

We need to know everything you know, Camden. Every little detail. For John and Ivy, you're going to show us.

"Now!" she said. "Ivy, Henry, now!

They took her hands. Once more, the darkness fell.

———•✕•———

Tipsy hears the commotion of an argument in progress, as if she turned on the TV in the middle of The Jerry Springer Show. Henry is to her right. They watch Ivy stomping around on the dock behind True Blue, which is, in this time, still painted white. Electric lightbulbs strung from the dock give off a yellowish glow. Moths swarm the bulbs. Their agitation adds to the overall chaos. Camden stands farther down the dock. His hands are in his pockets, as usual.

Alma More is in front of Tipsy. She's trudging across the yard. She's still wiry, but she's wearing glasses. Over a decade has passed since Tipsy last saw her. Her hair is shorter and grayer. She looks like she has dingy cotton balls glued to her head. There are two men with her. The younger man looks a hell of a lot like Bobby Brewton with his dark hair and strong jaw. It must be Saul.

As for the second man, Tipsy recognizes Bubba immediately. His hair is still dark, but his face is so weathered he resembles one of the alligators he proudly claimed to have throttled with his bare hands.

"What the hell!" she says. "What's Bubba doing here? I thought he disowned Ivy!"

"Maybe he did," replies Henry, "but he's here now. For good or ill."

Tipsy glares at Bubba's back. "I'm putting my money on ill."

The two men adjust their pace to Alma's shuffling, so Tipsy motions to Henry and they jog around them. They step onto the dock. Tipsy fights the urge to swat the whizzing bugs that can't reach her.

Ivy still wears her blue flowered dress. "You said it, plain as day!"

"Keep your voice down, you drunken shrew!" says Camden. "You'll wake the neighbors."

"You don't want to hear the truth. The closest neighbor is four acres away."

"You misheard me. You were talking about John. It made me sad and—"

"Murderer!" Ivy lunges at Camden. She's wearing her low-heeled shoes and she stumbles. She grabs for the dock railing and hauls herself to her feet. "How could you? And then walk around all these years like a normal man who didn't murder his best friend—"

Camden grabs her. Ivy struggles in his arms and her emotions batter Tipsy's own heart. Her rage and grief are even worse than in the last memory. So is her boozy mental fog. When she returned to the cottage, Ivy tried to drown everything in moonshine. She hides the booze in the broom closet in a wash bucket, because Camden never cleans anything and he'll never look there. Tonight even moonshine can't help her. Her despair makes Tipsy's sadness over Will feel like an everyday frustration. After all, John was Ivy's soul mate. She wasn't worried about settling or expecting perfection. In her mind, she had perfection. And Camden took it away.

Ivy wants to hurt Camden, and as she stops fighting him, she knows how. She leans into his face. "How do you think Bobby will feel knowing what you've done?"

"Don't you dare threaten my relationship with my son."

"You killed his true father. He. Ain't. Yours. No. More." Ivy's words spit her wrath and moonshine breath in Camden's face.

Tipsy turns to Henry. "Are you hearing this?"

Henry nods. "John fathered Ivy's boy. Not Camden."

"Holy hell. That means John is Pamella's grandfather—"

"Y'all!" Saul calls out. "What in the good lord's name is going on out here?"

"I'll find his ghost!" Ivy starts laughing. "I'll find his ghost and he'll tell me the truth—"

Camden grabs at Ivy's flailing arms. "Maybe it is time you get put away. I'm tired of your drinking and your theatrics." He turns on Ivy's approaching family. He points at Alma. "Get that loony old bat off my property! This is all her fault, getting Ivy riled up about ghosts—"

Ivy wrenches away from Camden and stumbles toward her mother. As she pulls away, Camden stomps back down the dock. He yells over his shoulder. "Since you started it, Alma, talk some sense into her. If you have any yourself."

Saul follows Camden, beseeching him to calm down. As for Bubba, he stands at the end of the dock and spits tobacco juice into the marsh. He's the calmest person there. In Tipsy's mind, that might make him the most dangerous.

Ivy takes Alma's hands in hers. "Camden killed Johnny."

"Do what now?" Alma's brow wrinkles.

At that moment, Saul walks back down the dock. "Daddy," he says. "Go talk with Camden. I'm getting him a cigarette and a bourbon to calm his nerves."

"Shit. Who do we spy on?" Tipsy starts babbling. "Alma and Ivy or Bubba and Camden? Henry, oh lord, Bubba turns up and she's dead. Somehow Camden thought he pushed her, but it must have been Bubba—"

"Calm down, now. There are two of us. I'll take the men. You take the womenfolk," says Henry. He follows Bubba toward Camden at the end of the dock and Tipsy turns back to Ivy and her mother.

"I heard him say it, Mama," says Ivy. "While he sat on the beach sobbing. He said he didn't know what came over him or why he did it, but he did it!"

As she talks, Alma's face lights up. It's an unnatural expression for someone in the middle of a conversation about murder. "Something came over him?"

"That's what he said."

"Oh, heavens to Betsy!" That quirky country-ism doesn't match the tone of the conversation any more than Alma's facial expression. "Well, I'll be. I knew it must have worked, but I didn't know just how."

"Mama. Talk sense for once. I just said Camden killed John. Killed him in cold blood. I can hardly believe it, but he was always jealous of John… or maybe he wanted Mr. R.J.'s money."

"That wasn't why he did it, Ivy. He said something came over him. Don't you see?"

"See what? Mama, please. My head is spinning. I need you to speak clear."

"The curse, honey. The curse is what came over him."

Ivy swallows. "Curse?"

"The curse I cast on John."

"I'm sorry… what?"

Alma smiles. This grin is more than merely emotionally tone deaf. It's pure batshit nuts. "I didn't necessarily want to kill him, but even a well-cast curse may decide its own path. I thought, maybe this cottage will burn down, so he didn't have no reason to come to the island no more. Or maybe the curse would choose to make him lose all his money, so you wouldn't want him."

"I didn't want him for his money. I loved him."

"You think that, but he was no good for you. That man was a walking, talking heartache. Besides, he was fixing to take you away."

Ivy squeezes her mother's hands. "Oh no, you didn't. Oh, no, no, no."

"I thought I tamped it down, but it turned out too strong again. Same thing with my old friend Lorraine."

"Wait now. You cursed Lorraine, too? You told me never to mess with curses myself, and you're casting them about, willy-nilly!"

"Your father had eyes for Lorraine after we married, and then she turned up pregnant! Happenstance? I think not. I couldn't sit back and let some tramp steal him from his family any more than I could let Mr. High-Falutin' Huger snatch you up. My family means all to me. What do I got without y'all?" Alma crosses her arms over her chest. "Don't look at me like that, Ivy. I didn't mean to kill her, either. Just make her go away, too."

"You're insane. You really are."

"Maybe so, but now we know I can cast a curse with the best of 'em." Alma is bizarrely smug. "My own father thought me weak, but looks like I got my own powers."

"No wonder you lost a screw when you saw Lorraine's ghost. Her death was your fault." Ivy grabs Alma by the shoulders. "My Johnny's death is on your hands, too!"

"Oh, pee-shaw, Ivy. I wasn't going to let him steal my daughter away from me just to break her heart."

"Mama, I told you back then. No one was stealing me away from you! Me marrying John didn't mean I had to leave you. Maybe you could have lived with us, or—"

"Ha. John wouldn't have wanted me any more than your other rich man did. In the end, you married Camden and left me anyway. You got to live in your mansion like you wanted."

"How can you say that? Do you know me at all?"

"You were gone and I had to say goodbye to my little house by the marsh and move up to dirty ol' Georgetown. Now I live in the shadow of a sawmill with my lungs full of wood dust. My, my. I suppose the joke was on me."

"How is any of this a joke?" Ivy scrapes her hands down her face hard enough to leave red streaks on her cheeks. "That's why you could see John... and Lorraine. Because your black magic did them in."

"To help you, honey. To save you from sadness when he left you."

"Stop it! John wasn't going to leave me until your curse killed him! You weren't trying to help me. You were trying to keep me trapped under your wing." Ivy's eyes bulge. They're the eyes of a deer with one leg stuck in a trap. "Something came over Camden, indeed. Your damn curse. Oh, poor Cam. He must have felt so guilty and confused all this time. Dear god, Mama. You ruined all our lives. You can't just go around cursing people!"

Saul walks out of the house. He calls his father and Camden from the dock. Ivy whispers to herself as the bizarre congregation meets on the cottage lawn. Camden's hands are in his pockets again and his eyes are puffy. Bubba spits tobacco juice into the grass. Alma stands there grinning like her pig has just won first prize at the county fair.

"Now that everyone has calmed down, let's let the man talk to his wife," says Saul. He offers Camden a cigarette and a bourbon.

Camden waves the drink away. "I've had too much already. I can't think straight. I need to go to bed. Ivy, we can talk tomorrow morning."

Saul hands him the cigarette. "That's up to y'all, but we're going to make coffee."

Ivy's family walks toward the house. Saul and Alma disappear inside, but Bubba stops in the yard. He removes his wad of dip and lights his own cigarette. The flame pricks the darkness like black magic fairy dust.

Ivy's arms hang at her sides as she watches Saul march her mumbling mother toward the house.

"What happened?" Tipsy asked Henry. "What did you hear?"

"What did you hear?" Henry asked her in return.

Before Tipsy can reply, Ivy takes Camden's hand and pulls him down the dock. Tipsy and Henry follow them as they both stumble and bump into each other. If Ivy is a drunk, Camden isn't much better, at least not tonight.

"We should talk now, Cam. It's important."

"If you insist, but...." He squints at his wife, and then closes one eye, as if he's seeing two of her. His voice is just above a whisper. "Saul told me how your mother imagines things. She got you all worked up with this silly ghost business. You know there's no such thing as ghosts."

Ivy looks at him blankly, and then bursts out laughing. "Oh, dear Saul. Trying to protect me and Mama as always." She touches Camden's cheek. "Cam, you did it, but I'm not angry with you."

He jerks away from her. "Goddamn it. I'm trying to make peace and you won't let it go? What the hell is wrong with you?"

"You killed him—"

"Stop saying that—"

"You did it but it wasn't your fault. My mother... how do I say it? You killed him because—"

"I didn't mean to kill him!" Camden hisses. He wipes one forearm across his eyes and looks over her shoulder at Bubba.

"I know—listen to me—there's an explanation. A reason why you killed him—"

Camden slaps Ivy across the face. "Shut up, goddamn you!"

He pushes her, and stomps past her down the dock. Ivy stumbles backward. She's still wearing her low-heeled shoes. One of the heels catches between the boards. Her bottom hits the low guard rail, and she goes over, head first.

Camden is shouting at Bubba. "Get your damn daughter! She's lost her goddamn mind. I'm calling the state hospital tomorrow!"

Bubba takes a drag on his cigarette. "I told you she's always been trouble."

"Bubba saw her go over!" Tipsy says to Henry. "He's not helping her."

Henry strides toward Bubba with his arms raised, as if he might control him the way he manipulated the rusty gate.

"That won't work, Henry! Just watch. We have to understand what happened."

For an interminable period that might be twenty seconds or twenty minutes, there's nothing but the still night air, and Bubba's cigarette. He finishes one and lights another. The light ebbs and builds as he drags smoke into his lungs, and Tipsy takes some relief in knowing those same tobacco sticks will eventually kill him. The smell of smoke nauseates her.

"Look," says Henry. He points toward the house. Alma and Camden are talking on the back porch.

"Stay here," says Tipsy. She runs toward the house.

Alma looks up at Camden with the fierce eyes of a cornered badger. "What did your wife tell you about me?"

"Always worried about yourself, aren't you, Mrs. More? Ivy thinks you're so silly and helpless, but I see through your song and dance."

"I don't know what you mean, Camden. I have no earthly idea."

"You're poison. I think you always have been, since Ivy was a child and you made her be a grown woman since you couldn't be one yourself. Crazy poison is the worst kind." Camden leans down into her face. "You'll get out of my house by dawn, or your daughter will regret it from her room at the loony barn."

"You'd do that to Bobby? Take away his mother? You're a bad man, just like your cousin."

"Get out, you witch!"

Alma laughs. "A witch, you say? Mayhap you're right. If you want me gone, I'll go. This witch won't stay where she's not wanted. I told Ivy that long ago." Alma calls to Bubba. "George! Camden said we can't stay here— Huh. Where's Ivy?"

Camden squints into the darkness. When he doesn't see Ivy, he walks toward the dock. Realization dawns on his face, and he starts running. Tipsy runs after him. Thank goodness she can't get out of breath in these memories.

"Bubba hasn't made a move to help her, damn him!" says Henry.

Camden sprints down the dock. Tipsy and Henry follow him and look over the railing.

"Oh, my god. Ivy!" Camden vaults into the darkness. It's low tide. He lands in the pluff mud and sinks past his knees. He's trudging toward a metal boat sitting in a few inches of brackish water. Ivy lays half in and half out of the boat. Camden thinks of John's leg sticking out of the bathtub and screams her name again.

She's facedown. There's muddy water pooled in the bottom of the boat. If Ivy was alive when she landed in there, she wouldn't have lasted long breathing in that sludge.

Camden cuts his hands on the exposed oyster beds. By the time he reaches her, he's bleeding all over her pretty blue and white dress. Her face is muddy and her head lolls. More blood gushes from the back of her head. Camden gags as he frantically tries to clear the mud from her mouth and nose with his bloody hands.

Bubba stays right where he is and smokes his cigarette. Alma has scampered across the dock. She looks down at her daughter and Camden. She takes in the full picture and starts keening. "Oh, lord. Oh, lord. Oh, lord."

Camden doesn't pay her any mind. He cradles Ivy and sobs. "I'm so sorry. Ivy. John. Ivy. John…"

Tipsy woke slowly this time, as if emerging from a deep daytime sleep. She'd never observed such a long and complicated memory. If she surfaced too fast, the details might fade like a normal dream. Or maybe if her eyes stayed closed, she'd float away into someone else's past problems and forget her current ones. Even the idea of tumbling into the nonsensical world of her own nighttime reveries appealed to her. She'd rather dream she'd shown up naked to her middle school math class than face her fight with Shelby, losing Will, Ayers's impending nuptials, or the embarrassment of being front page on the Mount Pleasant gossip tabloids.

"Now what was that phrase Miss Callie started using after the moon landing?" Henry's muffled voice. "Ah, yes. Earth to Tipsy!"

She opened her eyes. Henry and Ivy still sat in their kumbaya circle. Camden sprawled in the grass a few feet away. He sat up and cradled his head in his hands.

"You're catching flies, Tipsy," said Ivy.

Tipsy closed her mouth and smacked her dry tongue around like Granna after she removed her dentures. "Sorry, y'all… where were we?" She sat up straight. "Oh! Alma!"

"Ivy, do you remember?" asked Henry. "Once Tipsy brought Jane and I together to truly understand our deaths, she didn't have to explain it to us. We remembered everything."

"Yes. I understand now. My mother's curse started it all. All our loss and sadness and death." Ivy wiped away a sparkly tear. "Tipsy, I told you my mother wanted the best for me, but it seems her own wants were more important to her."

"She wanted to keep you in her pocket," said Tipsy. "Good lord. Alma didn't use her own hands to kill you or John, but her selfish scheming did y'all in!"

"So if we're correct in our hoodoo logic," Henry said, like a prosecutor summing up his closing case, "she cursed John, and the curse made Camden kill him. Therefore, she killed Ivy by proxy, because if she hadn't cursed John, she never would have married Camden, who ended up pushing her off the dock."

"Let's not let Bubba off the hook," said Tipsy. "He's just as culpable. He just stood there while she drowned in a puddle with her head bashed in. If he'd done something, maybe she could have been saved." She turned to Henry. "What did Bubba say to Camden, anyway?"

Camden spoke up from over Henry's shoulder. "He said he'd be happy to get rid of Ivy for me."

Henry nodded. "He commiserated with you. Said Ivy was always difficult. He was willing to take her off your hands for the right amount of money."

Ivy paled to the point of nearly translucent. "My father wanted to kill me? Is that true, Cam?" She clapped, twice. "Camden? Cam?"

Camden cast a rueful glance at Ivy. "No need to nag, Mrs. More." He scooted closer to them. "At the time I thought Bubba simply meant he'd take you away if I paid him. Back to Georgetown. Leave me and Bobby in peace. I honestly considered it for a moment, but I couldn't take Bobby's mother from him. I wouldn't even have had you committed, no matter how I blustered about it."

"Sounds like when he said get rid of her, he meant, *get rid of her,*" said Tipsy. "Bubba being there surprised me. Y'all were supposedly estranged, so why would he come help out in a family crisis? But it *totally* makes sense if he was using the opportunity to weasel money out of Camden. He didn't end up with cash, but he did get revenge on Ivy for crossing him. Y'all, my father is an ass, but Ivy's got me beat."

"What happened after you found me, Camden?" asked Ivy.

"Alma ran into the cottage for Saul. Bubba stood there until his son yelled at him to help pull you up. The three of us brought you into the kitchen. Alma was yowling enough to make me lose my own mind." Camden's mouth set in a grim line. "Ivy laid out on the kitchen table with her bloody head and mud in her nostrils— that shock sobered me right up. I sent Saul across the Pitt Street Bridge to find someone to help us. A doctor or the police. That gave me time to talk to Bubba and Alma."

"Did they want to turn you in for pushing her?" asked Tipsy.

"Alma said something of the like. I thought of Bobby left alone, with Ivy dead and me in jail. Being raised by Alma and Bubba. I warned her if she or Bubba ever said one word to anyone, I'd tell the police Bubba pushed her."

"The authorities would never believe the word of Bubba More and his crazy wife over yours," said Henry.

Camden nodded. "Exactly. I was a fine, upstanding citizen."

"Let's not forget that you were a *rich* citizen," said Tipsy. "They were dirt poor. That's American justice, even if in Bubba's case, he would have deserved whatever he got."

"He would have gotten sent to Old Sparky up in Columbia. Zippity-zip-zap. No more Bubba."

Tipsy grimaced at Camden's description of execution via electric chair. Even Ivy, who'd never harbored fond feelings for her father and now had plenty of reason to actively hate his guts, shivered.

"No one said a word about Ivy dying any way other than a drunken accident," said Camden.

"I don't think Saul even told his own son that Bubba was there when Ivy died," said Tipsy. "Seems Sandy would have mentioned it."

"Even families who hate each other often protect their own." Camden's jaw jutted. "Then I caught Alma at the funeral scaring Bobby with talk of spirits. Even said his own mother might be haunting the cottage. So I added her staying away from Bobby to the list of requirements to keep Bubba out of the chair and finally washed my hands of the Mores."

Tipsy turned to Henry. "I thought you and Jane had a complicated death. And let's hold on for a minute—John was Bobby's real father?"

Ivy and Camden exchanged a glance. He shrugged. "When the cat scratches a hole in the bag, you might as well let it out."

"Yes," said Ivy. "I told John about the baby that day you visited in my memory, Tipsy. The day Daddy threatened him. The last time I saw him."

"And then he disappeared, so you must have thought—"

"I feared he'd left me because of the baby, but then I found out he'd died. I was even more distraught. I didn't know what to do. Once I finally got out of bed, I went to the cottage y'all call True Blue. Camden found me crying on the steps."

"She told me a baby was coming," said Camden, "and I had no other choice in that moment. If John's baby had to grow up without him, I'd make sure the child had everything his heart desired."

"Did anyone else ever know? Bobby himself?"

"Only John's parents knew," said Ivy. "We told them after we got married, so they'd accept me and the child."

"With John gone, I got all this." Camden pointed up at the Huger House. "I even got a beautiful wife. It didn't take me long to understand why John loved you so much. But I knew you couldn't love me. How could any woman love someone else when she'd loved my cousin? On the best of days, I wasn't a very good husband. I certainly wasn't John Huger."

"Camden," said Ivy. "Those twelve years of missing John changed us both. I wasn't the best wife, either. My blue moods. My drinking."

Something clicked in Tipsy's mind. "Now I see why you and John were so quick to forgive Camden."

"Johnny didn't remember me telling him about the child, but once I did, he was relieved Bobby had a good life," said Ivy. "I'm sorry I didn't tell you, Tipsy. It's hard to reveal a secret kept so long. I thought my granddaughter might not want to know. The man she *thought* was her grandfather, killing her real grandfather, and then raising his child? It's rather scandalous."

"Pammy is used to scandal. She'll want to know."

"I don't understand though." Camden said, with a hint of desperation. "I loved John. How could I have killed him, curse or not? I still don't understand any of this. I was not supposed to hang around questioning everything I ever did in my life. Ghost are not supposed to have powwows in my backyard. Now y'all have brought curses into it!" He looked almost comically offended. "Frankly, it's not how I was raised."

"It *is* how I was raised," said Ivy. "Curses, now, they ain't no joke."

"Such a genuine use of the colloquial!" said Henry. "Really, Ivy, it suits you much better than your movie starlet act."

Ivy ignored him. "If the curse wanted John dead, it would have found a way. If not through Camden, through something or someone else."

Tipsy remembered John's disbelief when she'd reminded him of his own murderous plans. Yet in his memories, she saw firsthand how he coldly plotted to kill Bubba and wanted to strangle Camden that night in the barracks. Violence had settled over him and he'd inhaled it like supernatural mustard gas. "I think John was doomed from the second Alma cast that curse."

"Unfortunately, now I have a hunch it didn't end with John," said Ivy. "A potent curse can follow a bloodline for centuries. Wreak all manner of havoc."

Tipsy's brow furrowed. She thought of Bobby's lifetime of unhappiness, and Pamella's struggles with failed marriages and alcoholism. "Pammy is John's only remaining direct descendent. Do you think the curse is still working on her?"

"After listening to her sad story, I think it's surely possible."

"Oh, hell. How do we get rid of it?"

"From what I remember of Alma's teachings, the only way to get rid of a curse is to right the wrong it did."

"Right the wrong... the original wrong was against John. He died, and he and Ivy were separated. Do you think by reuniting them and letting them move on together, we can right the wrong?" Tipsy snapped her fingers. "Maybe that's why John can't move on! Yes, he knows Camden killed him, but he doesn't know the curse started it all. And you—Camden. You couldn't move on either. You know you killed yourself, but you've lived with this guilt about killing your cousin, when really, it wasn't your fault."

"Now you know the whole story, if Tipsy will give me license on more literary metaphors. The plot holes are filled in." Henry squinted at Camden. "So how do you feel now, sir? Any, ah, newfound sense of urgency about the next chapter of the afterlife?"

"Do you and Johnny truly forgive me?" Camden asked Ivy.

"John loved you. He still does. Now we know it wasn't even you who started it all, he'll want you to be at peace."

Camden blushed. "What about you? In the end, I shoved you off a dock."

"We both meant well, for Bobby. He didn't ask to be brought into this world, and we did the best we could by him."

"Especially if he was cursed, poor boy. Listen to me, talking about a curse as if Bobby was born with a club foot." Camden looked at his hands. "It has something to do with temperature, correct?"

"Yeah." Tipsy was tentatively hopeful.

Camden smiled. The deep lines around his eyes peeked out from the edges of his glasses. "It's always muggy in Charleston this time of year. I'd forgotten."

"Thank the lord." Tipsy felt like she'd unexpectedly found a last red jelly bean in a pile of yellow and green ones. "Please let John be able to move on, too."

"I hope y'all don't mind," said Camden, "but I don't want to dilly dally. Would you excuse me?"

Tipsy nodded. "Of course. Off to oblivion?"

"I used to want that. But now my heart is rather free. I'm hoping there's something better."

"My wife seemed to think so," said Henry.

"Jane was always astute."

"Ah, well. She did marry me."

"You're not the monster you think you are, Henry. Then again, neither am I." Camden touched Ivy's shoulder. "Give our Johnny my love. Perhaps I'll see y'all again. If that's how it works."

"I'm sure John would like nothing more," said Ivy. "If you see my mother… well, who knows where she is, after what she did."

"If y'all can forgive me, maybe we can all forgive Alma. Something about her was… not right."

"That's a polite way to put it, Cam, but she wasn't just not right. She was as wrong as hot sauce on ice cream."

Camden wasn't much interested in analyzing the rightness or wrongness of Alma More. After decades of apathy about the afterlife, he'd already switched from neutral to fifth gear. He stood and rubbed his hands together. He strode toward the carriage house with no hint of a shuffling, cowed old man in his step. He gamboled like a first year Hogwarts student skipping toward Platform 9 ¾. Like a future Gryffindor or Hufflepuff, he disappeared before he hit the brick wall.

"What about you, Ivy?" asked Tipsy.

"Do I forgive my mother? Or my father, for that matter."

"Uh, that too, but first I wanted to know—"

"My own parents killed me. My own parents."

"— if you can move on."

"Oh, yes, that." Ivy smiled. "I feel warmth, too. But I'm not going anywhere—"

"Without John. Yeah, I know."

"I'll return to the house to rest up, and then visit him. I'll tell him about the curse, and we'll be able to move on together."

"I hope so." Tipsy spoke around a growing lump in her throat. "All these ghosts leaving me is sort of traumatic."

"Would you like us to wait so you can say goodbye?"

"If y'all can finally go, I hate to delay you. On the other hand, if John is still stuck—"

Bridges, Tipsy. Bridges! Said Granna.

"We've already been waiting for a long time," said Ivy.

"Okay. Tomorrow I have to paint, and go to the bank to move money around so I can write a check for Jimmy. My truck is finally ready at the garage…" She scowled. "Wait. Maybe I'm cursed, too. You think?"

"I doubt it. There are few people left on this earth, living or dead, who know how to cast a curse."

"You could teach me before you go. A curse or two on my ex-husband might come in handy."

Ivy's pretty smile widened. "I never truly learned how to conjure them myself. Mama wouldn't let me. Deep down she surely realized it was all wrong."

"I'm kidding," said Tipsy. "I have enough supernatural yada-yada in my life. Probably best to let the art of curse-casting die with the dead."

"You don't have to be cursed to have challenges. Everyone has them, but a curse guarantees you won't be able to sort them out."

"So far, I haven't." Tipsy stepped onto the cobblestone path.

Henry followed her. "You've only existed for thirty-five years. You have to give yourself more time to fix your problems. I'm still working on mine, and I'd be… about one hundred and twenty-five, give or take a couple years."

"Thanks, Henry. But I hope I can work out my shit within a century."

———•×•———

Tipsy sat on the dilapidated back porch of the old barracks as the sun rose. Henry appeared beside her. He squinted into the morning light.

"Yesterday's adventures through time took it out of me," he said.

"It gets easier." Tipsy's breakfast hopped around in her stomach trying to escape, as if she were the whale that swallowed Jonah. "I feel sickish, but only because I'm so nervous. What if John can't go on? What if Ivy is stuck here waiting with him?"

As if on cue, the couple in question appeared before them. John and Ivy's spectral fingers wove together like tendrils of smoke from different fires.

"Good morning," said John. "We appreciate y'all meeting us here so early."

"No problem," said Tipsy. "I didn't want to keep you any longer than necessary. That is… assuming you can… that now you're…"

"Free to move on?" John grinned. "Indeed. I am, as you would say, *totally not* chill."

"Hallelujah!" Tipsy jumped to her feet. "Seriously? You're both really free?"

"We are," said Ivy. "Thanks to you. And you, too, Henry."

"If someone had said to me in 1920 or so, *John, someday you'll thank Henry Mott for your eternal happiness*, I would have told him to stick it where the sun don't shine."

"I'd have had similar sentiments for anyone who asked me to help you find your bliss," said Henry. "It's a happy day! Curses be damned! Are y'all excited?"

Ivy shifted from left to right. "I'm embarrassed to admit it, but I'm rather afraid."

"Why?" asked Tipsy.

"Deep down I doubted whether Tipsy could truly help me move on. Now there's another ending for me. It's unsettling." Ivy leaned into John until her shoulder almost disappeared into his bulky bicep. "I also wonder if I'll see my mother. I'm not sure I believe in heaven and hell anymore, like I did during my younger days."

"Being a ghost gives you a different perspective on the afterlife than what we're taught in Sunday school," said Henry.

"I don't know if I can forgive her for what she did, but I hate to think of her suffering for all eternity. She was my mother."

Tipsy thought of her own mother. She wouldn't care enough to cling to Tipsy or curse someone out of her daughter's life.

"I don't get the sense you're as worried about Bubba," said Henry.

"Can't say I am," said Ivy, grimly. "Mama had good in her. I believe that. Not so much my daddy. His god will decide his ending, and his god is a harsh one."

"I've told her to think of beginnings, not endings," said John. "If we find Alma, maybe we can make it right. Like we did with Camden."

"That's my Johnny. Always looking on the bright side." Ivy reached up and tapped John's nose. "Let's get a move on, handsome. I'm as ready as I'll ever be."

Tipsy felt a strange mix of sadness and relief, as if she were dropping her kids off at college. She'd done right by these ghosts. She'd be getting her money from Pamella. But she was saying goodbye once again to spirits she'd come to care about. She wiped her eyes and gave John and Ivy a smile. "I'm so happy for y'all."

"Goodbye, Tipsy. Thank you," said John. He turned to Henry. "And you, old man. I'm glad we met again in this world and I don't have to hate you anymore."

Henry chewed on the inside of his cheek. "I misjudged you too, John. How we all misjudged one another, for so long, in so many ways."

John reached out to shake Henry's hand. Henry offered his in return. Their fingers sparkled as they came together.

"Will you find Jane, and tell her I miss her?" asked Henry. "And I… I love her?"

"Of course," said Ivy. "But don't you think she'd rather you come along with us?"

"Tell her I'll be along rightly. I still have things to do here. She understands that."

"I hope you can finish your book," said John.

"I'll have less reason to roam around town now, so I can get back to work on chapter three."

"How many chapters are there?" asked Ivy.

Henry's cheek twitched. "Approximately thirty-five."

"Ahh. Good luck with it."

Ivy and John's subtly exchanged glances gave Tipsy their mutual opinion.

Good old Henry Mott, still as nutty as a squirrel's backyard, said Granna.

Yup. Bless his crazy ass heart.

Tipsy shooed John and Ivy. "Go on now, y'all. There's another life waiting for you."

"Where to, sweetheart?" asked John.

"I feel like it's that way." Ivy pointed at the marsh.

They turned and walked toward the water. As they strolled, Ivy's wind picked up and engulfed John. Her breeze lifted his hair and their edges blurred. They slowly faded, until they became part of the tall grass and the greenish water. It was as if the marsh itself had absorbed them. The island where they fell in love and lost their lives had called them home.

Chapter 18

Tipsy went back to Bennett Street that afternoon to prepare for the kids' return the next day. She changed all the sheets and went to Harris Teeter for groceries. As she strolled the aisles, she made sure to pick out everything they liked. Kiwis for Little A, assorted berries for Mary Pratt, and a giant pack of baby carrots for O-liv, who loved to douse them in ranch dressing. Carrots and ranch grossed out Tipsy, as she hated anything that smacked of mayonnaise, but O-liv was Ayers's child, too. That man had mayo running through his veins. She also filled her cart with all their favorite treats. Little A's chocolate ice cream, Mary Pratt's salt and vinegar potato chips, and O-liv's yogurt with little M&M's. Cheez-its were buy two get one free, so she grabbed three boxes. The salty orange bits of joy were really for Tipsy herself, although it would take an industrial strength winch to drag that admission out of her.

She went home and unpacked the groceries, and then she had nothing to do but wait. She'd finished Pamella's painting and had no ghostly mystery to solve, so she took the night off. She was sitting on the front porch with a deliciously fresh box of crispy Cheez-its, catching up on the latest terrible news of the world, when Lindsey texted.

HEY HEY HEY! I HAD A LATE LUNCH ON SHEM CREEK… CAN I STOP BY?

SURE, I'M HOME. COME OVER.

Ten minutes later, Lindsey sat across from Tipsy with a giant water bottle filled with ice cubes. She wore a long, flowy sundress and flat sandals. A very un-Lindsey outfit.

"Remember when we sat out here when you first moved in?" asked Lindsey. "This porch is divine. I'm so glad you've been able to stay here. And I'm proud of you for figuring out how to manage the rent and all.

I had it pretty easy with my settlement from Barker. Never had to deal with any of that, like, career-rebuilding and money stuff."

"Had to put my big girl panties on."

"Amen. We all have to do it in some way, even if they ride up your ass."

"Got to carry on even when life gives you a wedgie." Tipsy giggled, and it felt pretty good. Her new friendship with Ivy hadn't gotten to the belly laugh point before the ghost moved on. She'd missed Lindsey. She still missed Jane.

You really miss Shelby, said Granna.

As if she heard Granna, Lindsey asked, "You talked to Shelby yet?"

"A little."

Lindsey flopped back in her wicker rocking chair. "Y'all got to get over it. You're cramping my gossip style."

"I know, but we've never gotten in a real fight. When we lived together in the sorority house, we bickered. But nothing like this."

"Y'all have been friends for almost twenty years. You're long overdue for a blowout." Lindsey smiled. "Give me another year or two. You and me will throw down over something."

"I said some super nasty things. So did she."

"So apologize. She told me what you both said. You're right. *Naaaasty.* But you know, there's truth in all of it. Shelby has always been a train wreck with men and it gets exhausting listening to her. Her parents have always spoiled her. As for you, I've seen your old social media posts. You sure painted a sunshine and rainbows picture of your life with Ayers. A lot of perfect family *la-di-da.*"

"I was trying to convince myself we were okay."

"But Shelby always knew the truth, right?"

"Yeah. She warned me about marrying him, but I did it anyway. And she knew how unhappy I was."

"It was probably annoying, listening to you complain while at the same time, you had what she wanted. Marriage, kids, pretty house. Color coordinated family portrait Instagram pics."

"I still want all that stuff, but with my own income and with a healthy relationship. I'm closer to the former, but I've never felt further away from the latter."

"I know it's hard. Watching me get married and even seeing Shelby so happy with Brian, when Will was jerking you around. Now you're heartbroken. Ayers getting remarried doesn't help."

"I feel like an asshole though, Linds. I'm happy for y'all. I really am. But I'm still sad for myself."

"That's okay, sister. This is where you are right now. I've been there. When Barker left me, we were separated for a year before we even started working through the courts. Then two years in litigation. In the middle of all that, I've never been so depressed. And good lord, I made some questionable decisions."

"I can't imagine you being depressed or making bad decisions. You're always so positive and seem to have it all together."

"Girl, haven't you learned anything about this town? Everyone seems to have it all together, but most of us are treading water like crazy below the surface. I barely left my house except to take care of Emma for six months. She was like seven, and even going to the carpool line was a nightmare."

Lindsey's daughter, who was now almost twelve, attended Cooper Hall, a prestigious all-girls school downtown.

"I was *that mom*. My husband was one of the school's biggest donors and he left me for a much younger woman. No one wanted me around."

"I got some of that. You're put in divorce quarantine, like it's contagious. But I noticed that couples we knew still invited Ayers to join in things with the kids."

"Everyone feels sorry for single dads. People think they need help managing their own children. Single moms are expected to deal with it. Plus a lot of married women don't want single ladies around to tempt their man." She rolled her eyes. "Even if I had zero interest in their bald, dad-bod, loafers-with-no-socks wearing Cooper Hall School Father's Association husbands."

"What kind of bad decisions did you make?"

Lindsey snorted. "How long can you sit out here and listen?"

"So it was rough for you, too."

"It's rough for everyone, Tips. It will get better, but it takes a lot longer than you think. When you're fresh out of the cage, you think that's the end but it's really the beginning."

"I thought I was on an upward trajectory, and then everything stalled. And slid backward. Like Sisyphus and his stone."

"That's the guy who pushes the rock uphill, and it falls back down?"

Tipsy nodded. "I'm the single mom version."

"The difference is eventually you'll get the damn stone to the top. Hades or whoever has got nothing on Tipsy Collins, artistic genius and smokin' hot Supermom." Lindsey's phone dinged. She swiped over it. "It's Shelby. Can she come over?"

Tipsy scowled. "Y'all planned this, huh?"

"Who do you think I had lunch with? I had to talk sense into her. She went to get a pedicure while I talked sense into you."

"Okay," Tipsy said with a sigh. "Bring her on."

Shelby walked across the yard a few minutes later. She still had her little toe separators in. The sight of her old friend creeping across the yard made Tipsy tear up. Shelby hobbled up the steps like Miss Callie might have on her ninetieth birthday. Before she sat down, Tipsy was on her feet.

She grabbed Shelby and hugged her. Shelby stiffened for a second then hugged her back. They both started crying.

"Oh, lord, Shelby," said Tipsy. "I'm so sorry. I was so mean."

"No, no. Tips, *I'm* sorry. I was meaner."

"No, I was the meanest. I was terrible."

"I was even more terrible. I was the terrible-est."

"Okay, y'all. Okay!" Lindsey waved them both toward the wicker sofa. "You were both assholes. It's all good."

Tipsy and Shelby simultaneously reached out to wipe the other's face. They burst out laughing. Tipsy wanted to make up for lost time.

"Sit, sit. Or wait—you want a beer, Shelby? We can celebrate us both not being assholes anymore."

"Just water. I got the Niagara Falls of sweat waterfalls running down my back."

"Gross," said Tipsy, but she smiled. She got a couple glasses of water and returned to the porch.

Lindsey and Shelby looked up as she approached. "Listen, honey," said Lindsey, "we want to get something over with. Better you hear it from us."

Tipsy sat gingerly, as if thumbtacks covered the rocking chair. She knew where they were going.

"Will is dating Julia," Lindsey continued. "Like really dating her."

"I wouldn't be surprised if he's already introduced her to his kids." Shelby rolled her eyes.

"Right. Okay." There was not much more for Tipsy to say. "Thanks for telling me."

Shelby put a hand on her knee. "I'm so sorry, sister. I don't know what the hell is wrong with him. She doesn't understand the parent life. She spends her evenings at the bar, not at ballet lessons or soccer practice. Not exactly stepmom material."

"Maybe he doesn't want stepmom material," said Tipsy.

"I talked to P.D. about it," said Lindsey. "If anyone knows the enigma that is Will Garrison, it's P.D.. He thinks Julia is exactly what Will does want. It took him a long time to figure it out and he dragged you through it while he did."

"You know he dated a woman like this before you, right?" asked Shelby. "Younger. No kids."

Tipsy nodded.

"He ditched her because she wasn't family-friendly. Thought he'd try something different, right? He liked the idea of you, but the reality was too complicated. Ayers baggage. Three more kids. Even you yourself—you're a smart, grown ass woman. You have expectations and you want a man to at least try to meet them. He doesn't even want to be *asked* to do things, let alone told. Julia doesn't question him about anything. In fact, she's like, what's the word? All googly eyed?" Shelby clasped her hands under her chin.

"Enamored? Enthralled? Infatuated?" suggested Tipsy.

"All of the above. She's so infatur-ated with him she's all…" Shelby stared up an imaginary Will with wide eyes. "She's like, starstruck. I think he likes that. You were too much for him."

"I don't know—"

Shelby glared at her. "Tipsy Denning-Collins, you are a ten. You are gorgeous and totally unique and amazingly talented and a great mom. You're even kind of funny—sometimes."

"Funny is in the eye of the beholder," said Tipsy.

"We're serious." Lindsey crunched away on her ice cubes. "Will might be considered a catch around here, but he's a mullet to your marlin."

Tipsy sniffed. "Thanks y'all."

"You're the kind of woman a man is going to have to work to keep," said Shelby, "and Will Garrison realized he doesn't want to work that hard. So he went back to easy."

"It's his loss, Tipsy," said Lindsey. "I know that doesn't help, but it's true."

"It doesn't in this moment, but really, thanks."

"How many times did both of y'all tell me it was some jerk's loss?" asked Shelby.

"Ummm… at least ten," said Lindsey.

"You're relatively new on the Shelby scene. I told Shelby that… about ten *thousand* times?"

"That's a solid estimate," said Shelby.

"Y'all, can I change the subject?" asked Lindsey. "I'm dying to tell you—"

"You're pregnant," said Shelby.

Lindsey threw an ice cube at her. "How did you know?"

"That dress and those flip flops? Lindsey maternity wear."

Tipsy grinned at Lindsey. "Are you?"

She nodded. "Yup. Found out last week. It's so early but I had to tell y'all. I'm so nervous. We want this baby so bad. I'll need your support if something goes wrong."

"Nothing will go wrong, but we're with you regardless."

Shelby let out a long blast of air. "Now it's my turn to change the subject. Sort of. Ummm...."

"Just spit it out before you freak me out," said Lindsey. "Since you seem to have mystical pregnancy observation powers."

"I might be *really* with you. Like on the maternity ward."

Tipsy grabbed her hand. "Are you serious?"

Shelby's lip trembled. "I took a test this morning. I wanted to tell you both at the same time."

"Oh, hell, no!" Tipsy stood. "I cannot believe it!"

Lindsey and Shelby both started crying, and Tipsy joined them. They got to their feet and there was a big ol' hug out sob fest, the likes of which Miss Callie's front porch had surely never seen.

As they calmed down, Shelby told them about her plans. "Brian is so excited. It was a total surprise, but we both want kids. We're getting married next month, in my parents' backyard. Only close friends and family. Will y'all be my bridesmaids?"

"If I can wear a maxi dress and flip flops, I'm in," said Lindsey. "I'm not even eight weeks along and I already feel like every day is Thanksgiving. Like I ate five servings of mashed potatoes and my grandma's green bean casserole and finished it off with half a pecan pie."

"You can wear P.D.'s camo if you want to, as long as you're both there."

Tipsy and Lindsey, who had birthed four children between them, regaled Shelby with pregnancy and delivery stories. All the gory details no one but a best friend or a truly awesome mother will tell a woman pregnant with her first baby. Shelby laughed and squirmed at Tipsy's description of her twins poking her stomach with their little feet and fists like something out of *Aliens*.

"It was so creepy, like a stegosaurus rolling around in my belly. And when a foot gets under your ribcage—" Tipsy paused. "I mean it's all glorious and natural and all that crap, but it freakin' hurts. Too much?"

"I'm a be-prepared kind of mama." Shelby sighed. "I'm going to be a mama, y'all."

By the time they left, Tipsy had laughed and cried herself dry. She rode the high of the visit and her friends' happiness through her children's Facetime call from their last night in Florida with their cousins. She said a bittersweet hello to May Penny, Tripp, Mimi, and Jimmy. They weren't really her family anymore, but after so many years and everything the last two had thrown at them, they seemed more like family now than they had in the past. Sadness crept over her again by the time she climbed into bed. She thought about calling out to Henry for company, but he needed rest after their recent supernatural finagling.

Gotta learn to be okay on my own, she thought, as she turned off the bedside lamp and rolled over.

I'm still here, sugar, said Granna.

Tipsy smiled her thanks. The house was still and calm around her. She wondered if Ivy had found her mother in the afterlife, and what she might be feeling. Before she fell asleep, a memory crept over her. She wasn't quite sure why her brain or her supernatural power or whatever controlled the visions chose this particular scene from her thirty-five years of life. Maybe because she'd thought about her odd relationship with her own mother before Ivy and John left. Or maybe just to remind her that things would get better if she put one foot in front of the other.

Tipsy sits at the kitchen island in her pretty new house. Little Ayers, two years old, is watching a cartoon in the family room. Her newborn daughters, Mary Pratt and Olivia Grace, are blessedly asleep in their bouncy chairs. Tipsy can't recall the last time she's had a moment of peace, even though it can't have been that long, since the twins are only three weeks old. The

relative quiet is unnerving. If anything, it increases the sense of dread that's been closing in on her since she brought the girls home from the hospital.

Big Ayers isn't home yet. Sometimes Shelby stops by for an hour, but today she had to be at the GQB all day. Ayers's sister Mimi has three small children of her own. Tipsy thinks about calling her mother-in-law, but she can't handle May Penny's passive aggressive criticism of both her housekeeping and her parenting.

She holds her phone in her hands. She feels utterly alone, even with the three most important people in her world—her children—close by. She looks out the window. It's raining, and her lovely home suddenly feels like a prison. She thinks of her little studio in the old apartment on Society Street and her eyes burn. She'd walked through those French doors onto the piazza into creative bliss every morning. Now her creativity is washing away in the rain; in a flood of breastmilk and apple juice.

I have to call someone, *she thinks. She opens her contacts and scrolls through hundreds of random email addresses and cell phone numbers. She goes all the way to Z, and finds no one. She flips back up to the beginning of the alphabet, and the phone settles on the D's. She reads the name under her finger.*

Denise and Randy Denning.

Not Mom and Dad. Denise and Randy. Two people she barely knows, but for some reason, the urge to call her parents overwhelms her. She hasn't seen them in a year and a half, since their sole visit after Little A was born. They'd only come for the day, and her father spent most of the afternoon at Art's Bar and Grill, eating oysters and drinking beer. Her mother had feigned interest in her only grandchild, but she hadn't brought a baby gift. Instead, she asked Tipsy for money as soon as she walked through the front door. Tipsy can't remember if she's actually spoken to her parents since they drove away in their twelve-year-old minivan.

Sugar, I don't know if it's wise to call them. You seem rather fragile to me.

Tipsy ignores Granna and hits the call button.

The phone rings twice and her mother's raspy, cigarette-stained voice says, "Hello?"

Tipsy's heart pounds in her chest. "It's me, Mama. Tipsy."

Denise doesn't say anything at first, as if she's forgotten she has a daughter. "Look who decided to call. Randy, it's Tipsy."

There's a reply in the background, but Tipsy can't decipher it.

"Well, how are you?" asks Denise. "How's your boy?"

"Little Ayers is great. And I had the twins. I told you I was pregnant, right? They're both healthy and beautiful. Mary Pratt and Olivia Grace—"

"Those are fancy names."

"Mary Pratt has the same initials as Ayers's mother and Olivia Grace is named after his two aunts—"

"You didn't see fit to name either of them after anyone in our family?"

"I thought about Stella, after Granna, but Ayers wasn't a big fan. But anyway, they're both doing well—"

"Hold on." Denise's voice is muffled, as if she has the phone covered. "Daddy wants to know if your husband's father knows anyone in construction up this way. He's been laid off from the post office."

"Oh. Um, I think Tripp sticks mostly to South Carolina. Why was Daddy laid off?"

"Why do you think?"

Tipsy knows what she's getting at. Her father wasn't laid off. He was fired for being a drunk.

"We have my disability for my emphysema, but it's hard, Tipsy. We ain't so young anymore."

Tipsy's parents aren't even fifty, but her mother sounds as if they both have one foot in the nursing home.

"I can ask Tripp," Tipsy says, even as she knows she won't. She'll never ask Tripp to vouch for her father to any of his colleagues in the construction industry. "But, um. I called because… I've sort of been feeling…"

There's silence on the other end of the line. It dawns on Tipsy that this is the stupidest phone call she could have made.

"What? Speak up."

She has no choice but to keep talking. "I've been feeling a little blue, since the girls were born. I wondered… did you feel that way after I was born?"

Denise laughs. "Oh, honey. I'd just turned nineteen and I didn't know nothing. I hadn't planned on a baby and there you were. I don't know how I felt." Her voice is muffled again, but this time Tipsy can sort of make out what she says. "She wants to know how I felt when she was born."

Her father says something. Denise laughs again, but to her credit, she says, "Don't be an ass, Randy." She's back on the phone. "Sorry I can't be much help. But I don't know how you can feel sad when you're living in a big house at the beach with your rich husband."

"We don't live at the beach," Tipsy says, even though she knows in her mother's mind, anything east of Columbia is living at the beach. "But yes. We're blessed."

"You sound ungrateful to me."

Tipsy wants to get off the phone before she starts crying, so she says, "Mama, the girls are waking up. I have to go."

"Okay. Nice talking to you. Don't forget about us. We could use some help."

"Right, I won't. I'll, uh, see about Tripp."

"You could see about helping us yourself, too."

"Sure. I have your address. I'll send you a gift card or something."

"That would be nice. Say thank you, Randy."

A gruff male voice yells, "Thanks!"

"You're welcome. Bye, Mama."

"Bye-bye."

Tipsy hits the end button. She puts her elbows on the counter and silently cries into a dish towel. Granna doesn't say I told you so. She doesn't chide Tipsy for making such a dumb decision; for trying to get comfort from the woman who hasn't offered any since she was about ten, and wasn't too good at it before then.

"Mama?" Little Ayers's voice breaks through her fog. She wipes her face furiously and walks into the family room. Little A has somehow removed his pants and diaper. He's standing in a puddle of pee. He points at the floor. "May mess. Pee-pee potty. Bad."

"Oh, buddy. It's okay. You had an accident!" She scoops her little blonde son up into her arms. "No bad." She pokes his belly and smiles through the miasma of what she's starting to accept is not the normal baby blues. This is somehow more sinister. But her boy will not know it.

"Good!" Tipsy says. "Ayers is good."

He puts his hands on her cheeks and kisses her. A squeak comes from the bouncy chairs. It's Mary Pratt. She's already more demanding than her sister. As soon as Olivia Grace hears her, she starts in with her own mewing.

Tipsy's sore breasts sting at the sound of crying. She puts Little A on the floor and turns on another cartoon. He stands transfixed with his naked bottom hanging out as she takes M.P. out of the bouncy seat and sits down to nurse. O-liv screams louder, as if incensed that her sister is going first.

Darkness settles over Tipsy as she nurses one baby and then picks up the other while her son stands beside the pee-pee. Once both girls are fed and back in their chairs, staring up at their mobiles with slightly crossed eyes, she wipes the floor and gets Ayers a new diaper.

You made it, sugar, *says Granna.*

Made it through what? *asks Tipsy.*

The last hour.

There's another one ahead of me. *Her heartbeat picks up at the thought of trying to feed Little A while the girls inevitably started fussing. Dinner time is the witching hour.*

Where's their father?

He's hunting.

Granna's silent anger permeates their spectral connection.

I can't say anything right now, *Tipsy tells her.* I can't handle an argument.

He's not much help, but at least he could hold one of the babies.

I can't fight with him tonight. *Her hands tremble and her head throbs.* What's wrong with me, Granna?

Three tiny babies and a husband who'd rather sit in a deer stand than be a dad.

Ayers can't deal with babies. I think he imagined they'd be born as eight-year-olds he could play catch with and take out on the boat all day.

You need help, Tipsy. Not just Shelby stopping by or May Penny bringing over a lasagna.

I can do this. I can.

Even as she says it, Tipsy isn't sure. She's never experienced anything like this. In addition to the exhaustion and sadness and anxiety, she's afraid of her very emotions. She'd never been so afraid in her life, and the source of her fear is coming from her own mind.

She bites the inside of her cheek to snap herself out of it for the moment. She puts one foot in front of the other and makes it to the kitchen. She makes mac and cheese for Little Ayers and she gets him into the bath while the twins fuss in the background. She tucks him in and feeds the twins again. Olivia Grace first this time. As she looks down at their tiny faces, she prays whatever is doing this to her isn't somehow poisoning her daughters. She falls asleep on the floor beside their cribs to make sure they're okay. That's how Big Ayers finds her when he finally gets home, and that's how Tipsy makes it through her first day of postpartum depression.

The kids returned the following evening. Tipsy spent the next few days making Target runs for school supplies, hitting up Belk for school clothes, dropping them to visit with friends, and working on art projects in various stages of completion. She unveiled Pamella's painting for the kids in the living room where Henry and Jane were murdered, as had become something of a tradition. She set the painting on an easel and covered it with a sheet. The kids sat on the sofa with freeze pops.

"Not one drop of freeze pop juice on the sofa, y'all," she warned, as she took hold of the edges of the sheet.

Ayers held his freeze pop above his head, Mary Pratt pinched hers shut, and O-liv slurped down the last of hers.

"Okay. Ready, set, ta-da!" She pulled the sheet off the painting.

The kids tilted their heads like curious puppies. The painting's colors were mostly earth tones, contrasting with the shiny white of the house, the yellow flowers peppering the yard, and the bright orange of little Pamella's outfit. As planned, she stood barefoot in the grass and Bob Brewton sat on the porch behind her. As the foreground figure, Pammy's lines were sharper, but Bob's slightly imprecise face still revealed wry amusement hiding behind his 1970s mustache. The level of detail included a bit of haze in the air and the peppering of tiny, buzzing insects around the haphazard bunches of brown-eyed susans.

Little Ayers stood and approached the painting. "So here's what I like. This girl is super happy. But that guy—"

"It's her dad."

"He looks kind of mean."

"Not mean," said Mary Pratt. "Sad."

"Or tired," said O-liv.

"He wants to smile but he's not doing it," said Ayers.

"Do y'all wonder why?"

Because he's cursed, said Granna. *But best not to tell them that.*

"Yeah, sort of," said Mary Pratt. "But I'd rather play with the girl who looks fun than worry about her grouchy dad."

O-liv raised her hand. "It's a ten from me. Other judges?"

"Yes. A ten." Mary Pratt clapped politely.

Ayers squinted one eye. "Nine-point-nine-nine-nine-nine-nine."

"Thank you for your honesty." She patted his head.

"Really, Mama," said M.P. "It's, like, super pretty. I think your friend will like it a lot."

"Thanks, honey. She's on her way over here. When she gets here, y'all say hi and then let us chat."

The kids did as they were told, impressing Pamella with their *yes ma'ams* and *no ma'ams* before disappearing into their rooms to play. Tipsy led Pamella to the finished painting. She covered her mouth with her hands when she looked at it.

"I don't even know what to say."

"That's the best reaction I can ask for."

"Tipsy, you've outdone yourself. It's like the photo I wish I had, but no one ever took."

"I'm so glad you're happy with it."

Pamella sat on the sofa where the kids had doled out their discerning judgment. "So here you go." She fished in her purse for an envelope. "The full amount, now that my sweet Meemaw has moved on."

Tipsy sat beside her and opened the envelope. It contained a cashier's check written out to Tiffany Denning-Collins in the amount of $50,000.00 from the Pamella Anne Brewton Trust. She exhaled. The rent had come due and she could pay it.

"So you're staying at True Blue?" asked Tipsy.

Pamella nodded. "Thanks to you I can stay. And my Meemaw can be with Grandpa John again."

"Grandpa John. He'd like that. I guess you have two grandpas watching over you from the other side. Lucky lady."

"I don't know about that. If Camden Brewton killed my real grandfather and then killed Meemaw, I'm not sure I want him watching over me."

"It's a little more complicated than that. Less black and white. It always is." Tipsy thought about telling Pamella about the curse and Alma and Bubba, but she decided that for now, the simple version sufficed. "Camden took care of Ivy and your dad for a long time. You have your cottage because of him. He rose to the occasion."

"He had to, since he started it."

"Trust me. Give Camden a break."

"If you say so, but I want to talk about something else. Tipsy—about the other afternoon. I'm sorry I was such a mess."

"Jeez. Don't worry about it. I'd just had the most embarrassing night of my adult life, so I'm not judging."

"No. It's more than that. I've been going to AA meetings." She cleared her throat. "I'm an alcoholic."

"Wow. It's so brave of you to say that."

"It hasn't even been a week, but I haven't missed one day. I woke up the morning after we talked, thinking about Meemaw and how she died. I know Camden pushed her, but she was on Hammer Time. That surely didn't help matters. I don't want to leave my girls. I want to be someone's Meemaw someday. In this life."

"You will be an awesome Meemaw."

Pamella sniffed and waved her hand. Tipsy got up and grabbed a box of tissues from the kitchen. She handed them to Pamella, who blew her nose and grabbed another. "Doug and I are getting back together."

"That's amazing. I'm so happy for you."

"I truly believe we can work it out. It's shocking he still wants to try, but I'm not going to question him. He might wise up."

Tipsy suddenly sprung her own salty leak. She grabbed a tissue and dabbed her eyes.

"Oh, lady. You okay?"

Tipsy nodded. "Yes. I'm so silly. I'm so relieved about this money. And glad I helped Ivy and John and even Camden. I think about how much John and Ivy loved each other all these years. They were a match made in heaven, and I got to help them get there. And you're figuring out all this life crap and you have someone who truly loves you—" She sucked in a breath and waved her tissue before her bleary eyes. "It like, gives me hope that I'll figure it out, too."

"You will! You're only thirty-five. You're a baby."

"That's what Henry says, but I feel old."

"When I was your age, I still had two husbands in my future."

Tipsy chuckled. "If I ever have another husband, I hope it's only one. I'm sorry. I feel like a self-absorbed crybaby these days. People talk about their own crap, and somehow I make it about me."

"Don't be so hard on yourself."

"Shelby always tells me I'm too hard on myself and too easy on everyone else."

"I haven't known you that long, but I think that's true."

"I get so frustrated. I hate feeling helpless. A few weeks ago, Ivy and I talked about being patient and letting life sort itself out. I counseled my son about the same thing. Lindsey told me it takes longer than you think it will take to get over a divorce. And that I should accept that I'll make some questionable decisions." Tipsy rolled her eyes. "Like going out with Clarice. Or cussing out my ex-boyfriend via text. Let's not forget the worst hangover of my life. I always fancy myself cool, calm, and collected. Apparently not, since I got cussed out in public myself."

"Cut yourself some slack. People act out when they're hurting. As for Clarice and Kim and all that, remember what I told you about kissing Kermit earlier this summer."

"I know you're right, but it's so hard for me to take my own advice or anyone else's."

"Lady, you're talking to the queen of doling out wise advice while being a disaster." Pamella patted Tipsy's shoulder. "You're nowhere near my level of train wreck."

"I feel like there must be *something* I can do to *make* it all okay."

"That's what you're *doing*, every day. Even if it takes a long ass time like Lindsey said. Getting divorced wasn't a magic fix. You won't find one post-divorce, either, take it from me."

Tipsy nodded. Pamella's last statement really struck home. *There was no magic fix.* She had to keep doing her best and push her rock up the hill. Eventually it would crest the top of the knoll. She'd be strong enough to keep it up there, no matter what the gods of parenting and dating and work life balance threw at her.

"I'll remember that. Thanks for talking to me."

"Anytime!" Pamella wiggled her shoulders. "You call *Aunty Pammy* and we'll have a good chat. I don't have to work so I'm always available."

Tipsy laughed. Pamella's openness about her own good fortune made it impossible to begrudge her.

"Oh! I almost forgot." Tipsy stood and trotted into the kitchen. She brought a twenty by sixteen canvas wrapped in brown paper into the living room and handed it to Pamella. "Go on," she said. "It's a bonus painting."

"Wow, lady. You shouldn't have," said Pamella as she ripped away the paper. "You've been so busy. How did you have time to—" She froze as the paper fell to the floor. "Oh. Goodness. Is this who I think it is?" She stared at Tipsy with wide green eyes. "Is it them?"

Tipsy nodded as Pamella lay the painting on Ms. Callie's coffee table. It was John and Ivy, as Tipsy has seen them on the steps of the old barracks. Their faces were sharply defined, from the length of John's eyelashes to the freckles across Ivy's nose. Their bodies wrapped together in a mishmash of blues and browns. Pamella traced a finger over John's shiny golden hair and Ivy's red lips. Tipsy rarely wrote anything but her name on her paintings, but she'd been inspired as she worked on this one. Pamella traced Tipsy's neat writing, painted in strong black strokes along the bottom of the canvas.

Whatever our souls are made of, his and mine are the same.

"*Wuthering Heights*, right?" asked Pamella.

Tipsy nodded. "I've never seen two people more in love, even after almost a century apart. Like I said, the kind of love that gives hope to the heartbroken."

Pamella grabbed for another tissue. "Oh, Tipsy. Thank you."

"Every girl needs a picture of her Meemaw and Grandpa for when times get rough, right?" Tipsy pointed at a framed photograph of Granna and her PopPop, smiling in their tiny living room in the 1970s. When Granna's hair had still been dark, and PopPop had no reason to worry about his bladder unless he had to take a pee.

"I will *treasure* this. Seriously, lady." Pamella clutched the painting to her chest. "I have to meet Doug at our daily AA meeting. I'll come by with his truck tomorrow to get the big painting. You call me if you need *anything*, you hear? I'm glad I made a new friend out of this exorcism thing."

"Me too, Pammy." They walked to porch and hugged.

"I can't wait to get home tonight and sit on my own front porch like I used to do with Daddy. It's *crazy*, how I can actually feel that Meemaw is gone. The whole house is lighter." She hugged the painting again. "Everything is lighter, honestly. I've never felt so peaceful in my whole life."

Tipsy squeezed her hand. Once again, she thought about telling Pamella about the curse, but she had the sense it was already lifting. No use talking about an old curse when it was fading fast.

———◆✕◆———

After the kids went to sleep that night, Tipsy was lying in bed scrolling through memes when she got a text from Clarice Andrews. She sighed and opened it.

CLARICE: HEY. I KNOW YOU PROBABLY DON'T WANT TO TALK, BUT I WANTED TO MAKE SURE YOU'RE DOING OKAY AFTER LAST WEEKEND.

TIPSY: HEY. I'M GOOD. MY KIDS ARE BACK AND WE'RE GETTING READY FOR SCHOOL TO START. YOU'RE RIGHT I DON'T REALLY WANT TO TALK, BUT THANKS FOR HELPING ME THE OTHER NIGHT.

CLARICE: OKAY. I GET IT. I TALKED TO KIM, BY THE WAY. EXPLAINED TO HER THAT YOU'RE NOT TO BLAME FOR ANYTHING BETWEEN ME AND HER. SHE GETS IT. SHE FEELS KIND OF BAD. I'M SURE SHE'LL APOLOGIZE WHEN SHE SEES YOU OUT.

TIPSY: NOT PLANNING ON GOING OUT MUCH ANYTIME SOON, BUT THAT'S POSITIVE.

CLARICE: NOT THAT YOU NEED TO HEAR THIS, BUT I SORTED THINGS OUT WITH HER, TOO. NICELY, BUT I CUT IT OFF. YOU GOT ME THINKING. EVEN IF I'M STRAIGHT UP WITH PEOPLE, THAT DOESN'T LET ME OFF THE HOOK. THEY MIGHT NOT FEEL THE SAME WAY. I'LL BE MORE CAREFUL FROM NOW ON.

Tipsy smiled as she typed. LOOK AT YOU, LEARNING A VALUABLE LESSON. THAT'S WHAT THIS POST-DIVORCE LIFE IS ALL ABOUT, I GUESS!

CLARICE. I WISH I COULD SAY LET'S BE FRIENDS, BUT I DON'T REALLY WANT TO BE FRIENDS… SOOO… ☺

TIPSY: HAHA, SILLY. YOU'RE NOT TOO TERRIBLE, FOR BEING CHARLESTON'S BIGGEST WOMANIZER.

CLARICE: I'LL TAKE THAT AS A COMPLIMENT. IF I EVER DECIDE TO HANG UP MY TRAVELING SHOES FOR GOOD, I'LL LOOK YOU UP. NOT BEFORE THEN, I PROMISE. TAKE CARE.

TIPSY: HAHA AGAIN. YOU TOO.

He didn't reply, so she set her phone on the bedside table. She stared at the ceiling. Men. They were so weird. Between the living ones she'd dated the last couple years, and the man she'd married, she figured Henry might be the least crazy.

Bless their testosterone fueled hearts, said Granna.

It's honestly easier to accept them as they are than try to change them.

I never wanted to change your grandfather. I don't think Ivy wanted to change John. Find someone you like as he is.

And forgive the rest for being who they are.

She watched the ceiling fan go 'round and 'round for a bit before grabbing her phone again. She typed out Will's number. She spent a few minutes trying to figure out what she wanted to say, and then read what she'd written.

WILL, I KNOW YOU'RE DATING JULIA NOW. I WANTED TO SAY I WISH YOU THE BEST AND I HOPE THERE WON'T BE HARD FEELINGS IN THE FUTURE SINCE WE HAVE SO MANY MUTUAL FRIENDS. I CAN'T SAY I WANT TO BE "FRIENDS" AT THIS POINT, BUT I ALSO UNDERSTAND NOW WHY WE DIDN'T WORK OUT. I PROBABLY KNEW DEEP DOWN ALL ALONG, BUT SINCE YOU STARTED THIS NEW RELATIONSHIP, I TRULY GET IT. I WON'T SAY WE COULDN'T MAKE EACH OTHER HAPPY, BECAUSE WE REALLY SHOULD BOTH BE HAPPY ON OUR OWN. MORE LIKE I CAN'T BE WHO YOU NEED, AND YOU CAN'T BE WHO I NEED. I FORGIVE YOU FOR NOT BEING WHAT I CONVINCED MYSELF YOU COULD BE. I DON'T EVEN MEAN THAT IN A MEAN WAY— YOU ARE WHO YOU ARE AND YOU TRIED TO TELL ME THAT. JUST LIKE I AM WHO I AM, AND I CAN'T BE WHAT YOU WANT. I WAS STIFLING MYSELF BY TRYING. NOT GOOD FOR EITHER OF US. SO ANYWAY, MAYBE YOU WON'T EVEN READ THIS, BUT I'LL FEEL BETTER FOR SENDING IT. HOPEFULLY SOMEDAY WE CAN REACH A PLACE WHERE THE GIRLS CAN HANG OUT AGAIN. SORRY FOR THE LONG ASS TEXT AND NO NEED TO REPLY, SERIOUSLY. TAKE CARE, TIPSY.

She hit send, and got up to go to the bathroom. Her heart was still heavy, but she felt better, too. By the time she got back to her phone, he'd already replied. For a brief moment, she hoped he'd say something profound. Offer some proof she hadn't totally misjudged him. She swiped over his message.

THANKS, TIPSY. THAT'S REALLY NICE TO HEAR. YOU TAKE CARE TOO.

She chuckled. Same old Will. Somewhat disappointing but predictable. She plugged in her phone and went to sleep.

Tipsy spent the next two weeks getting back into the groove of the school year and working on paintings for the GQB. She interviewed for a new commission thanks to Vivian Greenblatt, one of her first commission clients, who hooked her up with another wealthy Kiawah Island art lover. Before she knew it, Ayer's wedding was upon her. Thankfully, the kids went straight to his house after school on Thursday. She didn't want to face dropping them off at his house, or at May Penny's, where there would surely be caterers and florists running in and out. She met Lindsey and Shelby for lunch on Saturday, and they did a solid job of distracting her. On Sunday, she had a non-boozy brunch with Pamella and Doug, who proved to be a handsome guy of almost sixty with a north Georgia mountain twang that made Tipsy feel like she was back in Martinville. Tipsy liked him immediately. Pamella laughed and talked their ears off. She even ate a cheeseburger and fries. Pretty good for someone only a couple weeks into a curse-free, AA lifestyle.

On Sunday evening, with the knowledge that her ex-husband was now fully remarried, she came back from a run and found Henry at the dining room table doing his writing-on-air thing.

"Hey," she said, as she strolled into the kitchen and got water. She walked back to him. "How's it going?"

"Starting chapter four."

"Jeez." She sat beside him. "Chapter three done already?"

"Yes. I'm picking up steam."

"Good. You should be able to return to Jane in... oh, about fifty years."

Henry grunted and started tracing his fingers over the dining room table.

"I guess that wasn't funny. Shelby said I'm only funny sometimes."

"It must be odd to have a man in your house who isn't your husband or father or brother."

"Not so much. In this day and age, people have roomies of the opposite sex all the time. I don't want you to go for my sake. I think about Jane, and you... I want y'all to be together the way you were in the memory you showed me, if you can. Because I love y'all."

He blushed. "It's hard to get used to hearing you say that. I know you want the best for us. And I do miss Jane. But she knows I still have things to do here."

"That's what you said to John and Ivy. But maybe this book is meant to live in your head."

"Possibly, but I'd still like to sort out the story, and I don't know what my head will be capable of on the other side. But it's not only about the book. Jane knows that."

"What is it about?"

"I told her I wouldn't tell you, but it seems like I should. Otherwise you'll think I'm truly mad. Woman I love waiting for me on the other side.... yet I sit here talking to myself day in and day out." He pointed at her. "It's about you."

"What about me?"

"Do you remember how you couldn't find me, those few days before you set us free?"

"Yes. You were hiding. I told Jane to look for you, and I kept calling for you."

"Jane found me, briefly. That morning. We talked about—" He held out his hand. "Once again, how about if I simply show you?"

So he did.

———◆✕◆———

Tipsy looks down at the top of Henry's head. He sits on the front porch stairs, muttering to himself. A voice from behind her makes her jump.

"Henry!"

She spins around, and there's Jane. The pale, ghostly Jane Tipsy knew so well, with her purple dress and bare feet. Jane walks toward Henry, and Tipsy gets out of her way. Henry gets up without turning and strolls into the yard. Jane follows him with her hands on her hips. Tipsy follows them both onto the lawn.

"Henry Mott!" says Jane. "I know you hear me."

He turns around slowly. "Yes, my dear wife. I hear you."

"Don't talk down to me. Tipsy and I have been looking for you. She needs to touch us both to see how we died, and—"

"No."

"For goodness sake. It's been a century. We can leave this house, finally!"

"Maybe I don't want to leave."

"Just like Tipsy would say, that's a lot of bullshit! You leave here all the time and fly around town like a red-headed bat, or whatever it is you do. Please, let her see."

"All these years, you knew you'd betrayed me. Did you love him, Jane?"

"I loved you, Henry. I always loved you, even when I loved someone else. You were the one who didn't love me." She crosses her arms over her chest. "Now stop changing the subject and cooperate for once. I want to get on out of here and see my parents and Connie and Luisa and all our other friends!"

"I cannot see myself kill you. I could tolerate watching me kill myself, but not you."

"Maybe I killed you!" Her voice gets shrill, as it always does during these surreal conversations about their own deaths. "Maybe we killed each other! Maybe it was a robbery gone awry—"

"If Tipsy can find a way to free you, I fully support it. But I won't participate."

"She'll make you participate. She's stronger than you, even if she doesn't know it."

"I know she is. If she forces me, so be it, but I won't go willingly."

"Damn you, Henry. You are the most insufferable man on earth!" She points up into his face. "I'll tell you one thing, if Tipsy figures out how to set me free, and you're still stuck here, you'll do me one last favor. You owe it to me, after all you put me through."

His nostrils flare, but he tips his chin in her direction. "If it's within my power, I'll do it."

"You watch over her. And help her. She's on the right path, but I sense it's still a hard road for a woman in her place. Even in this day. So whatever you can do to assist her, you do it. You hear me?"

"Yes ma'am. I'll do so, gladly."

"But don't tell her. She has too much pride to think she needs a protector."

"Tipsy and I have an overabundance of pride in common. I won't say anything."

"All right then. I see there's no more talking with you, so go back to your—" She twirls her fingers beside her head. "Whatever it is."

"Writing my story."

"Yes, well. I'll leave you now." As always, it's uncomfortable. How can two people who meant so much to each other, for good and bad, just walk away? Take care, old friend. See ya later, alligator. Catch you haunting around on the porch later.

"I'm sorry I can't do what you want me to do," says Henry.

"Won't. You won't do it."

She turns to walk away, but he calls her name. When she stops, he says, "I always loved you, too. I was terrible at showing it, but I did. For what it's worth."

"Thank you," she says over her shoulder. She walks toward Tipsy, who stands at the bottom of the porch stairs. Sparkly tears fill her eyes. She disappears before Tipsy has to move out of her way, or the tears spill onto her cheeks. Once she's gone, Tipsy wakes up.

———◆✕◆———

Tipsy's mood slowly improved. Getting past Ayers's wedding helped. The buildup to that event had been taking more out of her than she thought. Listening to the kids talk about their new house and the girls chattering about their flower girl dresses had drained her. She'd spent the wedding weekend anxiously trying to avoid photos on social media. The stress made her temporarily delete Instagram and Facebook from her phone.

Now Ayers was married and off on his honeymoon, and honestly, more power to him. She still harbored some jealousy that he'd found someone so quickly after putting her through hell for almost two decades. If there were any justice in the world, karma would have seen her get settled before him.

No one ever said life was fair, said Granna. *Plus, you wait until Kate finds out how much gum he chews.*

I'm thinking about what happens when he realizes this new marriage won't be the source of all happiness. With Ayers, malcontented angst is always around the next bend.

He's never learned. No quick fixes, right?

Right on, Granna.

In the end, Ayers's happiness was no longer her problem, except for how it affected her kids. For now, everyone seemed to be humming along, so she planned to live in that space and be good with it.

On Thursday evening, with Ayers and Kate still on their honeymoon in the Virgin Islands, Tipsy drove over to Ayers's house with all three kids so Little A could grab his favorite soccer cleats. As she pulled up, she noticed the "for sale" sign in the front yard. For the kids' sake she hoped the house sold quickly, so they could move into the new place down the street without everyone having to be crammed in here for long.

She pulled into the driveway behind a black Yukon she'd never seen. Mary Pratt pointed out the window. "Chloe and Tristan are here! Can we say hi?"

"Sure." Tipsy put the car in park and the girls tumbled out. "Who is that?" she asked Little A.

"That's their dad's car. They must be here getting stuff, too. I met him once. Dad still doesn't like him, but he seems okay to me."

"Ah, right." She tried not to look into the car beside her. Tristan and Chloe were climbing out.

"Can you help me with the key, Mom? It always gets stuck."

"Sure, buddy." As Tipsy got out of her truck the Yukon's doors slammed beside her. The five kids ran toward the house. Tipsy turned to face Tristan and Chloe's father.

He was tall, with dark hair, blue eyes, and a short, well-kept beard. He wore a suit and a medical badge hung from his neck. He was as handsome in person as he had been when Shelby and Lindsey stalked Kate on Facebook. Tipsy felt herself blushing.

"Hey," he said. "Tipsy, right?"

"Yeah. Hey." She pointed in the direction of the kids. They were all wrestling around with the key. Tristan had grabbed it from under a rock and jammed it into the lock. Mary Pratt cheered when the door opened and O-liv ran inside. "That's my brood."

"Right. Mine too. One less kid, just as much noise." His accent held the twangy vestiges of a mountain upbringing. Made sense, since Kate had moved to Charleston from Tennessee. He reached out to shake her hand. "Scott Brandt."

"Nice to meet you." Tipsy was suddenly grateful she'd been to the GQB earlier. She had showered and wore a sundress. It would be mighty embarrassing to meet her hot ex-in-law with sweaty gym hair in her painting clothes.

Is ex-in-law even a thing? asked Granna.

Probably not, but you know what I mean.

"So, they're moving?" He pointed at the sign.

"Yeah. I assume they need more space."

"Your kids okay with it?"

She sensed he meant not only the move, but all of it. "For the most part. They've lived here their whole lives, so it's sad for them to think of moving. On the other hand, ziplines and trampolines have been promised, so you know…"

He smiled. His teeth were very white in his dark beard. "Got it. A good trampoline bounce can be truly cathartic."

Oh, lord, Granna. He's hot and a doctor and has a good vocabulary.

"True, true," said Tipsy. "Besides, they adore your kids. And they like Kate."

Tipsy let the comment hang in the air. For a second, Scott did too. Then he said, "That's great. Mine like Ayers, too."

Of course, Tipsy was tempted to say something snarky. She figured he had been, too. She liked that he hadn't.

"It's good for them to have more people who love them, right?" she asked. "That can't hurt."

"No, it sure can't. The twins told Chloe you're an artist."

Tipsy nodded. "That's right."

"Fascinating. You got a card, or a web site? I bought a little house in I'On. Lots of blank white walls."

"Ah, yes. I do." She reached into her car and grabbed her business card from the console. She handed it to him. "Everything is on there. Website. Instagram." She cleared her throat. "Contact information."

"I'll check it out. Maybe you can help me with my white walls."

"If you like my work, I'd be happy to." She pointed at his tag. "What kind of medicine do you practice?"

"Neurology and psychiatry. I'm a two-for-one."

"Wow. Impressive."

"The human brain is impressive. Some doctors like bones or hearts. I like brains."

Tipsy giggled. "I'm sorry. *Baby Got Back* just popped into my head."

He grinned back at her. "It's true. I like big brains and I cannot lie."

Little Ayers ran back outside, followed by the twins and Scott's kids. They parted like the Red Sea at the two cars.

"Hey, y'all," said Scott. His kids stopped. "This is Miss Tipsy. Can y'all say hello?"

Tristan and Chloe, who were both attractive children with dark hair and blue eyes, smiled and said hello.

"Nice to meet y'all," said Tipsy.

Mary Pratt stuck her head out the window. "Hey, Chloe's dad!"

"Hi, there. I have to ask, which one are you?"

"I'm Mary Pratt. You can tell us apart because I'm cooler."

"Heeeeyyyyy!" O-liv yelled from inside the car. Her face appeared like a duplicate of the same photo. "She's just louder."

"Now that is saying something," said Tipsy. "Can y'all say hello nicely to Mr. Scott, please?"

The girls shouted their hellos. Ayers looked up from the iPhone his dad had gotten him before the wedding. "Hi," he said through the window.

"Hey, Ayers," said Scott. "Nice to see you."

"Yes, sir. You too." He returned to his phone. Tipsy wondered what he was thinking, given that his dad had apparently bashed this guy in front of him.

"Well," said Tipsy. "Gotta go feed the troops."

"Yeah, me too. I'll check out your work. See what I think with my very uneducated eye."

"You don't have to be educated. You just have to like what you see."

They stood there for a moment, and Tipsy felt it. There was something there. Something like attraction but also something like a kindred spirit. They were tied together by their kids, and Ayers and Kate's potentially traumatic but hopefully positive relationship.

But also, damn. This man is fine.

Tipsy....

Granna's admonishment cut the tension and Tipsy opened the car door. "It was nice to meet you," she said, as she slid into the seat.

"You too," he said.

She half hoped he'd add, *talk to you soon* or *I'll be in touch*, but he didn't. Probably better, since the idea of having the hots for her ex-in-law came loaded with weirdness and complication.

Now that is the gospel truth, said Granna.

She glanced at Little A as she backed down the driveway, but he was ensconced in his game. The girls were happily bickering in the third row. She reached the street and put the car in drive. Scott still stood in the driveway. He looked up from his phone, then smiled and waved. Tipsy replied with her own ungraceful half wave as she yanked on the steering wheel.

She drove down the street with a buzzy feeling in her chest.

No, no, no, said Granna.

I get it, seriously. No Dr. Scott Brandt for me.

Then why am I getting these happy vibes?

Tipsy thought for a minute. Attraction to someone other than Will was a good thing. She'd been attracted to Clarice, who was off limits. Now this guy was also attractive, and also off limits. That meant there would be another one. Or two. Or however many it took to find the right situation. She just had to be patient.

I'm not going to be alone forever, Granna. For a while, and that's totally okay. I think I need it. But not forever.

I could have told you that, sugar.

Even with your grandmother's wisdom, sometimes life has to show you before you believe it.

Four days later, after the kids were asleep, Tipsy and Henry sat on the front porch. She sipped a glass of icy lemonade. Her tongue tingled pleasantly from the tartness. She was trying to cut back on Coke. Lemonade somehow seemed healthier, even if it was just as sugary.

It was one of those rare September evenings that carried the first hint of cooling weather. In the Lowcountry, nature liked to throw out such teases every once in a while. The next morning it was *haha, you fell for it,* and it was one hundred degrees again. The salty air would return to the consistency of lukewarm chicken broth. Still, Tipsy wasn't sweating in this moment, and so she wasn't complaining as she watched the sun set behind her neighbors' picturesque houses. Red and gold shone through the limbs of the oaks and magnolias. The branches were black rivers drawn on a crimson map.

Her phone dinged. A text from Big Ayers.

AYERS: HEY! WE'LL BE BACK TOMORROW AROUND LUNCHTIME CAN I GET THE KIDS SATURDAY MORNING? NEED SOME TIME TO UNPACK AND GET SETTLED! WIPED OUT!

TIPSY: SURE. NO PROBLEM. HOPE Y'ALL HAD FUN AND CONGRATS!

AYERS: IT'S BEEN A BLAST BUT I'M TOO OLD FOR A WHOLE WEEK OF DAY DRINKING HAHA. THANKS! I'LL TEXT WHEN I'M ON THE WAY OVER TOMORROW

TIPSY: I HEAR YOU RE: DAY DRINKING! SOUNDS GOOD! ☺

Tipsy reread the simple messages. They said so much. They were both enthusiastic and unusually punctuated. Normally, she'd wonder if Ayers was being passive aggressive or trying to rub his happiness in her face. Something told her that wasn't the case. For now at least, married life must be agreeing with him, and he was genuinely content.

And how do you feel? asked Granna.

A happy Ayers means happier kids. Besides, he's my kids' dad. He was my first love. I'm happy for him.

Big of you.

He'll be driving me coo-coo again soon. I'll enjoy the peace for now.

For now is all you got, sugar. You always have to enjoy it.

I think I finally understand that.

As Tipsy conferred with Granna, she felt a sense of relief. She hadn't realized how much energy she put into the never-ending renovations on her fixer-upper life. Freeing to think of just living in it, even if the whole place needed a new paint job. Scary, but oddly liberating.

She remembered Bobby Brewton, painting his entire house haint blue to deter his mother's ghost. The Gullah-Geechee people's attempts to trick spirits with false water and pseudo skies, or imprison them in bottles, stemmed from fear of the unknown. She'd surely harbored her own terror of that nameless beast over the years, even if her list of personal fears didn't usually include ghosts for obvious reasons.

What better way to show the unknown who's boss than by controlling the outcome? asked Granna. *Maybe even with a curse or two, haha.*

Haha, sure. But like Ivy said, curses ain't no joke. Anyway, it's hard enough to let go of the past, much less control the future. It's exhausting, and I'm over it. Tipsy smiled. *For now, I'm truly all about* for now.

"Why are you smiling?" asked Henry.

"What? Oh, nothing much."

"I like your new drawing."

"Thanks." Tipsy's new commission included Colonial Lake and the line of pretty houses encircling it.

"When I was a child, my brother Edward and I would walk from our parents' house on Bull Street to the Pond. That's what we called Colonial Lake. We'd fish and paddle around in a canoe we left there all summer."

"So you and Edward did have some good times."

"When I was small, yes. Once he realized other boys' little brothers didn't talk to people who weren't there, I became even more embarrassing than your typical younger sibling."

"I'm sorry."

"There you go with another needless apology! Nothing to be sorry about, my dear. As I've said before, I didn't do much to endear myself to other children. I can see why he didn't want to be associated with me. Still, he never apologized for how he treated me when we were young."

"Not like Camden."

"Correct."

"He owned up to his mistake. Sort of like you admitting you misjudged John. Such humility."

"I've learned a thing or two from you in the past two years, Ms. Denning-Collins."

"Right back at'cha."

He pointed out into the yard. "Jane's tree is... how do you say it? Hanging out there?"

"Hanging in there," said Tipsy. The magnolia tree Jane had planted when she and Henry moved into the house in 1919 lorded over a corner of the yard. In June, it had been in its full glory, covered in fat white flowers like melting marshmallows. Three blossoms clung to the limbs in a testament to the tree's tenaciousness.

"It's been on this property longer than any living thing but the oaks. I'm not a living thing, so I'm not in the same category."

"Henry, you can move on. Seriously."

"Not yet, Tipsy."

"Why, though? I've gotten through life this far with only one supernatural chaperone, my grandmother in my head. I'll be okay. I promise."

Henry changed the subject. "What will you do this weekend when the children go back to Ayers?"

Tipsy wasn't going to get anything else out of Henry. He'd move on when he was good and ready, no matter how much she pushed him. Whether because of his book or because he promised the love of his life he'd look after her, she was stuck with him. Another comforting thought. "Hmmm. Weekend solo mama plan. Walk on the beach. Binge watch some TV. Paint. Oh, and Lindsey asked me to go on the boat with her and P.D. and Shelby and Brian. Sunday Funday with two pregnant ladies."

"No Wi-yum?"

"This time, he's left out. But it's all good. I'm just looking forward to a day in the sunshine on the water."

Tipsy and her undead guardian sat on the porch for a while longer, until the sun went down and the black branches faded into the night sky. She thought about Ivy and John and Camden, and was happy she'd helped them on their way. She also felt pretty good about her checking account balance. For the first time in years, she was sitting pretty in the finance department.

An idea dawned on her... what if she found another disgruntled ghost to remove for a paying customer?

Perhaps it was lunacy to think of making a living off ghostbusting. She should stick to finding commission clients, not exorcism clients, but Tipsy was too accustomed to the odd and unusual at this point to care. Painting would always be her bread and butter and her passion, but there might be some value in diversifying her portfolio of services. As she turned off the porch light and Henry disappeared to take his supernatural repose, Tipsy decided to keep an open mind. After all, she lived in Charleston, a beautiful city with a lot of ghosts and a lot of crazy. She was plenty sane enough to make the best of both.

The End

Acknowledgments

I must first acknowledge you, dear reader! It may be presumptuous to assume you read *Charleston Green*, the first installment of Tipsy's story, but if you did and you came back for more, thank you! I have been overwhelmed by the positive response to Tipsy and her friends and companions, both living and dead. As readers reached out to tell me how they connected with Tipsy, it was a no brainer to continue her journey. I truly hope I have done justice to your expectations!

That being said, I hope you'll all forgive me for how much grief I dole out to Ms. Denning-Collins. Sometimes I, myself, feel like I'm too hard on her! The truth is, however, that I've been in her position. I went through a divorce when my children were young. I had to rebuild my life, personally and professionally. I know firsthand how long the process takes, and I also see it every day in my work as a family law attorney. I have great confidence in Tipsy's ability to surmount all obstacles, but I would be remiss if I didn't force her to learn the hard and painful lessons that will eventually get her where she needs to be. All my fiction (including Tipsy's story and my fairy tale retelling, *The Cracked Slipper Series*) leans heavily into the idea that happy endings don't come simply. As women, we enter our adult lives with a set of expectations about the paths our lives "should" take, but life often has other ideas. All the lessons Tipsy is learning the hard way will help her understand and appreciate the good stuff that is coming her way (after I give her hell for one more book).

I'd like to again acknowledge that the primary metaphors in *Haint Blue*, both the title color and the "blue bottles," come from Gullah-Geechee traditions. I couldn't have imagined more effective imagery for story of trapped Lowcountry spirits and the frustrations of dealing with life's unexplainable road blocks. The Lowcountry's culture and traditions are beloved and heavily romanticized, but the simple truth is there would be no Lowcountry culture or traditions without the Gullah-Geechee people.

Thank you to everyone at Bublish, Inc., for your support and assistance getting my work out into the world. Thank you to my friends and family who always support my literary endeavors. Thank you again to every single reader and reviewer who has sent encouragement my way. Each bit of positive feedback is so appreciated in this tough business of creativity.

Lastly, as always, thank you to my husband, Jeffrey, who is endlessly supportive. You are my happily ever after.

Stephanie

Made in the USA
Las Vegas, NV
02 July 2021